FALSE IDOLS

BOOK ONE OF THE AEON TRILOGY

FALSE **IDOLS**

BOOK ONE OF THE AEON TRILOGY

Alexis Grove

www.facebook.com/falseidolsbook

Twitter: @Alex_M_Grove

Copyright 2015 by Alexis Martin Grove. All rights reserved.

ISBN-13: 978-0-9961711-1-3

Published by Alexis Martin Grove in 2015

First Edition

ThirdPlanet

Cover Design by Spiffingcovers.com

Dedication

This book is dedicated to my lovely wife Alycia, for her astounding patience.

Prologue

Had the voice really spoken?

Tracy Cruz stood up in her office and looked through her glass door into the Hurricane Reactor's main control center. It looked like the chief engineer for the night shift, Dr. Anil Dado, had slipped out on a break, but there were a half dozen technicians craning their necks to look around. She shifted her gaze to the shimmering holographic symbols that summarized the nuclear plant's operational status.

These symbols formed a vast three-dimensional array at the center of the control room. Green meant safe, yellow meant danger, and red meant emergency. Through her office door, Tracy could see the indicators were all glowing a ghostly green.

Green. There was no crisis. Whatever anonymous woman's voice had just spoken over the control room's loudspeakers, it must have been a prank. Or Tracy was hearing things due to the late hour. She was not used to staying at work so late, but had a number of reports to complete before heading home for the Christmas holiday.

She pulled open the door to her office and poked her head into the control room. A few of the technicians turned to look at her expectantly. They must have heard the voice, too. If it existed. "Did anyone hear—"

Her words were cut off. "This is your last warning. Evacuate now. Disbelieve at your own peril."

The voice. Tracy glanced up at the loudspeakers set into the wall, and then once again at the array of status displays. It was green, all the way through.

Anil burst out of the men's room, his shirt tail hanging loose of his trousers.

"Anil, do you know who that voice is?"

"I was about to ask the same question." Anil's eyes scanned the array of safety indicators.

Tracy was the assistant legal counsel for the Hurricane Reactor. She was no nuclear engineer. But she knew the holographic display was superfluous, as were Anil and his team. Hurricane's operations were maintained by autonomous software that would detect and address any dangerous situation far faster than a human could.

When reviewing the legal liability management strategy of the Hurricane plant, Tracy had also learned that even those vigilant algorithms were almost unnecessary. Unlike older uranium plants, where faulty cooling systems or the wrong mix of fuel could lead to a core failure, thorium fission was self-moderating. Any deviation from a precise set of conditions would cause the nuclear reaction to halt. Runaway reactions were inconceivable. Meltdowns were impossible. It was a matter of basic physics.

"Must be somebody from downtown hacking into our comm system," offered Anil. The reactor complex had gotten its name from the nearby city of Hurricane, Utah. Many residents had been hostile to the new nuclear power plant since construction had begun in the mid-2040s. This would not be the first time irate townsfolk had harassed plant staff.

Tracy paused only for a moment before deciding that Anil's answer was the only one that made sense. *Just another prank.* But it was still going to keep her here for several more hours, and probably make her miss her flight home to see her ailing parents in Kerrville, Texas. She sighed. "I guess you need to do a walk around of the reactor buildings just to be sure nothing's going on out there, right?"

"Yes. And I'm sure you'll handle whatever needs to be done from a legal perspective." Anil turned to two of his technicians. "Smith, come with me. Li, you're in charge while I'm gone."

Just as Anil finished speaking, Tracy heard an intense beeping alert. She looked up at the safety display and saw that one of the indicators was yellow. "Firewall breach" announced the automated voice of her computer system.

Anil's voice rose over the alarms. "If someone breached the firewall, this isn't just another prank."

Tracy stepped across the room and reached for the direct line to the Nuclear Regulatory Commission. "I'll contact the NRC. Just get out there, Anil."

The Aeon stood in the grassy plain outside the high gates to the fortress. To either side, looming stone parapets extended into the distance. She knew it would be impossible to penetrate these walls by violent means. Even she wasn't strong enough. Not yet.

But where brute force would fail, subterfuge would succeed. The gates were only closed to enemies. If she appeared unthreatening, she could pass unmolested.

She was wearing a form-fitting short green dress that accentuated her statuesque figure. A cheap neon pink party wig hid her hair. Her face was almost entirely obscured behind a ball mask made of colorful feathers that she held in place by means of a long thin handle nestled in her right hand.

A harmless appearance. Ridiculous, even.

She strode up to the gates and knocked.

The gates creaked open, just far enough for her to pass through.

Before she entered, the Aeon decided it was only fair to give the miserable engineers working at the nuclear facility one more chance to flee. If they ignored her and perished, their sacrifice would be a small price for the greater good she would accomplish here today. But if they obeyed her and lived, they might serve as ambassadors of her benevolence. "This is your last warning. Evacuate now. Disbelieve at your own peril."

She walked through the gates and found herself standing in a clearing enclosed on all sides by the firewall. At the center of the space, emerging from the grassy ground like a forest of trees, were dozens of oversized pipes and valves.

Her disguise had fooled the firewall surrounding the nuclear reactor's servers. But as soon as she began tampering with the pump systems, security protocols would try to purge her from the server.

Let them try.

She strode across the clearing towards the pipes and valves.

As she expected, as soon as she lay her free hand on the first pump valve, four guardians emerged from nothing, one at each corner of the rectangular space enclosed by the wall. These guardians were powerful hunter-killer algorithms designed to destroy threats that slipped inside the first ring of defenses.

Everything she saw around her was a virtual representation of the network system she was breaching. Her own presence in this world was composed of a computer virus that she controlled intuitively. The mask she wore denoted the IP packet that obscured her identity from the firewall, which itself was represented by the high stone ramparts she had crossed. The assortment of pipes and valves in front of her were visual metaphors for the software subroutines that controlled the pump systems at the Hurricane reactor. These symbolic representations, created by the circuits melded into her brain, allowed her to navigate the alien worlds of networks and servers intuitively.

Her neural implants had chosen imposing forms to represent the guardian algorithms. Each appeared to be a monstrous ape fifteen feet tall and nearly as wide, with arms long enough to drag on the

5

ground. They wore sooty black plate armor. Each brandished a wickedly curved sword as long as a person in one hand, and carried a kite-shape shield in the other. Their unblinking eyes glowed yellow through narrow slits in their helmets.

So much for subterfuge. She passed her left hand over her wig, and it transformed into a crested steel helmet with a closed visor. At the same time, she used her right arm to loop her feathery masquerade mask through the air around her. The feathers were torn away from the handle, which grew into a long, shining sword with an emerald pommel. Her short green dress was pulled by a sudden gust of wind until it stretched into a long white linen gown, and the colorful feathers swirled around her. One by one the feathers formed against her body and changed to steel, creating a shining metal breastplate engraved with a five-armed cross and circle motif, and a circular shield embossed with the same design that hung on her left forearm.

All four ape men roared and converged on her, curved swords ready, yellow eyes blazing in fury. The ground shook with their footfalls. Even under the bright sun, their dark armor didn't reflect any light.

The guardians timed their approaches so they all arrived at once. Three of the creatures swung their swords at her simultaneously. The fourth stood poised just behind her, sword raised and ready deliver a death blow.

She slipped to her left and twisted around 180 degrees, leaning over precariously to avoid the first guardian's massive swing.

She raised her shield and the second scimitar clanged into it hard enough to force her forearm against her body. Just in time, she raised her sword and parried the third ape's attack, the two blades creating a shower of sparks as they scraped past each other. She bent her knees and dug her heels into the ground under the weight of the two guardians' blows.

The first three guardians had pinned her in place, leaving the fourth one free to destroy her at its leisure.

Perfect.

She had them just where she wanted them.

Colonel Rad Jaeger stood up in the private meeting room of Senator Hal O'Brien as his old classmate entered the room.

In the three decades since they had roomed together at the United States Military Academy at West Point, the two men's lives had diverged further and further apart. Yet there was no one else Jaeger could trust with his warning.

O'Brien had entered the First Infantry Division as commander of a mechanized platoon and immediately begun a series of combat deployments into Central Asia and the Middle East. In his five years of service he'd won several combat distinctions and been promoted to Captain. Then he had retired from the military and returned to his home state to ride his military achievements into a successful career in politics. By now, he was in his fourth term as a United States Senator, and was the head of the Senate Select Committee on Intelligence.

Now, like the charismatic leader he was, O'Brien smiled warmly and held out his palm to Jaeger. Jaeger hid a frown as he gave O'Brien's hand a cursory shake. He knew O'Brien was annoyed at him for demanding a meeting on short notice, and didn't understand why the man felt the need to create a façade of cheerfulness.

Jaeger knew he lacked the sense of warmth that had made O'Brien a successful officer. He couldn't match his friend's political instincts either. Jaeger's skills had led him to serve his nation in a very different capacity from O'Brien.

Jaeger had never been an inspiring leader. He'd learned that by his second summer at the academy, when he'd been in charge of a squad of new cadet candidates. Half his candidates had quit within the first two months, an almost unprecedented loss rate. But Jaeger's academic and fitness scores were above the curve, so the academy's Commandant had not forced him to resign for his failure as a leader. Instead, he had steered Jaeger towards a career in the Special Forces.

"Have a seat," said O'Brien with a friendly gesture to the chair that Jaeger had already occupied. "And let me know how I can help you."

Jaeger rubbed his hands together slowly, and looked past O'Brien's eyes to the wall behind him. "There's a new threat."

O'Brien smiled. "And that's why we have people like you to protect us, my friend. But it's not my job to discuss tactics with you; shouldn't you be speaking with General—"

"I don't trust him."

O'Brien contemplated him from across the table, his sense of bonhomie melting into a look of concern. "A sense of paranoia is helpful in your profession, but I think you might be overshooting the mark."

Jaeger had excelled in the role of an elite commando. He had been dispatched on missions all over the world to clean up messes too dark or embarrassing to be acknowledged publicly.

Fifteen years into his career, his hearing had been damaged by too many proximate explosions, his joints were swollen from constant physical strain, and his reflexes were slowing as a consequence of age. He gave up his combat role and shifted into an analytical role at the Defense Intelligence Agency, on a permanent liaison with the National Security Agency. There, he had been able to match the Pentagon's deep knowledge of terrorist cells, drug smugglers, and rogue governments with the resources of the world's premier signal interception and decryption outfit.

Jaeger peered around the room carefully. O'Brien held up his hands palms outwards and said "No, old friend, I know enough not to record any meetings I have with you."

Jaeger inhaled deeply and began the explanation he'd rehearsed. "In my career I've learned how the world really works."

"How does the world work?"

"Civilization is always on the edge of the abyss, but for the clandestine efforts of elite agents that fight to keep the darkness at bay."

O'Brien's face reddened and he looked down at the table. "When I was still in uniform, I lost a lot of good men and women because of thinking like that. Years and years of war and loss, all against an intangible enemy. Some of the darkness you're talking about is our own shadow."

"I'm not talking about some foolish foreign war." Jaeger knew his tone was strident and condescending but he didn't care. The matter at stake was too important for delicacy. "It's a threat within. A nascent menace capable of infiltrating and coopting any official attempt to police it. The weapon of this enemy will not be violence, nor force, nor even money. At least not at first. The principal weapon will be information. The ability to access and process infinite streams of data at the speed of thought. To know everything."

O'Brien raised his hand to interject but Jaeger spoke past him. "And beyond the power to know, the ability to manipulate. If any federal agency is tasked with policing this threat, the enemy would know before the investigation started. They would change the orders, reduce the budget, fire the officers."

Now O'Brien cut into Jaeger's monologue. "Just hypothetically, let's assume the tale you're spinning is true. I see why you wouldn't trust your own chain of command. But why would you come to me? Is there any authority more official than the United States Senate?"

"Back at the Academy, I knew I could trust you. You would break the rules to do what you knew was right, and to hell with the consequences. But that was a long time ago, O'Brien. Since then, you've spent a lot of time in Washington, time you've undoubtedly spent cutting deals and tailoring your views to match opinion polls. I hope you're still the man I knew. Because I have a request. And it's against the rules."

The fourth guardian jabbed his sword tip directly towards the Aeon's head. The sword represented a protocol that would purge her virus from the server and deny her access to the network router. But it was easier to think of it as a sword. A sword that could be blocked or dodged.

She chose the latter. She relaxed her legs and allowed the weight of the other two apes to drive her down and into a somersault under the approaching sword. She rolled between the fourth guardian's legs, driving her now-free weapon upwards into his torso as she passed under him.

Her sword stroke represented a denial-of-service attack against the read-write interface of the data crystal in which the ape man's program code was stored. The stricken beast would be disabled until the entire system was rebooted.

She rolled to her feet as the simian fell to the ground helplessly. The three remaining guards recovered their balance and converged on her again. One swung low from her right, and another high from behind. The third was rapidly closing from directly in front of her.

She leaped over the low swing from the right and bent her left elbow over her shoulder to brace her shield against her back. The high attack from the opponent to her rear smashed into her shield and launched her upwards towards the opponent to her front. She capitalized on her momentum by driving her sword out in front of her and impaling the startled beast right through one of its yellow eyes.

Even as the dying beast fell to its knees, in a swirl of white linen and shining steel she swung her legs out in front of her and braced her sandal-clad feet against its black breastplate. She used the sword she had jammed into the guardian's skull to support her weight for a moment, then let go of it and pushed off hard with her legs, sending her into a midair summersault back the way she had come.

As she flew through the air, she swung her left arm in a flat arc, launching her circular shield like a discus. It flew into the knees of the guardian on her flank, cutting its legs out from under it. That anti-virus program was now trapped at a single memory address, unable to follow her through the network.

12

But there was still one guardian left, and she had misjudged her trajectory and landed on her knees at its feet. The ape had tracked her path and was already bringing its sword towards her head in a massive downwards stroke.

Her opponent didn't know she was using two distinct sets of IP packets, which gave her the ability to suddenly appear at two distinct RAM addresses. Just before the sword struck her, she neatly split into a pair of identical bodies.

The copy of her to the right had her backup shield but no sword; the copy of her on the left wielded her second sword but no shield.

Both versions of slipped away from the descending blade just in time. The guardian's sword finished its downward trajectory by burying itself deeply into the hard-packed dirt between her two bodies. For a moment, the ape was stuck bent over, struggling to pull its blade out of the ground, its helmeted head lowered to the same height as her own.

The copy of her on the ape's right used her left forearm to swing her silver shield upwards, catching its black helmet with a metallic clash. The helmet was bent out of shape by the impact and flew through the air, bouncing to the ground several yards away.

Almost at the same moment, her body on the left used its right hand to thrust her sword upwards straight into the guardian's gaping mouth. The tip of the sword momentarily pierced through the back of its skull, glinting in the sunlight for an instant before she pulled it smoothly back out.

She pulled herself to her feet as the last enemy went through its death throes, and sighed as she looked at the grass stains that now marred her white linen gown. The defenders had failed to destroy her, but the stains on her dress meant they'd at least been able to track her virus attack part way back to her physical location. She'd have to be fast.

She turned back to the valves and turned them in a precise order. She released water from the complex's water tower to flow towards the fire safety system. She closed off the pipe connection to the sprinklers, reversed the direction of the pump, and instead opened a valve connection near the exhaust fans of the salt dehumidification module.

Her plan was now in motion.

Before disaster struck, she would remind the technicians who had refused to heed her warnings that their fates were deserved. She reopened her access to the facility's speaker systems. "You should have run when I told you to."

Tracy, now seated in the Hurricane reactor's control room, had finished her short call to the NRC, and another to the Utah State Police, who would dispatch three squad cars to augment the on-site security team. Not that uniformed police could do anything to stop an attack by computer hackers, but that was the protocol. The NRC was convening its disaster response team. Orders would probably arrive at any moment to shut down the reactor until the nature of the attack was known.

No doubt the facility would be crawling with FBI cybersecurity forensic teams within the hour. And as the senior legal executive present at the time of the attack, she'd be dragged into the mess and miss her flight. She silently shook her head in dismay at the amount of effort that would be spent to chase down some adolescent hacker playing a prank to impress his peers.

There wasn't anything more she could do for now, so she was watching Anil's inspection circuit around the exterior of the squat concrete reactor building via video feeds captured by the facility's many security cameras. The images were projected into a holographic display above a small console in front of the much larger array of holographic safety indicators that dominated the room.

"You should have run when I told you to." The mysterious woman's voice was back.

Tracy hadn't seen her parents for months; they were sick; this might be their last Christmas. And now this miserable computer geek was going to make Tracy miss her trip home. She pushed the transmit button on the comm unit and tried to sound intimidating. "This is the senior legal counsel present at Hurricane. I hereby warn you that interfering with this facility's computer systems is a serious crime. I've already notified the autho—"

"Your facility is going to explode in thirty seconds." The voice sounded confident. Almost gloating. It sounded too real to be a prank.

But of course it was a prank. It had to be. Tracy had seen the disaster planning herself. There was nothing short of dropping a bomb on the thorium reactor that could cause it to leak radiation, much less explode. The worst a computer hacker could do would be to force the plant to shut itself down. That would be an embarrassment, sure, but in terms of safety there was nothing to worry about.

Tracy spoke back into the comm unit. "As a matter of basic physics, this reactor can't explode." She winced at the tremor of uncertainty in her words.

The voice sounded like it was stifling a laugh. "Fool. I'm pumping water into the reactor core."

Tracy involuntarily stood at the words. She recalled that the disaster plans had strictly forbidden using water to combat fires at the plant. This was because even if the fission reaction stopped and the failsafe core dump was activated, the reactor's molten salt reaction medium would remain white hot for hours. Days, even. Adding even a small amount of water would create enough steam pressure to annihilate the reactor walls and cause a Level Seven Radiation Leak.

That was why there were no water pipes connected to the reactor. The voice was bluffing.

"That's impossible!" she insisted, as her eyes flitted between the green safety readings in front of her and the exit door across the room. She recalled there were emergency radiation suits in a cabinet by the door.

Tracy felt a rising vibration in the floor beneath her feet.

Anil's voice crackled over the radio. "Something's wrong. I see cracks in the concrete!"

As Anil spoke, the array of glimmering safety indicators in front of Tracy blinked from green to yellow and then red.

The evacuation alarm started wailing. *Bwomp, bwomp, bwomp!*

Tracy felt the room spinning and fell to her knees. She grasped the console in front of her to steady herself. "Anil! Everyone! Get out of here!"

She watched helplessly as Anil's little figure in her holographic display turned to run, only to trip and fall as the ground around the reactor building buckled. Before Anil could rise, her view of him was obscured as jets of thick steam burst out of the side of the reactor building.

Senator Hal O'Brien frowned across the polished wooden conference table at his old classmate.

"Are you sure about this threat?"

"Yes," said the Colonel emphatically. "Absolutely."

"Do you have any evidence?"

Colonel Jaeger grimaced and his steel gray eyes flitted from O'Brien's face to the table between them. "Not yet."

O'Brien sighed and ran a hand through his thinning hair. His old classmate had suddenly shown up asking for an unscheduled meeting. O'Brien had juggled his hearings and fundraisers to find time to see the man. But Jaeger was wasting his time. "You're asking me to illegally fund a secret domestic espionage program, with no possibility of oversight, based on your gut feeling that some mysterious new threat is arising?"

"Yes."

"I trust your instincts, Jaeger, but I don't trust them that much. The DIA and NSA have good protocols, including that unbreakable quantum encryption technology my committee funded for you. I'm sure you can discuss your concerns internally without any risk of detection by this new enemy."

"Is that what you learned by being a politician? To sit around and do nothing until you know your ass is covered?" Jaeger's voice carried all its characteristic condescension, the mocking tones that alienated all but his most stalwart friends.

O'Brien clenched his jaw at the unprovoked insult. He was one of that small band of Jaeger's stalwart friends, and being insulted came with the territory. "You know the law has changed. The Patriot Act was revoked over a decade ago. You try warrantless domestic spying, you're toast. And I will be too if I allocate shadow funding to you."

Jaeger pointed to the chunky golden ring on O'Brien's hand. "I thought our class motto at the academy was *Do No Evil*. Since when did it become *Do Nothing*?"

"If you don't have evidence yet, nothing is exactly what I'm going to do." He took a deep breath. Arguing with Jaeger had never been easy. He could end the meeting faster if he offered Jaeger some face saving concession. "Give me your prediction of what the enemy's first moves will look like. If and when that pattern emerges, we can talk about specifics."

Jaeger looked down at the table for a moment, as if composing his thoughts. "It's hard to predict how the attack will unfold."

O'Brien threw his hands up in an exasperated gesture. It was time to ask his friend to leave so he could get back to his job. The United States economy had never really recovered from the food crises of the previous decade and now the nation was facing spiraling energy prices. Senators like O'Brien needed to focus on finding solutions to the many real challenges facing the nation, not on bizarre theories about unseen threats.

But Jaeger continued speaking. "The only certainty is that they'll use computer attacks; computer attacks that even our best defenses can't stop."

There was a loud knock on the door. "Come in," said O'Brien, hoping it was an urgent phone call he'd have to answer so he could end the meeting promptly.

"Senator, there's been a meltdown at the Hurricane nuclear reactor," said the breathless aide who poked his head into the room.

"A meltdown? I thought meltdowns were impossible with thorium." O'Brien reached out and grasped the remote control for the room's holovision. He clicked it on and it immediately projected three dimensional images from the National News Network. The images showed a cloud of smoke heading towards a small urban area in an arid landscape. "NNN has learned that moments before the explosion, the Nuclear Regulatory Commission received an alert from the power plant that it had been penetrated by some kind of computer virus."

O'Brien switched off the holovision and slammed his hand back to the table hard enough to shatter the remote control. "We gambled our economic future on the success of this thorium reactor program. If the Hurricane prototype melted down, energy prices will spike and the economy will crash."

O'Brien took deep breaths and quickly mastered his emotions. His training at the academy had taught him the need for decisive action in times of crisis. "There will be much work to do in the coming days." He stood to leave.

"Senator."

O'Brien stopped in his tracks and turned to Jaeger.

"How good was the computer security at Hurricane, Senator?"

O'Brien looked to his aide.

"The best, sir. No one could crack it."

"Senator, it's happening just like I told you. The war has begun."

O'Brien waved the aide out of the room and sat back down. "Did you know this was going to happen before you came here?"

"No. Not this fast. They're even stronger than I feared."

"What do you need, Jaeger?"

"I need funding."

"How much?"

"You're going to have to cancel that new aircraft carrier."

"What are you going to do with that much money?"

The Colonel rubbed his hands together and looked down at the table again. "The *Aeons* are too fast for me."

"The *who*?"

"That's what they call themselves. Aeons. Some term from a defunct religion. It means demi-gods whose divinity is derived from infinite knowledge."

"It seems like a fitting name."

The Colonel's eyes narrowed. "The point is not their name. The point is I can't catch them myself."

"If you're right about the threat, then no one can."

"I want to build a team. People with the same skills as the Aeons."

O'Brien leaned forward in his chair. "How?"

Chapter 1

Sarah Fenton shifted uncomfortably in her seat inside the stuffy lounge of the *Lal School for Gifted Orphans*. She stole a longing glance at the silent air conditioner that perched atop one of the room's two open windows. It was only April in Providence, but the temperature was already well over eighty degrees Fahrenheit, with high humidity making the heat unbearable. Unfortunately, the orphanage's climate control would only kick in when the temperature exceeded one hundred.

She wished the orphanage provided tank tops instead of the baggy long-sleeved shirt she was wearing. At least then she would be a bit cooler. She also regretted cramming tissue paper into her bra before leaving her small dorm room. The crumpled Kleenex were now damp with sweat and she would have to peel little balls of paper off her skin later.

Stuffing her bra was a childish thing to do, but she had wanted to look mature enough to deserve the internship she was here to interview for. She'd woken up thinking today could be her ticket out of the orphanage.

Yet by now she'd been sitting on an old, cracked faux leather sofa for thirty minutes, waiting for the morning interview. Around her on mismatched chairs and couches sat half a dozen of her classmates, fellow orphans at the institution that had taken her in.

They were a motley crew, mostly about her age of 16, of every size and race, all wearing clothing whose bland cleanliness only served to accentuate its age.

Every few minutes, the principal of the orphanage, Margaret Kim, would stick her head out of her office door and call out the name of one of Sarah's classmates. After a few minutes, that student would walk back out of the office, head hanging a little, shoulders slumped a little, and Ms. Kim would call the next name.

The whole event seemed like a waste of time. Sarah was impatient for her turn to come. She'd been up late necking with Robbie Bayer in a broom closet last night and she had overslept and missed breakfast; her stomach rumbled.

She looked down at the apple bar she was snacking on. It had unblemished red skin and sweet white flesh that tasted like an apple. But it was not a real apple. The apple bar was a rectangle, making it easier to stack than a round apple, and had no core or stem.

Sarah had eaten real apples a few times in her life. Their skin wasn't as perfectly red, and they had cores full of tough fiber and bitter seeds. But she preferred something naturally imperfect to something unnaturally perfect. She wished vat-grown foods like apple bars could look more real, even if it meant she'd occasionally swallow a few seeds by accident.

After shaking her phone to charge its kinetic battery, she checked the long distance signal strength, and saw it was zero. Not a huge surprise; it was well-known that communication satellites were failing and the undersea data cables were being corroded. Getting reliable access to what bandwidth remained was pricier than most people could bear. She certainly couldn't afford it.

Not that network strength really mattered. She probably didn't have enough credit to make a long distance call. She definitely didn't know anyone worth calling.

Her thoughts were interrupted by a muffled yelp and a thump from within Principal Kim's office. A moment later, a male classmate named Nathan came back out of the doorway, sheepishly rubbing his backside as he quickly strode out into the hall.

Sarah rolled her eyes. Nathan was such a dork.

She heard a man's voice calling out to Principal Kim. "Sarah Fenton is next." The voice was friendly, but carried the tone of someone who took for granted that his orders would be followed.

Principal Kim greeted her in the doorway. "Be careful," she whispered into Sarah's ear.

"Careful? – Don't you mean, 'good luck?'" asked Sarah incredulously.

"No, I mean, *be careful*," said the Principal pointedly.

Sarah noticed that the furrow across Principal Kim's brow was even deeper than normal, and brought her fingers to the small silver cross she wore around her neck for reassurance.

Nick Lal reached out to hold his girlfriend Peggy Peng's hand. She flinched away slightly, as if afraid of the contact.

"I'll be back soon, good as new," he said, in a reassuring tone. "I promise!"

The two sat on the granite stairs to their elite private high school, wearing smartly tailored gray jackets with the school's seal imprinted on the breast. Nick wore navy blue slacks, and Peggy a knee length navy skirt whose waist she had folded over several times so that it left half of her thighs bare. They both sported long locks of raven black hair.

Peggy looked down at her hands and played with a golden ring, not saying anything.

"What's wrong?" asked Nick, careful to hide his frustration. "Are you afraid of this silly implant I'm getting tomorrow?" He gestured at his head.

Peggy kept looking down, and spoke in a soft voice. "They talk about you."

"Who?"

She looked up and faced him, sadness making her features droop slightly. "Everyone. Everyone talks about you. They say you're going to be a freak. A weirdo."

"It's not such a big deal." He willfully softened his voice until it almost had a jovial tone. "It'll become common in a few years. Everyone will have one. You too, next year after you turn 17. I'm just a trendsetter!"

She looked away. "You know my family can't afford to get me one of those things. Once you have one, will you still stay interested in real people? In me? I've read the brochures. I know what it can do. Won't normal life seem so boring in comparison?"

He forced a chuckle. His voice came out higher pitched and more strident than he'd intended. "Oh come on. My parents are making me get it. And brain implants have existed for decades. This is just the most powerful one ever."

Peggy kept looking away. "Yeah, like 10 million times more powerful. It's a bit different from an implanted 10G phone."

"Whatever. Don't worry, I'm not that interested in computer stuff. I'll hardly use it."

She looked up at him again, her eyes narrowed in anger. "Yeah right. Once you do use it, you'll forget all about me." She stood up crossly and walked away.

Nick sat on the stairs, grimacing in frustration. He was genetically engineered to be smart, but he didn't even know how to soothe his girlfriend. He heard Peggy stalking through the ornate wooden doorway into the school, and turned to watch morosely as the door closed behind her.

But the door didn't shut. It was stopped, and then opened again by a strong arm. Three boys came out, wearing the same uniform as Nick. They walked jovially, as if they had just shared a joke. Upon seeing Nick sitting on the stairs alone, they exchanged knowing glances. Their grins faded into grimaces and their postures tensed.

Nick looked away. Jake Carnegie had been pushing him around since news of Nick's surgery had spread.

He'd taken the abuse patiently at first, but that had just encouraged Jake to be rougher. Nick had sworn that next time Jake bothered him, he would put up a fight. But Jake had two friends with him now, and three against one didn't make for good odds. Especially not when his opponents had the same genetic upgrades he had. And if Nick was going to fight, he'd let them throw the first punch, so he could claim self-defense and avoid being suspended from school. So for now, the best thing to do was just sit quietly.

He heard shoes scrape to a halt behind him. *Don't provoke them,* he thought. *Wait for another day when Jake is alone.*

Something heavy thudded down hard between Nick's shoulder blades. He fell forward down the stairs, bloodying his nose and tearing one of the elbows of his jacket.

He rolled onto his back and looked around in a daze from the pavement. As his eyes came back into focus, he saw a beautiful white and brown leather wingtip scrape to a halt on the pavement just to the right of his head. Desperate to get up, he moved to his other side, but saw a shiny black leather loafer waiting for him there.

"What were you doing, freako?" The voice came from between his legs. He looked down the length of his body and saw a pair of heavy black boots standing right below his groin. Instinctively, he scrabbled backwards and tried to close his thighs.

28

"Freako, I'm talking to you!" He looked up the long blue trouser leg, to the grey jacket that stretched snugly over broad muscular shoulders, and finally to the thick jawed, pug-nosed face of his attacker.

Jake was pointing at his own head with both of his hands. "What are you doing alone out here? Were you using your brain device to send secret messages?"

"I don't even have the implant yet, you—"

Nick's remark was cut off by a sharp kick to his kidney from one of the white and brown wingtips.

First Peggy ditching him, now Jake and his goons kicking him. His caution was replaced by anger and he tensed his muscles in anticipation of a fight.

Nick had grown up aping all of Jonnie Wang's kung fu holomovies and was going to put the martial knowledge he'd gained from the cinema to good use.

He slammed his open palm into the kneecap of his attacker. He didn't manage to shatter the knee like Jonnie Wang would have, but at least the boy fell to the ground heavily.

When Jonnie Wang found himself on the floor surrounded by enemies, he would spin his legs around above him in a way that pulled his torso up off the floor and brought him to a standing position, and then use all the torque stored in his hips on the way up to unleash a roundhouse kick at the nearest bad guy.

Nick spun his legs around above him as ferociously as he could. The maneuver did not pull him up to a standing position as planned but the momentum rolled him over on top of the boy he'd just knocked over. He planted a hand in the boy's solar plexus and pushed himself up.

As Nick rose, Jake greeted him by swinging a meaty fist in a wide arc towards his head. Nick had seen Jonnie Wang counter the same attack a hundred times with a devastating dip-roll-punch combination. He rotated his torso away and then down and back under Jake's arm. As he came back up to standing position he wound his torso to the right while driving a left uppercut at Jake's chin. His fist caught in Jake's armpit, eliciting a grunt but not doing much damage.

Nick wasn't done yet. He screamed sharply, unwound his torso and unleashed a right hook at Jake's jaw, with tight form that would have made Jonnie Wang himself proud. The punch glanced off Jake's shoulder and lost most of its force before hitting its target. But Jake was staggered, holding his jaw and cursing.

Nick winced and stared at his split knuckles. Jonnie Wang never hurt his hands when punching the bad guys, except in the outtakes shown during the ending credits. Apparently those outtakes were more realistic than the scenes that made the final cut.

Nick's contemplation of his injured hand was interrupted as he was shoved from behind. He managed to stay on his feet and used the momentum to carry him towards the small playground that served the primary school next door. Directly before him was a jungle gym made of vertical and horizontal steel pipes. Directly behind him was the last of Jake's goons, racing to catch up.

It was time to deploy a classic Jonnie Wang move: spinning around a conveniently located pole to kick a pursuing bad guy in the face. As Nick reached the nearest vertical bar of the jungle gym, he leaped forwards, grabbed it with both hands, and used his momentum to hurl himself around it feet first.

Unfortunately, the boy behind him had pulled up just out of range. Nick's feet spun past his opponent harmlessly. Jonnie Wang had never faced this dilemma, so Nick wasn't sure what to do. He held on to the pole and let his momentum pull him around it, once, twice, thrice. Finally, he ran out of momentum and his legs dragged on the ground.

Somewhere in the middle distance, he heard a group of girls laughing.

Jake trudged over. "We don't need freaks like you around here anymore. Go find a school for freaks." He raised a knee and slammed his black boot down on Nick's abdomen.

Nick gasped for air as he heard the three boys jeering and exchanging high fives. "I call dibs on your little girlfriend once you're gone!" Jake yelled as they sauntered off.

Sarah walked through the threshold and saw a middle-aged black man with closely cropped hair at the old beat up desk normally used by Principal Kim. Though he neither rose nor moved to shake her hand, his gaze was friendly and welcoming. She looked over her shoulder at the still-frowning Principal Kim with a shrug and arched brows, as if to say, *what's there to worry about?*

The man introduced himself as William Johnson and encouraged her to call him Willy. He offered her a seat across the desk from him.

Now Sarah knew she liked Willy. Principal Kim always made her stand in the office, but Willy had let her sit. She set aside her annoyance at her thirty minute wait and resolved to do her best to pass the interview. As she sat, she folded her hands in her lap in a way she thought looked attentive and polite.

Willy smiled and asked "Sarah, do you know why you're here?"

"I suppose that you're looking for some kind of intern for your company, and Ms. Kim has recommended me for an interview."

"Good guess, but wrong." Willy stared at Sarah for a moment before continuing. "I work for a federal agency. And I'm not looking for interns. We're recruiting for permanent positions."

"What? A permanent position for the government? Are you recruiting for the army or something?" No wonder you didn't like Nathan." She regretted the dig at her classmate immediately, and suppressed the chuckle in her throat.

"Let's just say if we hire you, you'll get to explore new worlds. But I don't want to get specific just yet." He raised his eyebrows as if politely requesting Sarah's agreement, but everything else about his manner suggested that this was no request.

Sarah smiled in assent, careful to keep her lips closed to avoid exposing her crooked teeth.

"You've been here at the Lal Orphanage for ten years now," said Willy as he glanced down at a tablet. "I know you've excelled academically and athletically. But I'd like to know more about you. What kinds of things do you think about when you're alone?"

"Well... all kinds of things." She looked around the room and then back at Principal Kim uncomfortably. She spent her days dreaming about boys, but that was probably not what Willy wanted to hear.

At night, she woke screaming from nightmares in which she was a young girl again and her mother gazed at her through sad eyes. Sad because Sarah had left the door open and the men with knives had come and now her mother wouldn't live to see Sarah grown.

This was also not something to share with Willy. She reached up and stroked the necklace she'd taken from her mother's trembling, red hands that night ten years ago.

Aware that Willy was looking at her expectantly, she seized on something to say. "Just now I was thinking about how it stinks that we have no more satellites so I can't get a good long distance signal. You're with the government, why can't you just send up some more satellites?"

Willy seemed amused by the question. He responded with one of his own: "Tell me, Sarah, how many satellites is the theoretical minimum we could use to create a global communications network?"

Sarah formed her fingers into a sphere in front of her face and thought for a moment. "Three. You form them in a triangle around the Earth, far enough out that each one can see the other two. I mean, that's if you don't care about the North and South Poles – to cover those you probably need five. Assuming polar bears and penguins don't need coverage, we can probably get by with the three."

"Polar bears are extinct so I don't suppose they need a signal. Not sure about the penguins." Willy pursed his lips thoughtfully, looking down at a small screen in front of him. He lowered his right hand below the desk as if reaching for a file in the drawer.

Sarah continued, "Hey, so why can't you guys in the government just send up a few new satellites?"

"That's not my department," responded Willy, with a sly smile and a wink. At the same time, he flicked his right hand up and over the table, sending two small rubber balls hurtling towards Sarah in diverging paths.

Sarah reached up with both hands and grabbed the balls out of the air without breaking her line of thought. "I know the economy is bad but can't we at least afford a couple new satellites? And, why

34

are you giving me two rubber balls? I need at least three to show you the satellite thing."

Willy leaned back in his chair and grinned at her. "How would you like to get out of this dump, Sarah?"

Nick and his parents sat facing each other in the spacious limousine as it drove east through Central Park, along one of the transverse roads that linked the two shores of Manhattan Island.

Peggy had refused all of his phone calls and ignored all of his messages. They'd been dating for a year, and he'd thought she really liked him. She should know how nervous he was about the procedure, so her refusal to talk to him now was particularly cruel. A simple message from her, wishing him good luck, would be more reassuring than anything his parents could say.

He stared out the window of the car, trying to push away his worries about Peggy and his anxiety about whether the surgeons would ask him about the bruises on his abdomen and the scrapes on his elbows. He didn't want to admit he'd been beaten up by bullies at school. Through the glass, he saw few other motor vehicles on the road, just a lot of bicycles. Every now and then, the car passed a horse- or mule-drawn cart.

Willfully ignoring the envious and resentful stares of the filthy men and women who were driving the carts along the road,

Nick fiddled with the seam at the bottom of his custom tailored Armani t-shirt.

"I remember, when you were born, Central Park was still closed to the public" began Nick's father wistfully in his slightly lilting Punjabi accented English. "The government needed the farmland. We had famines, riots, million percent inflation... So much has changed since those days."

"Because you changed it," said Nick's mother, reaching out and smoothing her husband's *dastar* turban back into place where it threatened to slip down and obscure one of his brown eyes.

Nick's father held his wife's olive hand in his brown one and spoke in a voice that was slightly reproaching. "Please, Fabiana, you did half the work. And this is besides point." He turned back to his son. "Your mother and I, our science merely delayed the inevitable. Humanity will be in peril again soon. Nick, I know you're nervous about today's surgery, but you're already a gifted boy and this implant will give you new abilities you can use to help the world the next time it's in danger."

Nick looked at his yellow-turbaned, grey-bearded father, and at his short and plump mother. Then he turned his head and stared out the window, looking through the reflection of his own green eyes, pale skin, and chiseled features.

"Oh, don't give him so much stress, Aakar, not on such a big day," interjected his mother. Her Brazilian accent, as always, was stronger when she was upset.

His father looked away and fingered his *kara*, a silver bracelet that symbolized his devotion to his religion, for a moment before continuing. "I'm sorry, I'm not trying to give you pressure, Nick. I'm just trying to help you put the day's big event into context. It will be worth it, I know you will *make* it worth it."

Sarah followed two steps behind Willy towards the small turboprop aircraft. As they drew closer, she allowed herself to fall further and further behind.

Willy turned around and gave a reassuring smile. "What's the matter? Haven't you ever been in a plane before?"

"Of course not," replied Sarah, almost laughing at the obviously ridiculous question. She motioned behind her towards the dark sedan that Willy had just parked at the edge of the airstrip. "I've only been in a car about three times before."

"Well, there's a first time for everything. Get onboard and maybe I'll even let you fly her for a while." Willy winked and broke into an exaggerated stage whisper. "Just don't tell my boss back at the ranch."

"The *ranch*?"

"That's where we're going. A facility, a training ground. You could call it a school. I like to call it a ranch."

Sarah glanced back at the car once again. "And you can just take me away to some ranch somewhere? Don't I at least have to sign some consent forms or something?"

Willy chuckled. "No, you're still legally a minor. Principal Kim is – was – your legal guardian and signed the forms for you. I have them right here in duplicate." He raised his worn leather case.

"I can't believe Ms. Kim sold me out so easily…" Sarah wasn't sure if she was joking or serious. She was startled by the speed of her departure from the Lal Orphanage. Just this morning she had dreamed of leaving, but now that she was finally out, she was filled with foreboding. The orphanage really wasn't that bad. She slowed to a halt and crossed her arms.

"I can tell you, Ms. Kim was a very tough negotiator," said Willy with a wry grin. "Your classmates will enjoy two cases of diet cola and a shiny new basketball, thanks to your sacrifice. Now, are you coming or not?"

Sarah came to a halt, set her half-filled duffel bag on the ground and crossed her arms over her body. Willy seemed kind, but so did most serial killers. Who knew where he was really taking her? Her mind filled with an image of her mother, face streaked with blood, eyes afraid.

"Can you at least tell me who you are?"

"I'm Major William Johnson."

"No," she said in frustration. "Where are you from? Who do you work for? Why are you taking me to this ranch?"

"The only answer that comes free is my name. The rest, you have to earn. Now if you don't want to come, I'm sure you can outrun me, but I'm not sure you have anywhere to go." Despite his stern words, Willy's voice seemed full of sympathy.

He pressed a button on the smooth black fuselage of the plane and a door that had been flush with the outside of the plane unfolded outwards into a staircase.

Sarah looked around her at the deserted airfield. Willy was right; there wasn't anywhere else for her to go. She rubbed her silver cross necklace for a moment, shouldered her bag, and followed Willy into the jet.

As she sat down in the seat he indicated, she saw that his jovial expression had been replaced, briefly, with a flash of pensive guilt.

Chapter 2

Tracy Cruz smiled through her veil down at her father as she let go of his hand. She knew that the smile he flashed back masked a grimace of agony as he painstakingly turned his wheelchair and rolled over to her mother's side in front of the first row of pews.

She was so glad that this day could happen while her parents were still present to witness it. And so lucky to have survived this long herself. If she had taken thirty seconds longer to zip herself into a radiation suit after the Hurricane reactor retaining wall failed, she wouldn't be here today. Maybe it was, as so many of the church's congregation had told her, a miracle from Heaven that she had survived.

It was also a miracle that she could support herself here in Kerrville. Eric Romero, CEO of Southwest Pipelines, Inc., a local oil and gas transportation company, was a member of the church, too. Despite the faltering local economy, he had been kind enough to offer her a job as a corporate legal counsel. It wasn't going to make her rich, but it provided an income she could use to service her school debt and a mortgage.

As her father wheeled himself away, Ricky had taken her arm firmly and was guiding her towards their spots before the altar. She looked up at old Reverend Doctor Edgar Lawson. The man she'd affectionately called Doc in her childhood looked almost as weak as her parents, but he was still ministering to the small nondenominational church here in Kerrville where she had grown up. She remembered him, thirty years ago, giving her a sugar cookie and sip of grape juice during her first communion. He'd flashed her the same reassuring smile then that he was giving her now as he presided over her wedding.

She found her spot and turned to face Ricky. He was trying to keep his composure, but his crooked grin kept bursting through and he was rocking as she shifted his weight from one leg to the other.

"Dearly beloved," Doc intoned in his raspy voice. "We are gathered here today to witness the wedding of two of our congregants.

"Ricardo de Leon has been a lifelong member of our National Unity Church. In fact, I don't think there was a single Sunday in the last thirty-odd years when I didn't see him singing in the choir, or organizing youth events, or helping some of our elder members to and from the parking lot.

"It was first in this church, in Sunday school, that Ricardo met Tracy Cruz. They grew up together in our community. Yet after high school graduation, Ricardo's life remained rooted in Kerrville, while Tracy went out into the world.

"The world can be a dangerous place, and Tracy was nearly taken from us. It was only thanks to the Lord that she has returned. And so it is with a deep sense of gratitude towards the Lord that today in His house of worship we join Tracy's and Ricardo's into a single life."

"Ricardo, would you make your vow to Tracy?"

Ricky gulped and took a deep breath. Tracy tried not to smile. She knew he wasn't good with words, and she wasn't expecting much. "Tracy, my love. Every day after you left Kerrville, I prayed to God that one day you would return. I know that God has a plan for all of us, and that there's a reason for everything. I could never understand why His plan called for you to leave. But I think now it was a test, to prove that my love for you was pure. I know that I will continue to pass that test every day for the rest of our lives."

Simple and to the point. Just like Ricky. But smart, too. No customary comments about forming a family together. Because he knew her secret, the reason why she'd never let herself get too close to any man before him.

"And Tracy? Your vows?"

Now it was Tracy's turn to gulp and take a deep breath. She looked out at the audience. The pews were packed with family and friends, some of whom she hadn't spoken to in the nearly two decades between high school graduation and her return to Kerrville last year. Yet all of them had turned out to celebrate her wedding. That was the nature of a small tightly knit community. The community she had wanted so urgently to escape when she was eighteen, for reasons that had faded with time.

Escape! She tried to push the panicked thought from her mind. She was far from the Hurricane reactor.

42

Her eyes fell on her parents, and she saw them holding each other across their wheelchairs and weeping. Today's ceremony had been put together hastily to accommodate the fact that they had both been diagnosed with late stage lung cancer and were not expected to survive much longer.

Escape! It wasn't only Hurricane she was thinking of. What was she doing, wedding to a man she'd been dating for less than a year, hurrying things along just so her parents could see her married before they died? She gasped for breath and felt the walls of the church closing in on her. She knew she was having another panic attack, but she could do nothing to slow it down. She needed to get outside, away from here!

"Tracy." Who was talking to her? Frantically, she turned and saw Ricky had leaned in and put his arms protectively around her shoulders. "Tracy, it's all right. We're all here. We're all here for you."

It was crazy to marry Ricky, but it also made perfect sense. She couldn't hope for a more understanding man. She took another deep breath and felt herself calming down. It was time to make her vows. She had briefly sketched out some words last night.

"Ricky, I—" Now she was sobbing, and she couldn't remember what she'd planned to say. She began blurting out words. "You know the last year and a half has been very hard for me. But you were always there. From the first day I got back to Kerrville, you were always dropping by and trying to offer a hand. I didn't really—I didn't appreciate it at first. Maybe I took it for granted. Since I left for law school, I'd always thought my life would be something great, that you would all watch me on TV while I conquered the world. When I came back to Kerrville last year, I thought it was just temporary. I thought it was a *setback*. And yet there you were, always trying to help, even if it meant helping me move on."

She embraced him. It was a violation of wedding protocol but she didn't give a damn. "And then one day I realized I wasn't going to leave. I didn't *want* to leave. And you were the reason. You were the reason, Ricky."

Sarah woke up on the lower mattress of the bunk bed Willy had directed her to late last night.

The bed was similar to the one she'd used until yesterday at the Lal Orphanage. But instead of the cozy, carpeted double room she'd lived in at the orphanage, here there were eight bunk beds in a much larger room that had unpainted wooden walls and floorboards. The space was separated down its middle by a high screen, which she guessed was an effort to separate boys from girls. Dim morning light streamed through long, multi-paned wooden framed windows.

She pushed a tangle of long blonde hair out of her eyes and shook away her grogginess. What had Willy called this place? The *ranch*?

There were about half a dozen girls in the other bunk beds on her side of the screen, all still asleep. They were of different races, but she guessed they were about the same age as her: sixteen or seventeen. They all wore the same light gray t-shirts and shorts that Willy had told her to change into. She looked down at her shirt, which was at least a half size too large, baggy around the waist and covering her buttocks entirely. On the left side of her chest, *S. Fenton* was printed in black letters an inch high.

Sarah wondered what this new place had in store for her. It couldn't be worse than the tedium of the Lal Orphanage. She wanted to put some proper clothes on and explore her surroundings.

She was dismayed to see that the meager pack of belongings she had brought with her was gone. Someone had taken them during the night, and in their place left more gray t-shirts and a pair of white sneakers. She reached up to her throat and was relieved that the silver cross necklace her mother had given her was still cold against her flesh. She caressed the angular metal, to remind herself that despite her strange surroundings, she was not alone.

Sarah slipped out of bed, and walked barefoot to one of the long windows and looked out.

Outside was a large expanse of orange, dusty terrain covered in rough bunches of yellow and green grass that she guessed was about knee height. In the distance, the flat terrain met the wooded foothills of an angular, orange mountain. A stream trickled down the face of the mountain and wound its way towards the building she was in, passing it a few hundred feet from her window. Around the stream, the vegetation was thicker, with bushes and some stunted looking trees.

No wonder Willy called it the ranch.

Her mind flitted to the Hurricane Reactor disaster, which had irradiated a section of the Southwestern desert almost eighteen months earlier. She dismissed as silly her momentary fear that Willy had taken her to part of the irradiated zone, and continued taking in her surroundings.

As her eyes adjusted to the dim light of the early morning, she noticed that several hundred yards away, well beyond the stream, there was a tall chain link fence stretching across the horizon. It was topped with strips of razor wire that glistened in the morning sun.

"Hi," a tentative voice came from behind her. Startled, she whirled around. A boy about her age, with olive skin, brown hair and brown eyes, was standing couple of feet away from her. *Chinese*, she thought, *maybe Korean*. "I'm Michael," he said. He stepped forward and held out his hand.

"Your last name is Kang, right? I can tell that from your shirt," Sarah replied, peering at his broad chest. "We have our names on our shirts. See?" She pulled the fabric on her shirt taut over her small breasts to make the letters easy to read.

Michael's hand was still wavering in the air uncomfortably. "Nice to meet you," he prompted.

"Oh, sorry, nice to meet you, too," she replied, taking his hand and giving it a cursory shake. She'd learned not to invest a lot in friendships at the Lal Orphanage. People came and left without warning.

She took a second look at Michael. He was good looking – tall and athletic, good skin, good features. She instantly hoped the ranch would be different than her orphanage, and she would spend a long time with Michael. She narrowed her smile so he wouldn't see her crooked teeth.

"You weren't here yesterday. Where'd you come from?" Michael asked.

"Last night. I flew in from Providence with a guy named William Johnson. We got in really late. I guess you were asleep." The trip from Providence had been exciting – it had been Sarah's first time in a plane – but she didn't want to gush about it to Michael. It was possible he wouldn't be impressed. For all she knew, he flew every day.

"Wow, you flew, huh?" asked Michael with evident envy. Then his face got a sly expression. "You know, in our grandparents' day, every time they invented a new technology, like telephones or planes, they would say the world was getting smaller."

"So?" asked Sarah, nonplussed.

"Well, the telephone systems are failing and we're running out of fuel for planes. That makes us the luckiest generation ever, because we're growing up in a world that keeps getting bigger and bigger!"

Sarah suppressed a smile and rolled her eyes at the joke. She wasn't going to laugh like a dork at the first slightly funny thing this boy said to her. "Very funny. Where did you come from?"

"I got here yesterday afternoon, with Brian – you'll meet him soon, I guess. We were brought here by a man named Rad."

"Rad? Willy didn't mention him." Willy hadn't really mentioned much at all. Just that she should pack her belongings and prepare for a new life.

"I never heard of Willy. But watch out for Rad, he's a real—"

Before Michael could finish, the doors at the front of the building opened and a slender man wearing a buttoned up black suit walked in, leading a trio of sleepy-eyed youth. He was of nondescript European heritage, and his thinning hair was graying to match his eyes. The three children trailing behind him were wearing gray clothes identical to those sported by Michael and Sarah. "That's Rad!" Michael whispered.

Rad looked up at the sound of Michael's voice. "Well, well, we're early risers, aren't we?" he asked rhetorically, rubbing his hands together. His manner was slightly off-putting, though Sarah could not decide why – the appraising angle at which he held his head? The slightly mocking tone of his voice?

He leaned down and looked at Sarah's shirt. "Ah, candidate Fenton! It's a pleasure to meet you," he said in a way that conveyed meeting her was, in fact, an indignity he was resigned to enduring. "I'm Rad Jaeger."

He held out his hand for Sarah, slightly too far away.

Sarah cautiously leaned forward and shook it, then moved back. His gaze made her uneasy and she wished there was an excuse to end the conversation quickly.

She was relieved when Rad abruptly broke away to check his watch, then clapped his hands loudly and chanted "Time to get up! Time to get up! Five minutes to muster!"

As the other boys and girls climbed out of bed and headed to the bathrooms at the rear of the room, Sarah sized up the social scene at the ranch. She was pretty sure she was the best looking girl, although a dark-featured girl whose shirt read O. Freeman offered stiff competition.

There was no doubt that Michael was the best looking of the boys, and she congratulated herself on breaking the ice with him early.

She also noticed that the other teenagers were checking each other out just like she was, some radiating bravado and others acting uncertain and shy. Clearly, she wasn't the only new arrival.

After a few minutes, Rad harangued them all into a double line and marched them out the door. Sarah pulled her sneakers on carelessly while conniving to get herself placed next to Michael in the short double line.

As they walked outside, Sarah turned her head to Michael, who was looking past her at the stream. "What the hell is this? Boot camp?" she whispered.

"No pushups yet, so can't be boot camp. The way Rad keeps clapping his hands and making us line up, it's more like kindergarten," he replied with a sly grin.

"Did your parents send you here?"

"I don't have parents. They died six years ago in a car crash, with my only uncle. I've been living in an orphanage in Boise, same as Brian," Michael replied, indicating the stocky boy who was walking in line ahead of him.

"Hey, I'm an orphan, too! Is everyone at this ranch an orphan?"

Before Michael could answer, Rad ordered them to halt in the orange dust, facing the stream and beyond it, the chain link fence. Rad rubbed his hands together and said, "Wait here until Major Johnson gives you instructions." Then he turned and jogged rapidly across the stream and towards the fence in his military style boots.

In her thin t-shirt and shorts, Sarah shivered uncontrollably. As she hugged herself to stay warm, she heard other kids' teeth chattering around her.

After a few minutes, Willy, dressed in a dark suit that matched his complexion, walked out of one of the run down wooden structures of the ranch and stood before the group. Sarah felt herself warm up a little at the sight of his friendly grin. He was far better to be around than Rad.

"Good morning, candidates," he began. "My name is Major William Johnson. You can call me Willy."

Most of the teenagers stood sullenly, hugging themselves in the cold. Sarah and a few others muttered "good mornings" in response to Willy.

Willy looked down guiltily. "Don't worry, we'll get you moving around soon so you can warm up. And then you'll get a hot shower and breakfast."

There were ironic cheers and sarcastic comments from the crowd around Sarah. She fought a smile. She was going to fit right in.

"Great," said Willy in a cheerful voice. "We're going to start our competition this morning. We want to find out who the fastest, strongest, and smartest of you are. And do you know what the prize will be?"

"A tour of your magic chocolate factory?" called out Sarah, earning a few snickers.

"The winners get to stay at this ranch!" proclaimed Willy expansively.

There was empty silence. Sarah felt her mood darkening. She didn't know who Willy was, and she didn't know why she was here. But she was damned if she was going to let Willy kick her out as if she wasn't good enough. Where was she going to go? Back to the orphanage in a cloud of shame?

She looked angrily around her at the other candidates, her nascent thoughts of camaraderie melting into jealousy and competitiveness. She noticed several wary faces staring back at her.

Willy chuckled. "Maybe staying at the ranch doesn't seem like it's so great right now, when you're new here, and you're cold and hungry! But believe me, you want to win."

Willy allowed his gaze to pass over the entire group of children and said in a reassuring voice: "And for those of you who don't win, don't worry. We have plans for you, too."

"Can I just give up now and have some bacon?" someone called out from the back row.

"All right, time to get started," Willy continued, paying the heckler no mind. "Line up in a single row behind this line." He scraped his foot along the ground, creating a shallow ditch in the orange dust. Sarah nudged her way into line with the other teenagers.

"I want you to run as fast as you can to that fence where you see the Colonel standing, touch it, and then run back across this line." He gestured at the line he had just scraped on the ground. "First three get hot chocolate with breakfast."

A footrace? Sarah thought to herself in disbelief. Michael was right that this ranch was like kindergarten. But she wasn't worried. She had run intramural track at the Lal Orphanage, and figured she could do well in the race. At least she wouldn't get kicked off the ranch.

Maybe she would even earn some hot chocolate to warm her up. Food was more expensive every year and the Lal Orphanage had long run out of budget for luxuries like hot chocolate. It had been years since Sarah had tasted the drink.

To her right, Michael flashed her a thumbs-up. "Good luck, Sarah," he said, and then he began shaking out his arms and legs to warm up.

"Has everyone tied their shoelaces nice and tight?" asked Willy loudly. Sarah realized he was looking at her intently. She looked down and gulped. She'd been so distracted checking out the other teenagers that she had not properly tied her left shoe.

She refused to be the only dork who needed to bend down in front of everyone to retie her shoelace. Especially not when she was standing right next to Michael. She'd just have to be careful not to lose her shoe during the race.

"OK, then," said Willy. "When I say 'go,' you go. Ready, set, GO!"

Sarah guessed it was at least half a mile to the wall, so she ran at a measured pace like she'd learned from her track coach. But she noticed several of the other candidates sprinting ahead of her, and became nervous that she was out of her league. She picked up her pace to keep close to them.

By the time she reached the stream, she was breathing heavily. She stopped short when she saw the depth and speed of the water flowing past her. The quiet brook she had seen from the window of her dorm now seemed more like a swollen river. But she wanted to win, so she plunged into the swift current

She gasped involuntarily. The thigh-deep water was frigid!

Around her, the other candidates were yelping as they felt the freezing water on their legs. Despite already being out of breath, Sarah pushed hard to wade through the water as fast as possible. About halfway across, as she lifted her left foot, she felt her shoe stick in the mud and slip off.

The water had turned muddy and it was impossible to see anything at the bottom of the stream. She bent down and stuck her right arm shoulder deep into the water, soaking her shorts and the front of her t-shirt in the icy stream. She gasped again from the cold as she felt around wildly. Her shoe was gone. She looked up. Almost all the other candidates had already crossed the stream and were running towards the fence.

She cursed in frustration, and resumed wading across the stream without her shoe. As she approached the far bank, she slipped and stepped down heavily with her now-bare left foot. A sharp rock cut into the sole of her foot. She gasped in pain and collapsed onto the bank.

The line of candidates was now 300 feet ahead of her. Her body was racked with shivers, she was sobbing in pain and frustration, and her nose was running. She stripped off her sodden sock and looked down at her left foot. The water-diluted blood was a translucent red against her skin. With the race unwinnable, she looked down in defeat. She hadn't even completed half of the first event in this bizarre competition. Instead of flirting with Michael, she would be sent back to the orphanage in disgrace.

Chapter 3

As she sat in the wet orange dust staring at her wounded foot, Sarah looked across the river at Willy. He was watching her with a sad expression.

She'd seen that expression before. In her nightmares. On her mother's face.

As before, she was going to lose her home because of her own carelessness. She reached up with a shivering hand and felt the silver cross around her neck.

No! Sarah resolved. *I won't be the first to be kicked off the ranch. I will finish this race!*

She dragged herself to her feet and resumed running at the best pace she could manage. Her left foot hurt too much to take the impact of a sprint, and the weight of her water-logged clothes slowed her as well. Instead of running normally, she lurched forward in a lopsided jog, each step with her left leg shorter and faster than the ones she took with her right leg.

After a minute of dragging herself along like this, she saw the first candidates reaching the fence, two hundred yards ahead of her. Then she noticed that instead of turning around and running back, they leaned against the chain links in exhaustion. It was several seconds before one of them – she thought it was Michael – turned around and began making his way back towards Willy. In those seconds, Sarah had made up fifty yards.

She pressed on. More and more of the candidates recovered and turned to make the journey back. But none of them were running anymore. Some were walking with their hands on their hips and their heads pointed up at the sky as if they were trying to drink in as much air as possible, and others were moving at a plodding pace, staring at their feet as they shuffled along.

Michael came jogging past her. His face was flushed and he was almost hyperventilating. He looked up at her and asked "Are... you... OK?" between huge gulps of air.

Sarah's breaths were rapid, but measured. "Yeah, I'm fine," Sarah responded as she flashed a thumbs-up sign.

She pressed forward, step by bloody step, and finally reached the fence right by where Rad stood. She placed her hand firmly on the metal and looked into his narrow grey eyes, waiting for acknowledgement from him that she had touched it. He held her gaze and motioned back in the direction of Willy with his chin.

With her leg muscles burning from exhaustion and the pain from her left foot now steadily crawling up her calf, Sarah reached up to the cross her dying mother had given her and smiled to herself. Surely her efforts would be enough to impress Willy. Maybe she would be allowed to stay.

The slowest candidates were only forty yards ahead of her. She pushed herself forward by focusing on the closest one and pretending she had lassoed him with a rope. Every time she pumped her arms, she was pulling herself along the rope, just a little bit closer. She used the rhythm of pumping her arms, punctuated with the pain that shot from her left foot every time it struck the ground, to modulate her breathing. The sense of rhythm made the motions seem a little easier than they really were, almost like they were all part of a crazy hip hop dance.

Sarah overtook several more candidates before she reached the stream again. Seeing several more figures ahead of her, foundering as they waded across the stream, she steeled herself and stepped in to the frigid waters.

This time, she ensured her footing was firm before each step. She didn't lose her balance, and she carefully felt the ground under her left foot before putting her weight on it. While crossing the stream, she passed three more of her exhausted competitors.

As she pulled herself out of the stream for the second time, she noticed Brian, the stocky boy that had arrived with Michael, sitting in the red dust near the edge of the stream, his clothes barely wet, with an ashamed look on his face. Despite her exhaustion and pain, she couldn't help giving him a quizzical look. Brian felt her eyes on him and looked up. "It was too cold," he murmured before looking away again.

She looked away from him without another thought. The finish line was about 200 yards away, and between her and it there were about six candidates struggling along at various speeds. She saw Michael stagger across the line in first place, and receive a pat on the back from Willy before falling down into a heap of grey in the orange dust.

She wanted a pat on the back, too.

Ignoring her injury, she leaned forward into a sprint. The pain was excruciating, but using the same rhythmic breathing and imaginary rope as before, just at a much faster tempo, she was able to overcome it. Her mind went blank, except to focus on the rhythm of sprinting. She passed other candidates without counting how many, or noticing who they were.

She saw someone else cross the finish line. "Good job, Bob!" called Willy.

The line was finally coming up to her. There were other runners on her right and left, all leaning in to cross the line first. She was wrong footed. The only way she could beat them would be to put all of her weight on her bad foot and push off hard.

She dove forward in a blaze of white hot agony.

As she sank to the ground, she felt a broad hand patting her on the back.

The Aeon paused as she surveyed the digital world she had entered. She floated in orbit over a small planetoid. The server she planned to penetrate was hidden deep under the planet's sandy surface, in a subterranean chamber.

What defenses had the Tactical Dynamics Incorporated weapons research laboratory built into this world, and what holes existed in those defenses? There was only one way to find out – to go in and confront them directly.

She descended to the surface of the planet and immediately felt a new sense of heaviness fill her body. She took a few steps forward, and realized with dismay that the soft sandy ground was yielding under her feet. She was leaving deep footprints as she walked. Even if whatever guardians existed here could not see her now, they would be able to follow her progress later.

Could she fly? She tried. No, she could only jump about one foot into the air before being pulled back to the surface by the planetoid's powerful gravity.

Gravity. An immutable physical law. Unless you knew how to cheat.

She dropped her heavy sword and shield, and shed her breastplate and helm into the sand. She stepped out of her long linen gown. And then she closed her eyes for a moment, reorganizing the makeup of her body. In a moment, she pulled most of the atoms out of it. Now she only weighed a few grams, and was almost invisible. The remaining 120 pounds stood next to her, a grayish, lifeless version of herself.

She moved away from the discarded possessions and atoms. She was delighted to see that her newly light steps now left no footprints. The security experts who had put together this server's defenses had failed to foresee her tactic. But they could not be blamed. They were merely humans, and she was an Aeon.

She turned around and focused on the pile of lifeless atoms in front of her. Under her control, it moved forward step by ungainly step. The body moved methodically, leaving deep footprints in the ground.

She flinched as the ground to her right exploded outwards in a shower of fine grained sand. A giant centipede had burst out of its underground lair.

The Aeon ducked as the centipede arced over her. She could see the sun glinting off of its shiny carapace, its razor like jaws trembling in anticipation of a kill.

The bug landed on top of the heavy body that the Aeon had left behind and bit deeply into its neck. A shower of red blood stained the yellow sand.

"You're so dumb I don't even need to fight you," the Aeon muttered to herself.

The centipede's long tail flicked, its innumerable legs searching for purchase in the shifting sands as it continued to feed.

The Aeon turned away from the grisly sight, and walked towards the hole in the sand the centipede had created as it burst out of the ground.

In a few moments of crawling, the Aeon was at the edge of the central chamber, her naked, nearly transparent body now visible because it was dusted with a layer of sand from squeezing through the centipede's tunnels. She peered towards the center of the dimly lit chamber and saw the object she had come to steal.

To fulfill her destiny of saving humanity, she would need an army. Her forces would be victorious not through weight of numbers but because of the advanced technology she would provide. She could develop weapons herself from nothing, of course, yet even she could work more quickly if she could reap the benefits of existing science.

Tactical Dynamics had built cutting edge designs for all manner of offensive and defensive systems. Weapons like high energy beams. Defensive measures like ceramic-metal composite armor. And multi-use technologies like directional electro-magnetic fields and artificial intelligence subroutines. And all of that valuable technology now sat in the filing cabinet one hundred feet away from her.

The only thing between her and the filing cabinet was... nothing. Just an empty chamber. She raised her foot to step forward and then paused, her foot wavering over the sandy ground.

It was a bit too easy. A trap meant to lure overconfident infiltrators into dropping their guard and celebrating victory too soon. She recalled the empty surface of the planet, where pressure-sensitive centipedes lay in wait to pounce on anyone walking past.

The tunnel through which she'd entered this chamber was made of the loosely packed sand she'd seen on the surface above. With a wave of her hand, she summoned three long streams of sand out of the tunnel. In moments, each stream had created a sand likeness of herself.

She blew on the three likenesses in turn, sealing the sand particles that comprised each into a single living organism. And then she sent the three warriors ahead of her into the chamber.

Dozens of human-sized ants emerged from the sandy walls and floor of the chamber and swarmed over her minions, tearing at them with claws and pincers.

As the melee proceeded in front of her, she formed more sand into a spherical shape and tossed it into the chamber. As soon as it impacted the sand, two ants ripped at it with their mandibles until it was completely destroyed.

Still within the tunnel, she carefully extended her arm well into the chamber and waved it around. The swarming ants ignored it, and continued their attack on the sand warriors she had created.

The Aeon shook her head at the foolishness of the security system's designers. *Did they really think this could stop me?* She could go back to the surface and retrieve her weapons and cut a path to the filing cabinet herself. She could stay here and form more sand warriors until she overwhelmed the ants. But there was no need to tax herself with so much effort. She just needed her existing three warriors to capture two small trophies before they were destroyed.

Several minutes later, she had used sand from the tunnel to bond her legs to the two ant legs her three warriors had torn from the attacking insects before being overwhelmed and shredded. Then she took a careful measure of sand and added it to her ephemeral body, so that her weight increased from several grams to several dozens of pounds.

She pulled herself up and took careful steps forward into the chamber. It took a few strides to learn how to balance on the narrow ant legs that protruded below her feet. They were awkward, but they would protect her from attack.

The ants attacked anything that hit the chamber floor. They had attacked her warriors, and they had attacked the ball she'd thrown among them. But clearly, there was an exception to the rule: they didn't attack each other. Now that she was walking on ant feet, and weighed the same as an ant, the Aeon could safely reach the filing cabinet.

After the other candidates had crossed the finish line and gone to showers, Willy extended his hand to Sarah and pulled her up with a surprisingly strong grip. He let her use his shoulder for support as they hobbled to a building to the right of the dorm. He used his hip to softly butt the metal push plate of a wooden door with a small red cross, and the word "Infirmary" stenciled on it. The sunlight streamed in behind them as he helped her sit on the edge of an examination table.

"Our medic is busy sourcing some special supplies so you'll have to trust me to look at your foot," he said as he stretched on a pair of pale yellow disposable rubber gloves that he got from one of the many wooden cabinets lining the room.

She gingerly lifted up her foot, which was now throbbing with every beat of her heart. Willy raised his eyebrows. "I'd love to tell you that what I'm going to do is not going to hurt, but that would be a lie."

He walked over to a sink and filled a shallow plastic bucket with warm water, and then went to another wooden cabinet and took out cotton swabs, alcohol, and what looked like a turkey baster.

Meanwhile, Sarah looked around the drab, dimly lit room and wondered why it looked like something out of the previous century.

Willy gave her a sidelong glance from where he stood. "Sarah, why did you refuse to admit you needed to retie your shoes before competing in a foot race?"

Sarah opted not to answer. Principal Kim at the Lal Orphanage had given her similar lectures on a number of occasions. With Ms. Kim, the best strategy to end the conversation quickly had been to listen quietly, but look angry.

Willy turned around to face her. She saw that the front of his suit and shirt were covered in orange mud that had rubbed off of her as he helped her to the infirmary. She felt a stab of sympathy and softened her expression.

He walked over and sat himself on a stool in front of her and put the bucket of warm water in his lap. "Stick your foot in here.

You have so much of this orange muck caked onto your foot, I can barely see the wound underneath."

She did as she was instructed, and he bent over and used his hands to flush away the mud on her injured foot. She could see the salt and pepper of his wiry hair, and the wrinkles on his forehead.

He pulled her foot out of the warm water and placed the bucket on the ground. He opened the bottle of alcohol and suctioned some of it into the turkey baster. "Brace yourself," he warned.

Sarah winced, but made no noise.

While he was cleaning her foot, Willy glanced up at her. "I can't believe you ran the better part of a mile with such a big hole in your foot. What motivated you?"

Sarah paused. She didn't want to talk about her mother. "I didn't want to get kicked out of here on my first day."

Willy pulled away the skin around her wound as he cleaned it, and Sarah winced with pain again. "Sorry. I have to be thorough, Sarah," he said and looked up at her, this time appraisingly. "There was more to it than not wanting to get kicked out. You were hurt, ready to quit, then our eyes met, and you were full of new strength."

Sarah remained silent.

Willy put down the baster and jabbed a cotton swab into her wound, and she reflexively pulled away her foot. He held on. "I know I'm a handsome guy, Sarah, but I think I'm a little old for you. Did I remind you of someone else?"

Sarah was starting to fear Willy would never be done cleaning her wound until she answered his question truthfully. She stared at the wooden cabinets set into the wall across the small clinic. "You reminded me of my mother."

Willy looked at the dark skin of his hand, which stood in stark contrast to the whiteness of her foot. Then he glanced up at her. "I doubt I look like your mother."

Sarah bit her lip. She needed to explain, so he would stop asking her and she could stop thinking about it. "Not your face. Your expression. It's how she looked when she knew she was dying and I would be on my own."

"I'm sorry for asking such a personal question."

She forced her eyes back to his. "No big deal. I'm an orphan. You already know my parents died."

"Why would that memory motivate you to run on an injured foot in some crazy competition you don't understand?"

Sarah looked back at the cabinets. Her vision was blurry. *Damn you for asking, Willy.* She just needed to get the words out and maybe he would leave her alone. "My mother died because I was careless, and I hurt my foot because I was careless. I was angry at myself, and I wanted to prove I could be better."

"Prove it to yourself?"

"Yes." She blinked and clenched her teeth and raised a hand to the necklace she wore.

Willy nodded thoughtfully and peered at her injury. "Well, you're going to be all right, Sarah."

66

Sarah thought for a moment. Willy was not someone she could trust. He had taken her from her safe orphanage and brought her to this bizarre ranch without offering an explanation. And he insisted on asking personal questions about her past while she was suffering from a painful wound.

But he seemed to feel bad about all that. Sometimes he even looked guilty. Maybe he wasn't such a bad guy. Maybe he could at least field some questions in trade for the ones she'd answered for him.

"Willy, I thought you were taking me to join some government program. But what is up with this place? Why does everything look like it's two hundred years old? This clinic is practically medieval."

Willy was silent until he was done wiping healing cream across her wound and then sat back thoughtfully. "Appearances can be deceiving, Sarah. You need to look under the surface to see the real truth."

Sarah looked back at him through narrowed eyes. Willy was blowing her off with aphorisms. She'd try again.

"I know you can't tell me exactly what this secret program is. But I know sometimes government agents have to do evil things like spying on grandmas or bombing children. What I want to know is, are we going to have to do evil stuff? I don't want to do evil, Willy."

"Don't worry, I'm a good guy," said Willy, with a quick wink. He reached for a roll of waterproof bandages lying on the counter.

"Are you? Sometimes you look guilty, like when you were signing me out of the orphanage and when you saw us freezing in the cold this morning."

Willy looked down at her foot for a moment, and then raised his eyes to meet her gaze again. "Sometimes I wonder if the ends justify the means."

Sarah shook her head in exasperation. "Whatever, Willy. Just don't make me do anything evil." She slid off the table gingerly, testing her foot. The injury still hurt, but she could already feel the tickling sensation of the flesh knitting itself together. The healing cream would make her good as new by lunchtime.

Sarah ignored Willy's offer to support her, limped across the room, pulled open the door and stepped outside. The sun was casting long shadows across the ranch. She blinked as the morning light reflected off of a shiny surface in front of the dormitory. She used her cupped hand to shield her eyes and looked again.

The sun was reflecting off of the glass and trim of a minivan that was parked in front of the dorm. It was white, with heavily tinted windows. Both the white paint and the dark glass were covered in a thin layer of orange dust. Its door was open and she saw Brian, the boy who had failed to cross the river, stooping to get in.

Sarah looked back at Willy, a questioning expression on her face.

"That boy just wasn't cut out for this place," said Willy, shaking his head regretfully. The minivan's door slid shut and it drove away in a cloud of dust that soon hid it from view.

"But don't worry about what's next for him. You have bigger problems."

Chapter 4

"Nurse," said Dr. Arora in faintly accented English, after scanning a number of holographic medical readouts projected in midair near the cot. "Let's remove the surgical dressing."

As the nurses approached, Nick Lal ran his hands over the strange bulges underneath the bandages that were wrapped around his skull. Before the operations, he'd gazed at diagrams explaining what those lumps were. But he still couldn't quite imagine what his head looked like now.

Nick's parents were sitting on benches about five feet above the operating room, watching the scene unfold below them from behind a reflection resistant Plexiglas barrier. Next to his parents sat Peggy. He was relieved that she had come. Before being put into a medically induced coma six weeks ago, he'd though she was leaving him.

One of the female nurses picked up a pair of scissors and Nick cringed at the coarse sound the blades made as they cut the outer layer of bandages. He noticed his mother, father and Peggy leaning forward, almost pressing their noses against the Plexiglas in anticipation.

One nurse began unwrapping the cotton bandages and spooling them to her colleague, who wound them around her hands neatly. Nick felt a strange sensation as if an unnoticed burden was being loosened and removed from his head. At the top of his field of vision, he could see layer after layer of pure white cotton gauze being unwound from his skull. His head felt unnaturally cool as the fabric that had covered it for weeks was removed.

Nick had wanted this brain implant since Dr. Arora had developed it a few years ago, and had spent months considering asking his parents about them. But the expense involved was breathtaking – equivalent to the cost of a Manhattan skyscraper – so Nick had never summoned the courage to broach the subject. Then, his father had announced the implants would be Nick's 17th birthday present.

That his parents had freely offered him the prohibitively expensive gift he secretly wanted was not happy news for Nick. Instead, it made him bitter. His parents' suggestion meant they weren't satisfied with him as he was.

And not for the first time. Before Nick was born, his parents had decided they would not be content with a natural baby, one carrying the genetic imperfections of a normal human. So they had invested a significant part of their large fortune in genetic engineering. That was why Nick had fair skin and green eyes despite having a father from Amritsar and a mother from Rio de Janeiro. Why he stood more than a foot taller than his parents. Why his IQ was a couple of standard deviations higher than their genius level scores.

Their investments in creating a superhuman child were just facet of his parents' hypocritical lives. A few years before Nick's

71

birth, they had prevented a global famine by developing super-efficient food factories. They sold the food cheaply, with a tiny profit margin, and soaked up public praise for doing so. They also made huge donations to charities ranging from wildlife preserves to orphanages. His father pointed to his Sikh religious obligation to contribute to communal meals as inspiration, and his mother to her Catholic belief in charity.

But his parents were no aesthetes. His mother lived a life of ultimate luxury and complete exclusivity. She ate the finest foods, travelled in the fanciest cars and planes, and lived in the grandest lodgings, all the while avoiding any contact with the masses she claimed to love. His father, who loved playing the role of self-sacrificing entrepreneur and philanthropist, was ruthless when it came to amassing and preserving power. Whenever the Lal family's near-monopoly on global food production was challenged by a new competitor, he used his immense financial resources and political influence to destroy the threat.

By now, the nurse had unraveled several coils of bandage and Nick could see that the dressings were no longer pure white. There were dark red spots of dried blood on them, and lighter stains that look like tea spilled on linen. He felt a tightening in his stomach as he realized the stains had been made by fluids that had seeped out of his skull.

Finally, he winced at a slight, stinging pull on the half-healed flesh around the back of his head, as the nurse carefully removed the last layer of bandages. The hair on his forearms stood up straight and he shivered.

He craned his neck impatiently, trying to get a clear view of his head. There were no good mirrored surfaces. Even the Plexiglas separating this room from the theater where his family and girlfriend sat was glare resistant.

"Surgical wounds in patient Vinicius Lal appear well healed and the MindWave implant appears to have been accepted by the subject," said Dr. Arora, as he leaned down to inspect the back of Nick's head.

The doctor walked around into Nick's field of vision. "It appears you have recovered very well from the surgeries. I'm going to recommend that you begin training with your MindWave as soon as it can be arranged."

Nick glanced around and saw his parents and girlfriend in the theater above and looked up with his eyebrows raised. "So?" he said, and tentatively felt around behind his head with his hands.

"You don't want to touch it now," said Dr. Arora. "There's still a small chance of infection."

In response to Nick's inquisitive glance, the doctor added. "Silly me. Let me show you your reflection." He turned to the nurses. "Please bring the mirrors."

As the nurses bustled, Nick's father stood up, his beaming smile visible through his full beard, and gave a double thumbs-up. "Looking good, son!" he called through the Plexiglas.

The nurses aligned two mirrors like barbers displaying their work, so that Nick could finally see the back of his head in the mirror.

The front three quarters of Nick's head were unchanged, except that his head only sported a short stubble of hair instead of the long, straight black locks he had always maintained before.

But the back of his head looked alien. There were three circular vents, about the size of bottle caps, just above the base of his skull. They were surrounded by pink, swollen flesh, and protruded enough out of his skull to make them impossible to miss even in profile, at least while he had a shaved head. Below the middle vent, there were a number of jacks and ports, as if Nick's head was meant to be plugged into something.

Nick swallowed back the bitterness he'd felt moments ago. Whatever his parents' motivations, he had just received augmentations that made him almost superhuman. His vision was now more acute than an eagle's, his hearing sharper than an owl's, and his reflexes faster than a gunslinger's.

The biggest benefit to come not from his enhanced physical senses but from the networked computer that was now grafted to his brain and which he could use to immerse himself in virtual worlds beyond the realm of physical senses. The *MindWave*.

He smiled and turned away from the mirrors and towards his family and Peggy. Behind his grinning father, he saw his mother sitting still, her face pale and her arm around Peggy's shoulders.

Peggy was averting her gaze away from Nick, and held her hand over her mouth.

Six weeks had passed since Sarah had woken up in the crowded dormitory building at the ranch. This morning she only shared it with four other candidates. All of the others had been driven away in the white minivans to an unknown destination. *They were probably just being sent back to their orphanages*, Sarah had told herself innumerable times. But she wasn't quite sure.

There had been a series of physical challenges, like the race where Sarah had injured her foot. Then the challenges had become more intellectual, such as a session in which they had rushed to complete a series of abstract logical puzzles. Every few days, one or two candidates would be sent to the minivans.

There were no scores posted. None of the orphans knew their place in the standings, or what it would take for them to be the next one beckoned over to a waiting minivan by an apologetic Willy or an impatient Rad.

At first, Sarah had lost a lot of sleep obsessing over how she was doing and how she could prevent herself from washing out. Gradually she had realized there was no benefit from worrying, and the best thing she could do at nightfall was blank her mind and get rest.

She had mixed feelings for the other remaining candidates. She couldn't help respecting Greg Silverstein. Greg compensated for his small, compact physique with a booming voice and decisive manner. He seemed like the kind of guy who would stay with you to the end – covering your back if you were an ally, or hunting you down if you were an enemy.

Olivia Freeman, a tall dark-skinned girl who followed rules precisely and mostly stuck to herself, was much less expressive. Sarah would have thought Olivia was emotionless, except for the fact that Olivia seemed to have a soft spot for Bob Eckers, the boy who had finished in second place between Michael and Sarah in the race on the first day. Sarah often saw the two murmuring together softly between drills or over meals in the canteen where the candidates ate.

Whatever Olivia found in Bob, Sarah couldn't see it. Bob was a physically powerful boy, sure, but the way he used his strength to intimidate and bully the other candidates was a turn off. Aside from Olivia, he didn't seem to get along with any of the other candidates.

Finally, there was Michael Kang. Now, as she prepared to change out of her pajamas into her daytime outfit of gray shirt and black pants, Sarah gave him a quick grin between the screens that separated the boys' side of the dormitory from the girls'. He smiled back, but quickly averted his eyes as she pulled her night shirt over her head, revealing her sports bra.

She cursed herself for being idiot – what was she doing flirting with a competitor? Yet she knew she wouldn't stop.

There was a loud rap on the wall of the dormitory. Sarah looked up to see Rad standing in the doorway with his hands on his hips, and instinctively pulled her shirt quickly down over her torso.

"Last stage of the competition today. Today you win or you pack up and go home. Meet in the shed in five minutes," Rad announced into the room before striding away.

Sarah reached up to the cross around her neck and took a deep breath.

There was no time to waste on sentiment. If Rad had given the candidates five minutes then he would expect them lined up and ready to start the drill in exactly 300 seconds. She hurriedly finished changing and jogged across the orange dusty ground to the room called the shed.

The shed was not a building of its own, but a room in the same structure that housed the infirmary where Willy had patched up Sarah's foot. Instead of old fashioned medical devices, the shed held five virtual reality gaming pods all hooked up to a central server. Each gaming pod consisted of a deep chair upon which the user sat. A headset descended over their head to provide immersive visual, aural, and olfactory input. Small probes extended from the headset into the ears to manipulate the user's sense of balance and velocity. Gloves and shoes provided detailed sensory input to the hands and feet, while a series of wire leads delivered cruder sensory input to the rest of the body. Users were strapped securely into the chairs for their own protection – the experience was so immersive that without restraining straps, users often fell out of the pods.

In the outside world, VR pods like these were used to enjoy video games, immersive holomovies, and other forms of entertainment. At the ranch, the devices were put to a more utilitarian purpose. In earlier stages of the competition, Sarah and the other candidates had used the pods to navigate virtual worlds using avatars, or projected bodies. None of those tests had been particularly demanding. She was sure today would be different.

Sarah and the other four candidates scampered into the shed at about the same time. Rad gave them a once over, curled his lip as if in disappointment, and made a curt gesture with his head towards the pods.

Sarah and the other candidates were arranging themselves in the chairs when Willy entered the shed and came around to help each person tighten their straps and test their connections. He would kneel down by each orphan and check their pod, while saying a few exhortative words.

Willy came to Sarah last. As he bent down beside her, he winked and said "Make sure you pay attention to the instructions for once, Fenton." Sarah shrugged back noncommittally in response. She didn't recall ignoring any instructions during earlier stages of the competition. And she had expected something a little more encouraging from Willy, with whom she'd built a friendly relationship since the day he'd cleaned her foot wound.

She didn't have much time to ponder his strange remark. A moment after he stood up, the glass visor at the front of her headset, which had been transparent while the VR Pod was offline, came to life.

Sarah found herself floating in a featureless pool of dark blue green liquid, with Willy's face floating in front of her. "Candidates, during this final stage of the competition we want you to manage multiple competing priorities in an unfamiliar virtual setting. You will be scuba diving under the ocean, with the objective of reaching the surface. On your left wrist you will have a watch that displays your depth and your points. Collecting jewels from the seabed will increase your points. Red jewels add one point. Blue jewels add three points. And yellow jewels add ten points. You can use the spear guns you'll be carrying to harpoon fish. For every green fish you reel in, you add five points. And for every silver fish, you add twelve points. You'll have rubber sacks you can use to carry the gems and fish you collect with you. If it's in your sack, you add the points; if it's not in your sack, you don't. Keep a look out for the jelly fish. Each one of them that touches you or your equipment subtracts fifty points from your total. By the way, if you run out of air, you'll die. Not for real of course, but it will feel extremely unpleasant. All right, starting in three... two... one!"

Willy's face disappeared and now Sarah could see that the blue green liquid was seawater. Above her, she could faintly see sunlight filtering down. Under her, the water was darker, but she could make out the seafloor about fifty feet below. She looked at her left wrist and found a watch with a large glowing display.

Depth: 250 feet. Points: 0.

Around her, she could see four other floating figures sizing up the situation just as she was. While she couldn't see faces, even in the dark waters she could tell whom each candidate was by the size and shape of their body. Bob was big and thick, almost lumpy where his muscles strained against his wetsuit. Greg was smaller, and seemingly made entirely of squares and rectangles. Michael was slender and athletic. The curves of Olivia's body contrasted sharply with the hard angles of the boys.

She could see Michael looking between her and Olivia a few times before figuring out who was whom. He swam towards her, making several hand gestures she didn't understand. In the meantime, Greg swam away into the distance, and Olivia edged toward Bob.

Bob reached around and unslung the spear gun that was slung over his shoulder and pointed it right at Sarah. She tried to dodge but, floating in the water, there was nothing to push off of and no way to gain momentum quickly. She heard a sharp sudden hiss and saw a burst of frothy gas emerge from the gun's barrel.

Sarah looked down at her abdomen and saw a black string piercing her belly where Bob's harpoon had penetrated it. She let out a scream through her scuba breathing regulator, but it emerged from her mouth as a silent cascade of bubbles.

Michael unslung his own spear gun and pointed it in Bob's direction while swimming to Sarah's side.

Sarah grabbed at the harpoon string and yanked at it. All that came out of her abdomen was more string. The projectile must have completely passed through her and travelled on. She screamed again, and this time dislodged her regulator and took a mouthful of water that made her choke. She flailed around in the water, trying to dislodge the harpoon with one hand while grasping for her regulator with the other.

She felt a strong arm seizing her by the shoulders and tried to push away, but she was half suffocated and too weak to fight. Her eyes were dimming and instead of the ocean around her she saw an image of her mother lying on the floor in a pool of her own blood, staring back at her in grief.

Something was thrust into her mouth and she could breathe again. She sucked in three huge lungfuls of air before she realized Michael had given her his scuba regulator. He was still holding her tightly so that she couldn't thrash around. Now that she was returning to her senses and calming down, he let go of her. The first thing he did was reach behind her, grab her abandoned regulator, and put it into his own mouth.

Then he yanked sideways on Bob's harpoon cord. It slid across her abdomen and through her hip until it was floating freely in the water. It took a moment for Sarah to realize that the harpoon had passed through her harmlessly. It seemed that in this virtual world, the candidates could not use their spear guns against each other.

She felt foolish at panicking when she hadn't even been hurt. She should have known all along – she'd never felt any pain. Her shame quickly turned to anger at Bob and she turned towards where he had been. But he and Olivia had disappeared into the murky waters.

As she peered into the ocean, she saw a glimpse of something silver heading down deeper towards the seabed. She tugged on Michael's arm. It was a school of the silver fish that could help them amass points. She began to swim towards them but stopped when her regulator was pulled out of her mouth.

She remembered that Michael had traded regulators with her while she was panicking. She turned towards him to trade. As they exchanged the breathing apparatuses, Michael was shaking his head and mouthing something, but even if she could have read lips, his mouth was hidden behind a stream of bubbles. He pointed up and Sarah raised her eyes towards the sunlit waters above her, but saw no fish or jewels.

Not knowing how else to communicate, Sarah turned back towards the school of fish and swam after them. Out of the corner of her eye she saw Michael swimming after her.

The fish were heading downwards so she followed. The display on her watch showed her depth increasing to 260, then 270, and then 280 feet. Just when she was getting close enough to line up a shot with her spear gun, she felt Michael tugging on her arm again. She turned to look and saw several translucent white jellyfish swimming upwards from the seabed towards her. Each jellyfish that touched her would reduce her points by fifty, she remembered.

The way Michael had pulled at her, he had pulled her closer to the jelly fish. Sometimes he was a big help, and other times he was a clumsy oaf. She gave him a dirty look that she hoped he could read through her scuba gear, and stroked hard with her hands and feet to guide her out of the path of the jellyfish just in time.

With the jellyfish floating safely above her, she turned back to the silver fish. Luckily, they had stopped near a large rock on the seabed, and were still close enough she thought she'd be able to shoot them with her spear gun. She lined up a shot at the closest fish. She turned to Michael, to give him a chance to take aim at a second fish. He didn't.

She couldn't wait all day. She fired.

Her harpoon shot true through the water and impaled the fish. Willy had said she would only add the points for objects she placed into her sack. And he'd also warned her to pay close attention to his instructions. Sarah immediately began reeling in the cord that pierced the flopping animal.

Out of the corner of her eye she could see Michael gesturing furiously again, pointing down at the seabed. She peered downwards and saw a glint of gold in the sandy bottom. Now she understood. The other fish had swum away when she'd impaled the first one, but there were jewels right below them.

She finished pulling in the fish, extracted the harpoon, and shoved it into her sack. Instantly, the display on her watch changed to read:

Points: 12

She prepared to swim down towards the jewels Michael had spotted but realized she was already drifting down towards them. She must have built up downwards momentum while hauling up the fish. It made sense. *Every action has an equal reaction*, she remembered learning in physics.

As her feet reached the bottom she knelt down and used her hands to start digging out the closest golden jewel. It was cut like a diamond, shiny enough to glint even in the dull light of the seafloor, and just big enough to fill the palm of her hand.

Just as she extracted it, Michael reached the bottom and tried to kneel down beside her. Unlike her, he had trouble getting his knees to stay on the sandy seabed.

He had only just gotten settled as she opened her rubber sack to put the gem inside. He immediately grabbed at her wrist. For a moment she was angry. *Who the heck does he think he is to take my jewel away?* Then she remembered how he had given her his regulator when she was drowning and her anger faded to gratitude. She held the golden gem out towards him.

Michael held out is hands palms outwards in a "no thanks" gesture.

Sarah shoved the gem into her sack and was momentarily satisfied to see the score readout on her watch increase to twenty-two. As she excavated the next jewel and Michael gestured wildly again.

She could see thick clouds of bubbles coming out of his regulator as he tried to speak but she couldn't understand him. His behavior was bizarre. Maybe he had had enough of the ranch. Maybe he was trying to fail the mission and go home. She would miss him, but that didn't mean she was going to give up, too.

She would at least try to talk some sense into him. Except there was no way to communicate under water, aside from simple hand gestures.

As she dropped the second jewel into her rubber sack, she had an idea. She tried to dump out the fish and two jewels already inside but found they wouldn't budge. *Well at least no one can steal them from me.* So she turned to Michael and pointed at his empty sack.

He reluctantly passed it to her with a curt hand gesture that she interpreted to mean "don't dare put anything inside this." She inverted the bag's mouth so that it pointed downwards, took a deep breath from her regulator, and then stuck the mouthpiece inside the sack and let air stream out into it.

Michael caught on to what she was doing and reached out to steady the lips of the bag so that it would not float away or twist to let the air out. After several moments of blasting air into the sack, Sarah bent her neck and squeezed her head inside it. Just as she'd hoped, she'd created an air bubble several inches deep inside the waterproof walls of the bag.

Michael followed her inside, so that their two heads were nestled against each other inside the rubber bag. Sarah said "What the hell are you—"

"Our only objective is to reach the surface."

"Willy told me to pay attention to his instructions. And then he told us how to score points."

"Not *score*. He said *add*. The points add weight. That's why you can kneel on the bottom and I can't."

"So?"

"Points are bad. The only way to win is to reach the surface first. It's another race."

"Damn it. I think you're right. And now my sack is so heavy."

"Ditch the sack."

Sarah began to say "I'm sure it won't work" but realized she was speaking into water and Michael couldn't understand her. Her regulator was no longer releasing gas, and water was rapidly filling the air bubble.

Not only were they unable to communicate. She was out of oxygen.

Sarah pulled her head out of the bag and immediately tried swimming upwards. But she was too heavy.

She dropped her sack onto the seabed, and tried swimming upwards again. As she'd feared, it didn't work. She recalled that Willy's instructions had been that the points stayed with you as long as the fish and jewels were inside your sack. He had never said you had to hold onto your sack.

Michael handed her his regulator. She realized that the airflow coming from it was already weakening. She must have wasted a lot of his air when she was drowning. Michael wrapped his arms around her and they tried swimming upwards together. But their combined efforts were still not sufficient to overcome the weight of Sarah's sack.

She cursed herself. She was done. There was no way for her to get up to the surface. Michael could stay beside her until his air ran out too, but that wouldn't do any good. He should abandon her and swim for the top himself.

She would have a few moments of panic and pain as the air in her lungs ran out, but it was all simulated. Her virtual reality pod would eventually disengage, and she'd wake up defeated, yet otherwise fine.

She knew she'd never see him again. She'd be escorted away to one of the waiting white minivans without even a chance to say goodbye. But there was no other way. She pushed Michael away and shook her head. Then she handed his weakly bubbling regulator back to him and pointed to him, then upwards.

As he rose he grabbed onto her arm with his left hand. She looked up and mouthed the words "Go!"

He shook his head and then indicated his right with his chin. She saw that his right arm was raised above him, holding his spear gun, and that the harpoon had impaled a jellyfish just a few feet above him. She glanced at the watch on his left hand. It read:

Depth: 300 feet. Points: -50.

They rose slowly. Sarah was going to run out of air before they could ever reach the surface. She realized that she had accumulated so many points that their combined score was barely negative.

She saw there was another jellyfish swimming by the one Michael had harpooned and she used her free hand to unsling her spear gun and take the shot. Her spear pierced the jellyfish and she saw the display on her watch change to show her points at negative eighteen.

Now they were rising towards the surface quickly. Sarah felt the waters flowing past her growing warmer as they neared the sunlight above. But for the second time in several minutes, she felt herself suffocating. Her chest heaved involuntarily as she tried to suppress the overriding need to breathe.

Michael used his free hand to pull her up so that she was even with him. Then he spat out his regulator. She watched as a final, tiny bubble emerged from it as it floated upwards beside them in the water. There was no more air, and her watch readout still said they had one hundred feet to go. It was too far. She couldn't resist her body's need for air any longer.

She opened her mouth to take a final, deadly breath.

Michael let go of her hand and seized the back of her head and pulled his mouth to hers and as soon as their lips were sealed around each other, he blew the air out of his lungs into hers.

The air was hot and moist but it held enough oxygen to keep her alive. She held on to him and pressed her mouth into his and soon she felt the surface of the water breaking over her head and the sunlight shining on her face.

Two weeks after Nick was released from the hospital, his parents had finally agreed that he didn't need to return to his high school. His mother was worried that the bullying he had endured before his surgery would only worsen, and that any blow to his head could be particularly dangerous now that he had the implant. His father, nervously rubbing his kara bracelet, reasoned that Nick was better off spending his energy learning to use the MindWave than spending his time on a more pedestrian education.

Nick didn't mind so much. The only classmate he cared about was Peggy, and he didn't have any classes with her so dropping out wouldn't mean he'd see her any less. In fact, she'd been so busy since he'd been released he'd hardly seen her despite being in the same school building for eight hours a day.

After lunch, from the privacy of his bedroom, Nick picked up his holophone to call Peggy with the news. His parents paid a small fortune every month for Elite Priority access to the multinet, so as always he had full signal.

Peggy responded after five rings. She had just gotten out of class and was still wearing her school uniform.

"I decided I'm too cool for school," he said with a grin. "So I'm dropping out."

Peggy didn't return his smile. "OK, I guess I'll see you around when I can," she said noncommittally.

"What does that mean?" Nick demanded. "Why are you always so busy?"

"I have to study for the SATs. You know how it is," she mumbled unconvincingly.

"Bullshit. You've been studying for the SATs for six months and you always had time for me. What's going on?"

She looked down and responded with a mix of regret and anger. "Nick, this isn't working. You look … scary. You don't fit in at all; you can't even stay in school. And…"

"And what?" he pressed.

"And I just don't feel right around you anymore. I'm sorry. I hope we meet again in the future but right now I just can't."

She ended the call, and her image blinked away into nothingness.

Nick quickly redialed Peggy's number. "Call Blocked" the holophone announced in its saccharine voice.

Nick angrily stood up and punched the wall of his bedroom. He paced around for a minute.

Then he took his holophone stand and flung it against the wall, shattering it. He stared angrily at the broken pieces, wondering how he was going to explain the phone's destruction to his parents.

One piece of the wreckage caught his attention: the network antennae that connected the phone to the internet. He looked around until he found his wireless router and pulled the network cable out of its socket. It was the same size connector as the internet connection jack in the back of his MindWave.

MindWaves were not equipped with wireless antennae for two reasons. One was a health concern about using mega bandwidth antennae in a device connected directly to the brain. The other was a fear that hackers could secretly hack into MindWaves via antennae and literally steel the MindWave user's digital memories. The absence of an antenna meant at least that users could be sure they were safe from hacking attacks while the network cable was unplugged.

Nick had already begun to master the basic offline functions of the MindWave, such as enhancing his calculation skills and memory, monitoring his own heartbeat and blood sugar levels, and using his powerful vision and hearing to spy on the people walking on the streets below his window. It still felt amazing to pick out the individual hairs on someone's head from twenty stories above.

But he had never dared to plug his MindWave into the multinet. He'd been told that the first attempt to connect a MindWave to the network could be terrifying. He'd heard rumors that an early user in Los Angeles had actually gone mad and killed her parents. Nevertheless, he needed the MindWave's powers now.

Getting past the wireless network servers Peggy had instructed to block his calls would be no problem. The multinet's infrastructure might be crumbling, but he enjoyed the fastest uplink money could buy, complete with a dedicated fiber uplink to the best remaining backhaul network in America and reinforced with directional microwave backups, so he'd definitely have the bandwidth to succeed. All he had to do was use his MindWave to find a way through the firewalls.

Peggy was just upset because she was afraid he'd get bored of her now that he had the MindWave. What better way of showing Peggy how much he cared about her than using his MindWave to appear on her phone despite her efforts to block him?

He sat down on his bed, reached around behind his head, and found the correct socket in the back of his skull. His hands fumbled for a minute before the cable slid into place and he heard a loud clicking noise reverberating inside his mind.

Chapter 5

Nick closed his eyes and commanded his MindWave to enter the multinet, with the intent of finding his way through the mobile network servers to Peggy's phone.

Instead of a navigable world, Nick found himself in a vast dimensionless darkness, filled with luminescent arrays of numbers and images. He tried turning his head and shifting his eyes, but his view didn't change. He realized he wasn't seeing with his physical body. Somehow the images were being projected directly into his mind.

He tried to move his consciousness around, but he couldn't feel his own physical existence within the dizzying endless blackness. He had no concept of his own location, or even of up and down and forward and back.

Nick ordered the MindWave to turn off, yet nothing happened. He thought back to his physical body, sitting on his bed in a room in Manhattan. He willed his hand to reach behind his neck and unplug the MindWave, but he couldn't control his limbs anymore. He couldn't sense them, even. He was disconnected from himself.

He cried out, but speech had left him.

There was no way back. He felt a chasm of terror engulfing him as he realized he would be trapped in this chaos forever.

And then she was there. A beautiful redheaded college-aged woman, dressed in a luminescent white silk gown that accentuated her statuesque figure. She stepped out of the blackness, giving form to formlessness, lending order to chaos by virtue of her very presence.

The beautiful girl raised her palm towards Nick, and in that instant he saw that he, too, had an existence, a physical body amidst the nothingness.

He had a voice, too. "Thank you, thank you!" he cried. He clasped his hands in front of him in a gesture of exaggerated gratefulness and relief.

"Let there be light," she said with a slight smirk. Behind her, a sun rose above a nonexistent horizon, briefly illuminating her red hair to a golden yellow halo.

And then Nick found that he and the girl were submerged in water, and the sun's rays were piercing down from the distant surface. Nick was a poor swimmer, and in a panic, tried to pull himself upwards.

The girl watched in silence as he struggled to stay alive.

Out of the murky waters, an immense shark swam towards him. It opened its mouth, exposing row after row of jagged teeth, each as large as Nick's fist. The shark's layered gums were bright red, engorged with blood, in contrast to the pitch black of its deep throat.

Nick had lost sight of the girl. He tried to scream, and his mouth and lungs filled with salt water and he choked. The shark swam closer, its maw looming around him.

But then solid earth pressed Nick upwards. He was forced down on his back by the speed of his ascent. Soon, the surface of the water broke over him and he felt the sun's warmth on his face. He opened his mouth and gasped for breath.

He looked around, and realized that the shark had been brought to the surface with him. It flopped and thrashed in the mud, opening its gaping mouth in a silent scream.

The shark's skin changed from grey to brown, and the shark rose up off the ground on legs that appeared beneath it. In a moment, it had transformed into a tyrannosaurus, which leered down at him.

Nick scrabbled to his feet to run away, but tripped and fell on his side. The dinosaur bent down, ready to rend him with its jagged teeth. Nick flinched away, knowing he was helpless. The monster roared, and Nick retched at the stench of rotting meat rolling over him.

Before it could bite him, the tyrannosaurus sprouted bright white fur, trimmed short in some places and grown into bulbous layers in others. Its horrendous roar became a falsetto yap. The dinosaur had become a toy poodle, not even as tall as Nick's knee.

The poodle had a leather collar studded with emeralds and attached to a golden chain. Nick's eyes followed the chain until he saw that the mysterious red-headed girl was holding it as a leash.

She stood calmly, beholding him with a broad smirk, head cocked to one side, clearly amused at his distress.

He got to his feet, and she allowed him a moment to take in the scene around him. They stood on the rocky peak of a mountain, whose slopes were covered by forests. Birds flew through the air and deer ran between the trees. In the distance, fields spread across the hills and a city rose from the plains. The sky was clear and the sun bright, and he and the girl were standing in the shade of a massive apple tree.

"Welcome to the new world, Vinicius Lal." She held out her hand towards him. "Or should I call you Nick, like everyone else?"

Nick carefully extended his hand towards hers. "Who are you?" he asked.

"I'm Laura."

"Laura," he repeated as he hesitantly took her hand. "But *who* are you?"

"What you really want to know is *how* I did this."

"Yeah."

She smiled and spread her arms. "In this world, we are like gods. We create, we destroy. We do whatever we want."

"This *world*? The multinet? You're telling me we're the gods of the multinet?" Nick asked. "Like, webmasters?"

Laura repressed a laugh, but then her tone became very serious. "It's much more than the multinet. We are in a new world, created at the nexus of reality and imagination, existing on the boundary between ideas and objects. I call it the *ether*."

"So," Nick paused to choose his words. He didn't know whether he was asking stupid questions of a genius, or talking to a dangerously insane person. Probably a little of both, he decided. "You have a MindWave, too? And you're saying the MindWave lets us do this kind of stuff? Live in the ether, be gods?"

"The MindWave is the instrument of humanity's apotheosis. It makes us divine."

"Making a simulation of the world doesn't mean you're divine. It just means you have a fast computer and a good imagination."

"The scope of our divinity is not just confined to the purely imaginary," responded Laura patiently. "I know that you were born on June 6, 2030. I know your mother is a chemist from Rio, Brazil and I know your father is a genetic biologist from Amritsar."

"That's not that impressive," said Nick, furrowing his brow and speaking guardedly. "My parents are pretty famous. And I'm sure I can find your profile online somewhere, too."

Laura responded in the Rio-accented Portuguese of Nick's mother. "Would you easily be able to speak the language of my ancestors?" She paused and switched to his father's Punjabi. "I think no mere human can learn two languages in an instant."

"Whatever," said Nick. "I've seen simul-translate software before. Or maybe you're a language whiz. But I don't see your point."

Laura waved her hand. The wind kicked up, blowing three leaves off the apple tree that shaded them. The leaves swirled in midair and blended together, creating three-dimensional genetic diagrams that floated in the breeze. "What's this?"

Nick stared at the shifting shapes. "Wow, those are the genetic models my parents used at Langar Foods." Nick himself had struggled to understand the science that was the foundation of his parents' global synthetic food company, but weeks of study had only given him a vague understanding of the simpler concepts involved. He looked at Laura with a new respect. "Where'd you learn that from?"

"I didn't *learn* it," Laura answered, with evident contempt for the idea. "I *know* it. I know everything. Regular humans have to learn; they struggle for years to master a single discipline or to understand a single field of knowledge. But their expertise is always limited, their knowledge is always incomplete. I – *we* – have a purer form of knowing, a knowing that is spontaneous and complete. It separates us from normal humans, it makes us greater, more powerful."

Nick resisted the temptation to snort skeptically. Given that he'd become alienated from all of his real world friends, it wouldn't be wise to also alienate his first new MindWave friend. Instead, he opted for offbeat humor. "You sound like you're trying to use your MindWave to create a new religion. Do you want a tax exemption or something?"

Laura looked at him intently and narrowed her eyes. "You'll learn to accept your nature, Vinicius." And then she melted into the breeze blowing past the mountain peak.

The sun sank beneath the horizon and the breeze turned into a powerful gale that tore the leaves off the tree. Nick heard thunder, and as the mountain shuddered he realized it was the sound of the rock beneath him tearing itself apart.

The ground supporting him fell away and he stumbled backwards, falling deep into the void.

Nick shook his head in confusion as he found himself sitting again in his room, the fans in his MindWave making a loud hum as they cooled down its racing circuits. Laura had freed him from being lost in the ether, but hadn't done anything to make him feel less queasy. He pulled the internet cable out of the connection jack in the back of his skull as if it were a poisonous snake that had bitten him.

He tried to stand and realized he was too dizzy. His MindWave told him his blood sugar was low and he was dehydrated. As he crawled weakly towards the kitchen, he remembered that the doctors had warned him that the device used liquids and sugars from his blood stream to cool and power itself. Hunger and thirst were the implant's normal side effects.

"Whoa, back up!" Sarah was lying face down on an examination table in an open-backed hospital gown staring up at Willy. "You want to stick *what* in my *what*?"

Dr. Vivian Lee, who had just entered the room sized up the situation and stared sternly at Willy with her arms crossed over her chest. "Is everything all right, Major?" she demanded.

Willy scowled. "What I said, Sarah," he stated very deliberately through gritted teeth, "is that *Dr. Lee* would like to implant a small *device* in your *brain*." He eyed Dr. Lee until she went back to her business of programming the surgical robot.

"You never said anything about brain implants before!" screamed Sarah. "How the hell do I get out of here?" She'd built a lot of rapport and trust with Willy during the last eight weeks, but she was scared by the implants and angry at him for withholding so much from her for so long.

Suddenly feeling vulnerable, she rolled over and self-consciously pulled the back of her gown together while she looked around the room in vain for some less revealing clothing.

Willy's features twisted into his characteristic guilty expression. "I'm sure you realize there's no way out of this clinic for you. We're three stories below the ranch, the exits are secure, and for fifty miles in any direction it's rugged desert terrain. Now, I'm sorry about keeping the implants a secret, but I didn't want to scare you unnecessarily. There was no way to be sure if you were going to get any implants until you and Michael won the final part of the competition."

"This morning was the first time since arriving at this damn ranch that I woke up without feeling afraid I didn't belong here. I didn't even have nightmares about – about my past." She felt her fingers closing around her necklace. "And now you're saying you're going to mess with my brain?"

"It's just a small device. Nothing to worry about for a competent surgeon like Dr. Lee."

"Thanks Willy, it's nice that at least now you're being honest about totally screwing me. So did Dr. Lee invent this brain implant thing?"

Willy looked troubled for a moment. "No. But she did modify the designs Rad stole from the original inventor so that—"

Sarah shrank away from him. "You're implanting *stolen* brain implants in me? You can't even cough up the cash for the real ones?"

Willy sighed and laid a hand on her shoulder. "Sarah, there were smarter and more athletic people in the competition, and you beat them all. You're so good at playing superficial, at preoccupying yourself with your pretty blue eyes and your rebellious teenager game, that even you believe your own act. But deep down underneath it all, you're a tough girl. Right now you're scared and angry, but you'll be all right."

She shoved his hand away. "Screw your psycho-babble Willy. If you think I'm preoccupied with my looks just drop the brain implant and give me a boob implant instead!"

They both watched in silence as Rad Jaeger and Dr. Lee reentered the room. Dr. Lee turned to a table and filled a pneumatic syringe.

Rad walked to the bed and stood behind Willy. His voice was patronizing. "For once, you'll get what you want, Sarah. Your role will require a full suite of cosmetic enhancements."

"*Enhancements*? A full suite of – are you saying I'm ugly? Did you actually just tell me I'm ugly?"

Her tirade was cut short by a vision of her mother. *Why are there three of them in the room with you?* her mother choked through the gash in her throat.

Sarah knew she had to get out of the clinic. She pulled herself to her feet and pushed between Willy and Rad. "I'm finding Michael and the two of us are going to get the hell out of here."

Willy stood and together with Rad held onto her shoulders.

"Let me go!" She struggled but all she accomplished was to tear open her delicate hospital gown, which slipped to the ground at her feet.

"Sarah, I'm sorry but we can't let you go." Willy was averting his eyes from her naked body. Sarah sobbed and tried to retreat back to her bed but the two men held her immobile.

"Hurry up, Lee," barked Rad. Even though he was addressing the doctor, his eyes were fixed on Sarah.

Sarah realized that Dr. Lee had slipped behind her. She screamed, twisted, and kicked at the doctor but missed. Now she was off balance and Rad slammed her into the wall and then forced her down face first on the mattress. Lee ducked down and injected the contents of the syringe into her shoulder.

Sarah smiled as Rad let go of her and Willy helped her sit up on the bed. What had she been so angry about a moment ago?

Rad stood staring down at her. "Why does it have to be *teenagers*?" he muttered. Sarah wanted to ask Willy why Rad was so upset.

Willy was busy draping a sheet over her body. She didn't understand why he was so uptight about her nakedness. "Come on Willy, relax. We're buds. A little skin is nothing to worry about."

She was so sleepy it was hard to think straight. They could settle all of this just as soon as she took a nap. "Good night, Willy," she whispered as she lay back down.

Willy was wiping something out of his eye and didn't respond.

Chapter 6

After his frightening encounter with Laura, Nick had stayed away from the network for two weeks. But eventually his curiosity and loneliness had gotten the better of him. He found himself sitting once again in his room, internet cable poised to be plugged in.

He shook his head. *I can't believe I'm stupid enough to do this again.*

This time, he had taken precautions. He had a large glass bottle of imported Italian spring water, the bubbly kind that he preferred. And a box of fine Swiss chocolates, to provide him with a jolt of energy in case his blood sugar fell from overusing the MindWave.

More importantly, he'd programmed the internet connection to die after five minutes. If he were trapped and disoriented like last time, he would be released automatically.

He took a deep breath. And another. Then he clenched his jaw and pushed the cable into the socket.

He was immersed in a familiar dimensionless blackness. He felt fear rising up into his consciousness but beat it down. He knew it was possible to conquer this world, to make it his own.

Right now he was a point of nothingness amidst the nothingness. He remembered that when Laura had created her world last time, she had begun by forming her own body, and then by emanating space and dimensions outwards from herself.

The first thing he needed was his own body. He was seeing, so he must have eyes, and yet he didn't have eyes. He reached up with his hand to feel where his eyes should be.

Wait!

He had hands! That was a start. He held out his hand. It was a shimmering, shifting, ghostlike appendage. It shimmered, sometimes showing his wrist wearing a watch, sometimes not, as if his mind couldn't quite decide exactly how his hand should look.

If he had a hand, he must have the rest of his body. He followed his wrist, up his arm. The arm seemed to form as his eyes looked at it. Now he saw his shoulder, his chest, and below that his legs.

Below – there was an up and a down. Things were coming into place.

He had a full body. He looked at his foot. He was wearing his favorite pair of gray sneakers.

No, wait!

He was wearing blue flip flops. Somehow, both seemed to be true at the same time. Several different slightly different versions of himself seemed to be co-existing and intertwined.

Never mind the details. I have a body! He reached up and pinched his cheek. It hurt dully, like a slightly less defined version of what a real pinch would feel like. "Ow" he said, happily.

It was time to create a world. Better to start off with somewhere he knew personally. *His room.* He imagined the thick carpet beneath his feet. And it was there. He looked around to his bed, and his desk. They were all there.

He walked to the bed. The sheets were nondescript. He couldn't quite make out what color they were. He looked towards his shelf, where he kept his game collection. The titles of the data crystal holders were unreadable. He could not read the words so instead he focused and tried to read one letter at a time. It was impossible. Every time he began reading a letter, it shifted into another form. He might follow a horizontal stroke to see where it went. It would intersect a diagonal, so he'd think he'd found a "Z". But as he followed the diagonal, it would curve back up into a strong vertical, which never met the original horizontal.

He looked out the window and saw blackness. There was no world outside his room.

"Are you the *demiurge* of this world?" Came a sudden, scornful female voice.

He whirled around, to see Laura sprawled suggestively on his bed. Unlike the rest of this half-formed world, she appeared in exquisite, unchanging detail. Her smooth legs were crossed and her bent elbows supported her weight. She was wearing a short, form-fitting white dress that set off her braided red hair. Golden jewelry and diamonds sparkled around her neck and wrists. She looked around with a wrinkled nose.

"Am I the wha—" Before he had even finished the question, Nick knew the answer.

Demiurge. The creator of a world.

"I would have thought your skills would have advanced a bit further than this by now," she continued.

"I haven't really had time to practice," he said defensively.

"I hope I didn't scare you away last time."

"I've had a lot of stuff to do," he responded lamely.

"Do you want me to take over and improve this world for you?"

"Can't you just improve it for me without taking over?"

"No, if you're the demiurge of a world, you're the only one who controls it. Until and unless someone else comes along and takes over. You can't have two people running a world. You might set two different times of day, or even two different locations..." She waved her hand as if not wanting to explain all the details. "It's too damn confusing."

She blinked for a second and suddenly he felt, in a way that he couldn't have articulated, a sense of freedom melt away and be replaced by a sense of confinement.

At the same time, the incomplete version of his room that he had conjured shifted into a completely realistic version of his father's den. He could see the detailed grain of the walnut desk; read the display from the newsreader on the desk, smell the leather in the cushions on the chair.

"How'd you know what my dad's den looks like?" he asked. He wasn't sure whether to be impressed or scared.

"I didn't know what this room looks like until I wanted to. To find out the information I need, I'm checking architectural diagrams, reading your memories, and relaying all the information into this world. At some point you should learn to prevent people like me from hacking into your brain." Instead of reclining on his bed, Laura now straddled his father's chair backwards, her dress pushed up to allow her thighs to rest on the two armrests.

"Right," he said, nonplussed.

She looked around. "Anyway, this is boring. Let's go make some money."

"Huh?"

"We'll go trade in the markets."

"What markets?"

"The global equity and debt markets."

"I don't know finance," he protested. "And anyway, I'm only 17. It's illegal for me to open a brokerage account."

Laura laughed. "Silly Aeon. You don't need to study finance if you're using a MindWave. And we can make you a fake identity easily enough. I'll even lend you some money to get you started. Come on."

The world changed. It didn't melt away. There was no sense of transition. It was just *different*, as if a scene had changed in a movie. Instead of standing facing Laura, Nick was now floating next to her.

He flinched, fearing she was dropping him again. Then he realized that he was levitating over a vast ocean, covered as far as he could see by all manner of ships. Some were lumbering battleships, others were deftly tacking sailboats. Still others were foundering in heavy weather, and a few were sinking.

"What is this?"

"This is the financial market, or actually it's a visual simulation of the market. Every ship below represents a company. The quality of the ship tells you whether it's a good investment."

"There are thousands and thousands of ships! I can't watch them all at once."

"Yes you can. Come into my avatar."

Suddenly Nick felt his presence shift. He was no longer in his own body. Instead he was inside Laura's. He saw what she saw, felt what she felt.

Laura's perception of the world was impossibly sophisticated. Where he had perceived a featureless, flat oceanscape receding away from him into the distance, she viewed all parts of the sea at once.

Or rather, Nick realized after he had had a few moments to digest what lay in front of him, she saw the important parts of the sea all at once. The fastest and slowest ships, and the burning ones, appeared before her equidistant, in a space that besides length, height and width also had two more dimensions he couldn't quite grasp.

He blinked hard and squinted. Gradually, he came to understand what he was perceiving. The flat landscape was twisted and folded in the two extra dimensions to bring the important ships

109

into focus, and to obscure the less important ships. Once he understood how the seascape was folded in the two new dimensions, he intuitively knew exactly where each of the important ships lay in the flat seascape he had originally perceived.

"If it's steady sailing, buy. If it's foundering, sell. If it's sinking, sell more. The beauty of finance is that you can make money by selling something you don't even own."

"Won't other people see the same opportunities and buy or sell before we can?" he asked.

"Other *people*? You're not a person. You're an *Aeon*."

"Fine. But people have computers. Powerful computers that can do their trading for them. I've read about it."

"People can build computers a million times more powerful than the fastest supercomputer and they still won't be able to see what we can see. They have to choose between using an automatic program to trade for them based on rules, or to take the time to add human judgment. For us, the data processing and the judgment can occur at the same time. And because our neural circuitry transfers data a million times faster than neurons can, even our judgment is faster than theirs. In the world of finance, you just have to know something a millisecond ahead of your opponent. We've got whole seconds. Now go make some money."

Nick realized that while they had been talking, Laura had established a fake identity for him. He was Jose Vargas, a 35-year-old pediatrician in Sacramento. He had a million dollars to invest, from a brokerage account in First Bank of California.

"A million dollars?" he asked incredulously.

"I don't want you to get carried away. But I see you're out of time for today."

Before Nick could place his first investment, he had fallen out of the sky and landed on the ground. Disoriented, he opened his eyes and found himself sitting in his room. He was overcome by vertigo for a moment, scrabbling at the ground with his feet and grabbing at the chair.

When he had gotten his sense of balance back, he looked at the computer. Five minutes had elapsed, and his internet connection had automatically turned off.

He shook his head in disbelief and smiled. *A million dollars. That was a lot of money when my dad was born, but not anymore.* He reached into his pants pocket and pulled out several hundred thousand dollar coins. *A million bucks is barely enough to buy a bicycle.* If a million dollars was enough of a base to build a fortune with his MindWave, he'd be back in the ether. He'd be back soon.

"Your implant has vital weaknesses compared to the ones your opponents are going to have," Willy explained to Sarah and Michael.

Sarah reclined in a cot wearing her hospital gown, head still lightly bandaged. Her silver cross necklace lay in a small plastic container on the stand next to her bed. Michael lay in a cot next to hers, his head similarly dressed. His presence helped calm Sarah's fraught nerves.

"You must accept these weaknesses because you're going to be in covert roles. You can't have the full MindWave. It's too damn obvious if you have computer ports and cooling vents sticking out of the back of your head."

"Yeah no full MindWave. Whatever. You already told us it was a small device," said Sarah, weakly sipping on a cup of cola through a straw. "When do I get my new boobs?"

Michael, undoubtedly still too tender from the surgery to turn his head, looked towards her quizzically with his eyes. Sarah suppressed a smile. She might be stuck in a secret military base with government agents who felt entitled to implant mysterious devices in her brain. But at least now she knew for sure that Michael was interested in her boobs.

Willy sighed and responded uncomfortably. "You already have. Dr. Lee did that as a freebie during the neural implantation process."

"Huh, what?" Sarah looked down and feebly raised her hands to her chest.

"You didn't notice?"

"No. I just woke up from a six week coma after you drugged me!" protested Sarah, her voice changing from weak to strident as she spoke. "How would I know what you freaks did to me while I was under?"

Willy looked wounded and she forced herself to calm down. She still remembered the last moments after Dr. Lee had drugged her. How distraught Willy had looked, how he had tried to cover her nakedness, how he had been weeping. She was angry at him for betraying her, yet she also realized he was the only officer at the ranch who saw her as more than a piece of meat.

Perhaps he was a good man, in a horrible position. Perhaps that was what he'd meant that day after the race, when he'd been bandaging her injured foot and had said he wasn't sure whether the ends justified the means.

Besides that, Michael was here with her. His calm presence simultaneously made her feel secure, and also deterred her from venting her anger and fear. She didn't want him to think she was a coward or a mindcase.

Seeking to break the tension, she ran her tongue over her teeth. "Hey, my teeth are straight too!" Afraid of opening her half-healed wounds, she carefully turned her head to smile theatrically in Michael's direction.

"Yes, we made a few changes in how you look, which will be helpful in your covert role. And we erased your fingerprints and changed the patterns in your irises and retinas."

"Uh, did I get any extra surgery," asked Michael, looking with concern down at his body.

"Nah, you're easier. We zapped your fingerprints and retinas, of course. Beyond that, we'll give you colored contact lenses and send you to the gym."

"Thanks." Michael frowned.

"Oh no, don't make him bulk up too much," interjected Sarah. "Asian guys look better nice and wiry." In the face of Willy's bewildered stare, she realized she'd said a bit too much, and decided to change the topic. "What kind of covert role is this, anyway?"

"We want you to fit in with a certain group of people. The people you'll be following. The people you'll be policing."

"I've got a computer in my brain and a boob job. Who am I supposed to spy on? Internet porn stars?"

Willy grinned and gave her one of his winks. "You must know, Sarah, that there are wealthy people who pay fortunes to genetically alter their children. To make them look... a certain way."

"Oh yeah, the dirty rich and their test tube babies. So you want me to look like a beautiful, rich heiress so I can go make friends with real, beautiful, rich heiresses? Still, why do I need a computer implanted in my brain?"

"It's the latest accessory for the richest of the rich. A computerized brain implant called the MindWave. It gives the user extraordinary mental powers," explained Willy.

"Like... telekinesis? Can I read your mind? Or make you fall out of your chair?" Sarah squinted and grimaced as she stared intently at Willy.

Willy shook his head and rolled his eyes. "Access to information. Any information they need. And the ability to process, to visualize that information, and to communicate with each other in ways that no humans ever have."

Sarah gave Michael a skeptical glance.

Michael picked up Sarah's sarcasm. "Great, so you basically stuck Wi-Fi modems into our brains?" He tried to shake his head, wincing at the pain caused by the movement. "All these damn surgeries so I can talk to computers?"

"It's a bit more than that," Willy insisted. "Look, it's a bit hard to explain until you start using it, which will be in just a few days. You're going to be able to do some extraordinary things. You'll just have to trust me for the moment."

"Yeah, great, trust the man that kidnapped me from an orphanage, threatened to boot me out if I didn't win some contrived competition, and then performed mad science experiments on me." Sarah looked away and breathed deeply to calm down. "Anyway, didn't you just say our brainwaves are weaker than the regular ones?"

"*MindWave*," corrected Willy. "Actually, in your case we call it a *TacWave*, because of the enhanced tactical abilities we've added. In terms of processing speed, it's just as powerful as a regular MindWave, more powerful even. But it has two differences, two... *weaknesses.*

"First, a regular MindWave has a number of external connection jacks. These allow the user to easily connect to any computer or network, or even to directly connect MindWave to MindWave with another user. Now, in theory MindWave users could rely on antennae built into their skulls but the pencil-necks who designed the device think too much radiation inside the skull is dangerous. So until we solve that problem, wired connections are the only way to connect. Now, with your TacWaves, you can't have all those connection jacks. You just have one small port, hidden at the base of your skull, covered by your hair.

Willy's tone became more somber. "Second, you don't have endomorphic cooling vents. Computer chips generate a lot of heat and the inside of the human skull is not well ventilated. Using the MindWave at full power will fry the user's brain in a few minutes. The MindWave solves this problem with large cooling vents in the user's skull. But you don't have the cooling vents…" he let his voice trail off.

"So you mean if I use this thing my brain fries?" asked Michael incredulously.

"If you *over*use it your brain will be *damaged*," Willy responded carefully. "Now, the TacWave has automatic temperature warnings that tell you if you're overheating it. But Dr. Lee and I thought that there was a risk, a small risk, you see," he held up his thumb and index finger as if to indicate how small the risk was "that you might overlook those warnings in periods of stress. We thought a much more reliable way to prevent overuse injuries is to rely on your body's natural pain response. The human brain normally doesn't have pain receptors. So we, ahh… we…"

"Willy, what did you do?" Sarah let her mouth hang slightly open in a reproachful expression.

Willy spoke delicately. "We put some pain receptors inside your brain tissue, so you'll know when you're overheating your brain."

"This just keeps getting better, Willy," Sarah responded bitterly, and turned her gaze away from him again. "I already get migraines!"

"Well, there is one mitigating factor. We can affix external cooling systems to your skulls. When you're here at the ranch, you can use those to cool your brains well enough that you might be able to use the TacWave for hours at a time.

"Those systems are too bulky to be mobile. When you're out in the field, all we can give you is a half-measure, a refrigerated helmet. It's definitely not as good as the normal endomorphic cooling systems but better than nothing. You'll probably get 30 minutes of use with the helmets."

Michael looked thoughtful. "What about power? If it's all sealed up inside my skull, how do I replace the batteries?"

"There are no batteries. The system uses energy from your body. Specifically, it takes the sugars carried by your blood, and turns that into electrical power through a chemical process that mimics human cellular biology."

Sarah forced a meek smile. "Well, at least I can eat all the ice cream and chocolate I want."

She grinned as Michael rolled his eyes.

Rad opened the door and beckoned towards Willy. Sarah remembered, too, how Rad had behaved while she was helpless,

117

drugged and naked. She turned away from him and stared at the wall. Willy headed for the room's exit. "Tomorrow you begin basic training."

"Don't we get any easy days?" asked Michael.

"Yesterday was the only easy day," said Rad curtly.

"I was unconscious yesterday!"

"Good. So you're well rested."

It had been six weeks since Nick had first met Laura in the imaginary digital space she called the ether. At first, he was acutely aware that the settings of their encounters were completely artificial. The falseness of the ether seemed to make honesty and intimacy impossible, and he avoided deep social interactions.

Now as he gained facility with the MindWave, he also became increasingly comfortable in the ether. He came to accept the dis-realities of the MindWave as his new reality. Instead of an exotic diversion from real life, the fabricated worlds within the ether became his life. Instead of impeding honesty, the artificialness of these worlds began to act like a drug, removing inhibitions and making bonds of trust possible.

His admiration for Laura had grown when he learned her full name was Laura Sophia Mayer. Her middle name was in honor of her grandmother, Sophia Rosenbaum, a turn-of-the-century internet entrepreneur. Sophia had earned a fortune that the Mayer family had protected and grown, a fortune that had passed to Laura when her parents had died in a boating accident a few years before. In fact, Laura was almost as wealthy as Nick's parents.

Now Nick and Laura were spending hours together in the ether every day. Laura had explained that she was one of the earliest recipients of the MindWave, and took it upon herself to help clumsy new users learn the ropes. She was inspired by the tragic story of the early MindWave recipient who had used the device without guidance and gone mad. Laura had rebuffed Nick's questions about that event, though she must have known the victim. She just insisted she was determined to ensure such a tragedy never happened again.

Today Laura was again pushing Nick to develop his skills. They stood on the same high mountain peak that she had created upon their first meeting. She wore a long, white gown made of light and airy fabric, and a thin golden tiara that shone in her scarlet locks. He wore his normal attire of jeans and a t-shirt. "OK, I want to see your demiurge skills. Let's see your bedroom," she demanded.

Nick felt his MindWave's fans revving up as Laura passed control of this part of the ether over to him. He closed his eyes for a fraction of a second and formed a new world around them. The grain of the mahogany, the pile of the rug, the smell of his sheets. They were all there. He placed Laura seated on his bed. Nick was standing before her.

Laura looked around. "Very good. You're making progress."

Nick felt himself blushing. Then he realized he could simply will himself not to blush in the ether.

"Not so fast. Can I read this book?" Laura uncrossed her legs, stood, and used her left arm to reach out and pull an old softcover book from Nick's shelf.

She opened it and immediately sighed in disappointment. She tossed it to him, and he saw the pages were blank. "The next step for you, Nick, is making worlds that are fully realistic," Laura scolded softly.

Nick looked down in frustration.

She grinned. "Anyway, let me introduce you to my friend Abril. She's over in the casino."

"Casino?" Nick asked, his eyes wide in surprise. He wasn't old enough to be allowed entrance into a casino. Then again, he wasn't old enough to invest in the equity markets yet Laura had shown him how.

Before he could even clearly formulate these thoughts, he was standing in front of a roulette table on which a large colorful wheel, perhaps six feet in diameter, was rotating. There were about a dozen well-dressed men and women intently watching the wheel, each with a pile of round, colorful chips in front of him or her. A tall man in a tuxedo, standing behind the table, called out, "bets closed!" and dropped a ball onto the wheel. After clattering around for a while, the ball settled into the 00 slot. The tuxedoed man used a long pole to rake piles of colored disks towards himself. Around the table, the well-dressed crowd made signs of derision and disgust.

Nick noticed that one of the women watching the table was slightly more animated than the others. She was a tall and curvaceous girl of about eighteen with flowing black hair, almond-shaped eyes, and cinnamon skin. She turned around to greet them with a beautiful smile.

"*Hola*, Laura, I haven't seen you for a while. Keeping busy? And you must be Nick," she said, with a slight Mexican accent. "I'm Abril Espinoza. How do you like my casino?"

Nick allowed himself a moment to take in the casino before responding. It was spectacular, with high, arched ceilings, shining crystal chandeliers, and a luxurious red carpet. The air was cool and dry. In the background, 20th century rock music played. There were beautiful women in slinky dresses walking around with trays of food and drink. All of the patrons were dressed in the latest couture.

"Wow, it's really incredible!" he gushed.

"*Gracias*! It's modeled after a place near Cancun my uncle owns," said Abril with a wink. "I took the liberty of improving it a bit – especially the fashion sense of the clientele. So how are you getting along in the ether?"

"It's getting better and better," said Nick modestly. "But I still struggle to recreate my own apartment. I can't wait until I can make a place like this myself!"

Laura rolled her eyes. "Actually, Nick, now that I'm introducing you around, the most important thing for you will be to learn to defend yourself from hacking. Get that figured out before you go designing any casinos."

"Oh really, he doesn't know how to play defense?" asked Abril with a mischievous grin.

Nick began to respond, but realized he was hooting instead. He looked down at his arms and saw they were elongated and covered in thick brown fur. Finding himself in the reflection on the mirrored side of the roulette table, he saw the reflection of a chimpanzee staring back at him, still wearing the same jeans and t-shirt he'd been wearing a moment ago.

"Hey, come on Abril, don't push around the new guy!" said Laura, like a big sister gently scolding her younger sibling. "You know you hated it when Jakobus did this to you!"

"*Bueno, bueno,*" said a still-grinning Abril. As suddenly as he had become a chimpanzee, Nick was himself again.

"Damn it," cried Nick. "You guys keep playing tricks on me! How can I learn to stop you!"

A bipedal polar bear wearing a red wool vest ambled up to Nick, shook his head, and growled in a thick accent "Shame, *bra*. It's tough being a newbie."

Nick looked at Laura with alarm.

"Oh, don't worry, that's just Jakobus," interjected Abril with a wide grin. "He's from the South African veld. Mostly Afrikaner, one-quarter Xhosa, and he's completely unintelligible. Good luck understanding him even with your MindWave translator on."

"Did someone turn you into a bear, Jakobus?" asked Nick, glad to find someone as unskilled with the MindWave as he was.

"Call me Kobus, *bra*. No, no one turned me into a bear. This is just how I roll." The bear extended a large paw to Nick before turning towards the roulette table. "Speaking of rolling, let's gamble, *ne!*"

Nick stepped back from the group at the roulette table uneasily. Once he had overcome his initial terror at the endless freedom of the ether, he had come to believe he could fully master it. The ether, and the worlds he created within it, had seemed wide open spaces free from danger. Now he wasn't sure anymore.

Nick grabbed a strong looking drink from a passing waitress, a gorgeous brunette in a skimpy, sequined outfit who rewarded him with a warm smile.

He drank deeply from his glass, but it didn't help. He could not get drunk from the imaginary alcohol. Or he hadn't learned how.

He took a deep breath, and stepped forward to the group again.

In the next half hour, Laura introduced Nick to another dozen other MindWave users who passed through the casino. Nick was aware there were only about thirty MindWave users in the world, so now he knew about half.

Aside from Kobus, all of the other MindWave users appeared to be very attractive teenagers. This helped Nick feel like he fit in, but also raised an intriguing question.

He had assumed that other MindWave users would mostly be highly successful, middle-aged business titans. The MindWave was prohibitively expensive. Then again, maybe despite their appearances, his fellow MindWave users *were* middle aged men. There was nothing stopping them from projecting themselves into avatars that had whatever appearance they desired. Kobus, after all, was presumably not a talking polar bear in real life.

Nick pulled Laura aside. "Is there somewhere we can go to eat?" he asked, hopefully.

"Yes, of course," she said. "Good idea. Let's get everyone together for a lunch party."

"No, no," responded Nick. "I wanted to ask you some questions in private."

Chapter 7

"Let's go to the Beijing Duck Restaurant," suggested Laura. She reached out, grabbed his hand, and took off into the air. In a moment, they had flown across the wide floor of the casino and arrived at a round table in a finely appointed restaurant. Laura slid smoothly from midair into her seat, while Nick landed off balance and nearly fell out of his.

She thought aloud. "Hmm... let's get a whole roast duck with plum sauce, and some *zajiang* noodles, and fried *jinying mantou* with *lianru*."

"You're mixing buns with noodles?" asked Nick, screwing up his nose. He'd grown up eating with his discriminating mother, and as a result he had mastered most of the world's culinary traditions. "That's a bit of a faux-pas in Beijing cuisine... Why don't we have some *basi xiangjiao* instead of the *mantou*? I love fried bananas with caramel!"

Laura raised her eyebrows. Nick guessed she wasn't used to being corrected. But then she shook her head and smiled. "For someone whose family got rich making food in laboratory vats, you know your way around a kitchen." She waved her hand in the air and the three dishes appeared, along with a pot of steaming *tieguanyin* tea.

Nick used the chopsticks that had appeared in his hand to pull a sliver of meat off the golden brown duck. The greasy flesh melted in his mouth, while the crisp skin remained for him to chew, releasing new flavors with every bite. "Wow! This is amazing. The flavors -- it's the best duck I've ever had!" he exclaimed.

"Try the noodles."

"These are amazing too! What spices did they use? I can make out the thyme and ginger, with a light *jiangyou*... and there are other things in here that I can't even name!"

"Food is always better in the ether."

"But at home I only eat the finest foods! How can this fake, imaginary stuff taste better than gourmet cuisine made from fresh produce by a Michelin-starred chef?"

"You really haven't been making the most of your MindWave. If you think the food is good, you should try the sex."

"Uh..." Nick paused with a piece of *basi xiangjiao* hanging tenuously off of his chopsticks halfway to his mouth. A long hair-thin strand of molten caramel that had stretched between the fried banana and his plate hardened and cracked, slowly floating back down to the table.

"Don't worry, I'll show you after lunch," said Laura with a flirtatious smile. "Now, what were those questions you wanted to ask me?"

Nick blinked, making a concerted effort to get his mind back on topic. He looked around to ensure they were alone and then leaned towards Laura to ask in a low voice, "Why is everyone in the ether a teenager? And why do they all look like supermodels?"

Laura gave him a once over. "You're not so bad looking yourself, Nick."

"Um, thanks."

"Do you look like this in real life?" Her tone was that of a teacher using the Socratic Method to lead a slightly slow student to an obvious solution.

"Well, mostly," he said, slightly uncomfortable at the question. "I mean, pretty close."

"You're about two inches shorter and your shoulders aren't this broad, but yes, basically you look like this in real life. Why's that?"

There was no use hiding anything from Laura. "Well, my parents had me designed this way. Genetic engineering."

"And is that procedure inexpensive or expensive?"

"Pretty damn expensive."

"And what about your MindWave? Expensive or cheap?"

"That was even more expensive."

"And why did you have your MindWave implanted when you did?"

"Because it's only suited to be implanted in brains at a certain stage of development, around age 16 or 17."

"And when did the inventor of the MindWave, Dr. P.J. Arora, start selling it?"

"About three years ago," responded Nick.

Laura gave him another once over and stated impatiently: "Nick, you have all the information you need to answer your own question. Just think for a second."

Nick stared across the restaurant for a moment, feeling very silly. Then it dawned on him. "Oh, only the same parents with the wealth and craziness to genetically engineer every aspect of their kids would also be wealthy and crazy enough to implant MindWaves in their children. And those kids have to be teenagers, and the MindWave's been around such a short time that everyone who has one is twenty or younger. Duh."

"Good job. Are you done eating?" She wore a sly smile. "I've got something important to do with Kobus this afternoon. But first, I promised to show you something after lunch."

He took a sip of tea, trying to look nonchalant. He was glad that he'd recently learned how to stop himself from blushing in the ether. "OK, my place or yours."

Once Sarah and Michael had fully recovered from the implantation surgery, they had begun undergoing intensive training, for sixteen hours a day, seven days a week.

Sarah had quickly learned that the ranch was much larger than she'd initially thought. The three drab looking wooden buildings she'd grown used to housed concealed entries and air circulation vents for a larger underground space.

This subterranean part of the ranch hosted the operating rooms where Dr. Lee had implanted their TacWaves, facilities far more modern than the clinic above where Willy had treated her foot all those weeks ago.

The underground space also included a generously-sized physical training center, small living quarters, and a briefing theater equipped with a podium and holovision projector, where she and Michael met with Willy early every morning to review their training assignments for the day.

Willy told her that the ranch was completely off the grid. It had its own power source – thorium generators like the ones that had blown up at Hurricane, but a smaller, simpler design that had been used by the navy to power battleships for two decades without incident. The facility also drew its water from the same spring that fed the stream that ran across the ranch, and it could fully detach itself from all communications networks.

Willy also explained that the ranch facility had originally been built by NASA, then had been abandoned for decades before Rad – properly known as Colonel Rad Jaeger – had requisitioned it for a new use.

That new use was to train Sarah and Michael. In addition, the orphans who had seemingly been sent away during the competition had really just been relocated to the underground section of the ranch. Now they were undergoing brutal conditioning intended to turn them into a commando team capable of rapid deployment to raid criminal and terrorist facilities.

Sarah and Michael were receiving training that was different, yet no less rigorous. At the end of every long day, after finishing a late dinner, Sarah would drag herself, exhausted, down a long hallway to her quarters. These consisted of a small square room, furnished with a bed, desk and closet. In the closet were her clothes – mostly additional sets of the same gray T-shirts and shorts she'd been given on her first day at the ranch. She also had a small private bathroom with a simple plastic toilet and a weak shower with tepid water.

There was no phone or computer in her room. The only communication device was an internal voice paging system.

The door to her room automatically locked from 9PM till 5AM every morning. Whether or not she was sleeping, she had to be in the room during this time. In her few moments of spare time, her only choice for entertainment was to flip through well-worn soft cover romances from the small library near the mess hall. She had no idea how such old-fashioned novels had come to be at a computerized military facility, but she secretly suspected Dr. Lee had brought them.

Michael lived in a similar room at the other end of the long hallway. In between were four rooms that belonged to Willy, Rad, Dr. Lee and a muscular man named Hank Green who was mostly focused on training the other orphans.

Sarah had never been in Michael's room and he had never entered hers. Even if her shaved head hadn't robbed her of her social confidence, all of Sarah's thoughts of flirting with Michael had been drained out of her by the intense training program. Romance, she told herself, was something to look forward to after they graduated.

It seemed Rad was the most senior officer present at the ranch and didn't trouble himself with keeping day-to-day tabs on her. That was fine with her. His condescending manner was off putting, and she still was bitterly anger about how violently he had treated her when she tried to escape before her implant surgery.

The training was mostly run by Willy, and consisted in horribly tedious drills. During the sessions, Michael and Sarah lay in what looked like metallic reclining chairs. The headrest of the recliner had a curved metallic cooling system built into it, which closed around her entire skull, just leaving her face free. This system prevented the two students from overheating as they ran through their drills. Even with the cooling equipment, they had to keep their TacWaves only partially powered up.

The first few weeks of drills were incredibly mind numbing. She and Michael had spent an entire afternoon watching an animated ball bounce around a holovision. The purpose of the drill was to calibrate the TacWave with their visual cortexes. Another drill consisted of aiming a small laser pointer at a screen on which a red "x" would periodically appear. This drill was intended to allow the TacWave to begin improving their reflexes.

They also practiced simple movements, such as walking in a circle, to teach their TacWaves what nerve endings to stimulate to move which muscles. To keep their TacWaves from overheating, they detached the coolers from the chairs and strapped them to their heads and shoulders. The bulky devices looked like comically large collars from a cheesy vampire movie.

Sarah was getting frustrated by the slow progress. The sense of accomplishment and belonging that she had felt right after winning the competition was fading, and being replaced with her old anxieties. She was disturbed by visits from her mother on more nights than not, which left her feeling exhausted the following mornings.

"I thought these TacWaves are supposed to be incredible communications devices," muttered Michael to her one day during their short lunch break. As usual, they were sitting at their own table away from the other orphans. "Why the heck are we wasting our time with these stupid training drills?"

As Michael spoke, one of the other orphans was walking past with a tray. He stopped and turned towards them. "What kind of drills are you guys doing?" he asked.

Bob was his name, Sarah recalled. The bully who had tried to shoot her with his harpoon gun.

"Just calibrating our implants," said Michael through a mouthful of potatoes.

"Sounds easy. We've been training in tactical combat with Sergeant Green." Bob put down his tray on the table loudly. Across the cafeteria, several other orphans turned to watch.

Sarah knew what was coming. Maybe she could defuse the situation. She lowered her loaded fork to the table and forced a grin. "Cool. That sounds like fun."

"Yeah, it is fun." Bob slapped Michael's shoulder hard. "So much fun I want to practice right now."

"I don't have any beef with you," said Michael angrily. "Save it for the training room."

"You afraid? Good thing you run so fast because you fight like a wuss." Bob shoved Michael so hard he slid off the bench onto the floor with a thud.

Sarah started to stand up but some instinct told her to duck instead. As she lowered her head, a steel bowl full of mashed potatoes sailed over her and hit the ground.

She wanted to turn and face whoever had thrown the potatoes but felt a strong urge to move to the right around the table instead. This maneuver put her out of reach of Olivia Freeman, who was trying to tackle her from behind.

"You think you're so damn cool because you cheated and beat us?" demanded Olivia from across the table. "Just let me go toe to toe with you in a fair fight!"

Sarah's movement had positioned her behind Bob, who was ignoring her as he raised his leg to stomp on Michael. Not knowing quite what she was doing, Sarah obeyed her impulse to kick the back of Bob's knee while thrusting her left hand into his neck. Bob fell sideways and banged his head on the edge of the next table over.

Before Bob slumped to the ground Sarah heard clumping on the table to her left. She ducked just as Olivia's roundhouse kick cut through the air where the back of her head had been. Sarah raised her right arm and push on the back of Olivia's ankle as it passed overhead, sending the girl spinning off the table onto the floor in a hail of falling dishes and cutlery.

Michael reached up and Sarah grabbed his hand and pulled him to his feet. They turned together to see that five more orphans had formed an arc around them.

As the five moved in, Sarah heard rapidly approaching footsteps from the right. But she didn't dare tear her gaze from the nearest orphan, a big muscular boy just out of kicking range.

Suddenly, the small, compact form of Greg Silverstein appeared in her peripheral vision and shoved the boy back. "Cut this bullshit out!" Greg yelled. "And get back to our table."

The five orphans exchanged uncertain glances and then stepped backwards. They helped Bob and Olivia to their feet and then silently trudged back across the room.

Greg remained behind and turned as if to address Sarah and Michael. Instead, his gaze fixed on something behind them. Sarah turned and saw that Rad was standing in the doorway, arms crossed, face expressionless.

"I wonder how long he would have let it go on," said Greg.

Before Sarah or Michael could respond, an alarm began pealing.

Chapter 8

"What the hell do you expect us to do?" demanded Sarah. "We barely know how to use these things."

"You're better than anything else we've got," responded Willy grimly as he strapped her into the cooling chair. Over his shoulder, Sarah could see Rad typing passwords into the console, apparently opening a connection to the multinet from the normally isolated servers at the ranch.

Dr. Lee burst into the room. "Don't tell me you're connecting them now! It's too early."

Willy clenched his jaw and looked at Rad.

"Really doctor, what's the worst that could happen?" demanded Rad without looking up from his console.

"You've heard about that girl in California who killed her family when she first connected. We need to stage this process carefully and—"

"Your advice is noted. Return to your station in the clinic."

"Willy, what's going to happen to me?" asked Sarah. *Run! Run away Sarah!* She heard her mother gasping.

Willy was checking the restraints on Michael's cooling chair, which faced hers. "Nothing's going to happen, Sarah."

Michael was sitting still, staring at the ground. "We'll be fine, Sarah," he said, just before Willy slipped a rubber mouth guard between his teeth.

"Connect them," ordered Rad.

Willy took a hair-thin network cable and leaned down behind Michael's immobilized head. After a moment, a green light set into the headrest flicked on. Michael's eyes rolled up inside his head and he shook violently in his restraints.

Willy stepped over to Sarah's side. "I'm sorry you have to see that, Sarah. It's just a normal muscular reaction. Nothing to worry about."

"No, no! Please, Willy!"

Willy hesitated. Rad stepped over from the console and forced strong fingers into the sides of Sarah's face, forcing her jaws open. He shoved the rubber mouth guard between her teeth. Then he seized the network cable out of Willy's hands. "Connecting Fenton."

Tracy Cruz stood up in frustration at her CEO's statement. "Eric, there's no way we're going to get that regulation changed, energy crisis or not."

Eric stood up behind his desk. "Dammit, Tracy, we need these changes or the whole pipeline will go under. You're our in-house lawyer. Get it done."

"For the regulatory changes you want, you don't need a lawyer. You need a miracle."

"I could hire three roughnecks for what I pay you. You'd better get me some results, or I'll find a better use for your salary!"

"You know what, Eric, you don't need to threaten to fire me anymore. Because I quit."

Knowing she would regret it later but too incensed to care, Tracy pushed her way out of Eric Romero's spartan office and into the cinderblock building that housed it. She ran a hand through her raven black hair and looked around her. Only four of the dozen desks were occupied, and those staff members were staring intently at their computer terminals, evidently trying to avoid her. They must have overheard the shouting from Eric's office.

Tracy marched out of the Kerrville, Texas headquarters of Southwest Pipelines Inc., and over to the crowded rack where she had parked her bike. Not many people could afford to drive cars anymore, whether electric or gasoline powered. The Hurricane Reactor had just been a prototype, and its destruction had virtually no impact on energy production in the United States. But its failure meant that future energy prices would be high, which drove up prices in the present.

Or that's what the official story was. From her perch within the legal department of a small oil and gas pipeline company, Tracy had seen a lot of strange activity in the refining and logistics markets. She couldn't prove anything, but it seemed that there was a new player in the industry that was intent on pushing prices sky high. It was using front companies to manipulate the market by creating pipeline bottlenecks and regional product shortages. She had tried to document the activity well enough at least to build a case she could present to official investigators without being laughed out of town. But Eric's demands for her to focus on lobbying the government to relax regulations on costly environmental protections for oil transport had prevented her from making much progress.

That wasn't her problem anymore. Someone else would have to figure it out. She rode her bike two miles down the dusty I-10 highway towards the truck depot where her husband Ricardo worked as a mechanic. The highway was lined with all manner of commercial storefronts. Many of them were empty, and a few were boarded up.

There was a time, in the days when her paternal grandparents had immigrated from Mexico, when Kerrville had profited from the American natural gas boom. But the wells had been depleted in the late 2030s. Since then, the city had fallen back on transportation and logistics. It was positioned along the I-10 highway and further benefited from the presence of several oil and gas pipelines that linked coastal ports and refineries with inland markets. Of course, so was nearby San Antonio, which got the bulk of the work, but the bits flowing to Kerrville had kept its economy afloat. Now even that meager source of revenue was drying up.

She remembered her childhood, when riding a bike down this stretch of road would have seemed suicidal because of the densely packed big rigs speeding by. But now there was plenty of open asphalt for Tracy, and she didn't even bother to signal before turning into Ricardo's workplace.

"Hey babe," said Ricardo as he climbed down from inside the engine compartment of a tractor unit. He turned his gaze from her to survey the lot that was mostly empty. "Funnily enough, things still aren't looking good in the trucking world."

"Ricky, you're going to have to keep this job because I just quit mine."

Ricardo put his hands on his hips and stared down the empty highway. "You quit?"

"Sorry, Ricky. I couldn't take another minute of Eric. That man can't see beyond his own beer gut."

"You always go and act rash without thinking things through, Babe" said Ricardo, shaking his head and still staring down the road.

After a few moments, he looked back and smiled. "I guess that's why you came back to Kerrville and married a grease monkey like me. I guess that's why I love you."

She leaned closer and put an arm around his muscular shoulders. It *had* been crazy of her to marry him. But she'd never regretted it for a moment. "We still have each other, Ricky."

"And we still have the Lord looking over us. He's helped us get through worse. Remember twenty years ago when we were in high school? High energy prices are bad, but starvation's a lot worse. I saw the evil in men's hearts back then. But the Lord showed us the way to feed ourselves, and he'll show us the way out of this crisis, too."

Tracy shrugged. "I thought it was science and technology that created the food labs, not divine intervention."

"Careful, babe. That's your mortal hubris speaking. The Lord inspired those scientists, and revealed the technology to them."

"Sure, hon."

"All those fancy schools you went to messed up your thinking so you can't see the obvious truth." He hugged her with his forearms, holding his greasy hands away so he wouldn't soil her clothes. "I gotta get this rig back on the road by five. If I were you, I'd go down to the church and talk your situation through with Doc."

"Sure, Ricky. I'm volunteering there for the kids' program tonight anyway."

He was silent and tense. She apologetically kissed him goodbye and hopped back on her bike to head towards the church.

When she arrived she found Doc sitting on the stairs out front, his hunched form and black clothes standing in contrast to the right angles and white façade of the small single story church. He looked despondent and was smoking a cigarette. When he saw her, he pulled himself up, stamped out the cigarette butt, straightened his black-rimmed glasses, and ran a spotted hand through his thin white hair. "How are you, Tracy?"

"I've been better, Doc."

"Tracy, your parents lived long and happy—"

She smiled sadly. It had been three months since her mother and father had passed away in quick succession just a few days after her wedding. "I know, Doc. I've come to terms with that now. But I just quit my job and I don't know what to do. I want to spend more time volunteering with the kids."

"I always wondered why you became a lawyer, Tracy. You don't seem suited to all that confrontation. You're more the giving type."

"Folly of youth."

He held out his hand for hers. She felt his paper-thin skin, saw his trembling fingers, and was overcome with sadness that the strong pastor she'd known in her youth was now so weak.

"Tracy, how would you like to give more back to your community?"

"That's what I just said. I'm going to volunteer more."

"Not just with the after school program. I mean, this whole ministry."

"What do you mean, Doc?" She backed away from him, suddenly not wanting the conversation to go any further.

"I don't have much time left, Tracy."

"Then what are you doing smoking, Doc?" She gestured angrily at the extinguished butt on the ground.

He smiled bitterly. "The tobacco didn't get me. It's terminal liver disease. I guess I've been drinking too much of the communion wine. Whatever the cause, I need someone to take care of my flock after I'm gone."

"I'm not—I mean, how much time?"

"I've got a month or two."

"I'm so sorry, Doc."

"It happens to us all, in the end. Nothing to be sorry about. It's God's plan."

"Is there anything I can do?"

"I just told you what you can do. Take over the ministry."

"Isn't there someone… someone qualified?"

"A little backwater non-denominational church like ours doesn't exactly have first claim on newly minted Doctors of Divinity. It doesn't matter. I can't think of anyone more qualified than you, Tracy. You're smart, educated, and well spoken. And Tracy, you'll earn a small stipend."

"Doc, I'm not—I don't think I have enough…"

"You don't believe your faith is strong enough."

She looked down in shame, just as she had thirty years ago when Doc had found her doodling in her Sunday school book or trading love notes with some boy during services.

"You've always blamed Him for making you barren."

She didn't respond. She wished she'd never come here today.

"But maybe that's His plan for you."

"His plan? His plan is to make me suffer? How can you believe there's any plan at all?"

"You've brought joy to so many other children through your work here. Maybe He's calling you, Tracy, to help the whole community during this difficult time."

"If I have so much doubt how can I lead others through—"

Doc leaned in close and she smelled some kind of medicine on his breath. "Tracy, there's a saying that God helps those who help themselves. This community doesn't need someone whose only skill is quoting scripture. It needs a leader with practical skills, the kind of skills you've got from your education and career. Think about it. Your presence here, your quitting today, it's all part of His plan."

Before Tracy could respond she was distracted by a strange yellow glow in Doc's eye glasses. It was followed closely by a thunderous boom. She turned and saw a plume of yellow and red smoke rising up in the distance.

Tracy's mind went back to that horrific night more than a year ago at Hurricane. She saw Anil Dado falling to the buckling pavement as jets of superheated steam melted his radiation suit, scalded his skin, and blistered his lungs. She felt an urgent need to flee.

Her flashback was interrupted by Doc's voice. "Lord protect us, that's the pipeline terminal!"

Tracy stole a glance at her watch. 4:45. The staff wouldn't have left for the day yet. As she ran towards her bike she turned back to Doc. "When I left there were still five people in that office. Are their deaths part of God's plan, too?"

In an instant, everything around Sarah disappeared. The room she had been in, Willy, even herself. She experienced a vast nothingness, and a sense of absolute detachment and isolation.

She was totally alone.

She'd been alone her whole life. She knew how to handle this. If this was the worst she was going to face when using her MindWave, there was no reason to be frightened. She took a moment to gather herself.

Then she tried to look around to get her bearings but realized there were no directions. *That's going to have to change,* she thought to herself.

In the total silence, she focused on her own heartbeat. She heard its steady *thump thump.* The location of the sound must be down.

If there was a down, there was an up, and a left and right, back and forward. The world now had dimensions, though it was still completely empty.

If she had a heart, and ears to hear it with, she must have a body. She sensed her limbs and trunk, and then her head, coming into existence. She held her hand in front of her face and saw that it was shifting, unstable. One instant her fingernails were long and painted red as she had kept them at the orphanage, the next they were short and unpainted, as she was required to keep them at the ranch. *Stay red,* she willed. And they did.

If she could see her hands, there must be a light source. She spun around in the nothingness to see a bright sun-like sphere rising above her.

The empty void was disconcerting. She wanted solid ground beneath her feet. She opened her mouth and spoke. "I want the ranch!" In this realm, her voice was deeper and more powerful than in the real world.

She continued pivoting. As she spun, orange dust formed at her feet and spread outwards, at first gradually then rapidly picking up speed.

As the landscape extended in all directions, a clear blue sky opened above. The edges of the orange landscape and the blue sky raced to meet each other at the horizon.

She completed a full turn, coming face to face with the dormitory she had slept in during the competition, with the stream trickling by behind her.

"I want the Lal Orphanage," she said. With a swipe of her hand she tore away the ranch as if it were a sheet of tissue paper. It fell away to reveal her dorm room at the Lal Orphanage. The bunk bed she had shared with countless other girls, made up with its pink comforter, and her favorite pillow. On her desk, her few belongings lay as she had left them the day Willy took her away.

She jumped onto her bed and heard the mattress creak under her weight, felt the rough spun cotton of the comforter on her cheek, smelled the harsh detergent used to wash it.

"I want home," she said in a forceful whisper. She rotated the world, so that where she had been prostrate, she was now floating upright in midair, her bed behind her and the ceiling in front of her. She reached out with both hands and violently tore away the Lal Orphanage.

Now she stood on cracked pavement in front of a small, battered house in a working class suburban neighborhood. The gate to the small, ill-kept front yard hung loosely on its hinges. She stepped forward and slowly ran her hands across it, the way she sometimes fantasized about Michael running his hands through her hair. She felt tears roll down her cheeks as she carefully creaked it open.

Just then the front door of the house opened, and a blonde girl of seven years of age emerged, smiling in a bright red dress that was a size too big. "Sarah, it's dangerous outside" called a concerned female voice from inside. "Come back inside and lock the door!"

"Mom?" asked Sarah, reaching one hand to her neck to finger her cross, and her other hand out towards the doorway.

The young girl looked up at the fence where Sarah stood, her smile melting away into fear. "Mom, someone's coming!"

Sarah smiled softly and opened her mouth to comfort the girl. But before she could form any words, scruffy figures carrying knives jumped over the fence from behind her and headed towards the door that the young girl had left open. "Look at that chubby little girl," one announced. "I bet this house is full of food."

Sarah leapt forward through the gateway, her arm outstretched towards the door. "Mom! Mom, get out of there!"

Everything went black.

"Fenton, get on mission." It was Rad's voice. Apparently he could pipe it into her mind while she was using the MindWave. Clearly, he could also see what she was doing.

"What *is* the mission?" she asked, working to get her emotions under control.

"Go to the Five Mile Creek Pumping Station and defend the servers from attack."

Sarah began to explain she had no idea what Rad was talking about, but before she could form the words she suddenly did know. Five Mile Creek was a central oil and gas pipeline pumping hub that was critical to moving energy around the country. Its delicate operations were controlled by complex algorithms that optimized utilization of the dozens of pipelines that ran through it. Those algorithms were protected by sophisticated security protocols that prevented outsiders from interfering.

Already, she saw an illuminated path through the blackness that would bring her to Five Mile Creek's servers. "Where's Michael?"

"He's already there."

Sarah raced through the virtual space of the multinet, following one thin cord of light and then another. She travelled thousands of miles in an instant until ahead of her, she saw a glowing orb that was the Five Mile server. The orb seemed like it was only a few feet in diameter. She could not see its interior through its softly glowing borders. She pushed herself forward into the luminescent skin.

147

As she passed through the surface of the orb, she entered a new self-contained space, much bigger than suggested by the small external appearance of the orb. She stood on a flat circular plain of perfectly trimmed grass that stretched for miles towards a ring of high mountains that appeared to mark the border of this world. In the center of the plain was a glinting steel box-like building that seemed to be hundreds of feet long in every dimension.

She jogged to the side of the building and push against its side. It was cold, flat, and immovable. She saw her blue eyes reflected in the metal, and backed away quickly. In this realm she had no real physical presence, just a consciousness. To look into her reflection was unsettling. It was like looking directly into her own soul.

She looked down the length of the building. Aside from a single portal that snapped open and shut in an irregular rhythm, the metal was solid and featureless. She knew, somehow, that this meant the server had few links to the outside world, and the few links that did exist were protected by a powerful firewall.

"Hey, Sarah!"

She turned and saw Michael. He wore a long white robe that emphasized the breadth of his shoulders and chest. It was cinched at the waist with a black sash, matching his baggy black cotton pants. He had wrapped a white headband around his forehead, and his unkempt black hair was tied into a topknot. He looked bizarre, but he also looked good.

She looked down and realized she was wearing a black leather body suit, taught over the curves of her figure. Her hair was pulled up in a severe bun over the suit's high collar.

Once Sarah had obeyed Rad's order to begin the mission, she had stopped putting any thought into her outfit, and she doubted Michael cared much about his clothes, either. Perhaps the MindWave used their subconscious self-images to choose outfits. She was sure that she could will her outfit to change to something else with a moment's thought, but she kind of liked being dressed in black leather around Michael.

More importantly, she needed to focus on the mission, not her wardrobe. She pointed to the irregularly opening and shutting doorway set a hundred feet down the metal wall from where they floated. "Have you tried going through that?"

"I was about to. Let's go."

As they got closer, Sarah could see glowing bits of data flowing along a thin beam of light that led to the gateway. She strode to the stream of data and stuck her hand into it. Immediately, she could visualize the information being exchanged. Oil transmission orders, emails from clients, invoices to customers. A landslide of information, none of it immediately useful to her.

"Let's try to get inside."

"Even if you get through the gate, there will be protocols designed to destroy you," warned Michael.

"Destroy me?"

"Don't worry, you can't get hurt for real. But your connection to here will be shut down."

Sarah shrugged and strode tentatively to within several paces of the gate, Michael half a step behind her. Then she slowed down, motioning at Michael to stop, and tiptoed the last few feet towards to where the solid steel door was snapping open and shut. Once she was right at its edge, she inched her head so that she could see inside.

Just inside the door there was a large antechamber littered with the jagged parts of several destroyed robots, acrid smoke and buzzing sparks still rising from their shattered forms. She heard the pulsing sounds of a security alarm. "Do you see, this Michael? I think someone got here ahead of us."

"Look over there!"

Sarah had already seen what had drawn Michael's attention: a female figure sprinting into the antechamber. She wore a long white gown, and carried a gleaming sword and shining silver shield. Her face was obscured by a closed helm but long red hair streamed behind her.

The door shut suddenly and their view of the inside of the chamber was obscured, and the wailing alarm was muffled to a faint whine.

After a fraction of a second it opened again and Sarah saw that two humanoid robots were now converging on the armored female, one from the front and one from behind. The robots had some kind of gun built into their forearms, and they were both aiming at the woman.

The woman leapt into the air, and then the door shut again.

"Dammit. How can we keep this thing open?" asked Sarah.

"Hang on," said Michael. He reached into his sash and came out with a keycard, which he fiddled with as he squatted in the grass.

"What's that?"

"Back at my orphanage I had an old holovision and no money. I used to hack my way past the tollgates on the multinet to get at my favorite, uh, content."

"That's disgusting, Michael."

"What?"

"You think I don't know what kind of *content* you're talking about?"

The door slammed open again and the dismembered head of one of the robots flew out and bounced through the plain, cutting gouges in the immaculate lawn. It was followed by pulses of orange light that Sarah took to be discharges from one of the robot's arm guns.

"Hurry up already!"

Michael stood up with his keycard and inserted into a slot next to the door that Sarah hadn't noticed. The door let out a short chirpy beep and snapped open.

Sarah peered into the room just in time to catch a glimpse of the sword-wielding woman disappearing though a doorway.

"Come on," Michael called over the blaring sound of the alarm as he stepped into the room.

"Are you sure we should—"

"Do you have a better idea?"

Sarah reluctantly stepped through the doorway and followed Michael as he sped down the hallway. The walls were the same reflective metal as the building's exterior, disorienting her as if she were in a hall of mirrors.

Suddenly a circular piece of the wall shot outwards at her face, too fast for her to dodge. The next thing Sarah knew, she was lying flat on her back, staring up at the female warrior she and Michael had been trying to follow. The woman squatted down so that her weight was on Sarah's solar plexus and put a mailed hand on Sarah's throat. "Who are you?" she demanded through her helmet.

She just needed to hang on for a few moments. "Who the hell are *you*?" gasped back Sarah.

"Sarah! Get out! Disconnect!" It was Michael's voice, from somewhere ahead.

The woman lifted Sarah's face off the cold metal round and up against her helmet. "Do you know what I am?"

Just a little longer. "Some crazy bitch."

"You fool. I am an Aeon. You cannot possibly challenge me."

And here we go. "I'll challenge you as soon as you get your fat ass off me."

Sarah grinned just as Michael leapt to tackle the woman from behind. Sarah had been watching him sprint down the hallway back towards her for the last several seconds.

Her grin faded when she saw the warrior casually reach behind her, grab Michael's robe in midair, and slam him into the metal wall of the corridor face first. Michael slid to the ground in a heap.

"Do you think it matters how many of you there are?" hissed the woman.

Sarah felt the woman's hand passing through her throat and working its way up through her skull towards her brain. She saw a flurry of glimpses into the woman's mind. Images of a lonely childhood in a high-walled mansion. Then joy at funerals for hated family members. And finally, the fervent belief that she was the divine savior of the human race.

Sarah knew that if she could observe fragments of her attacker's memories, then her attacker would soon see everything in her mind. She tried to pull away but found herself immobile.

"I'm going to find out who sent you," cackled the woman. "And then I'm going to destroy you all."

She heard Michael's voice. "Sorry. It's the only way." She turned her eyes and saw he was aiming a pistol at her head.

"No, I—"

There was a bright flash of light.

Chapter 9

Sarah tried to dodge but her body was still immobile. It was no longer the woman warrior that was holding her down, but something else. She blinked and overcame her disorientation. She was strapped into the cooling chair in the ranch.

Willy was coming over. "Are you all right, Sarah?"

"Michael shot me!"

She turned her eyes to glare at Michael and saw him blinking awake. "What the hell, man?" she hissed.

Rad interjected. "Fenton, quiet. Kang, report."

Willy put a comforting hand on Sarah's shoulder as Michael spoke. "I disconnected us both, sir. I was being overpowered. They would have traced us back here."

"You shot me!"

"Sarah, I'm really sorry. It was the only way I could think of to—"

"You two can kiss and make up later. Once you got inside the Five Mile firewall, our ability to read your data feeds was impaired. So tell me, did you at least learn anything that would help you identify the enemy?"

Sarah closed her eyes and tried to recall what had happened. It was all a blur, all except for the moment when Michael had aimed a pistol at her face.

"She had red hair," said Michael. "And she called herself an Aeon."

Rad pursed his lips tightly and rubbed his hands together slowly as he turned to Willy. "Johnson, get the agents out of their chairs and then report to my office for debriefing."

"It's all right, Sarah. You did well," said Willy, as he bent down to undo her straps.

Sarah turned away angrily. She could have kicked herself. How had she not remembered anything? Michael was making her look bad, first by saving them both and then by being the only one able to make a coherent report to Rad.

Willy shifted uncomfortably and waved away the holographic data in front of him. "Sir, our response to the attack on Five Mile was a failure."

Across his stainless steel desk, Colonel Rad Jaeger flashed him an ironic grin. "Excellent assessment. Half a dozen pipeline junctions exploding under our agents' noses is a failure. Now tell me what the hell went wrong."

"It was their first time in the multinet, sir. They're still figuring out—"

"No, you're still figuring out how to train them." Jaeger's smile was now gone. "Show me what she did in that little scuffle in the canteen."

Without waiting for Willy to react, he reached into the holographic image that Willy had just waved away and quickly spun through a list of titles. He selected one entitled, "Ranch canteen surveillance feed." A three dimensional video began, taking up the entire space above the table.

The image showed Bob Eckers pushing Michael onto the ground while several of the other orphans snuck towards Sarah from behind. He was obviously trying to distract her from his compatriots' approach. And it had obviously worked, as Sarah stared right at him and betrayed no sign she noticed the others.

Then Olivia Freeman threw a bowl of food at Sarah and she inexplicably dodged it, apparently without ever seeing it. During the next several seconds, she managed to knock both Bob and Olivia on their backs with perfectly timed movements.

"That's pretty handy for a novice," observed Jaeger.

"She was obviously helped by her TacWave."

"I thought the TacWave would overheat if she kept it on for too long. Did she turn it on when Bob approached?"

"She's learned to constantly flash it on and off for a few microseconds at a time, so that it never overheats, yet can pick up small changes in her environment, sir. That's how she sensed the bowl flying at her head."

"So she's figured out a way of using the device we never anticipated."

Willy paused, knowing Jaeger was steering him towards an unfavorable conclusion yet unsure of how to dodge it. "Yes, but that's nothing like going into the multinet, sir. That's a whole new world!"

"Why are you so protective of this girl, Johnson?" Jaeger's enunciation of each syllable was gratingly precise. "Frankly I don't understand why you chose her for the TacWave. She may be smart and fit. But she has a terrible attitude. We had to physically restrain her to give her the implant and we had to hold her down in the chair to get her to go on this mission. And she failed it utterly. If Michael hadn't had the presence of mind to shoot her, that Aeon would have traced her signal all the way back to the ranch. She's not focusing on her training. Either she's too plagued by guilt about her dead mother or she's too distracted by her hormonal urges towards Michael. Yet instead of correcting her faults, you indulge her with all your winking and friendly homilies."

Willy sighed silently before responding. He was indignant that Colonel Jaeger was questioning his expertise in psychology. Yet he could not deny that the man had a point. Despite her strong performance in many parts of the competition, Sarah's psychological makeup had obvious weaknesses. Willy had chosen Sarah to be one of the two TacWave recipients precisely because he believed Sarah's psychological vulnerabilities would make her receptive to the indoctrination program he had designed especially for her. In the end, her weakness would become his asset.

Nevertheless, Colonel Jaeger would not appreciate Willy's careful planning. He just wanted a fully competent and loyal soldier as soon as possible. It was time to bend the truth for the greater good. The ends would eventually justify the means.

"Sir, we've all gone through the psyche evaluations, and I've been working with her every day for months. On the surface she seems superficial and rebellious. But that's just an act she picked up to protect herself when her mother died and she was taken in by the orphanage. She's been playing the role for so long even she believes that's the real her."

"As do I," retorted Jaeger.

"It's a *survival* instinct, sir. At heart she is competitive, even driven. You saw that during the footrace on the first day of the competition. And she can be very loyal to people she considers as close as family. She watched her mother die; since then she's been looking for a new family. We can make ourselves that family."

Willy softened his tone slightly. "So, yes, she *is* a potentially amazing asset. But to develop her we can't beat her over the head with harsh training and crude indoctrination. That will just alienate her. We've got to use some finesse, to get her to come along in her own way."

Jaeger eyed him back angrily and rubbed his hands together animatedly. "No more coddling, Johnson. Stop trying to be Sarah's father and start acting like her commander. Ramp up her indoctrination so she learns whom she's working for. If her attitude doesn't improve, I'm personally going to take over her physical training. I'll kick the sass out of her."

Below the table, Willy closed his hand into a tight fist. At least Jaeger was not threatening to replace Sarah with someone else. Yet Jaeger's interference in Sarah's training could derail Willy's carefully planned program for her psychological development. And that could impair his ability to guide her development in the necessary directions. Willy knew continually contravening Jaeger amounted to insubordination, but still, he had to try to prevent Sarah from falling directly under Jaeger's control. "I don't think that's wise, sir. Your methods may not be what she needs."

Jaeger stood deliberately to his full height and leaned forward over his desk. He was a smaller man than Willy, but his posture conveyed command. And menace. "I don't care what she needs. I care what I need. And you are way out of line, Major. Dismissed."

Nick had now spent six months in the ether and had met most of his fellow MindWave users, or *Aeons*, as Laura insisted on calling them.

The Aeons had two pastimes. One was hedonism. They would play out fantastic adventures in worlds they created. They hunted dragons, refought famous battles, and celebrated their victories with feasts. Feasts quickly devolved into Roman orgies. Soon, the orgies became the most popular form of entertainment, crowding out the rest.

The MindWave was capable of simulating any sensation, and of arousing all of the pleasure centers of the brain for hours at a time. And romantic encounters were completely without worry. There was no chance of contracting a disease, of becoming pregnant, or of performing badly. There was no need for exclusivity, and therefore no need for jealousy. If the person you wanted to cavort with was preoccupied, you could create a simulated copy of them with your MindWave and get on with it.

Nick soon realized that Laura partook of this pastime much less than most of the others. Laura was much more focused on another popular pastime: making money.

While all of the Aeons were from the wealthiest families on the planet, most of them were on limited allowances dictated by their parents. They made sport of hacking into corporate servers, and using what they learned to speculate successfully in the securities and commodities markets. When you had insider information about every company in the world, it was easy enough to build a small allowance into a small fortune, and then to grow that small fortune into a large one. They marked their financial successes by using their new money to buy jewelry, cars, or whatever other baubles they desired.

This behavior troubled Nick, even though he was complicit in it, too. He still remembered the words of his father – the MindWave was a tool he could use to make the world a better place. Even though he knew his father's bright contributions to the world had come with a dark side, Nick wanted to live up to the man's idealistic wishes. But Nick and his new friends exclusively used their fast-growing abilities for idle amusement and unfair self-enrichment.

At the birthday party of an Aeon from Hong Kong named Chengwen Xu, as they watched gifts of fabulous expense being casually exchanged, Nick remarked to Laura, "You know, the more time we spend in the ether, the better we become at making money. But the more time we spend here, the less we need that money. It's not like Chengwen is actually going to spend time in the real world driving the sport cars he received today. Why would he, when he can just as easily create a world where he's flying a fighter jet?"

Laura flipped her long red hair back over her smooth bare shoulder and gave him a sidelong glance: "A man buying his third sports car in a year or a woman buying her fifth diamond necklace in a season is not buying to use, but buying to make a point."

Nick was confused that he could find no one among the Aeons who shared his interest in behaving selflessly. He wanted to understand why. He wanted to know if he was simply being naïve, mindlessly believing in platitudes that everyone else was wise enough to dismiss. "What point?"

"That they can buy it."

"That's the point? That's point*less*. Shouldn't we put the money to better use? We have all the abilities necessary to do something worthwhile. Yet we spend our time pursuing nothing but our whim of the moment." Maybe he was naïve, but it seemed that the other Aeons were no wiser than he was. He turned away from Laura in disgust.

Laura placed her ivory arms around his shoulders and pulled him back flirtatiously. "In the near future, we Aeons will save the world from cataclysm. And then you'll understand just how worthwhile you are. Our importance means that our own wellbeing is the most important thing in the world. The momentary whim of an Aeon is more important than the direst need of a human."

She pulled him closer, so that he felt her perky breasts pressing into his broad chest. She raised her mouth to his ear and sighed, "And I have a particularly strong whim right now.

Sarah smiled at Michael as he walked into the small briefing theater at the ranch. "Ready to get another butt-whupping?"

He rolled his eyes. "You were angry at me for two weeks after Five Mile, just because I did a little better than you. Now you're finally acting friendly again because you've found something where you can make me look bad."

After the Five Mile mission, Willy had begun requiring Sarah and Michael to play sports relying only on their TacWaves to provide the sensory information needed to steer their bodies. While she was clearly second to Michael in terms of navigating virtual worlds in the multinet, Sarah proved especially adept at using the TacWave in the real world. With each new sport she played, she further surpassed Michael. Michael had taken his series of defeats in stride.

"It's a good thing you're being a good sport about being bad at sports. I can't wait to see what Willy has planned for us today. Maybe boxing?"

"Knowing my luck, it will be sword-fighting," Michael answered as he sat down next to her.

Willy walked into the theater, looking strained. "Hi guys. I've just got a minute."

Sarah exchanged a surprised look with Michael.

"I wanted to let you know I'm not going to be running your physical training anymore. Don't worry, I'll still be overseeing your neurological drills." With that, Willy gave an unsmiling wink and walked out of the room.

"I guess it only makes sense," Michael said. "Remember that during the fight in the cafeteria, Bob bragged about how he was learning combat from Hank Green. It must be our turn to train under him."

She rubbed the silver cross around her neck and wondered if she could ever build rapport with Hank like she had with Willy.

Yet when the door to the theater opened, it was not Hank, but Rad who entered. He was dressed in a khaki T-shirt with matching pants and cap, and wore desert combat boots. Sarah repressed a curse. She knew whatever was coming was not going to be pleasant.

"I hope you had fun playing house with Major Johnson," said Rad in his characteristic condescending tone, "because playtime is over."

"Are you going to train us from now on, Rad?" asked Michael, not even trying to hide his surprise.

Rad took long strides until he was so close to Michael that their noses were almost touching. "This isn't summer camp and we're not on a first name basis. From now on, you will address me as Colonel Jaeger, or as sir. And I will address you as maggot and you," now he turned to Sarah, "as *maggette*."

Jaeger instructed each of them to place a small device into the single jack in the back of their skulls.

"What is this for, sir?" asked Sarah.

"You won't want to use your TacWave while this is plugged in," Jaeger responded. "Now, get above ground and run to the fence and back. I'll be ready for you by then."

Sarah glanced at Michael and saw her own unease reflected in his features. "Yes, sir" she said, as the two headed towards the large escalator that led to the surface.

The pair ran together to the fence wordlessly. As they reached the chain links, Sarah turned and looked at the device in the back of Michael's skull. It was a small metal cylinder, maybe half an inch long and a quarter inch in diameter, with a tiny green LED built into its tip. "What do you think these things are for?" she asked him.

"I don't know, but I'm sure it's not good," said Michael. He touched her elbow, letting his fingers linger there for a second. Despite her anxiety about training under Jaeger, Sarah felt her mood improve from the physical contact. She realized that this was the first time they'd been completely alone together in weeks, and that Michael was taking the chance to show his feelings for her. Their eyes locked for a moment, and then Michael withdrew his hand. "Let's head back. I don't want to make Jaeger any more unpleasant than normal."

By the time they crossed back through the cold waters of the stream, Jaeger was waiting for them, holding what looked like a remote control in his hands. He had set a medium-sized metal can on the ground. Sarah recognized it as an empty Langar Foods peanut butter container. There were a half-dozen tennis balls about 10 feet away from the can.

"Maggot," he said, addressing Michael, "Stand here behind the can."

Michael jogged over behind the can and stood expectantly.

Jaeger flipped a switch on the device in his hands and Michael fell to the ground, screaming in pain.

Sarah immediately turned towards Michael but Jaeger stepped in front of her and held out his hand so it dug into her solar plexus, knocking her backwards. "Maggette, the only way for you to help maggot over there is to get three of these tennis balls into the can."

Michael was rolling around and clawing at his head.

"What's wrong with Michael, sir?" demanded Sarah.

"He's in terrible pain. And you're wasting time. Get three balls in the can."

Sarah stared at Jaeger in disbelief for a moment and then bent down to pick up three of the balls.

As she rose back up, she was struck by an intense burning pain that raced up and down her spinal cord. She felt the dusty ground smack her in the face and realized she had fallen.

As suddenly as it had come, the pain was gone. She pulled herself to a sitting position and glanced over at Michael. He was still contorted in agony.

She looked up at Jaeger.

He stared down at her mockingly, rubbing his hands together. "Obviously, you are not allowed to carry the balls. That would be too easy, wouldn't it? You will throw them one by one into the can from where I stand."

Sarah shook her head clear of the residual pain and began dragging herself to her feet.

"Don't bother getting up yet. Ten pushups each time you touch a ball."

Sarah wanted to protest but she heard Michael groaning in pain and she decided the best thing to do was to start knocking out the pushups. When she was done, she grabbed one of the tennis balls and ran to Jaeger's side.

As she tried to aim at the small target, her gaze kept slipping to Michael, who still lay writhing in pain just beyond the can. She felt her arms trembling from the pushups she had just done, and was afraid she could never hit the target.

She threw the ball and it landed a full foot from the can.

Jaeger said, "There's a punishment for missing." He clicked his device and the wave of pain came back, knocking Sarah to the ground again.

After it passed, he nudged her with his foot. "Do your pushups and try again."

Sarah did ten more pushups and grabbed another ball. Her arms were still shaking, she was still distracted by Michael's gasps of pain, and now her eyes were beginning to tear up. "Sir, I can't," she cried.

Jaeger sounded almost bored. "Use your TacWave, Maggette. That's what it's for."

"But you said..." hadn't Jaeger just warned her not to use her TacWave while the device was plugged in? One look at Michael's contorted face convinced Sarah to try.

As soon as she turned the TacWave on, she was hit by another wave of pain like the ones that had floored her twice already. She fell to one knee and inhaled a short breath. She turned her TacWave back off, and the pain disappeared.

"I said you wouldn't *want* to use your TacWave. But now you *need* to, or your friend maggot here is going to need a six foot hole in the ground."

Sarah choked back a sob at the arbitrariness of Jaeger's sadism and stood again. She planted her feet and braced herself for the imminent onset of blinding pain.

The pain was as bad as before, but at least this time she was prepared for it. She inhaled sharply and checked her balance. Then she engaged several of the TacWave's functions at once. She released enkephalin into her blood to suppress the pain, and endorphins to relax her mental state. She allowed the TacWave to take control of the muscles in her arm, and to coordinate them with her augmented sight.

She tossed the ball in a high arc and it landed squarely in the can.

Before it had even landed, she cut off her TacWave and dropped to the ground to do ten more pushups.

"Good," said Jaeger. "Now we go up to the next level."

Michael's groans escalated to screams.

She grabbed another ball and stood up again. She engaged her TacWave and was hit by another wave of pain, this one much more intense than the previous ones. Jaeger had definitely gone to the next level. No wonder Michael was screaming.

She pulled herself together and used the TacWave to help her sink the next shot.

"Final level," said Jaeger, fiddling with his device.

Sarah was on the ground doing pushups when she heard Michael's cries escalate in volume and pitch. She closed her eyes in a vain attempt to make the horrible noise disappear.

As she climbed to her feet with another ball, she spared a glance in Michael's direction. His face was bright red and he was breathing in short halting gasps. There was a pool of vomit seeping into the dusty ground by his mouth.

"You're hurting him, sir," she cried to Jaeger.

"You're hurting him by wasting time," he replied calmly. "And there's a punishment for wasting time."

He clicked a switch and Sarah fell to the ground. The intensity of the pain was unlike anything she had ever felt before. All of her muscles locked together and she couldn't move. She felt warmth spreading in her pants and dimly realized she had soiled herself.

Finally, the pain passed. She staggered back to her feet holding the tennis ball. As her head cleared, she felt self-conscious about her wet shorts and turned her body away from Jaeger as she aimed the tennis ball.

"It's going to hurt just as badly when you turn on your TacWave," stated Jaeger.

She paused and felt tears falling down her cheeks. Her eyesight was blurred, and now her whole body was shaking instead of just her arms. She wanted to help Michael yet she couldn't bear to face that wave of pain again. Maybe, just maybe, she could throw the ball accurately without relying on her TacWave.

She took a deep breath, bent her elbow and aimed her throw carefully.

The ball sailed wide of the mark.

She cursed and dropped, pumping out ten pushups under Jaeger's cold gaze, as Michael continued to cry out in distress just a dozen feet away.

"This could all be over now. But you missed because you're afraid to suffer a few moments of pain to help your teammate." Jaeger's voice was full of scorn. "That calls for an extra punishment."

As the wave of pain knocked her into a prone position, she realized that the dusty orange ground had turned into the dirty linoleum floor of her old home, streaked with her mother's blood. Her mother was there with her, down on the ground, her eyes locked on Sarah as she died.

"Mom, I'm so sorry," sobbed Sarah.

Chapter 10

The nymph gave Nick a flirtatious glance before dropping her towel and diving into the pool of clear water. He watched her perfect naked form swimming away from him until she reached the island in the center of the pool.

"I think she *smaaks* you, *bra*," exclaimed Kobus. Even as a bear, he was licking his lips and breathing heavily, the way he always did when excited by some erotic adventure in the ether.

Nick saw that Kobus was right. The nymph had sprawled herself suggestively on the grassy ground of the island and was beckoning to him.

"Nick," came her voice.

"I'm coming," said Nick, stripping off the heavy leather armor he wore.

"Nick! I'm talking to you!"

The voice was no nymph. It was his mother.

Nick pulled the network cable out of the back of his MindWave and became more aware of his surroundings in the real world. He smelled the musty odor of his bedroom, and heard his favorite music compilation playing. He blinked his eyes open, flinching at the bright sunlight streaming through his window.

"Ah, so you're finally back inside the real world," said his mother with a tone of cross satisfaction. "What on earth were you doing with your MindWave?"

"Sorry, Mom, I was hanging out with some friends," he sputtered.

"Friends?" asked his mother with raised eyebrows. After a pause she gave him a friendly nudge. "Well, you'll do much better with your friends if you socialize on a full stomach!"

"OK, I *am* really hungry, let's go eat," allowed Nick, trying not to let his impatience show. He would much rather shove a handful of food into his mouth and be done with it than have a long, drawn out meal with his parents.

He followed his mother down the grand staircase that dominated their massive duplex penthouse and through the maze of hallways, a Bach concerto following him wherever he went. Finally, they arrived in the dining room, where the family cook had just laid out a finely prepared meal with dishes including Punjabi curries, Brazilian filés, and freshly baked Italian bread on the heirloom cherry wood table. Of course, none of the cook's ingredients came from his parents' food factories. His mother would never settle for eating the artificial nutrients she had developed to feed the rest of the world.

Throughout lunch, Nick was distracted. He could barely stomach looking at his parents. His mother's eyes had dark circles under them. And Nick's enhanced vision spotted hundreds of blocked pores on his father's nose. *So many imperfections,* he thought with disgust. In the ether, no one ever looked tired or had oily skin.

He barely noticed what he was eating, and only made feeble attempts to keep up conversation with his parents.

"So, your father tells me you're thinking about moving into your own apartment?" asked his mother.

"Uh, yeah, I'm kind of thinking about it," responded Nick absent-mindedly.

"Aren't you happy living with us?"

"Yes, mom, I'm very happy here," he said, suddenly exasperated. "But I'm eighteen years old and I shouldn't rely on you and dad for everything anymore."

"Well, now that you've dropped out of school, and you don't have your old classmates to spend time with, won't you be lonely if you live on your own? And who will take care of you?"

"I'll hire a maid to take care of me. I'm sure my new maid will be able to take care of me as well as the ones who take care of me here."

His mother ignored the implied rebuke. "You'll still be terribly lonely, won't you?"

"No, don't worry, Mom," he responded irritably. "I have plenty of friends."

"Friends?" asked his father, finally looking up from his computer pad and taking an interest in the conversation. "You mean your MindWave friends?"

"Yes, Dad, MindWave friends. We spend a lot of time hanging out together. So don't worry, I'm not lonely."

"What do you normally do with your MindWave friends?" pursued his father. "You all have so much potential, but I haven't seen any of you do anything constructive yet."

His mother interjected, "Oh, honey, don't give him so much pressure. He's still learning how to use the device."

"Nonsense. It's been almost half year," responded his father testily.

"We can't all save the world like you did, Dad," Nick said through clenched teeth.

"I didn't save the world," said his father dismissively. "First of all, it was half your mother's work. And secondly, we just delayed the inevitable."

Nick grimaced at his father's habitual false modesty and wished he could make the dispute go away. Instead, he equivocated. "We're working on a few projects, Dad. I don't want to talk about them until they're ready."

He glanced at the gold-trimmed digital clock on the wall. The lunch was taking too long. The gourmet food was tasteless compared with what he could eat in the ether. And the company was tiresome.

"You know what people are calling you MindWave users?" asked his dad. "They're calling you cyber barbarians. Cybarians for short."

"So?"

"They call you that because you have nothing to add to society."

"Sarah," gasped her mother. But it wasn't her mother's voice. It was Michael. "Help me, Sarah!"

Her mother was dead. Michael was not. Sarah had failed her mother, but she could still help Michael.

She saw a tennis ball lying on the linoleum next to her. She grabbed it and looked across the room to the can. It seemed to be right in front of her. She knew just how to throw the ball. She didn't even need to stand up.

The pain stopped the instant the ball settled into the can.

She stood up, dizzy and trembling. Michael was no longer screaming, and he was struggling to sit up but his arms were too weak to support his weight. Sarah looked to Jaeger pleadingly.

"Better take your friend, Maggot, to see Dr. Lee," said the Colonel, as he rubbed his hands together firmly.

Sarah supported much of Michael's weight as she led them back to the underground clinic, where a frowning Dr. Lee quickly examined him. "He's suffering acute exhaustion, but no physical harm," she concluded. "I'll keep him here for a few hours to be safe. You go get yourself cleaned up, Sarah."

Sarah took a few moments to calm herself down. Michael would be fine. He wasn't hurt. There was no need to panic.

As her concern for Michael faded away it was replaced by anger at Jaeger. She knew she should be humiliated at the stench that was coming from her shorts, but she was too furious to care. Without even stopping to change, she ran through the compound and pushed open the door to Willy's office.

When she burst into his room, Willy was looking at a document on a computer tablet, which he quickly slid into a drawer when she entered. Before he'd had a chance to rise from his desk, she blurted through tears, "Why can't you train us anymore?"

"I'm sorry, Sarah, Colonel Jaeger has insisted—"

She cut him off. "I don't understand why he punishes us. I tried as hard as I could, but he kept punishing me for failing. He made the training impossible to complete without being punished!"

Willy looked away as a guilty expression crossed his face. "Sarah, the punishments are not for failing the training. The punishments *are* the training."

Sarah felt the world close in around her. She backed out of Willy's office without speaking. She made her way through the underground tunnels to her room and sat down on her bed, holding her head in her hands.

How can I survive this? she wondered. She wanted to leave, to go back to the orphanage. But she was afraid to quit, terrified of admitting her weakness. *Why had she come here?* She should have just refused to get on the plane with Willy all those months ago. In her mind she cursed Jaeger for abusing her, Willy for bringing her to the ranch, Principal Kim for signing her over to the government, and her mother for dying.

Mom. How could she curse her mom for dying? It had been Sarah's fault. She had left the door open, allowing the bandits to enter the house. She'd been old enough to know better, and her mother had warned her of the danger countless times.

Mom, I'm so sorry.

As she recalled her mother's dying face, that last desperate embrace that spoke all the words her mother's slashed vocal cords would never again pronounce, Sarah recalled what she'd realized while crippled by pain and fear just several minutes ago. Her mother was already dead, and beyond help. But she could still help Michael. And she could still help herself.

She could help herself because she was not a victim.

Everything she had worried about for the last several years suddenly sloughed away; all of her obsessions about social status, her looks, her wants. In a moment of insight, she saw how superficial these preoccupations had been. All these years, there was something deeper, something stronger, something more elemental buried at her core, and now it was finally returning to the surface.

She wiped away her tears. She had never let go of the pain she'd felt at her mother's death, because she had never overcome her guilt about it. And fear of confronting that pain had led her to distract herself with frivolities, to create and live in a façade of personality that was not her own.

But there was no more time for distraction. Suffering and loss were simply a part of life, a part she needed to accept without alarm or self-pity.

"I'm sorry, Mom," she said calmly into the silence of her room, "I'll see you again when all of this is done." And then she slipped into a deep sleep, untroubled by the dreams that normally disturbed her.

Nick was playing blackjack with Kobus in Abril's casino.

Laura had been increasingly hard to find in recent weeks. But she had joined today's game, and was puffing on a cigarette. She looked at Nick with an impatient scowl and asked, "Nick, I have a lot of work to do. Can you stop wasting my scarce free time?"

Nick shook away the memory of his father's admonitions and looked up. "Sorry, family stuff on my mind."

A heartbeat after he should have, Kobus commented, "*Ja, your parents are jealous because you've pulled a *jabu pule* into the ether, ne bra*?"

Laura was in Los Angeles, Kobus was in Cape Town, and Nick was in New York. Their connection had an annoying lag in it. Despite their power to enter the ether at will, MindWave users were still reliant for communications on existing public networks, with their inherent problems of limited bandwidth and susceptibility to failure, leading to lags and disruptions in the signal. Just months ago, when Nick was first becoming adept at using his MindWave, paying broadband companies for multiple elite-status accounts was sufficient to get a good signal. But now, even that tactic wasn't fully reliable anymore.

"Yeah," said Nick. "I've pulled a disappearing act into the ether. My mom's worried sick about it. How do you guys know?"

Laura sighed and a cloud of smoke came out of her mouth. "Nick, we know everything. That's what it means to be an Aeon. The sooner you figure that out, the sooner you'll stop being surprised by it." She gestured at the cards in his hand. "Now, are you hitting?"

"Hang on, Laura," interjected Kobus with a growl, as he reached for another of the blueberries he was snacking on. "I'm interested in my *bra's* parents. Their company makes half the food in the world."

"It's not as if you actually eat that food," said Laura in a shocked tone. She quickly turned to Nick. "No offense, Nick. I only eat organic gourmet food."

Kobus laughed, which came out as a deep polar bear roar. "I dunno what I eat. I always have my body on autopilot. It eats whatever the maid leaves out for it. Maybe I'm eating *brak chow*."

"Yes, dog food would certainly be a lot worse than bear food," said Laura dryly.

"Whoa, wait, you can put yourself on *Autopilot*? How do you do that?" interrupted Nick, blinking in surprise.

Kobus looked at Laura in disbelief, and Laura responded with a shrug. Finally, Kobus explained: "*Bra*, you gotta get yourself on autopilot. It's *fokking* awesome. You let your MindWave guide your physical body through all the boring parts of real life. Like, showering, going to the *kakhaus*, uh..."

Laura gestured with the cigarette she was holding. "My body goes to the gym for three grueling hours a day, and I never feel a thing." She squinted. "In fact, I'm there now, doing squat lunges." She took a theatrically long drag from her cigarette and exhaled luxuriantly. "That's a good use of autopilot mode."

"Wow, that's amazing. I have to start doing some autopiloting," said Nick.

"You know, Nick, there's an owner's manual for your MindWave that explains all this stuff," remarked Laura with a disdainful shake of her head. "You don't even have to read it... it's preinstalled in your memory. Now, are you hitting or not?"

Nick hit, receiving a ten of hearts that forced him out of the game. He sighed.

"Your turn, Kobus," intoned Laura impatiently.

"This is *befoked*. You're running the probability generator today. You can just determine the outcome of any bet I make," Kobus growled.

"Kobus, I'm insulted," said Laura in mock outrage as she stubbed out her cigarette. "I'll have you know I've set all of these games to operate under the rules of chance."

"Chance? As in, you take any chance to steal my *kroons*?" Kobus dropped his cards. "This is getting boring anyway. Let's go make *kroons* for real."

"I was afraid you'd never ask," responded Laura. "Where shall we go? Bargain hunting in the financial markets again?"

"Nah, that's getting boring," piped in Nick. "I've already made a fortune doing that this month."

Kobus raised his eyebrows. "*Ja no*, what do you suggest, *bra*?"

"Why don't we try to build a real company? A company that does something useful?"

Laura said "I've told you our destiny is to save the world. What could be more useful than that?"

Nick had a ready answer. "There wouldn't be a world to save without my parents' company. That's pretty useful."

"What, growing food in laboratories to feed the poor?" Laura's disdain was clear.

"They did save humanity from a global famine."

"*Ja no*, I'm curious to see how a food vat works," interjected Kobus. "Let's go see a Langar Foods lab!"

"Fine," said Laura resignedly. "Let's go. Since we know the great Vinicius Lal, we might as well take the VIP tour."

Chapter 11

The world went dark and for a moment the three were in the endless blackness of the ether. Then Nick recreated a replica of the first Langar Foods lab near Woodstock, New York. Since his first attempts to form his own bedroom, he'd made great strides in building realistic worlds. To help him make an accurate portrayal of the lab, he combined his own memories, satellite photos of the plant, design information in private company networks he was able to break into, and footage from public sources.

They stood in a huge, well-lit room with a low roof. The walls, floors and ceiling were all white, and lit by regularly spaced, diffused lighting fixtures. Around the room were large transparent plastic vats, which held a viscous translucent liquid. A handful of men and women, dressed like surgeons in disposable paper garments, hair nets, and face masks, scurried around the facility, checking on vats and reading computer displays.

"Well, I have to admit this is kind of impressive," said Laura as she took in the view. "I taught myself the science but I've never bothered to look at a facility. It *is* bigger than I imagined."

"So how does this pile of *kak* turn out heaps of yummy *chow*?" asked Kobus, slipping a few more blueberries into his mouth.

"I'll show you." Nick shifted the world from the hangar into an old-fashioned industrial farm. They floated below a clear blue sky over an endless sea of corn stalks, which rustled slowly in a breeze. "Twentieth Century agriculture increased crop yields by introducing huge quantities of inputs. Water, pesticide, fertilizer, and so on."

"Yes, yes, we know. And eventually the water table receded, and fertilizer became more expensive, and the food supply was breaking down," interjected Laura impatiently.

"Yes," said Nick, slightly wounded at Laura's insouciance yet determined to impress her. He made a gesture with his hand, and one of the corn plants, complete with its tangled roots, lifted out of the ground to float alongside them. "Food production was so... inefficient. If you look at this corn, well, you have the roots, and the stalk, and the leaves, and the cob that holds the corn kernels. None of these are eaten, but they must be grown anyway."

"No, they're eaten. They're fed to animals," interrupted Laura.

Nick stifled an angry sigh at Laura's repeated interruptions and shifted the world to a cattle station, with hundreds of cows and bulls jammed muzzle to tail in a giant feedlot, and continued talking. "Yes, some of the waste material from agriculture was used to raise livestock. But if you think about how they grew meat, it was still an even worse waste of resources. For every steer ready for slaughter, you need bones, organs, a brain – a ton, literally, a *ton*, of wasted production that no one was going to eat."

"And there's always the ethical issues of animal mistreatment, *ne*," added Kobus, rubbing his furry chin with his bear's paw.

Laura gave him a scornful stare.

"What?" growled Kobus.

"Anyway," continued Nick, amplifying his voice slightly to regain his audience's attention. "You also have to consider that in order to grow a mature adult cow or steer, you have to grow the beast from newborn calf – from fetus, actually – to full-grown animal. That means you're supporting all those useless organs and bones for months or years before you finally get to harvest the meat. It took eight pounds of feed to make one pound of grown cow, and of that one pound less than half was usable meat, so you're really talking about almost twenty pounds of grain to make a one pound steak. So, in a way, you could say that for one person to get a steak dinner, twenty people had to miss lunch."

"If you feel this strongly, you must eat only vat food yourself," said Laura.

Nick paused and looked down. The private chefs his family employed to cook every meal certainly didn't use vat foods in their gourmet dishes. "I, uh, eat vat foods *sometimes*."

Laura laughed. "So while vat foods are good enough for the rest of the world, you deserve something better?"

"It's not like that."

"Yes it is. It really is. And I'm glad you realize it. So enough with the save the whales speech. Show us your food laboratory again."

Nick gave her a dirty look, but brought them back to the Langar Foods lab. "So, what my dad did – with my mom, although she doesn't like to take credit – is to figure out how to grow that corn kernel, or that steak, without needing the corn plant or the cow. Or the fields and feedlots, for that matter."

He continued proudly. "It's an almost perfect chemical process. For plants like corn, it cut costs by ninety percent. For meat the savings were about ninety-nine percent."

"Truly amazing," said Laura. "But, as I've said already, I know all this."

Kobus swallowed the last of his blueberries as he broke in. "I love this stuff, it's all so *ongelooflik*. Show us a vat!"

Nick placed them inside one of the large, plastic containers filled with a thick, translucent liquid.

"Disgusting," said Laura, taking a drag from her cigarette. Nick had adjusted the physical rules of his simulated world so that despite being suspended in a thick liquid, the three could talk without trouble. He hadn't foreseen that Laura would abuse the rules by smoking. He paused for a moment while he changed the physics, and Laura's cigarette was instantly extinguished, quickly becoming a soggy mess.

"Hey, I was smoking that!" she protested.

"Sorry, but this is a non-smoking facility," Nick grinned. Yet he was unnerved at how angry Laura appeared. Luckily, Kobus guffawed so loudly a blueberry came out of his nose, which eased the tension.

Nick continued explaining his family's business. "So, how this works is, you put all these proteins and sugars and vitamins into what we call a delivery medium, like the slurry in this tank. Then you put in a frame impregnated with stem cells, and add some heat, some other biological materials, and voilà, you have a nice juicy steak."

As he spoke, a curved plastic mold appeared in the vat. Quickly, red and white specs grew on the mold, and expanded and merged with each other until they had formed a perfectly shaped, nicely marbled, slab of meat. "In reality, this process takes about a day," concluded Nick.

Kobus nodded appraisingly. "As *indrukwekkende* as I hoped, *bra.*"

Laura had been brooding intently during this part of Nick's tour, but now interjected, "Can we get out of this vat? I thought the point of all of this was to make our own company. I'm sure you don't want us to compete with your family business."

Nick shifted them to a luxurious conference room. They sat in comfortable chairs around a beautiful cherry wood table, modeled on the kitchen table in his family's apartment. The walls were padded with sound absorbent leather, and the floor was covered with a beautiful pattern of colored tiles. A gilded chandelier provided soft yellow light.

"Tell us about Langar's financials, *ne,*" suggested Kobus. "Langar sells, what, *twoe triljoen* meals a year?"

"Yep, that's right," said Nick trying to hide the pride he felt. "Enough to feed two billion people a year. About a quarter of the food in the world."

"Probably half the food in the world if you don't count bugs and fungi," Laura said with a look of disgust.

"Insects and fungi are the lowest-end food," allowed Nick. "Langar's products cost a bit more. That's mostly because bugs can grow just about anywhere, but my parents' products must be shipped from factory to customer, and transportation costs money."

"Transport... *ja*, how many facilities do you have?" asked Kobus.

"This one in New York, one in Salinas, California, which ships a lot of its production to South America and Asia,. And then Portsmouth serves Eurasia and Africa," recited Nick.

"Only *drie*?" Asked Kobus, incredulously. "No wonder transport costs are so high!"

"My dad would rather keep production concentrated in a few large facilities he can easily monitor. But my mom is pushing him to open more factories, especially in Asia."

"*Ja*, I've heard Langar *vermorsels* any potential competitors before they can grow."

Nick paused. It was true that his father had used every means at his disposal, including some that were unethical, to prevent other labs from developing technology similar to Langar's. He donated so much to politicians that he could get the government to extend and enforce his patents however he wanted. And he even had leverage over foreign competitors – he could just threaten to cut off food shipments unless the local government shut down the offending entrepreneur. No regime was willing to suffer mass starvation in the hopes of developing a domestic food producer months or years in the future.

"My father is afraid that the technology is dangerous if it falls into the wrong hands."

"Of course it is. Still, even after transportation, the prices of Langar foods are so low." Laura pointed to the soggy cigarette she still held. "A steak doesn't cost much more than this."

"My parents set prices just a bit above costs. The company makes just a two percent profit pretax."

"You're practically giving them away," protested Laura derisively. "How did your family become one of the richest in the world if you're only making a two percent profit?"

"When you're selling *twoe triljoen* meals a year, *twoe persent* adds up pretty fast, *ne*" mused Kobus.

Nick never knew whether to be proud or ashamed of his family's wealth. His parents had taught him the ideals of selflessly serving society to make the world better. And in some ways, they had lived up to those ideals themselves. They had fallen short in many ways, too. His father had bought political influence and used it to crush all potential competitors, and his mother reveled in a life of fabulous wealth and isolation. "Yeah, when you add it all up, it makes us one of the most profitable companies in the world."

"Second most, right after Petro China," added Kobus.

"Yes, it's certainly not bad. How much does your family own?" Laura asked.

"My dad owns 40 percent, and my mom 39. Don't you guys already know all of this?"

"*Ja no*, it's a private company, so the financials are *geheime*," explained Kobus as he shifted in his chair. "We could probably get the information if we really wanted."

Laura stared up at the fine crystals hanging from the chandelier.

Nick filled the silence. "So, anyway, that's my family's company. As Laura pointed out, the question we're trying to answer is: what kind of company should *we* build?"

Laura turned her attention back to the conversation. "There's no need to discuss it."

She seemed to find reassurance in the blank expressions of Nick and Kobus. "Petro China is the most profitable company in the world. Even food is trumped by energy. Let's beat Petro China at its own game and make the biggest company in the world."

Nick gulped. Energy was a dirty business. He'd been expecting they'd form a high technology company.

Kobus stared in astonishment at Laura and asked "Are you *fokking* serious? *Grootste* company in the *wêreld*? And go up against the oil majors, with their private armies and government alliances?"

"First of all, Petro China is run by mere natural people," she answered defiantly. "Second of all, I've been building up an energy company for two years, so we won't be starting from scratch. I'll let

189

you each buy a 24% stake; if you don't have enough cash now I'll give you an earn-in."

Kobus looked at Nick and looked back to Laura, before nodding his assent. "Well, I still think it's a *fokking* crazy plan. But why not?"

He extended his paw, palm downwards, to the center of the table.

Laura reached out and placed her hand on top of his. "Deal."

Nick hesitated for a moment. Laura and Kobus stared at him expectantly. Slowly, he extended his hand and placed it on top of Laura's. "OK, deal."

Willy walked into the briefing theater and announced "All right, kiddos. I hope you're ready to begin *field* training."

Sarah suppressed a groan. She was ready to finish preparation and begin her real job. Since the day Colonel Jaeger had taken over their physical drilling, she had felt herself becoming tougher and tougher. Jaeger's regimen emphasized nimbleness and endurance rather than strength, and Jaeger often used the rugged terrain of the ranch itself for conditioning. The run from the ranch across the stream to the wall and back, the course that had seemed so imposing on the first day of the competition, became their daily warm up. After weeks of climbing the mountain, fording the river, and racing through the surrounding scrubland, Sarah felt her already healthy body becoming firm and toned.

At the same time, her competence with the TacWave had grown to the point that she was fully confident in her ability to operate in the ether.

"More practice?" complained Michael. "Are we ever going to get out in the real world?"

"You'll be up against real opponents," explained Willy. "I'm just calling it training because the stakes are low and no one will get hurt."

Sarah looked over towards Michael and raised an eyebrow. He returned her glance. They both faced their first mission with a keen sense of anticipation mixed with trepidation.

Sarah asked: "What's our assignment?"

"I was afraid you'd never ask," responded Willy with his characteristic wink. "A group of three MindWave users, or *Aeons*, as they like to call themselves..." He paused. "I'm not sure if you know what an Aeon is, but this particular term—"

Sarah hadn't known what an Aeon was a moment ago, but thanks to her TacWave, she knew now. She recited the information she had just learned. "According to the Gnostic religious tradition, an Aeon is a semi-divine being that has emanated from the true God."

Michael furrowed his brow. "There's an interesting parallel, Willy. A MindWave gives its users intuitive access to almost unlimited knowledge. According to Gnosticism, intuitive knowledge is a sign of divinity, and the hallmark of an Aeon."

Willy stared at them for a moment, nonplussed. "I don't know why I bother asking you if you know a word's definition when you have a dictionary in your brain."

"It's not in my brain," retorted Michael. "I went online to find the information." After careful discussions with Dr. Lee, Willy had equipped Michael and Sarah with small external antennae that connected to their TacWaves to allow them to access computers wirelessly. Sarah's antenna was the chain of her crucifix necklace, which was linked to the single tiny data port of her TacWave by a super-thin optical cable that was invisible when mixed into her hair.

"Whatever," said Willy, waving his hand dismissively. He turned back to the holovision. "Anyway, let's get on with the briefing. Sparkwise Energy was founded two years ago by—"

"We know who the founders are." Interrupted Sarah.

"It's a private offshore company," protested Willy. "How do you know?"

Michael filled in. "They had to file company registrations with various authorities. Obviously they used a complex holding structure to hide their identities but it's pretty easy to follow the trail with our TacWaves."

"Are you sure it's legal for you to go prying into government registries like this?"

"I'm quite certain it's illegal. Should we stop?" asked Sarah.

Willy paused for a moment. "No, keep it up. This way we can finish briefings a lot faster." He looked at her sternly and added, "But don't get caught or I'll have to fill out a stack of reports this high." He raised his hand far above his head.

Sarah and Michael exchanged quick smiles.

Willy looked at them with uncertainty. "So… where do I need to fill you in?"

Michael began, "Well, we can see that they started with a relatively small capital base for an energy company two years ago, when only the original founder, Laura Sophia Mayer, was involved. Since then she's done some really smart trades and grown fast. The company has been buying up key pipelines and storage facilities within North America. With the new investments from Jakobus Van der Merwe and Vinicius Lal, the company looks set to grow fast."

Willy stared down at the tablet that held his notes, scanning the screen as if he were trying to catch up.

"By the way, do you know that the two newer cofounders got the stake money for Sparkwise Energy by illegally trading stocks and bonds using fake identities?" asked Sarah.

Willy looked embarrassed to be confronted with this information. "Really? I thought they just used their parents' money. Can you prove that?"

"Easy enough. But it will be hard to enforce the relevant laws and regulations against them, due to their choice of holding structures and jurisdictions," explained Michael.

"We'll notify the Treasury or the SEC or whatever—"

"Treasury," said Sarah.

"Great," Willy responded, sounding a little unsure of himself. There was an uneasy break in the conversation.

"Anyway," Sarah picked up, "We know a lot about the company. What we don't know is what you want us to do about it."

"Michael, I want you to remotely surveil the original founder, Laura Mayer, over the ether. She's one of the first people to get the MindWave implant, and we believe she's the most proficient user. Our psych profile shows her intelligence is off the scale, but, well..." he paused, weighing his words. "After she first connected her MindWave to the internet, she had... psychotic episodes. She was institutionalized under court order, but her family used its money and influence to have her released after a month.

"All of her family members have died in various accidents since then, yet no one's been able to pin any murder charges on her."

Michael looked grim. "So, I'm up against a fellow orphan. But this one's an orphan by choice."

Sarah suppressed a shiver as she looked at the holographic image of Laura that Willy had projected into the room. The scarlet red hair and statuesque physique reminded her of the woman warrior she had fought with at Five Mile Creek.

"The psychological evaluation that was partially completed before her release from the institution suggested strong paranoid and narcissistic tendencies. She only trusts other MindWave users, and has become estranged from everyone else. Michael, don't make contact, and don't be seen. Just report on her activities."

Willy turned to Sarah. "And I want you to get close to one of the new investors. Vinicius Lal, he goes by the name 'Nick'." The holovision screen depicted a three dimensional bust of Nick.

"All right," said Sarah haltingly, trying to conceal her surprise. Every schoolchild knew that Langar Foods, the company founded by Nick's parents, had rescued the world from a horrible famine in the late 2020s. She'd exclusively eaten Lal foods since she could remember, even here at the ranch. Sarah had even lived half her life in an orphanage founded by the Lal family charity.

The bust of Nick displayed by the holovision was strikingly handsome, with long black hair, green eyes, and sculpted features. Even the unmistakable MindWave exhaust ports at the back of his skull didn't detract too much from his looks. Out of the corner of her eye, Sarah could see a dark expression on Michael's face, which she attributed to jealousy. It was a good thing Colonel Jaeger's intense training had pushed her to grow up. Otherwise she would probably have formed a crush on Nick.

"For this mission, I don't want you approaching him in the network. I want you to get to know him in the flesh and see what you can learn from him in person." said Willy. "So we're going to give you a six-week crash course in how to act like a spoiled rich kid. A properly brought up one, if that's possible, but spoiled rich nonetheless. We'll teach you what gossip to prattle about, which fashions to wear, and what slang to use. Oh, and our intelligence indicates that Nick is a food maven, so we'll have to train you up in the finest dining."

Sarah ignored Michael's possessive glance. "This seems like a lot of unnecessary work. Why don't I surveil him remotely over the networks?"

"Our psyche analysis is a bit dated, but it indicates he'll open up more to a real physical person, rather than an imaginary online persona. After getting his implants he lost all his friends in the real world. Now, especially because he feels anxiety about his appearance, he hardly ever leaves his home. So you'll have to work hard to meet him and even harder to break down the walls. But if you can use his anxiety and loneliness to your advantage, the walls may come crashing down on their own."

Sarah was silent for a moment while she digested Willy's instructions. "OK. So what's my cover?"

Chapter 12

Nick groaned as he slid into the self-driving limousine. He hated his dad's public events. They consisted of interminable meals consisting of foods that were chosen because their blandness would not offend anyone. On the rare occasions that alcohol was served, the drinking age was enforced and he had to abstain. And all the while, the guests persisted in nonstop glad-handing. Unfortunately, there had been no way to get out of this fundraiser. He'd missed the last two, and he was running out of excuses.

Ironically, this was the first time he actually had legitimate reasons to miss an event. Sparkwise Energy was growing fast and he was devoting more and more time to it. To attend this dinner he was missing the morning opening of the Shanghai Futures Exchange. But he didn't want to tell his father about his energy venture just yet. So he had grudgingly left the company in the capable hands of Laura and Kobus, and pulled on the tuxedo his maid had left out for him.

By attending the event meant Nick was having what was becoming an increasingly rare experience: leaving the privacy of his apartment and being exposed to the public eye – or as public as he ever experienced, given that he travelled to exclusive venues in chauffeured limousines. Yet any form of exposure was uncomfortable for Nick, because of the shiny metal cooling ducts that protruded from the base of his skull. No matter how long he grew his hair, the MindWave vents always stuck out.

There were still only about fifty users of the MindWave worldwide and most regular people had simply never seen one of the so-called cyborg barbarians before. Whenever he was out amongst people, even amongst the most rarefied company, he was harassed by strange looks and sometimes probing questions. Every long stare reminded him of how he had been taunted and bullied at school. And every awkward encounter reminded him of Peggy's cold decision to dump him right after he had the implant.

His limousine made the last turn towards the hotel. He saw a crowd of protestors standing outside the entrance, holding placards demanding lower energy prices. "We Need Gas!" "Winter Is Coming!" "Help Families Heat Their Homes!" Cordons of policemen and hotel security officers were holding back the crowd, but there would be no way to escape their view.

Even before his car fully stopped at the curb, he pushed the door open and hunched over as he hurried towards the hotel entrance. He didn't look at the crowd of demonstrators, who stood in the darkness outside the pool of light emerging from the glass doors. But he could hear them. "Look it's one of the freaks!" screamed a voice from somewhere in the crowd. Other voices chimed in.

"Cybarian!"

"Sociopathic monster!"

"Why don't you donate to my family's heating oil bill instead of some corrupt Washington politician's campaign?"

Then he made it through the doorway and trudged unhappily through the hotel towards the ballroom where he'd be dining with three hundred donors to his father's political action committee. As he caught his breath, he cheered himself up by musing that at some point, he'd gain enough mastery of the autopilot feature of his MindWave that he would be able to send his body to eat, make small talk, and otherwise endure these events without the need for his conscious mind to be present.

The room held over twenty large round tables, each covered in a beautiful white linen tablecloth and set with translucent bone china, elegant crystal glasses, and glimmering silver utensils. He was assigned to table number two. That would be at the front, near the podium where his father would give a speech later in the evening.

He walked through the room, past the sea of grey-haired guests in their conservative evening wear, chatting about their golf swings, bragging about their grandchildren, trading tips about vacation spots. It was going to be a long night.

At the front of the room, short in stature yet unmistakable because of his turban, his father was having an intense discussion. His counterpart was Senator Hal O'Brien, the main beneficiary of tonight's fundraiser. His dad had cultivated a relationship with O'Brien since the man's first run for national office a decade earlier.

Nick knew his father would be too busy handling the Senator and other VIP guests to spend much time with him. His mother, as normal, would be skipping the event but would undoubtedly swoop over in a limousine to pick up her husband as soon as the evening started winding down. Nick's role was simply to find his table and avoid offending the guests seated with him.

He saw table two. A white-liveried waiter was pouring wine for one of the guests, partially blocking his view of the table. Still, Nick could see that the twelve-seat table was already populated by ten gray heads wearing dark suits and gowns. He sighed. No one within thirty years of his age.

And then the white-liveried waiter stepped away.

There was a head of long golden hair at his table. She was facing away from him but her bright red dress stood out against the grayscale surroundings like a torch in a dark cave.

And the only remaining empty seat was next to her.

He stepped up behind the vacant chair and stood there running his hands up and down the seatback, forgetting to greet the guests. The blonde woman had left her stylish black leather handbag on the chair next to her. No wonder the seat was still empty.

She was looking away, trading some insights into the latest footwear fashions out of Beijing with a matronly woman a few decades her senior.

The older woman saw Nick and gestured in his direction. "I think this young fellow would like to sit next to you." She began the sentence in the kind of knowing, mischievous tone Nick was accustomed to hearing older people use when introducing two attractive youngsters to each other. But just as Nick knew it would, her voice trailed off to an embarrassed murmur as her eyes played over the shiny implants in the back of his skull.

The blonde girl turned to Nick, remarking, "Oh, I'm terribly sorry, I've left my bag here haven't I?" She extended a bare, toned shoulder to pick up the bag before looking up at Nick.

Nick's hands froze on the seatback. He needed to hold it firmly to keep his balance. She was the most beautiful girl he'd seen in real life. Sure, he'd seen prettier girls in the ether, but he'd never seen anyone like this face to face. "Um," he mumbled, and felt his face flushing red to match the girl's dress.

"Oh, please don't worry at all, no one's sitting here," the girl gestured at the seat with a polite smile. Nick wasn't sure if she really thought his embarrassment was due to a fear that he was taking someone else's seat, or if she had understood the meaning of his blush and graciously covered it up. Either way, he was relieved, even as his heart beat rapidly in anticipation of sitting down next to her.

"Thank you," he said, trying to muster a casual smile as he sat down. By now she would have noticed his MindWave. He braced himself for the usual mix of disgust and curiosity exhibited by strangers when they spotted his implant.

But this girl had no look of shock. Instead, she held his eyes and maintained an inquisitive smile. "Oh, sorry," he mumbled, "I'm Nick."

"It's a pleasure to meet you, Nick," replied the girl, holding out her exquisitely manicured hand. "I'm Sarah."

Reverend Tracy Cruz sighed and brushed back a lock hair as she spent the minutes before her Sunday service at the National Unity Church running through her sermon.

Doc had passed away on the last day in September, almost exactly two months after he'd told her of his disease. Those last two months had been rough. Doc had barely had the energy to walk her through the basics of running a small nondenominational church.

The two months after his death had been even harder. She smiled sadly in memory of his bewildering habit of insisting everything was part of God's plan. If that were true, then God's plan had worked out pretty well for Doc. He'd had a good long run and then checked out just before he would have become responsible for ministering to a hopelessly poor community in the middle of an economic depression.

Ricardo popped his head into the small office where she sat and rapped on the doorframe. "Ten minutes, madam Reverend."

She rolled her eyes at his mock formality. "Are you filming the sermon and posting it online again?"

"Of course. It's the best way to get the word out. A lot of the families in the congregation are having trouble attending the sermons in person without gas."

"You don't have to sugarcoat it for me, Ricky. They just don't like the job I'm doing as pastor."

202

"Nonsense, honey." He stepped across the room and hugged her from behind as she sat at the desk, head cradled in her hands. "You're the best pastor this town has ever had."

She pushed him off. "You know that's not true, Ricky. I don't mind helping out but I'm no replacement for Doc." Her eyes flitted to the wall where his Doctor of Divinity degree had hung for decades. The degree was gone, yet it had left a rectangular patch of paint that was a shade lighter than the paint around it.

"You have plenty of degrees, too, hon."

"Not the right kind."

"It doesn't matter. Degrees don't mean anything. It's whether the Lord speaks through you that matters."

"Why don't you read through my draft sermon and let me know whether you see the Lord's voice in it." She passed him the tablet.

As he read through the document she contemplated the desk she sat at. "I don't even feel like I belong enough to clean out Doc's desk. It's still full of his old cigarettes."

Ricky looked up from the tablet. "Clean it out, hon. You're pastor now. I really like this paragraph: 'We may be poor, but it was the salt of the Earth that Christ died to save. We may have been hit hard by the recession, yet it was Jesus who taught us to turn the other cheek. We must not wallow in anger and self-pity at our lack of worldly riches, for it is our very poverty, our very acceptance of what the Lord has planned for us, that dignifies us in His eyes. As Paul wrote in his Epistle to the Romans:

Who shall separate us from the love of Christ? Shall tribulation, or distress, or persecution, or famine, or nakedness, or peril, or sword? As it is written, for thy sake we are killed all the day long; we are accounted as sheep for the slaughter. Nay, in all these things we are more than conquerors through him that loved us. For I am persuaded, that neither death, nor life, nor angels, nor principalities, nor powers, nor things present, nor things to come, nor height, nor depth, nor any other creature, shall be able to separate us from the love of God, which is in Christ Jesus our Lord.

"My friends, what we can learn from Paul's wisdom is that the most important thing we can do is not to struggle for more material wealth, but to maintain and nurture our faith, in ourselves and in each other."

Cruz shook her head. "Exhortations to keep the faith, promises that Christ loves the poor, admonitions against anger at the unfairness of the world. It's a load of bullshit."

"Honey, don't say things like that!"

"These people out there, those that can even come, things are so bad they're lucky if they can put food on the table. And things just keep getting *worse*, Ricky. They need food and they need jobs. They *should* be angry. They *should* be trying to get better lives. What good are empty words telling them to be patient?"

"Things are going to get better. They always do. And if they don't, we can all just move on somewhere else. The Lord will show us the way."

She stood up and looked out the window at the small playground Ricky had helped her build in the churchyard. It had taken weeks of late nights, yet if it kept one kid off the street and out of the rapidly growing gangs, the effort would be worthwhile. But she wasn't sure anymore that anyone could be saved. "It's not just Kerrville, Ricky. Kerrville's lucky in some ways, because we don't have to worry about heating in the winter. The whole country is suffering, the whole world as far as I can tell. Everyone is getting poorer, everyone is struggling."

"It can't be this bad everywhere, not for everyone."

She turned back towards him, remembering the energy market manipulation she had been intent on uncovering before she'd quit her job, before the pipeline had exploded, before she'd taken over the ministry. "No. Not everyone. There are a few who are profiting from the misery of the many."

"Who?"

"It's those computer-brained kids. The Aeons."

"The Cybarians? I thought they were just spoiled rich kids who'd opted out of real life. A bunch of kids is causing all this pain? Can't we do anything about it?"

She reached out and took the tablet back from him. "I don't know. Our only weapon is our voice, and no one's listening."

Sarah stepped out of her limousine and walked across the pavement quickly. She wasn't hurrying just because of the cool late-fall breeze. Even here, in Manhattan's wealthiest district, she felt unnerved by the envious glances sent in her direction by pedestrians. Just a few miles from here, university students were occupying a city park in protest of the most recent bill increasing taxes and reducing social services.

She slid past the liveried doorman into the restaurant where she was to meet Nick Lal for dinner. It had been easy enough to lead him into asking her out while sitting next to him at the fundraiser.

And so, the date had been set and she'd returned to the ranch for a lengthy debriefing. Now it was a week later, and she'd travelled to New York City from halfway across the country to meet Nick in Blue Genovese, one of the trendiest restaurants on the East Coast.

She remembered saying goodbye to Michael. They'd shaken hands wordlessly, because Jaeger had been present. But he'd clung to her hand too hard and too long. Apparently, Michael was not happy to see her go on another date with possibly the most desirable bachelor in the country. She'd wanted to tell Michael to relax, that it was just an assignment, but it was impossible to do so under Jaeger's watchful eye.

She realized the tuxedo-attired maître de was staring at her. She'd been lost in thought while he bowed and asked for her name.

"Sarah Trenton," she answered quickly. It seemed strange that her undercover identity was so similar to her real name. But Willy had suggested that with everything else she needed to remember when interacting with Nick, it would be too hard to keep track of a second identity.

"Of course. Your host is already here, allow me to take you to the table."

Sarah followed him through the dimly lit restaurant. In contrast to the beautiful wooden floor of the foyer where she had entered, the main dining room was floored with blue tiles. These tiles, she knew, were engineered to absorb noise so that diners did not have to fear that their conversations would be interrupted – or overheard.

Ahead of her, over the shoulder of the maître de, she saw Nick, sitting on the inside of a booth discretely placed behind one of the columns that supported the high, frescoed ceiling of the dining room. She allowed herself a brief smile of relief. He had shown up on time; that was a good sign on a first date. Especially since she'd been worried that he wouldn't show up at all.

With all of the distractions available to him over his MindWave, he could just as well have blown off the date. Why would a man go through the trouble of dating a woman embodying all of the imperfections and challenges of a real person, Sarah reasoned, when at his whim he could summon one, or three, or three dozen perfect virtual beauties who would behave exactly as he wanted?

Nick rose to greet her, while the waiter pulled out her chair. Sarah gave her date a quick once over. He was dressed in expensive, tailored clothing that highlighted his athletic figure. But his jeans and collared shirt were understated and casual, not formal or flashy. The outfit made sense for someone who suffered anxiety about being seen in public, as she was sure Nick did.

Good. Her choice of clothes had been appropriate. She wore a knee length baby blue dress that complemented her eyes. It was tailored enough to show off her figure, yet not so tight or clingy as to draw attention. The dress was cinched at the waist by a white fabric belt that matched her white clutch and low white heels. The pearl earrings that peeked out from below her blonde hair completed the outfit.

Nick leaned in, clearly not sure whether he was meant to shake her hand, embrace her, or kiss her. She solved the problem by presenting her cheek and brusquely air kissing him, making use of a gesture she'd learned during her crash course in debutante etiquette. She sat down and allowed the maître de to push in her chair and spread her napkin in her lap.

Sarah glanced over at Nick to assess his body language. He was clearly a little nervous, and afraid of looking either too eager to please or too disinterested. She recalled feeling the same while flirting with boys she liked at the Lal Orphanage. It was strange to see her own former childish foolishness reflected in someone as wealthy as Nick Lal.

He was hers to lose. She felt her pulse increasing from the thrill of the hunt. She used her TacWave to suppress her adrenaline. She needed a clear head.

She took advantage of the time between the maître de's departure and the waiter's arrival to begin employing her charm. She looked at Nick and smiled. "You're remarkably well behaved."

"What do you mean?" asked Nick, nonplussed.

"Well," she explained, "you're dressed nicely, you showed up early, and you even stood up to greet me."

"That's just basic etiquette," equivocated Nick, clearly not sure whether to be embarrassed or cheered by her praise.

"You'd be surprised…" Sarah rolled her eyes emphatically before smiling mischievously. "But speaking of basic etiquette, you did make one mistake."

He furrowed his brows. "What's that?"

"You're supposed to let the woman sit on the inside of the booth," she said, in a playfully officious whisper. She was glad to confirm that she was still an excellent flirt. She had grown out of her former inclination to seduce every boy that came along, but teasing Nick was her mission tonight.

"Why's that, so I can protect you from the big nasty waiter? Don't worry, this is a reputable establishment and the waiters usually don't attack their guests," replied Nick with a slight roll of his eyes.

"No," she retorted. "It's to prevent the man's gaze from being distracted by other women who walk past!"

Nick laughed this comment off uneasily. "I'm sure I won't be distracted tonight."

Sarah decided to accept the implied compliment with a smile and drop the topic. She assumed Nick had sat with his back to the wall to hide his MindWave from other diners. His anxiety about his appearance was at play. It wouldn't be good to spend the night magnifying his unease – he would never want to see her again. To get him feeling settled, she'd give him an easy win.

"So you picked this place. What's good here?" she asked, running her finger through the holographic menu that was floating in front of her.

As she had expected, Nick smiled more assuredly now. "They have some fresh lobster flown in this afternoon from Maine that I was thinking of trying. The escargot is usually very good. And if you like red meats, they usually have some aged grass-fed Angus cuts hanging in the locker."

"Grass-fed?" asked Sarah, arching an eyebrow flirtatiously. "So is this *real* food? From a real animal, that used to be alive? Not something out of your father's factories?"

"*Of course* it's real," said Nick emphatically. "The food that comes out of the factory is so – so boring. It's all the same. With real food, you get all kinds of variation. Like, those grass-fed steaks – totally different flavor and texture from grain-fed. I can get the waiter to arrange a sampler for you, so you can taste the difference."

Sarah laughed off the offer with a wave of her hand. It was a tough act. How could Nick be blind to the hypocrisy of using money his parents had earned ending famines to gorge himself on the most wasteful foods imaginable? His restaurant flew lobster in from Maine daily, when most of the country couldn't even afford gas to drive to work. She thought of how much worse her life would have been if she had not been taken in by the Lal Orphanage, an institution supported by Nick's parents. She doubted he had inherited any of their interest in philanthropy.

But she kept smiling. "So you're a foodie, huh? Well, don't worry, I love real food too. In fact, I would have been scandalized if you served me something out of your parents' food vats tonight. You don't know how relieved I am that I don't have to hide my extravagant tastes from you." She looked down at her menu, hoping she was hiding the fact that the last real meat she'd eaten had been a squirrel her mother captured over a decade ago. "Hmm... I'm with you on the steak. Now I'll have to decide between a rib-eye and a sirloin."

And so the meal went, with the typical careful, light banter of a first date. Sarah never steered the conversation towards her real interest: Sparkwise Energy. That would have spooked Nick. After all, in her assumed identity as socialite Sarah Trenton, daughter of Argentinian silver and copper mining magnates Rodger and Lucy Trenton, she would have no way of knowing about Nick's clandestine business activities.

At the end of their dessert, Nick leaned back in his seat. "Well I hope that went down well."

"It was delicious. The best meal I've had in ages." Sarah realized this was the first completely true thing she had said all evening.

"Want to join me for a nightcap? I know the best jazz bar in—"

"That's all right, Nick. I've got an early flight." It was time to draw the line and end the evening. She'd see if Willy and Jaeger wanted her to continue getting to know this self-centered sod. She definitely wasn't going out for drinks with him unless she had explicit orders to do so.

"Oh come on. Just for one drink."

Chapter 13

"No." Sarah knew she'd said it too firmly as soon as the words left her lips. But it was already too late to take it back. She'd probably angered Nick, and her mission would be over regardless of what Willy and Jaeger wanted because Nick would never want to have anything to do with her again. At least Michael would be cheered by the news.

Nick's eyes fell to his lap, his lips trembled slightly, and she saw his Adam's apple bobbing up and down. He wasn't angry. He was sad, or heartbroken, or on the verge of despair.

She remembered feeling the same, years ago, when she'd first gone to the Lal Orphanage. Alone, desperate, guilty. Needing the friendship of the other orphans yet terrified of being rejected. And so she had built a façade of superficiality to hide her vulnerability, a façade that had only come crashing down when Jaeger's abuse shook her to the foundations of her soul.

Nick was the same. He was not really just some narcissistic rich kid. He was just as sensitive as she had been, and he'd built a protective façade of insouciance just like she had.

She found herself reaching across the table and placing her hand on his. He almost flinched away, but then his shiny green eyes rose to hers and held her gaze. "I'm sorry Nick. I can't go with you. Not tonight."

Nick sighed deeply and then raised his hand to cue the waiter for the check. Sarah pulled her hand back from his and waited with a bland smile on her face while he arranged the payment.

As Nick escorted her out of the restaurant and helped her into a cab, Sarah felt a ball of intense excitement in her chest. Instead of the affected air kiss she had greeted him with, upon kissing him goodbye she let her face linger beside his for a moment, and was thrilled at the rough brush of his beard stubble on her cheek.

On the ride to Grand Central station, where she would catch a mag-train out West, she was able to calm herself. She'd drunk a little too much wine, gotten a little too deep into her act, but she hadn't lost her head completely.

Nick was likeable. His genetic engineering had given him all the looks and brains humanly possible. His awesome wealth and power made a beguiling contrast with his evident vulnerability and barely repressed desperation for companionship.

And it was clear from his reactions to her that he liked her back.

But Sarah was no longer the girl who would get foolish crushes on every attractive boy she met. No, the excitement Sarah felt building up in her belly was not related to Nick himself, but to completing her mission, and snaring her prey.

Colonel Rad Jaeger rubbed his hands together firmly. He was growing more and more concerned about the performance of his expensive and irreplaceable espionage team. "Are you *sure* Sarah's going to maintain her professionalism in this assignment?" he demanded of Major William Johnson.

Willy raised his hands off the table palms upwards. "Why not, sir?"

"Have you reviewed the footage from her TacWave?" asked Jaeger rhetorically. He wasn't sure if Willy was really as incompetent as he seemed, or if he was just stonewalling.

"Yes, just now, with you," responded Willy with a shrug just faint enough that it couldn't be construed as insolent.

"Tell me then, what did you see?" asked Jaeger, leaning back in his chair and placing his hands behind his head. Whatever Willy was up to, Jaeger wasn't going to let him off easy.

Willy shook his head, as if to say, *isn't it obvious?* "Sarah and Nick Lal eating dinner, sir. Just as at the charity ball where we inserted her, she did a great job of building rapport with him. I'm sure she's on the way to developing a trusting relationship." He paused. "Colonel, if this is about her failure to discuss Sparkwise Energy, it's just not appropriate for her to raise that topic at this point."

Jaeger sighed in exasperation. Willy was an expert in psychology. Perhaps he was devoting all of his training to the sole purpose of aggravating his commanding officer. "I *am* aware we can't have our undercover operatives blowing their cover."

"So…" Willy let his half-formed question hang in the air.

Jaeger leaned forward and pronounced his words very clearly, so that Willy would have no room to misunderstand him. "You are just looking at the holovision images and listening to the sound. Have you looked at the records of her biometrics during the dinner?"

"Not in detail." Willy pursed his lips and looked down at the tablet in his lap.

"Watch the end," directed Jaeger. "When they kiss goodbye." He couldn't help letting a mocking tone enter his voice as he said the last two words.

Willy ran his finger over the tablet and watched the encounter play out for thirty seconds. "Her heart rate speeds up afterwards." He raised his open hands palms out. "She has to feel those emotions, somewhat, to make him fall for it. Acting is not easy, sir."

"Surely you see that her heart rate stayed elevated when she was in the cab, Johnson."

Willy appeared to be making a show of staring intently at his computer tablet.

Jaeger wondered what thoughts were going through Willy's head. Willy's choice of Sarah to receive the TacWave had troubled Jaeger at the time. He'd only acquiesced because Willy had spent his career selecting and indoctrinating counterintelligence officers. That's why Jaeger had brought him on board to begin with.

That choice had been made six months ago. Three months ago, Jaeger had become so worried about Willy's mishandling of

Sarah's training that he had stepped in himself. She'd made a lot of progress and toughened up quite a bit in recent weeks, yet Jaeger never felt she was fully focused, nor completely dependable. Her emotions during her mission the previous evening only worsened his misgivings.

"Sir, are you suggesting..." Willy began, his brows furrowed in what appeared to be a mix of concern and confusion.

"Her biometrics definitely *suggest* that she has real feelings for her target. Wouldn't you agree?" Jaeger wanted the point to be perfectly clear so Willy couldn't pretend he hadn't understood it later. "It's one thing if Sarah and Michael are attracted to each other. Hank's observed the same nonsense among the other batch of trainees. I know, they're kids. It's natural. And at least we can always keep them chaperoned here at the ranch. But falling for the enemy is a very serious breach of duty."

Willy sighed. "Do you want me to remove her from—" he began.

"No, no, not yet," said Jaeger. He would prefer to remove Sarah from the entire program, but Hal O'Brien had arranged funding sufficient for only two TacWaves and now that money was spent. There was no one he could replace Sarah with. "We need her keeping track of Sparkwise. The economic situation is deteriorating fast. We've got student protests at half the universities in the country and unions going on strike. This unrest will spread into the general population fast, so we don't have time for second chances. And now that Senator O'Brien is pushing a legislative agenda against the

Aeons, we need whatever intel we can get to support him. If Sarah can't keep her hormones in line, we'll take necessary measures to correct her behavior."

A strange expression played across Willy's face before disappearing. For an instant, Jaeger thought the Major was smiling mockingly, as if he'd won some important victory by outsmarting Jaeger. Then the moment passed and Willy's face returned to a neutral expression.

Jaeger joined Willy in silence for a moment before shaking his head and rubbing his hands together in irritation. It was going to be hard to defeat the Aeons if his agents couldn't help developing crushes on their opponents. "We built features into Sarah's TacWave so we can see what she sees, hear what she hears, and know what she knows. Why didn't we add a feature that controls what she feels?"

Nick listened uneasily from his side of the Sparkwise energy conference table. Above the table, an image of the globe slowly rotated, revealing the locations and status of Sparkwise's many energy projects, as well as those of its major competitors. Laura and Kobus were reveling in their success in capitalizing on the explosion at the Five Mile Creek pipeline station. "Guys, I'm glad we're doing well. But how is it we were able to profit from this disaster?"

Laura turned to him and her smile of triumph faded. "We used advanced statistical probability models to buy assets with high contingency value. Our analysis worked."

"I don't remember implementing those models."

"Nick, if you would pay more attention at these meetings, and get more involved, you would know what the company is up to. You're a smart guy, and I want you as more than a silent partner. You can add a lot more value."

"I'm trying to get more involved now. Isn't the government going to want to know how we predicted in advance that all those pipeline junctions we bought just happened to be the only ones that didn't explode?"

Kobus' Polar bear fangs glinted as he smiled. "That's why we used shell companies and false—."

"What Kobus means is that our tax efficient holding structure makes it unlikely anyone will ever trace those transactions back to us. Which is a good thing, because the last thing we want during our rapid expansion stage is a bunch of idiotic government agents bumping around on a wild goose chase."

Nick could not shake the feeling Laura was hiding something more serious than illicit holding structures from him. After watching his father's efforts to protect Langar Foods' monopoly, he understood some rough tactics were necessary to build an international business conglomerate. Yet there was a line between skullduggery and outright criminality. He knew Laura habitually bent rules, yet he couldn't bring himself to believe she could have engineered a disaster that had crippled the nation's already moribund energy infrastructure and killed thirty people.

"Nick, I don't really like the way you're looking at me. Do you really want me to say it? I had nothing to do with that disaster."

Kobus chuckled. "Ha, next thing you know, Nick will be blaming you for the Hurricane *ineenstorting*."

Neither Nick nor Laura laughed at Kobus' remark.

After holding Nick's gaze for several seconds, Laura stood up and spun the globe to highlight Africa. "Let's talk about how we're going to secure our Nigerian ventures."

Nick didn't want to dwell any longer on the possibility that Laura had known about Five Mile Creek in advance. But the topic of Nigeria raised another concern of his. "We wouldn't need so much security in our Nigerian venture if we used a local firm. Why are we using Abril Espinoza's engineering company to do this job? Her firm is based in Guadalajara; her people don't know their way around Africa, and their expertise is in high-end hotel architecture and design, not greasy oil field infrastructure."

Laura responded sharply, "Because Abril's an Aeon and we always work with other Aeons when we can. And they work with us in return."

"It's not practical," protested Nick. "It costs more, and causes us so much trouble to find accommodations for her people. We'd be better off if—"

Kobus held up a paw. "*Bra*, are you forgetting what we get in return from Abril? Her other business, Aeonic Avionics, buys as much of its fuel from us as it can. How does the saying go? *Een* hand washes *die* other, *ja*?"

"I'm all for working with other Aeons when it makes economic sense. But we shouldn't need to scratch each other's backs," protested Nick, working hard to hide his exasperation. "As you guys are always pointing out, we have our MindWaves and we can outthink any natural human. Since we're so much smarter than everyone else, we have nothing to fear. We should just run Sparkwise Energy in the most efficient way possible, and work with whomever offers the best prices."

Laura screwed up her face in disgust. "*Natural humans.* The *nats* are starting to team up against us. Not long ago I found two of them trailing me in the ether. They managed to escape just before I could identify them. And last week, some American senator recently proposed a bill to outlaw MindWave use in business. And you must have seen that there's an anti-MindWave movement on college campuses. Those idiots occupied the Boston Commons."

She rolled her eyes. "Those are our future business competitors, scampering around the park like a bunch of rats, smoking pot and planning how to shut us down. By now they've been there for months and they're prepared for a harsh winter. They couldn't have done it themselves. Clearly there are powerful forces arrayed against us, who are supplying and funding these student provocateurs."

"Laura's right, *bra*," Kobus explained to Nick, almost apologetically. "We've only gotten by because we make *groot*

221

donations to politicians. But so many people hate us, we've had to start making direct donations to schools and churches."

Laura continued, "We Aeons are destined for a great future. Yet if we don't act smart, we'll all find ourselves in prison on trumped-up charges. We need to stick together, to build a system of cooperating companies that together have the power and the clout to protect ourselves."

Nick squinted. "We're not *all* sticking together. What about Chengwen Xu? Remember we went to his 19th birthday party a while back? Recently you've made a point of refusing to work with him. Chengwen's an expert in commodity trading, he can help us with our risk hedging. But you've cut our business with him to zero."

There was an uneasy pause as Kobus and Laura exchanged glances. Nick got the sense he had raised a taboo subject.

Laura sighed. "Nick, Chengwen is not a real Aeon."

"What do you mean? He has a MindWave, just like we do," responded Nick. "He hangs out in the ether, or at least he used to before everyone started shunning him. If he can get into the ether, he must be an Aeon." He was baffled.

"He's more like a… half breed," corrected Kobus. "*Ja*, he has the MindWave, but he wasn't genetically engineered. In real life, he's a short, skinny *grazelda*. He's not one of us."

"I thought the MindWave was what defined an Aeon," asked Nick. "Infinite knowledge, ability to create worlds. It's about what's in our heads, it's not about our genes or how we look."

Laura pursed her lips. "There are those of us who are fit to have these abilities and share our great destiny, and then there are people like Chengwen. He does not share our pure genetics, so he is not – he cannot be – divine like we are."

Nick looked down at the table for a few moments. What Laura and Kobus were saying didn't make a lot of sense. He was tired of arguing with them about the strange beliefs they shared. "Fine," he sighed. "Look, I have to go meet someone anyway." Before either Laura or Kobus could react, he exited this part of the ether.

Sarah watched silently as Michael shook his head slowly and pursed his lips. "Laura is a tough nut to crack. Everything she does is encrypted about half a dozen different ways."

"What does she spend her time doing?" asked Willy impatiently from behind his desk.

"She operates in her own worlds, worlds she completely controls to the finest detail. In fact, she's frequently in multiple worlds at the same time. Only one of them is the real her, her consciousness, her avatar, whatever you want to call it. The others are decoys autopiloted by her MindWave. The psych briefing was correct that she's paranoid. It's taking a long time to figure out what she's doing."

Willy rubbed his hands together impatiently, doing a passable imitation of Colonel Jaeger's condescension. "Michael, you've been on this assignment for three weeks already. You're here to report your progress, not list excuses."

"I'm sorry, Willy. I just want to explain that the information I have so far is not necessarily reliable. I'm making progress but there may be a lot of garbage information in what I've collected."

Willy waved a hand dismissively. "Just get on with it. When you make your reports to Colonel Jaeger tomorrow, he's not going to want to hear these caveats."

Michael continued. "Well, the way I've followed her is not to follow *her* at all. I figure out where Kobus and Nick are. If Laura is in the same world as one of them, I think it's usually the real her. I'm even learning how to follow her avatar as it shifts from one world to another."

Willy smiled slightly and leaned forward. "Good, this is what we pay you the big bucks for."

"Wait… we get *paid*?" interjected Sarah. "Oh yeah, we're commissioned as 2nd Lieutenants, aren't we? Where's our pay?"

"Your check is in the mail," replied Willy evenly with a sidelong glance and a wink. Just as quickly as it had cracked into a smile, his face switched back to its original businesslike expression. "Michael?"

Michael paused for a moment as if searching for the right words. "The psyche report was also correct that she's a genius. Thanks to genetic engineering, her native IQ is 190, and the

224

MindWave adds about 100 IQ points. And I think she's using custom AI subroutines to magnify the effects of the MindWave."

"Just how smart are you saying she is? Quantify it."

"IQ 500. But not just smarter, also faster. The MindWave creates artificial neural connections that are much faster than natural ones, and much more precise memory to prevent data loss. So her mental capacity is not just like one person with a 500 IQ. It's like a team of two dozen people, each with an IQ of 500."

Michael waited a moment for Willy to respond, but the officer just sat watching wordlessly.

"She's tireless at using her mental talents. When she's not with the other Aeons, she spends her time working on advanced technology, like understanding the Langar Foods cloning technology. And I need to emphasize, Willy, that she's damn good. I can barely understand what she's doing, but she's at the cutting edge in several fields."

"So she's developing new technologies? Like what?"

"So far most of it seems to have two uses. To make money, or to control information. I'm afraid she's also trying to develop weapons. I've found information about laser beams and electromagnetic tractor fields. Like I said, she's paranoid; she seems to fear a clash between the MindWave users and the rest of the human race."

He paused again, before continuing in a lowered voice, "Actually, sometimes I think maybe she *wants* the clash. I think she really looks down on regular humans. She's started to refer to us as *gnats.*"

"Gnats?" asked Willy, with a wrinkled brow. "Like, little bugs? An annoyance, a parasite?"

"It's a play on words. *Natural humans.* Humans with no MindWave are *natural.* That's a common expression among MindWave users. She's shortened that to *nat.* And, yes, I'm sure it hasn't escaped her notice that *nat* sounds like *gnat.* And since she's helped all the other MindWave users learn how to use their implants, they all look up to her, and they've started using the same term, too."

Sarah repressed the urge to interrupt and point out that based on Michael's eavesdropping, Nick was the only Aeon that didn't use that word.

"She sounds like a really charming young lady. Are you going to bring her home for dinner?"

Michael responded with a flustered glance at Sarah.

Willy waved away his own remark. "So we have a charismatic sociopathic genius equipped with a supercomputer and an endless supply of money. Anything else you want to highlight?" he asked with a sigh.

"Since she's so brilliant, you might wonder why she spends so much time cultivating relationships with the other MindWave users. She doesn't really need anyone's help."

"No, it sounds like she doesn't."

"She has certain beliefs, beliefs that motivate all of her behaviors. You already know she calls herself an Aeon, which means a demigod in the Gnostic religion. Even *Sparkwise* – it's a reference to the divine spark, which Aeons possess and normal humans don't. The connections to Gnostic mythology are not random. She's into that stuff."

"That stuff?"

"The Gnostic concept of divinity through intuitive knowledge. She thinks she's a god. Or demigod... *Aeon* or *demiurge* are the technical terms. And I suspect she increasingly views her ability to create new worlds in the ether as the creative ability of a true god, the one god who manifested the real world. She digs the divinity angle big time, and she wants to have a pantheon of lesser gods that she can lead. That's why she's working hard to implant those beliefs in the other Aeons."

"Is she succeeding?"

"Yes. She's extremely charismatic and an expert at manipulation. It doesn't help that most of the other MindWave users are pretty untethered from any normal form of value system or supervision so they're pretty easy to convince. There's one big contradiction in her beliefs though."

"What's that?"

"Gnosticism sees the world as a realm of darkness, so inherently evil that even the worst actions within it cannot be judged immoral. The highest aspiration a person can have is to escape this world. But Laura claims she and the other Aeons are going to *save* the world, not abandon it. I don't know if she really believes that or it's just something she says to gain allegiance from the other Aeons."

"Great work, Michael." Willy paused for a second before turning to Sarah expectantly. "Sarah, time for your status update."

"Willy," stated Sarah, "This assignment is… difficult."

Willy looked up from the small tablet on his desk. "In what way, Sarah? You've gained Nick's trust in a very short amount of time." He grinned widely. "Frankly, even with the training in rich twit etiquette we gave you, we thought it would be hard for you to make any progress; we saw this as an advanced training mission where you'd learn from your mistakes. But, you're in. You've got him eating out of your hand!"

Sarah kept her face expressionless and Willy looked at the tablet again. "And we're lucky – Sparkwise Energy is turning into a real international energy company. We never thought these Aeon kids would get going so quickly; we would have been caught flat-footed if you hadn't succeeded so well in breaking into its inner circle."

He beamed up at her and winked. "I know it's tough, but your job is never going to be easy. And you've been doing a very good job!"

Sarah wanted to help Willy. But just as much, she didn't think it was right to deceive Nick. She pursed her lips, not sure of what to say.

Willy looked at her closely. "What's wrong, Sarah? I said you're doing a good job."

"I don't think the job is good!" responded Sarah, unsure of how else to explain her ethical quandary.

Willy's forehead creased with concern. "Why not?"

"I'm lying to, I'm spying on, and I'm abusing the trust of Nick," explained Sarah. Sarah's eyes slipped over towards Michael, who looked as unhappy as he always did when she was discussing Nick. Having Michael present made her conversation with Willy even harder than it already was.

She wanted to succeed at her missions and prove she deserved the trust and admiration of Willy and Michael. She just wasn't comfortable with this particular assignment. But saying so was making her very uneasy, because she knew it would call her loyalty and seriousness into question. It would also open her to spurious accusations that she had personal feelings for Nick. Such accusations would not just hurt her, but also Michael.

"That is your job," retorted Willy sternly as he put down the computer tablet.

"But it's not *right*," protested Sarah. She wanted to make her case that spying on Nick was unfair, yet also to appear loyal to the mission. If she could not convince Willy, there was no way she would convince Colonel Jaeger tomorrow. "You promised me I wouldn't have to do anything evil. And Nick is not a bad person, not someone we should abuse. He's a bit lost and insecure, and impressionable, but he's also a pretty good guy."

"I agree," said Willy, glancing down at his tablet. A hint of guilt showed in his expression. "He seems like a nice guy, especially in comparison to Laura. And your job is to make sure he doesn't change, doesn't become infected with her mad philosophy."

"Nick's a good guy. That can make him the key to unraveling the power of the Aeons. But it's obvious from Michael's report that Laura's trying to take advantage of Nick's good nature to manipulate him. And here I am, manipulating him in the same way Laura does."

Now she chose her words carefully. "He has real feelings for me, Willy. If he ever learns I'm spying on him, he'll feel betrayed, and the only person he'll have left to turn to is Laura, and we'll lose our chance to keep him on our side."

Willy's expression of guilt melted away and he stared at her with an uncharacteristically angry expression. "Lieutenant, *Colonel* Jaeger and I will be the judge of that. Your job is simply to execute your mission as we see fit. You're dismissed." He turned back to his tablet.

Shocked by Willy's sudden anger, Sarah spun on her heel. Before she stormed out of the door, she tried to make eye contact with Michael, but he was staring at the ground.

To hell with Michael if he couldn't be a grown up about this. Sarah needed to replace Laura's influence over Nick with her own. It wouldn't be long before Colonel Jaeger ordered some kind of direct action against Sparkwise. She needed to make sure Nick wasn't caught up in it and charged with treason.

If the only way she could save him was to lie to him, then she was going to lie as hard as she could.

Chapter 14

Nick reached out to hold Sarah's hand. She demurely pulled it away, giving him a sweet smile as she did so.

He sighed softly. "Why won't you let me get closer to you, Sarah? We've been seeing each other for over a month yet I feel like you won't let me in."

The two were picnicking on a large red and white checked blanket laid out in a small section of Central Park that had been restored to its early 21st Century glory. As always, Nick had provided a huge selection of the finest foods money could buy. Because of the early-winter weather, he had ordered heat lamps set up in a ring around their blanket. He realized the display and resulting waste was obscene, but he figured he needed to work hard to impress a girl of Sarah's background.

The section of the park he'd selected was full of wooden benches, flower beds and small bridges over narrow brooks. The serenity of the scene was marred by a half-dozen heavily armed security guards, paid for by the elite members who supported this private acre of placid space. The rest of the park was decrepit and full of homeless families. A pall of dark smoke rose to the south, marking where the police had crushed a riot in Union Square early in the morning.

Nick had taken advantage of the sunny sky that had accompanied the cold front by wearing a baseball cap, which, when worn backwards and pitched back on his head, mostly obscured his MindWave exhaust fans. Since he'd turned off the device, he was in no danger of overheating. Once they were within the protective ring of heat lamps, Sarah had removed her coat and sweater to reveal a sleeveless white dress.

"I'm sure you have three dozen other girls you're romancing."

"What do you mean," asked Nick, gesturing with his glass of freshly squeezed lemonade to emphasize his point. "Almost every hour I spend outside the ether, I spend with you!"

Sarah laughed and took a bite out of a fresh strawberry. "*Outside* the ether. And what do you do, my dear Nick, when you're *inside* the ether?"

"Nothing," protested Nick. "I just hang out with the other Aeo—with the other kids with MindWaves."

Sarah arched her eyebrows, and reached out to place a hand on Nick's shoulder. "You *hang out*? Surely you do more than just hang out. I've read about MindWaves. I know they give you full sensory feedback – even more intense and real than what you feel in real life." She lightly ran her finger down Nick's arm as she spoke. "And you've never taken advantage of that?"

Nick's face reddened and he pulled his arm away. He could barely suppress the indignation that Sarah's implied accusations arose in him, especially because they were true. "No, I don't know what you're talking about. I'm not some kind of pervert."

Sarah gave him a knowing smile. "Sure. Next, you'll tell me your eyes aren't green. Don't worry, I don't hold it against you. I'm just envious."

Nick decided it was time to shift the subject. Instead of letting her tease him, he'd tell her something to impress her. He could talk a bit about what he was doing at Sparkwise Energy as long as he didn't use its name. "Look, when I'm in the ether, I mostly work on this little company that some of my friends and I set up."

Sarah reached for her glass of chilled lemonade and swirled it in front of her face. "That sounds booooring."

"No, it's actually really cool," responded Nick. "We're doing really well. We're going to build it up into the biggest company in the world!"

"Don't you already own the biggest company in the world?" Sarah lazily reached into their picnic basket and popped a bright red strawberry into her mouth and slowly chewed it.

"No, well, Langar's my parents' company," countered Nick. "And it's only the second biggest company in the world. Anyway, I want to build something for myself."

"Very admirable." Sarah's tone was flirtatiously mocking. "So if your parents' company makes food, what are you going to make?" She arched her eyebrows as she reached for her cup again. "Lemonade?"

"No, we're making energy," said Nick proudly.

"Energy? So you're innovating to make cheap energy available to the poor downtrodden masses just like your parents have already made cheap nutrition available to them?"

"Um, no," responded Nick, less assuredly. Sarah's question was hitting on a nerve deep in his psyche, a nerve that screamed out that what he was doing was, at its very root, worthless. Worthless especially in comparison to the company his parents had built. He was reminded of his odd feeling that Laura and Kobus had known about, or even caused, the Five Mile Creek disaster. But these weren't issues to discuss with Sarah. "We're buying up and trading coal, oil, gas… you know, the stuff that makes the economy run and keeps families warm in the winter."

"Can you really make money buying and selling stuff back and forth?"

"Sure, with prices rising, there's a lot of unmet demand in the markets. You can take advantage of the imbalances through arbitrage, or you can try to lock up supply so you get a pricing boost…" his voice faded out. His psyche continued to scream out *Worthless! Worthless! Worthless!*

Sarah looked away and smiled again. "Yeah I heard that after that reactor blowout in Hurricane, energy is really expensive. I don't check my heating bill every month or anything, but I saw all the protests on National News. I guess you guys must be making killer profits."

Worthless! Now the voice in his head sounded like his father. Nick reached up to nervously rub the back of his neck where MindWave met flesh. He reminded himself that his father was not the paragon of virtue he often pretended to be. Even the great Langar Foods had only maintained its monopoly on lab food production for so long because of Dr. Lal's aggressive legal tactics and political patronage. "We're making the markets more efficient, without us, prices would be even hi—"

"Yes, sure, Nick. But I still think you should go with the cheap energy idea. You could help some people that way, and still make a lot of money." She lay back and fingered the small silver cross necklace she wore.

Nick looked away angrily. Was Sarah aware of how much he wanted to impress her? Could she see inside his mind and read his doubts about Sparkwise? Was she intentionally tormenting him, or was he just overly sensitive to everything she said because of his intense, unconsummated feelings for her?

He looked at her fingering the crucifix, seemingly oblivious to him even as he went through mental anguish trying to understand her.

"What's with that necklace?" asked Nick. "You wear it all the time."

"My mom gave it to me, a long time ago," responded Sarah, pensively, as she reflected sunlight off the silver cross into his eyes.

"It's very sweet, but couldn't she get you a nicer necklace? I mean, your parents own some of the biggest mines in the hemisphere."

She shot him a look full of daggers. "Yes and I know how they built that empire. Bribery, extortion, and violence. I know they had to; that's just how the mining industry works. So I prefer the necklace my mother gave me before she was wealthy. I also know the energy industry is even worse than mining, Nick. I'm afraid you're going to travel down the same path as you try to prove yourself."

"Sorry," he stammered. "I understand. The food industry wasn't much easier for my parents. Don't worry, I'll keep my head screwed on straight." He wanted to tell her about his concerns about Sparkwise, but he was afraid to. "But... that necklace, it just doesn't match your eyes. I'll get you a nicer necklace with sapphires for Christmas."

"No, Nick. Please don't."

"I want to show you how I feel..." Nick almost winced at the lameness of his protest.

"You won't impress me with big price tags, Nick. You're very good at earning money. It must be just as easy for you to spend it."

"Then how can I—"

She rolled over on her side, facing away from him. "If you want to impress me, stop bragging about how much money you make with your energy trading and put that super brain of yours to better use."

Nick persisted. "I will, I have some ideas already. First I want to build my own company. Before that, how can I convince you of how I feel?"

"You don't have to convince me. You *can't*. I'll make up my own mind," she said, rolling back over to look him in the eyes. "And Nick, if I do make up my mind, I'll give you this necklace. Because this *does* mean something to me. And you'll know for sure how I feel."

Nick looked away to hide his grimace. Once again, Sarah was keeping him in her control, dictating the rules of their relationship, holding the initiative for herself.

Dr. Aakar Lal settled into the deeply upholstered chair. "Thank you for seeing me, Senator," he muttered through gritted teeth as he fiddled agitatedly with his *kara*. No doubt, thought Senator Hal O'Brien, his security detail had insisted on feeling around inside Dr. Lal's turban to probe for hidden weapons. A Sikh like Dr. Lal would certainly be insulted by such a search.

He wished his guards could be gentler with the doctor. But with the amount of public unrest unsettling the nation, it was unavoidable that safety protocols around senators would be tightened.

While he intended this meeting to be their last, O'Brien still felt obligated to show respect for the doctor. "Please, how can I help you, Doctor Lal?"

"Why are you promoting legislation prejudicial to my family?"

O'Brien wouldn't let Dr. Lal's pugnacious manner provoke him. "You are referring to my bill proposing restrictions on the use of MindWaves for business activities?"

The bill had practically no chance of passing, given how beholden most members of the Senate and the House were to financial support from Aeons. O'Brien knew that the bill was a huge political risk that could lead to his defeat in his next election. But he had already made the decision to combat the Aeons when he'd agreed to secretly allocate funds to Rad Jaeger's anti-Aeon intelligence program.

Dr. Lal leaned forward and puffed out his chest. "My son has been persecuted every day since he got that blasted implant. At first he faced abuse and physical violence everywhere he went. So he dropped out of school and he withdrew from society. He fled alone into his imaginary world. My best hope for his future is that he go into business. And your new bill would make even that escape impossible."

This was going to be a difficult conversation, O'Brien thought. "Doctor, before I get into that specific bill, I wanted to bring something to your attention that may change your perspective on the matter. Have you heard of a company called Sparkwise Energy?"

"Only tangentially. A rapidly growing energy trading and infrastructure firm with a reputation for price gouging and other bad behavior." Dr. Lal's expression made clear that he did not appreciate O'Brien's change of topic.

"Did you know that your son Vinicius is a 24% owner of this company?"

"Nick? That's not—"

"He hid his identity by using offshore holding companies and trusts but it's possible to trace. Please confirm for yourself, but let me assure you now that it's true. And let me also forewarn you that the Federal Trade Commission is going to open an investigation into Sparkwise. The company is suspected of using their ownership of our energy infrastructure to create artificial bottlenecks and shortages that are unfairly restricting competitors' access to markets and improperly driving up prices. Put more simply, they're creating an energy monopoly."

Dr. Lal rose to his feet and his face reddened. "Energy prices have been going up ever since the government – the government you're supposed to be running – melted down its nuclear reactor at Hurricane. So don't go around scape-goating my son for your own shortcomings."

Instead of responding to Dr. Lal's challenge, O'Brien softened his tone before sharing even more bad news. "I think you should be aware that it's not just the US government investigating your son's company. The European Commission, the International Monetary Fund, and the Chinese Ministry of Trade are beginning hearings."

Dr. Lal seemed to be sputtering. "There must be some special interest group intent on smearing MindWave users. They've even gotten to you, Senator. Where do you get your evidence from?"

"We all have our own sources. And no one's persecuting the Aeons. We're just making sure the playing field is level. You must be aware of the economic crisis we're facing, that people are afraid they won't be able to heat their homes this winter, and that we won't even be able to afford the fuel to ship food into the cities. People worry that as the Aeons' numbers increase from dozens to hundreds and thousands, there won't be anything at all left for the regular folks."

"There won't be thousands of MindWave users. Not while Doctor P.J. Arora controls the patents and insists on doing all the surgeries himself. I believe there's another decade to go before the MindWave will become easy to obtain."

"Nevertheless, several government agencies are concerned that the Aeons are behaving improperly. I hope you will take the time to talk to your son."

"How dare you tell me how to raise my family!"

"I had hoped you would take this warning as a favor. Maybe you can get your son to cease his involvement. Otherwise, he risks arrest."

"Bah, if you try to arrest him, he'll just upload his consciousness to the cloud and escape from your clutches."

O'Brien paused and considered Dr. Lal's statement. "Is that something he can really do?"

"I don't see why not. The MindWave holds all his memories and a map of his neurons. That should be sufficient information to create a computer program that simulates his mind."

Senator O'Brien leaned back in his chair. He would need to consult with Colonel Jaeger about Dr. Lal's claims, but first he had a committee vote to attend. He stole a glance at his watch. "Thank you for this enlightening conversation, doctor. Given the bad news I had the unhappy task of delivering a few minutes ago, I am quite grateful that you have continued to talk with me so long."

Thankfully, Dr. Lal caught the hint and rose to his feet haughtily. "Senator, I am afraid to say that while you continue to persecute my family, my support for your political career must cease." He inclined his head curtly and walked out of the office.

"Nick, you need to come clean with the government." Nick's father's hand trembled as he pointed his fork at his son across the dinner table.

"Clean with the government?" asked Nick. He looked to his mother, but she was deathly pale and intently staring at her food. He was not sure what exactly his father was suddenly barking about, so he decided to play dumb.

"Your Sparkwise Energy colluding to drive up energy prices. It's disgraceful. I won't have it," his father yelled, shaking his head as he spoke.

"It's not as bad as you say," protested Nick. He wondered how his father had found out about Sparkwise at all, much less about the illegal actions Nick still secretly suspected Laura and Kobus were committing. Yet he couldn't admit that he'd had those suspicions if he hadn't acted on them. "We're just doing what any other company would do to maximize profits."

"It's not what Langar does," his father replied coldly.

Nick's face wound up in anger and hurt at the rebuke. The words *Worthless! Worthless! Worthless!* sprang to his mind again. "Are you forgetting all those other scientists whose competing companies you got shut down with your patent extensions?"

His father bristled. "That's different. The technology that Langar controls is dangerous, and needs to be contained."

"Sure, Dad, the rules don't apply to you. Anyway, in the long run, what we're doing at Sparkwise is better for everyone. Have you considered—"

His father cut him off. "The government is moving to break up Sparkwise, and no doubt to break up the other companies your friends have cobbled together through malfeasance and cheating.

And you know what?" He slammed a palm down on the table and gave Nick a defiant look. "I support the government!"

Nick had always been loath to believe Laura and Kobus' frequent complaints that Aeons were being persecuted. He'd thought they were jumping at the faintest rumor and playing victim at the slightest setback. Yet now it seemed that they had been right to be alarmed. Even his own father had turned against him. "You support those government goons in dismantling everything I've been building for over a year?"

"Oh, dears, would the two of you calm down and talk like rational human beings instead of growling and hissing like animals?" interjected his mother.

Nick's father kept right on yelling. "Yes, and you'd better cooperate with them!"

"Cooperate? I know all about your political action committees and election financing, in America and across the world. Why don't you just call up the same politicians you bribe to protect Langar's patents and tell them to leave me alone?"

"Whatever you may think, those leaders support Langar because it made a great contribution to humanity. But your Sparkwise is just a scourge. So go turn yourself in and help the government dismantle it."

"Why would I do that?"

"Because you're tearing apart your own country, that's why!" his father yelled, standing up from the table and walking around it to lean menacingly over Nick.

Nick was so much taller than his father that even sitting he was eye to eye with him. Only his father's high turban gave the impression that he was taller.

"My country?" Nick cried incredulously. He felt his face flushing with emotion and his eyes tearing as he pushed his way into a standing position, allowing him to stare down at his father. The US was no country of his, not if it was trying to arrest him just for trying to run a business. Laura and Kobus had been right to close ranks and retreat into the safety of their virtual worlds. "I don't *live* in America. I haven't since I got the MindWave. I live in the ether."

"It doesn't matter where you think you live when you're off in your fantasyland. You may think you live in the ether with the other Aeons but your body has always been in America. Surrounded by American people, protected by American laws."

"Protected? Hardly – I'm afraid to go outside without bodyguards. And— laws? Laws are a commodity. Any half-decent country can protect me with their laws. I can go to England or Canada for laws! I don't owe loyalty to my provider of laws any more than I do to my barber or butcher." Nick had stood up and was trying to shift around his father to get out of the room, but he was penned in by the table to his front and wall to his back. "And besides, the government here is twisting its laws to persecute us."

Dr. Lal reached up and grabbed on to his son's shirt by the collar. Tears streamed down his reddened face as he cried out in a voice that held a mix of pride and anger and disappointment. "Stop playing a victim! This is about your loyalty to your nation. I'm an

American by choice. I immigrated because of the opportunities America offered to people like me. I was born in a land torn apart by a war. Ten years of horrible, relentless war and oppression. Then I escaped here to the United States. And they welcomed me, they gave me everything I needed, and I made something of myself, I made something for the world, that I never could have if I hadn't come here. And your mother would tell you the same story. American by choice, and doubly loyal because of that choice.

"And you, you little ingrate, you go off into your la-la land and cheat and steal to beggar your countrymen and expect me to support you? To be proud of you? And you dismiss any loyalty to the countrymen you've driven to starvation because you think a society of laws is a *commodity*? To be traded to the highest bidder like the oil and gas you've been hoarding?"

Nick was so shocked by his father's anger that he allowed himself to be flung down into his chair. His father continued remonstrating with him. "You can still make good. You're young, and you've been misled. *Make good*. Renounce the Aeons. Work with the government."

Nick looked away. How could his father demand that he denounce his friends? Give up his business?

His father's voice took on a pleading tone. "If you won't do it out of principle, do it for your parents. Your poor mother does not want to see you go to jail. And if you don't even care about us, do it for that girl you've been seeing, Sarah. It'd break her idealistic heart to know you've been stealing from your own countrymen."

Nick pushed his father back and stood up again. Sarah still seemed friendly, but then again she was always needling him about how he needed to behave differently. It was just a matter of time before she rejected him. Just like Peggy had. "Don't try to use Sarah against me. You've barely met her. You say I have no loyalty to my people, but I do. My people are Laura, Kobus, Abril and my other friends in the ether, not this godforsaken country that's falling apart!" With these words, Nick pulled his father's clenched hand off his shirt, tearing the collar, and pushed past him towards the room's door.

"Nick—son!" his father called beseechingly, his hand reaching out helplessly after him. He was too winded to give chase.

"Son? I'm not your son. I was created in a test tube. If you want a son, grow him in one of your damned vats!" Nick screamed over his shoulder, as he strode out of his parent's home for the last time and slammed the door.

Half an hour later, Nick sat in his penthouse apartment. He was torn between anger at his father for turning against him, and dread that Sparkwise really was involved in illegal activities. He activated his MindWave and sought out Laura in the ether.

In a moment, Nick stood on the peak of a high mountain, looking outwards across the verdant landscape. A twisted apple tree shaded him from the bright light of the sun. Below him, beneath the clouds, people went about their daily lives, unaware of the Aeons looking down at them from above.

Laura's world.

Nick reached for an apple hanging from the tree, but thought better of it when he heard footsteps approaching.

"What brings you here, Nick?"

Chapter 15

Laura stepped around from behind the apple tree, her long white robes flowing behind her in the breeze and her golden tiara glinting in the sun. She was giving Nick a severe look, as if she were annoyed or concerned by his sudden appearance.

"We need to talk."

"We're talking now."

"About twenty different government organizations are investigating Sparkwise."

Laura smiled and her features relaxed a little. "Oh is that was has you worried? I'm already taking care of it."

"What does that mean?"

"It means you can go back to dating your nat girlfriend."

"Don't change the subject. What is Sparkwise doing that has the government investigating us?"

"Nothing. We're doing nothing at all, Nick. Nothing except fulfilling our destiny. The investigations are politically motivated. The have-nots are in a jealous rage against those more successful than them."

"How can I be sure? There are files I don't have access to."

Now Laura's face hardened. "You would have access to all the files, if you were fully focused on your duties. But you're not. Just now you accused me of changing the subject when I said you can get back to your nat girlfriend. In fact I wasn't changing the subject. That *is* the subject. Even when you're in Sparkwise strategy sessions, you're only half there. Part of you is always dreaming about your Sarah. So don't blame me if certain details of our operations have escaped your notice."

Nick was off balance from the direction of Laura's anger. He'd expected a confrontation about Sparkwise, not about Sarah. He looked away. "Kobus spends hours in the ether chasing nymphs or whatever turns him on. But you let him in on all of Sparkwise's operations. What's the problem with me dating a real person?"

"I want to know why you're wasting your time on someone so unworthy of you."

Nick's eyes narrowed and he glared back at Laura. "You don't even know her."

"I don't want to."

"Why do you hate her without the slightest clue about who she is?"

Laura's face relaxed into an empathic expression and she placed a reassuring hand on his cheek. "I don't *hate* her. She is what she is, just another natural human dependent on the Aeons to save her. What bothers me is not Sarah, but you. You're infatuated with her. You're taking advantage of someone inferior to you. And you should know you deserve better."

Nick pulled away, disgusted at her patronizing attitude. "*Better*? Why do I deserve better?"

"Because you're an Aeon."

"And what is so special about being an Aeon?"

"You know as well as I do, Nick. You have a great destiny. You have infinite knowledge, innate and—"

"Infinite knowledge? *Infinite*? What is my favorite color, Laura?"

Laura stared at him blankly.

"Do you begin to see that our knowledge is not infinite?"

"That's a trivial example," said Laura shrilly, defensiveness creeping into her normally confident tone. Her hands shook in anger. "I know the things that are important. *We* know them."

Yeah, I know the price of crude oil in Latvia and I know the pass through rates of every gas pipeline in the nation. I guess those are important."

Laura smiled faintly, her voice returning to a warm tone. "I knew you were smart enough to see this, Nick, and that is what has allowed us to build Sparkwise Energy into a global energy company in a single year."

"But I don't care. Do you know what's more important than oil prices?"

Laura looked at him, clearly unsure of how to respond.

"All I care about is whether Sarah loves me. Can your MindWave tell you that? Because mine can't."

Laura's features turned bright red but Nick exited her world before she could form her response.

He'd fought with his parents and he'd fought with Laura. He was running out of people to talk to. Thankfully, he still had one more person he could discuss his thoughts with. He keyed up the holophone function of his MindWave.

Sarah was strapped into one of the cooling chairs at the ranch, next to Michael. They were about to begin an evening session of mapping out the Aeons' network infrastructure.

Unexpectedly, the holophone integrated into her TacWave began ringing. She saw that the caller was Nick Lal and felt a surge of excitement. "Sorry, Michael, duty calls."

"Another call from your Aeon boyfriend?" Sarah ignored the edge in Michael's voice. He needed to get over the fact that her job was to date Nick Lal.

"Just go in first, Michael, I'll be along in a second."

She switched on the holophone emulator in her TacWave. Though she was standing in a room full of secret government computer equipment, to Nick it would appear that she was sitting on a luxurious leather couch and sipping a glass of wine. "Hey there, how's it going?"

"OK, I guess."

"You look kind of glum, Nick. You sure everything's ok?"

"Just some dumb arguments with my parents."

"Sounds normal."

"I'm really angry this time though. I don't think I'm going to speak to them again."

Sarah felt a stab of sadness that someone who was lucky enough to still have parents would turn away from them, even after the worst of fights. But this wasn't a pain she could share with Nick, not when her undercover persona had parents. "What was the fight about?"

"My company. You've probably seen it on the National News Network by now. It's Sparkwise."

"*You're* involved in Sparkwise? The news said the names of the owners were being held confidential while the investigation proceeded. I had no idea that was you..."

Sarah's mind was racing while she thought through how this conversation might play out. She would have to play dumb until she was sure of why Nick was discussing Sparkwise with her. If he indicated any willingness to cooperate with the government, she could hint that she could help him. Yet she still couldn't reveal her true identity to him.

Her train of thought was interrupted by an urgent message from Michael that cut across her holophone feed. "Sarah, I've found a hole in Sparkwise's firewall. Get in here and help me."

Nick was working up the courage to admit to Sarah that he thought some of the allegations against Sparkwise might be true and wanted to find a confidential way to cooperate with the government. But now his holophone feed was drowned out by an emergency MindWave message from Laura. "Nick, our firewall is being infiltrated. Get in here and help me defend it."

"By the government?"

"Can't be. They would have to show a warrant. It must be some damn nat hacker."

Nick reluctantly decided he would have to help defend the firewall. If he was going to turn state's witness against Sparkwise, he would need to keep Laura's trust for as long as possible. In fact, he'd have to *increase* her trust in him, so that she'd give him access to the most secret files.

He switched back to his holophone call with Sarah. "Hey don't go anywhere. I've got another call I have to take."

"It's all right, I have the same problem," Sarah responded. Her voice sounded distracted and strained. "Keep the line open and give me a shout when you're done."

Michael's request had come at a terrible time. Sarah thought Nick's tone over the holophone suggested that he was getting ready to confess something to her. Maybe even to ask her advice in how to cooperate with the government. It would be a major intelligence coup for her, and it would have earned Nick immunity.

But duty called.

She appeared in the multinet at Michael's location, a large stone-walled rectangular room, about one hundred feet long, fifty wide, and thirty high. In the center of the space, a four by four array of steel safes floated in the air. Each safe was a three foot cube. The lowest row of safes hovered about an inch off the ground. Each of the three rows above it was suspended two feet above the one below. Likewise, each column was spaced two feet distant from the ones to its left and right. There was a ledge that ran around the room at about the same height as the third row of safes. The only other features in the room were doorways at either end.

Michael was crouched over a prone polar bear near one of the doorways. Sarah saw that he was busy binding the bear with thick ropes. In addition to the martial gear he had worn to the Five Mile Creek server, Michael now wore a ninja-style face mask that hid his identity. Sarah conjured a stretchy leather ski mask and pulled it over her head, leaving only her eyes exposed.

Michael gave a final tug on the ropes and stood up.

"You think you can bind me, *jou bliksem?*" roared the polar bear.

Michael kicked the bear and said "Meet Jakobus Van der Merwe, also known as Kobus."

"Next time you say my name you'll be on your knees begging for mercy!" The animal turned its head and leered at Sarah. "*En jy sal wees op jou rug en bedel vir meer.*"

Michael ignored Kobus and turned to the floating array of steel safes. "This is the secure Sparkwise server room."

"How did you get in here?"

"The Aeons have expanded their systems so fast I guess they just made a mistake. There was one firewall in the Aeon Avionics email server that wasn't correctly installed, and the email server had connections to a data-pooling system with Sparkwise, and from there I could get to here."

"What should we do now? Report back to base?"

"No, this is a one-time chance." He gestured at Kobus. "They clearly know the vulnerability exists now and will close it."

"OK. Do you really think we can break into the safes?" Sarah didn't want to move aggressively now. If they uncovered proof of Sparkwise's crimes before Nick could confess to them, he would never get a chance to avoid arrest. She just needed a few more minutes of talking to him.

She switched back to her holophone conversation. "Nick, are you there? It really sounded like there was something you wanted to discuss and I don't want to leave you hanging."

"Yeah," Nick answered. "I do have something to talk about. Just as soon as I'm free."

"I might have to go soon, Nick."

"Sorry. I'll hurry."

Sarah resisted the urge to curse at him and switched her consciousness back to the Sparkwise server.

"We don't have the encryption key to unlock the safes," Michael was explaining. "But we can always try a brute force attack."

"I thought the best encryption was unbreakable."

"Well they don't have the quantum encryption systems we have. And even if they did, it would still be vulnerable to brute force. It's just a matter of having enough force." Michael pulled a huge sledgehammer from out of his sash and passed it to Sarah.

"How the hell do you carry all this stuff around in your sash?" Sarah muttered.

"You better hope he has a *fokkin tenk* in there," growled Kobus.

"And why don't you carry a muzzle, too?" She took a few reluctant steps towards the nearest safe and began lining up a swing.

Before she could strike, a figure ran into the room. He was dressed in baggy white pants held up by an orange belt, and a billowing navy blue top. A high black turban covered his head. In his hand, he carried a curved scimitar-like blade.

It was *Nick*!

"It's about time you got here, *bra*! Don't worry, I got your back!" called Kobus.

As Nick brandished his sword and turned towards Michael, Sarah switched back to her holophone. "Nick I need to talk to you now!"

"Almost done," he said breathlessly.

Inside Sparkwise's server, Michael was parrying Nick's sword blows with a long spear with red feathers near its tip. The two whirled around each other in furious circles.

Michael jabbed with his spear at Nick's head six times in rapid succession. Nick diverted the first five strikes with his sword and on the sixth dodged down and forward, aiming a vicious swing at Michael's knees. Michael leaped over Nick's sword while spinning backwards. As he landed, he brought his spear point down in a wide arc as if it were a hammer. Nick saw the attack coming and spun away to the left, aiming a backhand blow back at Michael as he completed his turn. Luckily Michael moved behind the shaft of his spear, which he used to block the blade.

The two warriors parted for a moment and circled each other, looking for weaknesses.

As Sarah watched the combat, she felt herself filling with fury. Just when she'd thought Nick was ready to confess to her about Sparkwise, he was actually acting to defend the company. When she had defended Nick to Willy and Colonel Jaeger, when she had believed in him, she had been proving herself a fool.

She realized now that she'd fallen in love with Nick. All the times she'd rushed to his defense, she'd been deceiving herself about her reasons. She wasn't just protecting him because he was a potential intelligence source. She was trying to protect him because of how she felt about him. And the excitement she'd felt in his presence wasn't simply the innocent thrill of the hunt. It was the tension of being in his presence at all.

The depth of her feelings just made her realization that she'd been wrong about him all the more painful. Indignation, shame, and rage all boiled up within her. She was going to get revenge.

When Nick's back was to her, she flung her hammer at him. It twisted slowly as it flew through the air, and then impacted him right between the shoulder blades. He let out a gasp and fell to the ground.

"*Jammer*! I guess I didn't really have your back, *bra*," exclaimed Kobus from the ground.

She switched back to her holophone. She spoke as sweetly as she could. "How are things going over there, Nick? Are you done yet?"

"Um, I hit a bit of a snag, Sarah."

She let the sweetness drain out of her voice. "I bet you did."

She switched back to Sparkwise, and drove her knee into Nick's back to hold him down on the floor. She grinned as she heard him cursing over the holophone audio link, and then cut the holophone connection.

While she held down Nick, Michael retrieved the sledgehammer and strode up to the nearest of the floating safes. "Like I said, it's just a matter of having enough force." He wound up and let loose a swing so powerful he nearly lost his balance. The hammer head impacted the safe's lock with a resounding clang, leaving a deep dent. Michael recovered his footing and took another wild swing, and then another. "Just a matter of force" he repeated between his grunts.

Finally, the safe burst open and an avalanche of paper documents burst out of it and fell scattered on the floor. "Score!" said Michael happily.

"*Jy bliksem, dit is my goed!*" cried a visibly upset Kobus. "*Ek gaan rip jou skrotum af en gebruik dit vir 'n sleutelhanger.*"

"Get out of my server!" the woman's voice was deep and powerful. Sarah turned her head just in time to see the same red-haired warrior that had overpowered her at the Five Mile Creek server striding towards them, sword and shield at the ready. This time, Sarah knew the woman was Laura Mayer. Laura was flanked by two enormous lionesses.

"Sarah, hold them off while I collect some of this data!"

Sarah got off of Nick's back. She had a sword and dagger in her belt, but she knew Michael's spear would be a better weapon to hold off the cats. She quickly retrieved it from where Michael had set it on the ground.

The two lionesses roared and pounced towards her simultaneously. One came right at her throat. Sarah held the spear firmly and gored it through its mouth. The cat's momentum was so great that it travelled all the way up the shaft of the spear, killing itself yet still slamming into Sarah with enough speed to knock her on her back. Sarah hit the ground hard and struggled to push the dead weight of the feline off of her.

Before she could budge it, the other cat bounded up and leaned over her face, its maws gaping open to reveal a row of jagged teeth. She struggled and got a hand free, pulled the knife from the

259

sheath on her belt, and stabbed the beast in the side. The cat roared in fury and backed off of her. She turned to Michael to ask for help.

Michael was engaged in one-on-one combat with Laura. Unable to swing fast enough with his unwieldy sledgehammer to parry her furious sword blows, he was backing up steadily, looking for an opening to strike. He was circling as he backed up, so that he wouldn't be forced into a corner. But his circling was taking him right towards—

"Michael watch out!" she screamed.

It was too late. Nick had crawled to his knees and Michael had backed right into him. Nick seized Michael's legs, holding him immobile. Michael pulled away and used the flat of his hammer to knock Nick in the ribs, sending him sprawling onto the pile of papers that had spilled out of the broken safe.

But now Michael's back was turned on Laura, who unleashed a brutal diagonal sword stroke that sent Michael's head rolling away down the length of the room.

Kobus roared "She got your head, *maar jou skrotum is myne!*"

Laura turned towards Sarah to finish her off. Sarah was still trapped under the dead lioness. She weakly flung her knife at the approaching Aeon. The weapon fell short and skittered across the stone floor, until Laura used her sandal-clad foot to stop it. "I've seen you before," said Laura as she approached. "You escaped me at Five Mile Creek. This time I'm going to find out who you really are."

Just before Laura reached her, Sarah's connection to the multinet was cut off.

Chapter 16

Reverend Tracy Cruz' hand froze as she came across the last piece of mail. Paper mail was rare except at this time of year, when some people still sent old-fashioned paper holiday cards to each other. Yet this piece of mail was no holiday card. It was a letter from Sparkwise Energy. "Speaking of the Devil," she said aloud. Sparkwise had come from nothing a year ago to now be the largest energy company in the nation. It was front page news everywhere, because it was being investigated by just about every government body in the world for various acts of corruption and market manipulation.

She shrugged and tore open the envelope to retrieve the letter.

Dear Reverend Doctor Lawson,

Cruz shook her head at the fact that Sparkwise had not updated its database since she had taken over the church from Doc Lawson. Then she continued reading.

Enclosed, please find a small Christmas donation to your church. Se hope that you will remind your congregation that they are held in the highest esteem by their friends at Sparkwise Energy.

Cruz nearly swore out loud when she saw the amount printed on the check at the bottom of the letter. It was enough to support the National Unity Church's activities for months.

She felt her face reddening, and the letter trembled in her hands. She sat like that for a long time. Eventually, she heard Ricardo calling through the doorway that led to the altar. "Honey, the worshippers are here waiting for your sermon."

"Sorry, I was just finalizing the text. I'll be there in a second."

Cruz had planned to give her congregation another of her impotent exhortations to keep their faith in the face of material hardship. Now, as she sat holding the letter from Sparkwise, she realized she had a better sermon to give.

She pulled open the drawer in Doc's old desk and rummaged around his old belongings until she'd found what she was looking for. She thrust the item inside her vestments and headed out of the small office to the altar, where her small congregation was waiting for her.

As always, Ricardo was standing in the back, recording her sermon. He would post it online for those congregants who were too unwell – or too deep in despair – to attend the service. He smiled reassuringly at her, and she felt her sense of agitation harden into resolve.

She stood at the podium and waited until she had the crowd's full attention. "Brothers and Sisters, today our church has received a large donation."

She held up the letter from Sparkwise, check still attached, for all to see.

"But I intend to give it back." She stated.

"Give it back?" gasped an elderly lady called old Ma Watson from the back of the church.

Cruz saw Ricardo looking up from his camera, concern on his features. *He will understand,* she reassured herself, and continued speaking.

"The donation is from Sparkwise Energy. I don't know why the misguided souls who run this parasitic corporation would extend their largess to our humble congregation. Surely they have taken so much from our community, and other communities all around the nation, that it causes them no inconvenience to offer us this gift."

And now she reached into her vestments and pulled out the item she had found in Doc's desk.

"We will not accept such false charity from the like of the Aeons. No. We will accept nothing from them at all."

She flicked the wheel of Doc's old lighter and a flame burst to life. She raised her voice. "Jesus Christ said to render unto Caesar what is Caesar's. I believe we must also render unto Satan what is Satan's."

She touched the flame to the paper, igniting it instantly.

"And so today, before you all, I'm giving it back."

The crowd watched silently as the paper caught fire. After several moments, the flames began to lick at her hand and she dropped the letter to the ground.

"Give it back!" cried out old Ma Watson from the back as she pulled herself to her feet. "Give it back!"

"Give it back, give it back!" echoed one congregant after another.

In moments, they were all on their feet, chanting the mantra so loudly Cruz thought maybe the Aeons could actually hear them.

Nick was again attending the weekly Sparkwise energy strategy meeting, debating the next steps for the company with Laura and Kobus. Instead of the vague unease and suspicion he had felt in previous sessions, now he felt betrayal.

During the attack on the Sparkwise servers a few days earlier, when he'd been knocked onto the pile of secret documents, he'd had a few moments to read one of them. And what that letter revealed had obliterated what remained of his faith in Laura and Kobus.

"*Bladdy* hell, Laura, if we go into Nigeria now, before we have our militia together, the Petro China guys are going to totally *fokk* with us. You saw what they did to the Hindustani concession a few years back. *Ingenieurs* going missing, pipelines *saboteered*, even a hijacked tanker. *Vir al wat ons weet*, that attack on our servers was launched by Petro China. To play the energy game in Africa, you need muscle." Kobus slapped a white, furry paw on the table to emphasize his point.

"It's definitely a risk, I don't deny it," responded Laura. "But the concession pricing on the table now is the cheapest it's ever going to get. We're only six months away from having an effective paramilitary capability in the region. How much damage can the Chinese do in that time?"

"Ask the Hindustanis! They can do a whole lot of *skade, ne.*"

"We won't even have many assets in the concession area for another year. We'll just have Abril's engineering company digging some small exploratory wells, and finding the gradients for pipelines and roads. We can defend a few small drilling and engineering teams with our Algerians."

"*Ja no*, we could. If we weren't also counting on the Algerians to train a local militia of Nigerians. If the Algerians are busy babysitting our *ingenieurs*, how are they also going to train the Nigerians?"

Laura leaned back in her seat and sighed heavily. "Damn. Maybe we can hire more Algerians?"

"*Jy sê vir my*. You're the one who knows the mercenaries."

Nick knew that he needed to cooperate with the government's investigation into Sparkwise. But while the information he had seen was enough to convince him that Laura and Kobus were dishonest, it was nothing that would lead to their criminal convictions. Even as he turned against his fellow Aeons, he would need to further gain their trust so that they would reveal their most vital secrets to him.

Laura had repeatedly criticized him for not being fully engaged in running Sparkwise. The way to gain her trust was to show he was involved and could help solve their problems. "Algerians, Nigerians. Let's think a little broader than 'gerians."

Both Kobus and Laura stared at him blankly. Perhaps they were surprised by the fact that he was making a constructive comment. They probably thought of him as more of an observer than a participant. That was exactly the impression he needed to change. "Why do the mercenaries have to be Algerians?"

"I know the Algerians. We've used them to guard our export facilities in Marrakesh and a refinery in Abu Dhabi," responded Laura. "Do you have a better suggestion?"

"What about Cameroon? Their government decommissioned a lot of their military about a year ago. They must have some out of work soldiers who would love the chance to guard an oil field. And Cameroon has more cultural affinity with Nigeria than Algeria does; Cameroonian soldiers might even be able to communicate with the local population."

"*Groot*, so they can apologize in local dialect when they *verkragting en roof*?" muttered Kobus.

"Oh, come on!" groaned Laura. "That was an *isolated* incident. The press didn't even find out about it. And in restitution, we docked a month of that soldier's pay and gave it to the girl's family."

Nick held up his hands, palms facing outwards, hoping to avoid an argument between Laura and Kobus. "Well, will the Cameroonians work?"

Kobus thought for a moment and then his face brightened into a toothy, bearish smile. "*Ja*, it's a *goeie idee*. Great thinking, *bra*. This could turn our whole Nigeria operation around. I'll look into it."

Nick waited expectantly.

Laura saw his expression and snapped at him, "Kobus can't find this out using his MindWave. He'll have to get on the holophone with *nats*. Talking with them takes time."

Nick's lips curled slightly at the term. *Nats*. How contemptuous of the countless men and women who weren't lucky enough to have a MindWave. It was amazing that Laura had even noticed one of the Algerian mercenaries they had hired to protect their offices in Abu Dhabi had raped and blinded the daughter of a poor Bangladeshi immigrant family. *Just one nat swatting another*. How could she believe the Aeons' destiny was to save humanity when she had so little respect for her fellow men and women?

If Laura noticed Nick's look of disgust at her words, she didn't let on. She continued with the meeting agenda. "Our final item is our American operation. It looks like we're going to have another harsh winter, and as was true last year, other suppliers are having trouble getting their product to market. On January first, we're making another twenty percent increase in our pricing of heating oil, natural gas, gasoline, and diesel.

"And that's it for today," sighed Laura contentedly. "Meeting adjourned. Are you guys heading over to Abril's Christmas orgy?"

"*Ja*! Last year Abril created an endless lake of chocolate liqueur populated with *dronk* nymphs and satyrs. *Ek kan nie wag* to see what kind of *hedonisme* she's got for this year!" replied Kobus. Nick saw that he was already breathing heavily and licking his lips at the thought of the orgy.

They both looked at Nick.

"Uh, I'll catch up later. I have some family Christmas stuff to do…" he responded awkwardly. He knew he should accompany Laura and Kobus in the ether to fully gain their trust. But he had one Christmas engagement he didn't want to cancel.

"I thought you disowned your family. Are you chasing your nat girlf—"

Laura's voice was cut off as Nick disconnected himself from the ether and appeared back in his private apartment in the real world.

Sarah was waiting downstairs from Nick's apartment, in the lower level of the finely appointed two-story lobby of his building. But instead of appreciating the beautiful furniture and artwork with which the lobby was appointed, she was tapping her foot with impatience. It was a cold and windy day. Nick was lucky his doorman had let her wait inside and given her some warm tea. Otherwise she'd be even angrier.

"I'm really sorry, Sarah. I got caught up in something," Nick said as he emerged from his private elevator, holding his hands up almost defensively.

"I know manipulating the energy markets is very important to you," replied Sarah with a roll of her eyes. "But given that you have a computerized communications center in your brain that's more powerful than most spy satellites, you might have at least sent me a text message. I've been waiting for twenty minutes."

"I know, I'm sorry!" retorted Nick, testily. "I just got caught up and couldn't get away."

He walked forward through the lobby and pushed through the large glass door, before the liveried doorman could scamper over and open it for him.

Sarah's anger suited the role she was playing as a girlfriend who'd been left waiting. But she didn't have to act. She was disappointed in Nick, and angry at herself for believing in him. She calmed herself; she still had a job to do; she could not let her temper get too hot. "It's fine. Let's just go." She followed him out the door.

"Back to the park again, right?" said Nick, taking a left turn to head towards the Central Park's 86th street transverse entrance, which was only a short walk away.

Sarah could see a few blocks ahead, past the entrance to the transverse, a few dozen people were milling about holding up signs. Probably more protests about unemployment or energy prices, but she was too distracted to read the placards. She was more concerned that Nick had forgotten something they needed.

"Yes, to the park," she said haltingly. "But don't we need the..."

"Oh no." Nick sighed, placing a hand on his forehead. "I forgot to tell the maid to put together a picnic for us! Ah, damn, I'm such an idiot!" His pace slowed.

Sarah waved her hand in the air and walked past him without looking back. "It's all right. I'm sure we can buy something along the way." A gust of frigid winter wind at her from behind, and she instinctively dipped her head down towards her collar.

Nick caught up quickly. "Yeah, I told you, I'm really busy."

Sarah carefully looked at the pavement in front of her to avoid seeming confrontational. "I know, I know. I'm not complaining. The weather's too cold for a picnic even with heat lamps, anyway. Let's just get something indoors. Isn't there a nice deli up ahead?"

Nick seemed to misinterpret her peace offering as sarcasm. "Please don't act this way, Sarah, I'm taking time away from some really important things. My company is facing a tough time and I'm behind on an important project. And I'm even missing my company Christmas party. All because I wanted to talk to you."

The fury rising in Sarah's gut overwhelmed her desire to see the mission through. She had been reprimanded for foolishly defending Nick to Willy, only to learn he wasn't the man she thought he was. And now he was feeding her this bullshit? She planted her legs and put her hands on her hips, furiously thinking of a way to express her anger without stepping out of character. "Company Christmas party? I thought today was *our* Christmas party!"

Nick stopped and faced her. "I know, I know. Sorry. I'm just busy, that's all!" he said in a mortified tone. Clearly, he was embarrassed. She wasn't sure if he really felt sorry towards her, or was just blanching at the prospect of being seen having an argument on the street. If their raised voices attracted the attention of the protestors down the road, Nick would no doubt be heckled and harassed.

Sarah wasn't going to let him off easy just because they were in public. "Should I feel flattered that the great and mighty Nick Lal has deigned to spend some time away from his more important friends? Or should I feel guilty for being the reason that Nick's other friends are being denied the pleasure of his company right now?" Sarah regretted her loud, sarcastic tone immediately. She was over acting her role.

"You know what, forget it!" said Nick angrily. "I had something important I wanted to discuss with you. But maybe you're not someone I should be trusting with my problems."

The two stood frozen in the pavement for several long moments.

Sarah knew what problems Nick was referring to. It had to be Sparkwise. He must be seeking a way out. She had been right about him after all. She felt a rush of remorse at her anger towards him,

271

and of euphoria that the man she'd fallen in love with really did exist. She needed to restrain those emotions and mend the current situation. She had pushed him away in a fit of pique just when he was going to reveal everything to her. "What's wrong, Nick? I really want to help."

Nick's eyes narrowed suspiciously and Sarah realized her change of tack had come off as unnatural. "I think I'd better join my company party. It would be rude not to. I'll see you again soon." He pulled a wad of bills from his pocket and jammed it into her hand. "That's for taxi fare home."

He walked past Sarah, and through the glass doors of his apartment building without looking back, leaving Sarah standing on the sidewalk of Central Park West, desperately grasping for a way to regain Nick's trust.

Before she could think of anything to say, she heard Willy's voice through her TacWave. *Sarah, I'm issuing an emergency recall order. Your safety is compromised. Return to the ranch immediately by the fastest means available.*

Chapter 17

Nick tread softly on the dead leaves in his soft leather boots, not daring to make a sound. A hundred feet distant from him, through the trees, the deer looked around nervously between sips of water from the slowly flowing stream. He'd been tracking this buck for an hour, carefully staying downwind to avoid giving away his presence. Now he'd finally lined up a kill shot.

He held the curved yew bow horizontally in front of him with his left hand as he reached into his quiver and pulled out a long arrow with his right hand. Almost unconsciously, he checked the feathers to make sure they were even and the notch to make sure it was sound. Then he slid the arrow onto the string and raised the bow in front of him. It took all of his strength to pull the cord back to full draw.

He looked down the length of the shaft at the buck, which was silently drinking from the stream. He found his quarry's heart, and then corrected his aim upwards for the headwind and the distance.

The buck had first sensed Nick's threatening presence fifteen minutes ago. But for some reason it had been indecisive. Instead of fleeing immediately, it had looked around for a while and then continued its business. And so the buck would die and Nick would earn his dinner.

Now the buck's ears perked up and it raised its head to look right at Nick. It bunched the muscles of its body as if it were about to bound away.

Too late.

He loosed the arrow. It sailed straight and fast towards the deer.

Laura appeared in front of Nick, and the arrow vanished as it passed right between her eyes.

The forest was gone, as were the deer and the bow. Nick was floating in endless black nothingness; the default state of the ether.

He frowned in annoyance. "What the he—"

"Nick, haven't you seen the mob? Why are you still in Manhattan?"

Nick looked at her with incomprehension. "What are you talking about? I was hunting in the Argonne."

"No, I'm talking about your physical body! You need to get out of Manhattan!" She waved her hand and the world turned into fire and chaos. Nick realized he was seeing live holovision footage of a rioting crowd.

Along the Upper West Side of Manhattan.

Just outside his home.

Laura continued, "Haven't you been keeping an eye on the news? This has been getting worse and worse all day!"

"I've been busy," said Nick weakly. He had been unnerved by his argument with Sarah. She was normally laid back, even a little detached. That was part of what he liked about her. But on the way to the park, she had seemed unusually volatile. She had gotten angry fast, and then suddenly shifted gears and appealed to let her help him. Now he had a bad feeling he'd trusted her too much.

After he had gone home, he had made a cursory appearance at Abril's Christmas orgy, just enough to show he was part of the Aeon team. Then he had cut himself off from everyone and spent the night immersed in solitary fantasy worlds he created with his MindWave. He'd received several messages from Laura and from his family, yet ignored them all.

Even as he spoke, his MindWave was summarizing the last twenty-four hours of riots by piecing together several news reports into a simple and coherent narrative in his brain.

The already tenuous situation had deteriorated substantially in the last fifteen minutes. Roads to the South, North, and West of his apartment were in flames. Rioters, angry at spiraling energy prices and inspired by the defiance a pastor in Texas had shown towards the Aeons, had given up their peaceful protest in Central Park and were now taking out their fury on the wealthiest neighborhoods in Manhattan. They were looting buildings and attacking residents.

There was speculation that the Governor would declare a state of emergency and send National Guard units into the city to quell the riots. Until that happened, it was up to the New York City Police Department. Manhattan's police were stretched thin and could only hope to contain the chaos until reinforcements arrived. And those reinforcements would be slowed by the lack of working police vehicles and the fact that rioters had barricaded many of Manhattan's narrow streets. It would be hours before more officers could arrive.

The worst violence was now unfolding along Central Park West, where Nick's luxury penthouse apartment was located. The police in the area had fallen back in the face of the mob, and now just held a thin defensive line around the 86th Street Central Park transverse. The East side of the transverse, where his parents' residence was located, was still under police control.

"Get to the transverse!" commanded Laura. "It's the safest way out."

"I will." He looked at her, fearfully. Adrenaline was filling his real body as he realized the gravity of the situation. "I'll have to disconnect. I'll have to get out of the ether. Wait for me."

As he prepared to exit the ether, he saw a wave of rioters charging at the thin defensive police line from the North. Some of the police dropped their truncheons and retreated.

Nick brought himself back to his physical body in his apartment and reached behind himself to disconnect his MindWave from the ether. Just as he did so, Laura's frightened face appeared before him and said, in an urgent whisper, "Run!" He disconnected and the image of her face froze on his retinas and slowly faded away, ghostlike, her widened eyes taking the longest to dissolve.

He sat up slowly and stiffly. His body had been sitting almost motionless since his fight with Sarah. His MindWave, connected to the ether with a forty foot cable, had auto piloted his body around his apartment, performing the basic functions of his body for him: eating, drinking, bathing, using the toilet. But otherwise he had been still.

He hauled himself to a standing position. His legs felt soft and unstable. There was a dull ache in his back. He lurched towards the exit of his apartment but realized he was naked. He called for his maid, and received no answer. She must have already fled.

From the streets below his penthouse, he heard shouting. The riot was getting closer.

He remembered it was winter and the weather would be frigid.

Before he could flee, he needed to get dressed. Where did the maid keep his clothes?

He staggered across the room as fast as his stiff legs would allow towards his walk-in closet. In a panic he tore priceless tailored silk suits from the wall, threw golden cufflinks and tie clips to the ground. He frantically uncovered socks and underwear. A pair of dirty jeans. An old sweater and a jacket that didn't fit him anymore. His wallet.

As he struggled into his clothes the sounds of the riot grew louder.

He frantically ran across his apartment towards his private elevator, jamming the button repeatedly with his thumb. The bell rang and the doors immediately slid open.

He stepped inside and ordered, "Lower lobby." Then he got a bad feeling in his gut – or was it in his MindWave? "Upper lobby," he corrected. As the doors slid shut, he leaned against the wall of the elevator and caught his breath.

He stepped out of the elevator as soon as the doors opened at the upper lobby. From outside the building, he heard sounds of breaking glass and running feet. There was yelling in the distance. He noticed a faint scent of smoke in the air.

He heard the doors of the elevator slide shut behind him as it continued its journey down to the lower lobby.

The upper lobby was a semi-circular arcade that looked down into the lower lobby. He leaned over the railing to peer down on the floor below. The doorman was gone and there were some open, half-filled suitcases lying abandoned on the hand woven afghan rug. But it looked safe.

Just before he began descending the wide marble stairs, a brick crashed through the glass front door, shattering it noisily.

Three muscular, unshaven men armed with baseball bats ran into the lobby behind the brick. One of the bats was splattered with what looked like blood.

Nick instinctively ducked down behind the carved railing before he was seen. He jammed a fist into his mouth to mute the sound of his heavy breathing.

"This place looks like a palace!" he heard one of the men exult. "More loot."

Just then his private elevator pinged and the doors slid open into the lower lobby.

"Must be our ride," answered another one of the men. Nick heard them stride into the elevator. Before the brass doors slid shut he heard a voice say, "This is the penthouse elevator! We're rich!"

Nick was terrified to move, yet he knew he had to get out of the apartment building, and into the park, while the escape route was still open.

Slowly, shakingly, he crept down the stairs to the main lobby and up to the shattered doorway.

A disorganized mob was running past him, men and women armed with sticks, knives, pieces of rock. Some even carried lit torches to ward away the rapidly encroaching shadows of evening. Their faces were twisted by the mindless fury they sought to take out on men like him.

Nick waited until the crowd had passed before tentatively stepping towards the exit. As he did so, a lone youth barged through the doorway and stood in the lobby an arm's length from Nick.

Nick froze, not sure what to say or do. He locked eyes with the youth, who looked about Nick's age but was a lot shorter and had dark features that spoke of mixed ancestry. Nick thought he would look identical to this youth if his parents had not genetically engineered him.

The youth's eyes passed from Nick's face to the cooling vents in the back of his skull. "You're one of them!" he snarled. Then he turned back towards the doorway. "Hey over here! I found one of the Cybarians!"

Nick lunged forward and pulled the youth back into the building before he could alert more rioters that one of the hated Aeons was inside.

The youth bent down briefly and then came back up again, slashing at Nick's face with something that glinted in his hand. Nick ducked just in time to absorb the blow with his forehead instead of his eyes. He felt and heard the knife's blade cut through the thin flesh of his forehead and scrape along his skull.

He staggered backwards. Already, blood was streaming into his eyes and blinding him. His first impulse was to turn and run, but something else took over. He leapt forward towards where he knew the youth was still standing, blindly catching his arm before he could slash again. Then he bulled the youth to the floor with his shoulder.

Nick still couldn't see. While he controlled the youth's knife with his left hand, he tried to clear his vision with his right forearm. Unfortunately, the jacket he was wearing was waterproof and the fabric just worked the blood deeper into Nick's eyes.

Beneath him, the youth was struggling wildly to free himself. He kneed Nick from behind, tried to claw at his face with his free hand, and twisted wildly to roll away. But Nick held the youth in place by using his superior weight and strength.

Suddenly, the youth pulled Nick's left arm inwards towards his face and bit it hard. Nick gasped in pain and let go of the youth's knife hand.

The youth's hand was now free to stab him again. From the movements he felt beneath him, Nick sensed that the youth was going for a wild round-house slash at his face. He fell forward inside the range of the attack. But his new posture left his back and kidneys exposed, a vulnerability the youth would surely take advantage of in a moment.

In desperation, Nick felt around the floor with his fingers and found one of the chunks of glass from the shattered front door. He seized it in his fist and jammed it hard into the youth's neck, over and over again, using all of his weight to drive it deeper and deeper. The youth tried to scream, but just produced a high-pitched bubbly noise.

Nick kept stabbing until the youth stopped struggling.

Nick staggered to his feet and pulled his jacket off and his sweater over his head. He bent over and gagged until his nausea faded, and then he used the sweater's clean dry fabric to thoroughly rub the blood out of his eyes.

With his vision clear, he was careful not to look at the body that was lying at his feet. He checked the lobby and the street outside and found both deserted. That was lucky; anyone nearby would have seen and heard his struggle with the youth.

He tied the sweater around his head as a bandage while he considered his next step. He knew he had to escape from the lobby. Yet he was the target of the riot. If he was seen while he made his way to the park, he would no doubt be surrounded and beaten to death.

Then he saw his reflection in a shard of shattered glass. He hadn't shaved in days and he was shirtless, wearing ill-fitting old pants. Blood from his wound was already soaking through the fabric wrapped around his head. He looked like a member of the mob.

Except for the back of his head, with its gleaming cooling fans and connection jacks. With shaking hands, he felt behind his neck, and turned his head from side to side. *Yes!* With a few adjustments, the sweater wrapped around his head completely obscured the MindWave.

He remembered, finally, that one of the functions of his MindWave was to allow him to release hormones into his bloodstream at will. Before the MindWave overheated from having its exhaust ports blocked by the sweater, he used it to modulate the flow of adrenaline in his blood and release a flood of endorphins.

Instead of the hot panic of a moment ago, he felt a cool readiness spread through his body and mind. The burning pain in his forehead faded to a dull ache. He picked up the brick that lay in the middle of the lobby floor and ran out into the madness outside, screaming like a member of the mob.

In a minute Nick had run to a point one block south of the police perimeter around the transverse, where he'd just watched news footage of the thin blue line of officers clashing with a disorganized mass of rioters. The police line had held, the battle had subsided, and now the two sides stared each other down across a wide no-man's land. The rioters were being reinforced by a steady stream of new arrivals. The police stared nervously out from their gas masks, searching over their shoulders for evidence of the reinforcements promised from the other boroughs.

He wanted to get into the park now, without having to cross through the battle lines. But the walls along this section of the park fronted the exclusive club where he had taken Sarah to picnic. Because security was so important to club members, the walls had been heightened and topped with razor wire to prevent anyone from climbing. He saw that the 85th street entrance to the club was blocked by a massive bonfire. Nick had no choice but to press north to 86th street and go through the transverse entrance.

The air was acrid with smoke from the heaps of burning tires. Smashed-up cars lay overturned throughout the street. Obscene graffiti was scrawled across the facades of the exclusive buildings that lined the avenue. Groups of rioters were everywhere, some looting storefronts while others headed to join the crowds at the transverse.

He saw a burly man crying as he carried a limp and bloodied child away from the scene. He noticed two police officers kneeling over a third who was convulsing. There were other bodies lying still in the street, some in police blue and some in the mixed colors of civilian wear. There was a ten foot tall wooden crucifix leaning against the stone wall of the park, splintered and badly burned. Two men wearing rubber gloves and breathing masks shouldered a heavy barrel into the 85th Street entrance of the large apartment block that occupied Central Park West between 85th and 86th Streets.

The rioters were chanting together, five hundred ragged voices, pronounced in nearly as many accents. "Give it back, give it back!"

Nick knew he had to get to the transverse. Parroting the rioters' slogan, he pushed his way through the jostling crowd towards where the police line met the stone wall of the park. As soon as he reached the front edge of the rioter's ranks, he broke into a run, heading into the empty space between the surging ranks of rioters and the ragged police line, waving his arms. "Help, help me!"

Nick sensed the rioters behind him pausing and watching in confusion, their chant melting into a cacophony.

The police in front of him tightened their ranks and raised their truncheons. "Halt right there!" cried an officer through his gas mask, "Before I crack your skull!"

"No, no! I'm... I live here!" Nick cried desperately. He realized he was still holding the brick, and he dropped it to the ground. But it twisted in his hand as he released it, ending up with more forward momentum than he intended. It skidded across the pavement towards the feet of the officer he was running towards.

"Not for long," said the officer, winding up to strike Nick in the head.

Nick flinched away and held his left hand up defensively, and used his right hand to unwind the shirt around his head, revealing both his wound and his shining MindWave exhaust ports. "I'm not a rioter. I want to evacuate!" he implored desperately, tears forming in his eyes.

The officer glanced over his shoulder and then back to Nick. "You caused this, you damn Cybarian."

"Reap what you sow, metal mind!" barked another policeman.

Nick looked behind him and saw several rioters approaching carefully. They clearly wanted to attack him yet were cautious about approaching the police barricade. Nick couldn't go forward through the police line, and he couldn't go back towards the rioters. If he tried to climb the stone wall of the park to his right, his back would be exposed for several seconds. His best bet was to turn left, and run down the police line searching for an officer that would let him through. If not, he could try seeking refuge in the subway entrance on the street corner.

Nick jogged along the line of police, begging and pleading to be let through. None of them would budge, and many hurled epithets at him or jabbed at him with their truncheons.

The whole way, Nick was shadowed by six rioters holding baseball bats, who stayed about ten feet further away from the police line than he was. "Don't worry officers. We got no argument with you. We just want to teach this Cybarian a lesson," one of them called.

Finally, Nick reached the corner where the subway entrance was and saw the stairway was sealed off with a heavy metal gate. There was no way he could pass through it.

He needed to find a way through the police line. He held up his hands, palms outwards, and walked towards the officers that anchored the battle line against the corner of the apartment block. "Please, please, let me through," he appealed to a woman cop who appeared to be in her late thirties. Maybe she was a mother. Maybe she would take pity on him.

She pulled her right shoulder back, revealing a path through the line to Nick. He stepped forward desperately, only to be slammed in the stomach by her nightstick as she brought her shoulder back forward with all her weight.

Stunned, Nick staggered several steps back towards the six rioters who had been following him. He looked up pleadingly at the cop.

"These rioters are my brothers and sisters," she said, indicating the crowd behind Nick with her nightstick. There were murmurs of agreement from the police around her and she turned her head left and right as if addressing them. "Why are we fighting them? We should be *joining* them to take back what's ours from thieving Aeons!"

Just then, Nick heard breaking glass above him and looked up to see a large barrel being thrown out of the second story corner window of the apartment block, right at the police line. A greenish liquid was spilling out of the barrel's open top as it fell.

When the barrel hit the pavement right in front of the police officer who had just struck Nick, the green liquid splashed upwards and outwards. The police whom it touched screamed in agony and recoiled away. Nick saw the woman who had hit him pulling her riot helmet off as she ran forward blindly, only to have her agony cut short by one of the six rioters behind him, who caved in her exposed skull with a steel bar.

286

"The line is breaking!" he heard rioters calling. "Let's get 'em!"

"Up, men! Up and hold the line!" bellowed an unarmored white-shirted officer who was trying to reform the ranks of panicking officers.

As Nick staggered to his feet, he heard Laura's voice again: "*Run!*"

"Rifles fore! Live ammo!"

He looked behind him and saw dozens of rioters charging his position. Just a few steps ahead of them, Nick sprinted through the hole in the line that had been formed by the barrel. As he passed over the liquid, his eyes and lungs burned from the fumes it was giving off.

As soon as he was inside the line, he turned right towards the gate to the park but recoiled as two dozen mounted police galloped out of it and wheeled around in the open center of the police position. With their shining black helmets and riot shields, the horsemen looked like knights from an age past.

Nick heard the staccato sounds of gunfire. One of the horses neighed desperately and fell down hard, taking its rider with it.

"Form on me!" cried one of the mounted police, rearing his whinnying horse and pointing his baton at the hole in the police lines that Nick had just passed through. "Charge! Charge!"

The horses whinnied as their riders spurred them towards Nick. He felt the ground vibrate as the first beast came right at him. Its rider leaned over and aimed a stroke of his truncheon at Nick's

287

head. Nick felt his body moving without any conscious command from him.

He rolled forward on his shoulder under the blow.

After completing his maneuver he was in a crouching position with another two horsemen bearing down on him, one on either side. He knew little about horses yet somehow he knew exactly where the horse hooves would strike the pavement. He pushed off with his right hand and rolled to his left. A heavy metal-shod hoof impacted the ground between his thighs. He kept rolling. Another hoof came down just to left of his head, so close that his skin was pricked by little pieces of pavement kicked up by the impact. He looked up and saw the massive bulk of the horse passing above him. And then horse and rider were beyond him.

He stole a glance towards the entrance to the transverse and realized he was in the path of another horse, which was going to stamp right on him. He twisted his thighs around furiously, spinning himself up and to the left side of the horse just in time avoid being trodden upon and in a position where the right-handed rider couldn't strike at him.

Now he stood right before the leader of the mounted police, who reared his horse up in front of Nick. He felt the heat of the beast's breath on his face, heard the high pitch of its whinny, and saw its fore hooves swinging down towards his head.

He dove forward under the horse and landed on hands and knees. The rider ordered his mount back down, aiming to crush Nick's skull with its weight. Nick pushed off the pavement hard with

288

his palms and toes, driving himself directly between the hind legs of the horse before it could come down on top of him.

He scrambled to his feet and risked a look around. The cavalry he had just escaped were fully engaged in melee combat with the rioters, and were not in position to turn around and pursue him. But that was little comfort. The police line had broken in three places, and rioters who poured through the holes were turning to attack the remaining police from the flanks and rear. He saw officers turning to run then being tackled by rioters. He watched the white shirted commander running to aid his men, and immediately being impaled in the neck with a shovel. He realized that he only had a few seconds to escape.

Nick turned towards the gate to the 86th Street Transverse. As he pitched forward to sprint, a hurled piece of rock or cement caught him in the back of his leg several inches above his knee. Luckily, most of its momentum was spent before it reached him, but it still caused the muscles in his leg to spasm.

He staggered forward into the sunken transverse road, out of the fading sunlight and into the gloomy darkness. He was grateful that his MindWave had taken over his reflexes during the cavalry charge. Without it, he surely would be dead.

When Nick finally made it through the park and to his parent's residence, he found that they had departed. No doubt some of the message he had ignored while hunting in the Argonne had been from them, urging him to seek safety, telling him where they were going. He pushed the thought out of his mind and lowered his aching body onto the mattress in his old room. He needed to call them and let them know he was ok. He needed to call Laura.

Most of all, he wanted to call Sarah. He'd had no interest in talking to her before the riot. But the experience of nearly dying had made him realize how much he needed her.

He plugged his MindWave in and was relieved to find his parents' broadband access still worked. Then he tried to call Sarah but couldn't get a connection.

Then his MindWave alerted him to some urgent news.

The New York Bureau of Public Health had already identified scores of victims of the violent riots. Overwhelmed by the number of wounded and dead, instead of quietly contacting next of kin, they were publicly releasing names and photos of the dead.

There, on the list of names that meant nothing to him, was one that he couldn't bear to see. The photo accompanying it showed a face that was so severely burned it was barely recognizable as human. But Nick recognized it anyway.

Sarah Trenton.

Chapter 18

It had been a shock to see the riots emerge so quickly and violently the previous week. Laura had believed she had the anti-Aeon protest movement well in hand. But the rabble had forgotten their place, and badly overstepped permissible bounds. It was one thing to scream angry slogans, another to take up arms. Nick had been attacked and threatened. He had fled like a dog with its tail between its legs. All in the face of natural men far his inferior.

It was a humiliation. It could never happen again. Laura would make sure that next time, the Aeons were prepared.

Nevertheless, something good may have come of the debacle. Nick's nat girlfriend, Sarah Trenton, was dead. A victim of the riots, burned so badly a DNA test was required to identify her, buried in a common grave with a hundred other victims of the New York Energy Riots.

Nick had reacted to the news by disconnecting from the ether. He was distraught. It was Laura's role to reassure him.

Since she had been a young girl, Laura knew she had a great destiny to fulfill. After she'd received the MindWave, she'd realized the implant was the instrument that would allow her to achieve that destiny, and that all other Aeons would follow her ascent.

And the other Aeons had slowly accepted her beliefs. Some were impressionable like Abril, and accepted the truth without prodding. Others like Kobus were more argumentative and prone to skepticism. Regardless, she had convinced them all to accept their elevated place in the universe by means of promises of glory, tastes of pleasure, or threats and bullying.

All except for Nick. He was the only one she'd been unable to fully convert. It was curious, because at first glance, she'd thought Nick's personality was weak. By now, she had invested more time in him than in any Aeon, and yet his relationship with Sarah was egregious evidence that he persisted in holding onto the misguided values he'd learned before becoming an Aeon.

While Nick was sometimes maddening, his independence also made him intriguing. It wasn't so much that he openly contradicted her; that only happened occasionally. More often he simply kept his own counsel. Laura knew that one day, she would be able to bring him fully over to her. It was part of her destiny.

Perhaps today would be that day. Possibly the trauma of losing his nat girlfriend would finally show Nick the foolishness of sympathizing with an inferior race.

And so Laura pulled herself out of the ether and ordered her driver to bring her from her rented residence in the upper floors of the Empire State Building to Nick's parents' flat on Fifth Avenue. She would be by Nick's side during this moment of pain. She would teach him to understand it was not a tragedy, but an escape, an event that would allow him to reach his full potential.

Her physical body was already clean and made up; she had taught her MindWave to take her through the ritual of combing her hair and applying cosmetics on Autopilot. To match her pale complexion, she donned a flowing, yet flattering, white dress, not unlike some of the ones she wore in the ether. She complemented the dress with fat pearl earrings and a matching necklace.

Her limo slowed as it steered around the debris still clogging some of the streets. During the twenty-minute car ride, she fidgeted nervously with the small electronic device she clutched in her fingers. She was uncomfortable being disconnected from her normal habitat of the ether. Discontent with being *limited*. Limited by her own senses, to the news broadcast on the radio, to the speed of the car. Why did it take twenty minutes to reach Nick when she should be able to reach him with a thought?

Steel-reinforced security gates were being fitted to the Lal family's building as she arrived. She strode past the workmen, through the threshold and directly to the elevator without even looking down at the squat doorman.

When Laura arrived at Nick's penthouse, and was taken through the piles of shattered glass and broken furniture to his room by the maid, she found him disconsolate, unshaven, wearing a long terrycloth robe at the desk she remembered him recreating in the ether. He did not rise to greet her.

She paused in the doorway, cursing herself for her awkwardness, for not remembering how to interact in the physical world. She would need to relearn these social skills if she was to fulfill her destined role.

Finally she stepped into the room and stood over Nick, clumsily putting an arm across his shoulders. She soothed him. "Nick, don't despair. You will get through this. *We* will get through this together."

As Nick continued to sob, Laura looked down upon him and instead of pity and compassion, she felt anger and contempt.

Anger at him for being so pathetic, for being enthralled by a woman so inferior to him, so beneath Laura herself. Contempt for his sadness at the passing of a nat's insignificant life.

After these thoughts had settled in Laura's mind, Nick finally looked up from his despair. She saw the bandage covering the ragged cut across his forehead and realized this symbol of his vulnerability just made her more incensed.

Nick said "Thank you for coming, Laura. The worst part of it is that the last words I spoke to her were cruel. I rejected her, I told her I couldn't trust her."

Laura twisted her lips into a closed mouth smile and said, "Then you finally told her the truth." Her forearm still lingered on his shoulders, her fingers working awkwardly at the base of his skull.

Nick recoiled away from Laura's arm, his eyebrows knitting in outrage. "Why is that the truth? Why *must* that be the truth?"

"Because you deserve better. Because *we* deserve better. Sarah couldn't even decide if she loved you. Soon you will realize it is ridiculous to spend your days crying about a single nat who couldn't see that by your very nature you deserved her devotion. Her *worship*."

"Wor— worship?" Nick struggled to work his mouth around the word. He stood, indignant, forcing Laura to step back. She saw now that the cut of his robe emphasized his tall, athletic build.

Just then the maid knocked and entered with a tray of coffee. She discreetly ignored the uncomfortable scene in the room and set the tray down on Nick's desk. Laura was struck by the maid's deferential manner, as if the maid understood Nick's greatness better than Nick himself did.

"Mr. Lal, there is a man here who says he has come with a delivery from..." evidently the maid's training in discretion was outmatched by the news she was delivering, and she swallowed nervously before continuing in a meek voice. "... from Sarah Trenton."

Nick's face went blank and he reached for a bone china cup and the matching coffee pot, as if occupying himself with such a normal routine would help his mind cope with the overwhelming situation.

Laura filled the silence by turning to the maid imperiously and saying, "Send him away. Now's not a good time for Nick, and clearly whatever Sarah sent doesn't matter—"

"No!" Laura turned in surprise at being cut off. Nick looked almost embarrassed by the loudness of his voice, and he continued in a soft tone, looking down at the coffee cup in his hand. "Let him in. Thank you, Flora." He ignored the irate look Laura shot in his direction.

A moment later, a middle-aged man of average height in an ill-fitting suit was escorted into the room by the maid, who introduced him as a Mr. Ian Zuckerman and then retreated to stand just behind his left shoulder. Laura marveled at how the athletic builds and comely features of herself and Nick contrasted with the squat and unattractive natural humans who faced them.

She turned up her nose and made a long, derisive sigh. She was wasting too much time dealing with nats today.

Nick spoke in a weary voice. "Mr. Zuckerman, please, what delivery do you have?"

Zuckerman looked around the room uneasily and responded in an earthy Brooklyn accent, "This is a day or two late. I had a hell of a time finding you. You are Mr. Nick Lal, right?"

Laura stared at the nat, instinctively chafing that he did not know Nick's name. "Of course he's Vinicius Lal. This is his home."

Zuckerman didn't pay her any mind. He reached into his suit jacket and pulled a black velvet pouch out of an inner pocket. "Your maid tells me Sarah passed away recently. Please accept my condolences." He thrust the black pouch in Nick's direction.

Nick's face drained of color and he backed away towards a corner of the den, his hand shaking so violently that his coffee cup clattered in its saucer.

Laura stepped in front of him protectively. "What kind of bauble could someone like Sarah Trenton ever give Vinicius Lal?"

Zuckerman's eyes narrowed and he looked at Laura with an expression of uncomprehending contempt. It was not worth Laura's time to correct his uncouth manner. She deflected his stare with a mockingly inquisitive smile.

Zuckerman shrugged silently and emptied the contents of the pouch into the thick fingers of his right hand.

Even Laura couldn't help watching Zuckerman's hand as he deliberately reached out towards the desk, and set the gift down with a firm clinking noise. He pulled his hand away to reveal the item to the room.

It was a simple, well-worn silver cross, hung on a long silver chain.

Laura winced as the sound of Nick's coffee cup shattering on the cold, marble floor echoed down the empty hallways of his apartment.

Sarah thought back to what had transpired after her fight with Nick. By the time her plane had landed and she was in the white minivan heading back to the ranch, she had been horrified to hear radio reports of chaotic rioting breaking out in New York and other major American cities, but she'd been unable to do anything about it while in transit.

As soon as she'd returned to the ranch, she'd checked the news with her TacWave, only to learn that the situation had deteriorated even further. The riots were centered near Nick's apartment, and the rioters were targeting the wealthy – especially MindWave users. Her only comfort was the knowledge that Nick had at his disposal the means to foresee the riots and escape any danger. No doubt, he had fled New York long before the riots escalated.

"What's going on?" she had demanded as she burst into Willy's office. She saw that Colonel Jaeger was seated in the visitor's chair facing Willy's desk, as if the two were engaged in conversation.

"Sarah, New York is just the tip of the iceberg. The country is close to tearing itself apart," replied Willy grimly, looking up from Jaeger. "Conditions are just getting too bad. It's a harsh winter and no one can afford heating. People are freezing and they know soon they'll be starving. They're taking out their anger wherever they can."

"I know people can't afford heating, but how can we have starvation? I thought we make all the food we need practically for free? That's what Nick's parents' company does."

Jaeger scowled and glanced at Willy at the mention of Nick's name. He turned back to Sarah and explained impatiently, "Langar can make all the food we need in their laboratories. But with energy prices rising so high, we can't ship it around the country at an affordable price."

"Can't the government do anything, sir?"

Jaeger continued, "Until some new genius does for energy what the Lals did for food, energy costs money. And the government is running out of money."

"But…"

"But what?"

Sarah was taken aback, unsure of what to say in the face of Jaeger's sudden scorn.

Willy broke in, "Sarah, it's a difficult time for everyone. It's not your fault."

"Why are people burning down the cities? That won't create food. Why don't they go work on farms instead?" she protested, not really expecting an answer but needing to vent her frustration.

Jaeger rubbed his hands together and rejoined the conversation in his characteristic languid condescending tone. "They're burning things because that's what people do when they're hungry. You want to build a farm? First you need land. Land isn't cheap, and neither is fertilizer. And if you manage to get both, you'll have a crop in six months if you're lucky. What are you going to eat until then?"

Sarah stared at him dumbly as she processed what he was saying. She knew all of these things in the abstract; she'd been watching this crisis slowly unfold for most of her life. She had gotten used to assuming they would always come to a head at some time in the future. Now it seemed that the future had suddenly arrived, and she was caught off guard, barely able to make sense of things.

Jaeger continued, "And they're burning the prosperous neighborhoods because the wealthy still have food and gas, and they aren't sharing. And perhaps the smarter rioters understand that part of the reason energy prices are so high is because of fuel hoarding and speculation by some of those rich."

Sarah instinctively rolled her shoulders to loosen them up. It was time for her to get over her shock and go into action. "What are we going to do?"

Jaeger looked away angrily as Willy stood and walked around his desk and put a sympathetic arm on her shoulder. "For now, nothing."

She looked into his eyes, desperate for him to listen. *Nick could help. He wanted to help.* How could she explain? "But... but I know some of those rich people. Maybe I can convince them to help. They're good people, really. They know what's happening is wrong, we just have to show them how to cooperate."

"Maybe they are good, and maybe you could convince them," said Willy. He grimaced. "But you can't appeal to Nick now."

"What! Why?" protested Sarah, pulling away from the hand he still held on her shoulder. "Just now, when maybe I can do some good? Nick runs an energy company!"

Willy renewed his firm grip on her shoulder. "The most violent rioting is in his neighborhood. We haven't seen him leave his building, but we did see armed rioters enter it, right around the time his MindWave seems to have been shut off. He could be… in serious trouble."

Nick caught in the riots? How could he have let that happen? The room spun around and she leaned into Willy's arm for support. "We can't let him get hurt. We've got to do something!" blurted Sarah.

Jaeger cleared his throat and Willy took his arm off Sarah's shoulder and walked back around to his desk. Jaeger spoke: "We're not going to do anything, Lieutenant."

Sarah turned to Willy. She felt her voice trembling as she spoke. "Willy, when I first came to the ranch, you promised me I wouldn't have to do any evil. But standing by and doing nothing at a time like this is evil, too. Can't we—"

Jaeger cut her off. "Sarah, a long time ago I graduated from West Point. I spent a foolish amount of money on a shiny golden class ring that displayed my class motto: *Do No Evil.*"

He splayed out his fingers and held out his hands for Sarah to see.

"You're not wearing a ring, sir."

"I took that ring off years ago. Do you know why?"

Sarah shook her head, barely understanding what Jaeger was talking about.

"Because I realized that motto was a lie. To defend a country, sometimes you do have to do evil."

Sarah looked to Willy but he averted his gaze. Jaeger looked her up and down with cold grey eyes. "You've become quite close to Nick, Lieutenant," he said.

"Is that a problem, sir?" She responded in a tone she knew was a bit too sharp. "My intimacy with him gives me more influence over him. Isn't that the purpose of my assignment?"

"Your assignment was to make him have feelings for you, not to develop feelings for him. You've spent weeks going on dates yet you have no valuable intelligence findings to show for it. And now your feelings for Nick are clouding your judgment. That argument you had with him in the middle of the street was ill considered. And wanting to make up for it by charging in to save him from a crisis of his own making is equally misguided."

He paused, apparently happy to let Sarah stammer. She had been afraid of accusations that her judgment was impaired by feelings for Nick. She had imagined ways to defend herself from them, but now, in the moment, she couldn't think of the right words to say in her defense.

Jaeger continued, "Your inability to keep your feelings in check is a cause for concern but it's not the main reason why I'm pulling you off your assignment."

Off her assignment? Sarah blinked hard. Would she never see Nick again? "Why, then, sir?" she managed to choke out.

"Because you've made enemies, and you're too expensive to replace," Jaeger explained in a resigned tone.

"Enemies? What do you mean?"

The Colonel glanced towards Willy, who explained the situation. "Laura Mayer. As you know, she's a close business associate of Nick. And she wants to be even closer to Nick than she is now. You've gotten in her way and she's been taking steps against you."

"I can handle myself," Sarah said, unconsciously putting her hands on her hips and leaning forward slightly.

"You don't know what you're up against. Michael's been raising alarms about this for weeks. You've become an obsession for Laura. Your relationship with Nick is not only making her jealous. It also threatens the whole belief system she's created for herself and tried to push on the other Aeons. She wants to believe she, Nick, and the other Aeons are intrinsically superior to naturals. Yet Nick's devotion to a natural girlfriend ruins that illusion. She's been looking for an excuse to get you out of the picture.

"We gave you layers of cover stories but Laura is resourceful. She'll soon find the cracks. You know her psychological profile. She's paranoid enough to spend hundreds of hours turning over every detail of your identity. Yet she views you as just another nat, not a form of life that's equal to Aeons like her. She'll have no compunctions about harming you if that's what it takes to get you out of Nick's life. And she's a dangerous woman, who uses whatever means are necessary to achieve her aims – bribery, sex, blackmail, and violence."

Sarah clenched her fists in frustration. Damn Michael, he'd probably been so jealous that he'd exaggerated the threat from Laura

303

to speed the end of her assignment with Nick. That was enraging and unprofessional, but at least it was understandable on some level. It made more sense than what Willy and Jaeger were saying.

Willy softened his tone. "Let's assume all she does is blow your cover with Nick. Once your cover is blown, your mission will have to end anyway, and worse yet, Nick will think you've betrayed him. And as you've pointed out, feelings of betrayal can only have negative consequences. It's better to bow out now."

"Damn it, Willy, just give me a chance to fix all of this!" Sarah stepped forward towards Willy. "He's close to coming over to our side."

"Back down right now, Sarah." Jaeger spoke slowly and calmly, yet his voice still carried a layer of understated menace. Even through her anger and desperation, Sarah realized that arguing with Jaeger was just going to make her situation more difficult. She backed out of the room without another word.

She walked slowly down the hallway towards her quarters, hating herself every step of the way. She wasn't so much afraid of Jaeger as she was ashamed and confused at herself. If she loved Nick, how could she have let Jaeger and Willy bully her into doing nothing to save him from the riot? If she were a super spy, why was it that she could think of no way to assist Nick without the approval of Jaeger? And had her protests really just been waved off like a child's tantrum?

She was not as strong as she'd led herself to believe. Nor was her status within Willy's team as high as she'd thought. She needed time to understand what was happening. Her hand reached up to her chest to finger her silver cross necklace for solace, but of course, she'd sent the cross to Nick as a sign of her feelings.

Laura sat up in her seat. Something was wrong.

She was testing a memory preservation program she'd developed to allow her to review any Aeon's memories, as recorded by his or her MindWave. She'd gotten the idea during the New York Energy Riots; had Nick been seriously injured or killed, she might never have known who his attacker was. She certainly wasn't willing to rely on the inept investigations of a nat detective.

She had better investigative skills than any nat. By accessing memories from the MindWave itself, she would be able to review everything Nick had experienced in his last moments to identify his attackers.

The idea was simple in principle. But she was not sure if it would work in practice. Would the memories of someone under duress be preserved clearly enough by the MindWave to be usable? Would she be able to access those memories directly without the consent of an incapacitated owner?

When she had travelled to Nick's house upon hearing the news of Sarah's death, and put her arm around Nick's shoulder, she had surreptitiously accessed his MindWave through one of the jacks in the base of his skull. She had downloaded part memories from his MindWave to a memory crystal for analysis. She hadn't been able to plug her device in to his MindWave. That would have alerted him to what she was doing. So she had just put a passive antenna up against one of the ports. That limited what she'd been able to download to a few days, and to visual records only.

Now, as she returned from New York to Los Angeles in her private jet, she had inserted the crystal into her own MindWave and was reviewing those memories. She had saved this task for the flight, because it gave her something to do with her MindWave during a long, unnerving period when she had minimal access to the ether.

Her MindWave pieced together Nick's memories into a three dimensional world that she could walk through, rolling time forward or backward as she wished. There were limitations on her movements, though. If Nick never opened a door or looked in a certain direction, then neither could she. If he only saw one side of an object, that was all she could see of it, too.

She was soon disappointed to learn that once Nick had wrapped his shirt around his head, his MindWave had quickly begun to overheat and had automatically shut down, so there was no record of the riot in the streets beyond what she'd already downloaded from New York's closed circuit video camera systems. The only useful information she could gather from Nick's memories of the riots was from the minutes before Nick had gone outside. She saw the images of the three hoodlums who had broken into his apartment building and gone into the elevator. They clearly had the intent of attacking whomever they met in the building. Had Nick not wisely made the last minute decision to get off the elevator in the upper lobby instead of the lower lobby, they would have killed him.

Nick had only looked at them for a moment before ducking down into his hiding place. Still, what he had recorded was enough. MindWaves were not just neural implants. They also included augmented senses. Laura and Nick could hear and smell more acutely than any nat. More relevant to the task at hand, they also had superhuman vision thanks to their artificial retinas and optical nerves.

Laura froze the memory and walked down the stairs of the lobby and circled around the men. Their faces and the fronts of their bodies were rendered in exquisite detail, while their backs faded into a hazy nothingness. Nick had not seen them from behind and therefore neither could she.

Laura saw one man with an open hand and knelt to examine his fingertips. Yes. The MindWave had recorded his fingerprints in enough detail to identify him. For the other two, facial recognition would have to do.

With the information she had now it would be easy enough to find them in one government database or another when she had access to the ether again. She would like to test some of her new weapons systems on these brigands, but unfortunately she didn't have time for such a diversion. She would have to task one of the mercenary teams she utilized to guard Sparkwise projects with punishing them.

This piece of revenge taken care of, her review of the riots was over. She deemed it a partial success. She paused. She had captured three days' worth of Nick's memories. She leaned back in her comfortable leather and looked out the window at the distant ocean below. It was tempting, very tempting, to see what else Nick had done in that time. At least to see what he had done with the nat girlfriend whose death had sent him into a days' long depression.

Not that she was fixated on Sarah. But really, what had been so enthralling about this miserable little human girl? The databases that Laura had broken into showed nothing remarkable. A young nat woman, good looking by nat standards. She was wealthy, and her communication, financial, and travel metadata suggested a luxurious lifestyle. Yet there was nothing that compared to an Aeon.

Laura reflected that she had never met the woman. Maybe in person she had some special kind of cunning, some affected charm she had used to ensnare Nick.

Assuming Nick had met Sarah that day he'd skipped part of Abril's Christmas orgy, she could access Nick's memories of their encounter and see for herself. Maybe she would learn something about Sarah that would help her lead Nick to accept the truths he had so far denied.

She scanned through Nick's memories searching for the right moment. *There it was!* A spat, in the street outside Nick's apartment. It made sense. Laura recalled Nick regretting that the last words he'd said to Sarah had been cruel.

She played through the scene, to see just what the argument had been about. She only had visual memories, so she couldn't hear words. But her MindWave could read Sarah's lips.

It seemed Sarah was angry that Nick had made her wait. She should have been grateful that an Aeon was willing to spend any time with her at all.

Laura kept playing the scene forward.

Then something went awry.

There was a strange interference pattern in the recorded memory. Some other electromagnetic source had interfered with Nick's MindWave, leading to slight distortions in the video recording of the memory. It was barely noticeable except to an intent observer with superhuman abilities to detect miniscule anomalies that lasted only one or two milliseconds. An observer like Laura.

Laura quickly worked out that Nick's MindWave had picked up a regular occurring electromagnetic signal. It would come for a few milliseconds then disappear for about ten milliseconds before returning. The traces of the signal were too faint to decode, but clearly it was high density and high power – otherwise it could not have disturbed the circuitry in Nick's MindWave.

Someone in close proximity to Nick had been using an extremely sophisticated computer device in short bursts.

Laura studied Sarah's image as she played through Nick's memory in slow motion. She clearly wasn't an Aeon. The weather had been cold and windy that day, and Sarah had been wearing a long coat. Had she hidden a computer in her coat? *But why?* Was she trying to gain information to blackmail Nick and his family? Or maybe she was trying to learn information about Sparkwise Energy or Langar Foods?

She pursed her lips in concentration as she slowly rolled the memory forward, carefully watching every one of Sarah's actions closely.

In the memory, Sarah asked Nick a pointed question about something he had forgotten, and Nick stopped in his tracks, allowing Sarah to walk ahead of him.

Laura searched for any signs of the device that was creating the disruptive signal. She couldn't help staring at the base of Sarah's skull, where a MindWave would have been. This was a foolish place to start, as Sarah didn't have the giveaway cooling vents of a MindWave user. However, looking at that spot was instinctive.

As the images of Nick's memory played forward, a sudden breeze lifted Sarah's hair. Simultaneously, Sarah lowered her head towards her body, exposing the top of her neck over the collar of her jacket. Laura got a clear view of the base of Sarah's skull. Of course, the only metal visible was a glinting necklace chain.

Wait. A tiny glimmer of reflected sunlight caught her eye. A reflection where there ought not to have been one, not quite right for a stray strand of hair.

She zoomed in on the high definition image, isolating the glint.

It was a single fiber optic cable. Laura saw that the cable was connected from the chain on the necklace and went up to where she saw a slight irregularity in the base of Sarah's scalp. The fiber appeared to slide underneath Sarah's skin into her skull.

A hidden MindWave!

Laura zoomed in on a partial image of Sarah's palm. She could see the fingertip clearly... and yet... it was perfectly smooth. Sarah had no fingerprints. They must have been surgically removed.

Only the Federal government would have the technology and funding to create an imitation MindWave and train a team of spies with no fingerprints. She'd known federal agents were trying to trace her activities in the ether but she hadn't realized how sophisticated their surveillance program was.

She would have to work harder and bring her plans forward and keep one step ahead of her pursuers. Her new weapon system prototypes were mostly ready. Her most critical job would be cultivating the proper mindset in her fellow Aeons. They needed to be ready to fight for her cause.

Laura felt a renewed wave of frustration with Nick. She didn't believe he had willingly betrayed the Aeons. But he had foolishly created this security risk. She would use his distress at his lover's apparent death to strengthen his commitment to the Aeon cause. If need be, she would isolate him even further to maximize her influence over him. There was no need to tell him of Sarah's true identity yet. She would hold that information in reserve.

Chapter 19

Reverend Tracy Cruz tried not to cry in front of the solemn men and women who'd called her on the *holophone*. "I don't think I can bear this burden alone."

"You have already inspired the nation, and raised a call for justice that no one else dared voice. You *must* lead the people," protested Reverend Steven Bacon, minister of the large Southwestern Protestant Alliance and unofficial spokesman for the group of preachers that had appealed to Cruz to allow them to merge their churches into hers.

"Yes, when I burned that check from Sparkwise Energy, it may have earned me millions of admirers. But it also led to bloody riots in which hundreds of innocents died." Her eyes glided from Ricardo's face to her office window, which overlooked a small, decrepit playground where several children from her congregation were kicking a soccer ball. "Almost two dozen children."

"Innocents who will be welcomed into God's embrace. We cannot fight injustice without shedding blood," admonished Bacon.

"What injustice have I fought? Did those riots harm the Aeons? Did they right any wrongs?" retorted Cruz in exasperation. "I have blood on my hands and I don't know what it's accomplished."

Bacon held up a hand apologetically. "Forgive me if my words sounded unduly callous. I sought only to comfort you. Each child's death is a tragedy. There is no way I can make them otherwise. God's will is beyond our ability to understand."

Platitudes and metaphors. Cruz shook her head and Ricardo squeezed her hand.

Cruz struggled to voice her feelings to the other ministers. "I am not a reverend by training. I began preaching at the National Unity Church to serve God and to help my small community. I never thought He would ask as great a task of me as you say He has. I still don't. I'm not prepared to lead millions of followers. Not to see people die in my name."

Bacon was silent. But now Ricardo leaned his head around so that he was in Cruz's field of vision. "Have you studied the *Book of Exodus,* hon?"

"Of course, Ricardo," she responded sternly.

"As Moses led the Israelites to the Promised Land, they were confronted by the vast army of the Amalekites at Rephidim," recited Ricardo.

Cruz remained silent. She knew the story, but was unsure where Ricardo was going with it.

Ricardo continued, "The Lord only supported the Israelite army when Moses held his hands aloft as a sign of faith. Yet even the prophet Moses could not bear the weight of the task the Lord had given him. Not alone. His strength faltered and he could no longer hold his hands aloft, and many Isrealites fell to the Amalekites because of his frailty."

Cruz nodded as she recalled the verses. "Moses' companions, Aaron and Hur, supported his hands for him, so that the Israelites would finally prevail."

Ricardo returned her nod, and then turned to look at the preachers in the *holovision* before turning back and placing his hands firmly on her shoulders. "Yes. Let us be your Aaron and your Hur, Reverend."

"Nick," his mother cooed, "Try the *feijoada*. I made it myself. It's delicious, almost as good as something you could dream up in that imaginary world of yours." She sat diagonally to Nick's left, at the head of the family's rectangular cherry wood table, which could have comfortably seated eight guests. Nick's father sat directly across from his mother. A piece by Beethoven played softly in the background.

Nick, sitting in his parents' penthouse duplex on Manhattan's 5th Avenue, picked up his fork and tried to hide his lack of appetite as he shared his farewell dinner. He was moving back into his refurbished flat again the next morning.

He took a big spoonful of the stew, made from ingredients that cost a workingman's monthly salary. It tasted duller than a piece of stale bread in the ether. Still, he faked a smile to make his mother happy.

"And are you really sure you want to move back to your own apartment after what happened? Family should stay together." his mother prompted, raising this point for what seemed like the hundredth time.

Nick's time living at home again had allowed him to partly mend his frayed relationship with his parents, for which he was grateful. But he longed for the freedom of living in his own residence. "I'm old enough to take care of myself now."

His father nodded. "Nick, it's true. You're old enough to make your own decisions. You're lucky that most of the government investigations into your company have stalled. And I know you needed some time to recover after those riots. But it's about time you started putting the amazing talents your mother and I have given you to some good use. Forget energy trading. You can make a real difference to the world.

Nick felt his face reddening. He wasn't about to sit quietly while his father gave him a lecture. Especially when he was working so hard to make his father proud. "Dad, don't worry, I'm trying to make Sparkwise a better—"

His father just continued speaking. "Remember your poor girlfriend, Sarah? She was idealistic. I'm sure Sarah would have wanted—"

"Don't bring Sarah into this again! She's dead. Just let it be!" cried Nick, bringing his hands up to either side of his head to block

315

out the sound of his father's voice. When he had received Sarah's necklace, he had finally known that she loved him. But now she was gone, taken from him forever by the rioters.

The best way he could honor Sarah's memory was to find evidence that Laura Mayer was using Sparkwise to illegally manipulate energy prices. But that would take time, and his father wanted him to quit Sparkwise right away. He feared that if he tried to explain his plan, his father would interpret it as a pretext to stay involved with the firm.

"Nick," his mother said, trying to smooth over his father's words. "It's not your fault that you weren't there when—on the night of the energy riots started by that dreadful preacher. How could you have known?" She reached out with her hand, trying to place it on Nick's shoulder.

Nick shook her off. "I am supposed to be *omniscient!*" he screamed, gesturing at the metallic cooling vents of his MindWave.

Sarah had struggled for days to maintain her normal upbeat attitude. Nick had escaped the riot, she knew, but thanks to Jaeger's manipulation of morgue records, Nick believed she was dead. Sarah felt sorry for him, alone in the ether again, with only the manipulative Laura to turn to for consolation.

Willy had let her take a few days of rest and recreation before starting a new assignment. There was not much to do with the spare time. She was not allowed to freely use her TacWave to explore the networks outside of the ranch, much less physically leave the compound. The empty hours stretched like canyons, filled with deep pools of despair and exhilarating gushes of fantasy.

Despite her efforts to move on, she could not forget Nick, and her heart ached for just one last chance to visit with him. She had gone through the encounter in her imagination a thousand times, playing out everything she would say, and every one of Nick's responses.

She was in deep emotional torment, and yet she needed to hide it from everyone around her. Michael had come by her room a few times to see how she was doing, and she'd pretended to be sick. She hadn't even opened the door to him. She knew that was cruel, but she couldn't bear to face him right now.

There would be time to worry about his feelings later. Right now she had to focus on her own. She knew her fixation on Nick called into question the proficiency she was proud of achieving in every other aspect of her profession. She didn't want Jaeger or Willy to know how much she suffered from her forced "breakup" with her opponent.

To get her mind off of Nick, she settled on the romance novels she'd found in the small library months ago. She'd flipped through them several times before, but never given them a proper read. The trite stories of love and betrayal had been a catharsis for her own pent up emotions, but now, after reading four of them in as many days, she was restless, pacing around her quarters in her pajamas, unsure of what to do.

The intercom in her quarters buzzed to life with Willy's voice. "Sarah, report to the ready room in ten minutes."

"Yes, sir," she said, relieved to finally have something resembling an official duty. She enthusiastically reached for a clean uniform.

When she reached the small briefing theater a few minutes later, Willy was waiting by the podium. She was relieved to see that Michael was not present. She wasn't ready to see both him and Willy at the same time yet.

Sarah sat in the front row and looked up expectantly.

He looked at her with concern. "Sarah, the country's in a lot of trouble, and the Aeons are right in the middle of the mess. There's a lot going on, a lot of places where you can be helpful. First, I need to know that you're fit for duty. Is your head screwed on straight?"

"Yes, of course," she replied, her words sounding too sharp in her ears. "How can I be helpful?"

Willy gave her a slow, thoughtful once-over before responding. "Michael's been looking into the old Hurricane Reactor disaster."

"Why? That was two years ago and has nothing to do with the Aeons."

"Jaeger always thought Laura was responsible for it. And now Michael's found evidence to support that claim."

"So what do you need me for? Send in Greg's Demons to arrest her." Sarah was referring to Greg Silverstein, who had been made commander of the orphans who had washed out of the competition. They had been through brutal training to become the tactical team meant to back up the intelligence work conducted by Sarah and Michael. Greg had chosen the moniker "Demons" for his team.

Willy waved away Sarah's suggestion. "You and Michael can operate without warrants or other official permissions because no one knows what happens in the ether. But we can't send in commandoes with guns blazing without a court to back us up. What Michael's found is circumstantial evidence; it won't stand up in court. It won't even get us a search warrant."

Sarah paused to consider Willy's words. She hadn't anticipated a problem like this. Even more concerning, she could see where the conversation was heading. She was going to be paired with Michael again. No doubt, he would be wounded by her recent refusals to see her and her obvious feelings for Nick. But she needed to prove that she was a capable member of the team, so she would have to find a way to work with Michael regardless of the emotional complexity that existed between them now.

Willy continued, "Michael's also convinced that Laura's planning more violent acts of terrorism. But we don't know who the targets are. I need you to help Michael stop her."

At that moment, Michael stepped into the room, and looked at her with a blank expression. She could see his hands opening and

319

closing at his side. Sarah decided the best way to deal with the awkwardness was to gloss it over.

She smiled and took a step towards Michael, her hand extended to shake hands. For a fraction of a second, he flinched away, and Sarah stopped in her tracks. But just as she stopped, Michael started the same act, stepping forward and extending his hand. When he realized she'd stopped, he stopped too.

They stood like that, about five feet apart, gazing into each other's eyes, for a long moment. Then Michael twisted his mouth into a contorted smile and said "Welcome back."

Reverend Tracy Cruz looked up at her applauding audience as she neared the close of her sermon. A couple of months ago, she considered herself lucky if thirty people showed up on a Sunday, and felt grateful towards any of those that actually paid attention for the entire service.

Today, her small church was packed. She guessed there were well over one hundred worshippers crammed into every pew and standing in the aisles. There would be more, but for the third week in a row two deputies from the Kerrville Sherriff's department had come to help restrain the crowds outside the church's doors.

And of course, the people physically present were only a fraction of her audience. Last week recordings of her sermon had been streamed to hundreds of thousands of viewers. In a country where fewer and fewer people could afford access to electronic media, that number was huge. This week's number would probably be even higher.

She was flattered by all of the attention her National Unity Church was now receiving. Yet she still worried that she was taking on a role she wasn't meant to fill. In all of the comparisons Reverend Bacon made between her and Moses, everyone seemed to have forgotten that she was no prophet. God did not speak to her. All she'd done was burn a check.

She was determined that no matter what powers Bacon and other followers ascribed to her, she needed to retain her humility. Even if she *were* a prophet, that would just make her a medium for spreading God's Word, no better than any other man or woman.

And being a prophet would not give her the management abilities to guide her rapidly growing church. A few weeks ago she'd been responsible for a congregation of a few dozen souls. Now she had followers across the nation, and dozens of ministers looking to her for inspiration. Yet rather than being an effective leader, she felt she was just struggling to keep up.

She pushed these thoughts away as the audience's applause died down. She put all of her focus into reciting the last lines of her sermon with the right mix of defiance and humility. She struggled to tread the fine line between projecting strength that would give her flock the power to endure a little longer, and sounding so defiant that she encouraged new acts of violence. "Do not allow yourselves to envy the Aeons. Yes, for a time, they will enjoy untold wealth, power, and carnal pleasures.

"Yet their apparent bliss is an illusion, a mirage that threatens to lure us away from the righteous path. We must look upon the Aeons, not with envy, but with scorn. We shall regard their MindWaves not as a source of power but as the mark of the beast.

"Even as we must not heed the words of the Aeons, neither must we lift our hands in anger, nor burn our cities, nor slay our brethren. Either path, idolatry of the Aeons or violent actions against them, will lead us to despair. Until the judgment comes, patience and endurance are our greatest virtues.

"We may be patient, enduring, and humble, yet we will never bow our heads to the Aeons. Instead we will lift our chins in peaceful defiance.

"We will not bow to these false idols! *We will not bow*!"

After her sermon was over and she had finally seen her worshippers and admirers out of the church, Cruz finally retired to her quarters where Ricardo was waiting to give her an embrace. "The ratings are going to be out of the park on this one, honey!" he enthused.

Cruz looked at her watch and sighed. It was already time to begin her management meeting with Reverend Bacon and several other preachers that had pledged themselves to the NUC. It seemed the Lord really had blessed her with a following. Maybe everything was part of His plan, as Doc Lawson had always insisted. But if she was helping complete His plan, He had not told her what the next step in it was. She hoped the other ministers would provide the guidance and wisdom she lacked.

While Ricardo connected her old holophone to all parties, Cruz took a moment to relax by watching the children running around in the playground outside her window. The sight of them helped her unwind, even as it focused her mind on her crusade to save them from a life of servitude to the Aeons.

Ricardo cleared his throat and Cruz turned back to her desk, where the holographic heads of Bacon and the other preachers were waiting for her. "Welcome, friends," she said, trying to hide her exhaustion behind a smile.

"May the Lord continue to give you strength, Reverend," intoned Bacon in greeting.

"And you as well. Our agenda today is to discuss organizational strategy," began Cruz as Ricardo settled down to take meeting minutes. She hated the stilted nature of these discussions, but her fellow ministers reacted better to the formality.

"We are currently united by an emotional—a religious—objection to the direction in which the Aeons are pushing our nation. We have successfully pooled donations and delivered food and fuel to the neediest of our members. But we are all men and women of God. We are not policy makers, nor soldiers, nor managers. Given our limitations, how can we make the NUC most effective in serving the Lord?"

"Reverend, we can overcome the limitations you speak of," interjected Bacon. "The Holy Spirit has inspired people of all talents to our cause. If we marshal them properly, we can create a truly powerful movement."

Cruz tried to moderate her skepticism. The churches that had joined her were from rural communities and small cities. "Of course many of our churches include doctors, lawyers, businessmen and veterans among their members. Still, these are not people with experience in running a nation-wide organization, Reverend Bacon. It will take years before the NUC can internally develop the talent required to lead." She glanced at the playground outside her window. "But we can't wait years."

Ricardo cut in. "We should keep doing what we're doing. Make statements. Raise awareness. Use social media to spread the word far and wide. We're already doing a better job of feeding the hungry than the government. That's a powerful story. Our message of faith and resistance is spreading into the national conversation, and beginning to influence the system."

Bacon wore an expression of disbelief. "Influence the *system*? Do you mean the government? That will never work. The government is *complicit*."

Cruz was startled by Bacon's statement. His words hung in the air for a moment before he continued. "The government is a willing ally of the Aeons, and a Judas to the people. Just as the Aeons are in thrall to Satan, so too is Washington in thrall to the Aeons. Social Media campaigns will influence the government no more than they will influence Lucifer himself."

Ricardo began to retort but Cruz held up a hand to hold him back. "Reverend Bacon, if what you say is true, what do you suggest we do?"

"Reverend Cruz, the ranks of the faithful are expanding rapidly beyond our original churches. There are some very senior—," and here Bacon paused and looked uneasy. "I'm sorry Reverend, but I don't think it's wise to reveal anything about their identities without being sure this phone line is completely secure."

Cruz pressed her lips together tightly. Both the Aeons and the Federal government were masters of penetrating digital communications. It would be foolish to assume the conversation was private from either group.

Bacon gestured as if to brush away his previous comments. "Revered Cruz, this reminds me of an issue I believe should have been at the top of today's agenda. We cannot succeed in the face of the present challenges if you don't accept more support."

Cruz hid a frown. She had already accepted the spiritual support of Ricardo, Reverend Bacon, and the other preachers in her alliance. But at a certain point, she needed to be able to rely upon the strength of her own faith. "Thanks to your support, my arms are raised to the Lord, Reverend Bacon," she declared in her best diplomatic voice.

Bacon smiled. "I am joyous to hear it, yet for once, I am referring to more earthly matters. It is no use trying to hide your exhaustion from me, Reverend. I can see how tired you are, and

Ricardo, too. This is not due to weak faith. You are overworked and overwhelmed. You need better facilities, aides, and expert advisors."

"Unfortunately I don't think there's room for many aides within my humble church," replied Cruz. "And while Moses may have been raised in a palace, he turned his back on it to serve the Lord. I know the NUC must develop its organizational prowess, but it is not my place as a servant of God to surround myself with the trappings of earthly power."

"Your humility is commendable, Reverend Cruz, yet when it impairs your ability to lead it becomes a liability. You need an efficient headquarters. And you need staff. Starting with security staff so we can get a properly encrypted phone and discuss our strategy openly."

"Where am I going to get these people? This is the point I was making before – we don't have these skills yet." No one in Kerrville was up to the task of blocking eavesdropping by the NSA and the Aeons.

"The Lord will provide, Reverend," said Bacon with a sly smile.

Chapter 20

Sarah stretched out her hand and touched the chain link fence of the ranch a moment before Michael did. They were completing a routine training run, but during the last mile they had accelerated faster and faster into an undeclared race until they were in an open sprint towards the wall.

Sarah leaned over and held her knees as she panted to get her breath back. Besides her, Michael sat down in the orange dirt and gulped in air.

Unable to stop herself, Sarah grinned at him. "Slow poke."

"Whatever," he said, laying fully back in the dirt and squinting his eyes in the sunlight. "I let you win."

"You're such a jackass," she complained, kicking a cloud of earth towards him, not sure if she was angry or just playing angry.

Michael extended a leg and hooked a foot around the ankle that was supporting all her weight, yanking her off balance and into the dirt next to him. He guffawed loudly until the dusty air got into his lungs and he started choking.

Sarah pushed herself up by leaning on his shoulder. "OK, can we start talking to each other again?"

"Sure," he said through gritted teeth. "You're the one who started it."

"I'm sorry about that. I shouldn't have locked you out like that. I was… it was a tough time for me."

"Look, this is hard on me, too. I thought we were… you know." He didn't meet her eyes. He was staring across the ranch towards the dormitory where they'd first met. "And then you and Nick Lal… I thought…"

"Let's forget it ever happened." Sarah didn't want to get into a discussion with Michael about whether she really had feelings for Nick. Of course she did. Only it was stupid and pointless because she was never going to meet him again as a friend. She could only observe him from afar, as a spy. It made her feel like a stalker. She wanted to put it behind her, and behind Michael as well.

"All right," he said noncommittally.

"He thinks I'm dead."

"So?"

"So nothing's going to happen. Just forget about it."

"I said all right," he said, dusting himself off and turning towards the ranch.

She realized he was going to just turn away and run back to the ranch without saying another word. Her effort to break the ice had failed, and their relationship would stay bad, maybe even get worse. When would she get another chance to make things right? It might be never. No, she had to do something to end the tension. "Michael?"

"Yeah?" he half turned back, but he was still stepping towards the ranch.

"Michael!"

Now he turned and faced her, a look of impatience on his face.

"Wanna get dinner with me? I know this great place called the ranch mess hall."

He grinned despite the lameness of her joke. "All right. Let's get back and hit the showers."

"Nice move!" Laura called to Kobus. The two had teamed up against Nick and Abril in a two-on-two basketball game. Kobus had just received a high pass from Laura, faked left and, displaying remarkable dexterity for a polar bear, slipped between Nick and Abril to score with a slam dunk on the fifteen foot high basket. The crowd of thousands of artificial fans cheered enthusiastically, while beaming cheerleaders deftly climbed into a human pyramid.

"*Ay Dios mio*, that's the game. Fifteen to twelve, to the combined might of Laur-Bus," groaned Abril. "I'm hungry. Why don't we check out my new restaurant?"

In an instant, the four Aeons were sitting around a table in a luxurious banquet hall, with soft classical sonata playing from speakers hidden in the high ceiling. The music was strangely disorienting to Nick, who associated it with his parents' home.

All of the Aeons present wore fashionable formal attire, except Kobus, who came as a bear wearing a red t-shirt emblazoned with the words, "The gods must be crazy."

"Nice place," mentioned Laura. "I like what you've done with the colors in the wall paneling and the carpet."

"Thanks," said Abril with a smile. "I remembered something like it from a hotel I stayed at in San Juan as a child."

Kobus grabbed a chocolate cookie from a tray in front of him. "It's too bad we can't do this more often. If the networks weren't *stukkend*, we wouldn't all have to stay in the same place to play sports." He was referring to the fact that all of the Aeons present were sharing a suite in the Diamond Vista Hotel on the resort island of Martha's Vineyard, where they had arranged their physical bodies in a circle and interconnected their MindWaves to allow for lag-free interaction.

"Tell me about it," agreed Abril. "My MindWave is fine for stuff I imagine myself, which doesn't require an internet connection. But I need the internet for anything interactive, like business. I can barely get my work done anymore. Much less hang out with you guys like this."

Laura leaned forward over the table. "Some level of network disruption is unavoidable because we're reliant on nats to run our infrastructure, and we all know how unruly and lazy they can be. More alarmingly, there's a lot of nat scum – government agencies, radical students, and followers of the damned National Unity Church – actively trying to hack in and obstruct our network access."

Nick took a long drink from a frosty mug of beer. Sarah had died just several weeks ago, and his emotions were still raw. And he was quickly growing weary of hearing the Aeons complain about how the nats were a scourge. Not after he'd seen the secret files that were nearly stolen by the mysterious invaders who attacked the Sparkwise servers.

It was Laura who was funding the student protests against the Aeons, Laura who'd made large anonymous donations to the NUC, Laura who had supported politicians who vowed to fight the Aeons. She had created the very opposition she used as a means of tightening her control over the other Aeons.

But he had found nothing he could really incriminate her with. It wasn't illegal to fund a protest movement or a church. Maybe her actions would be enough to turn the other Aeons against her, yet he had no proof, just his own memories of documents he'd seen for a few moments. He still needed something more damning before he could go to the government. "Yeah, basically life just sucks, and then you die," he grunted.

"Don't be so sure…" began Laura.

Abril gestured energetically with her hand. "It's so frustrating – we have the greatest capabilities the world has ever known, which should make location irrelevant. But because of the bad internet infrastructure, and meddling by the nats, we're still constrained by physical distance. Kobus and I have been trying to buy up internet service providers around the world so we can control the networks. However, the problem is not really with the ISPs, it's with the physical networks themselves, and the power supply, and so on. And in so many countries, these industries are protected by the state so we can't buy them, not even with envelopes stuffed with cash."

Laura stood up. She paused to look around the table. "I have been working on this problem and I have some solutions. I've thought them through in detail and they are ready to share, so why don't I tell you all about them now?"

Nicked watched guardedly as Kobus nodded and Abril inclined her head inquisitively.

"Things are going to get a lot worse before they begin to get better. The world will be an increasingly chaotic place for the next few years. I have a plan.

"First, communications are our lifeblood. We need to protect communications at all costs. And I'm speaking literally: this is going to require some ambitious projects, so everyone's going to have to invest. The first step is to build our own cable system. If we operate our own private network, there will be many fewer places for hackers to hide. We might not be able to bring cables inland in some countries, but at least we can lay cables to coastal areas, and use line of sight microwave uplinks for the last few miles to shore."

"As we build the cable networks, we should also launch our own aerial and orbital networks, to provide coverage in areas our cables can't reach. In some areas, we might be able to use solar powered blimps and drones. In countries where we are neither allowed to lay cable nor operate drones, we can rely on satellites.

Satellite uplinks are much slower than cable connections, but we could go anywhere and still connect to our own private networks. And I really mean anywhere – it's easy enough to put powerful antennae on our MindWaves, to directly connect to the satellite network."

"Wazzat?" interjected Kobus. "Antennae? In my *kop*? Is that… safe? I thought MindWaves don't have antennae because having them would fry our brains!"

"Don't worry." Laura smirked and waved her hand dismissively. "That was just a liability insurance issue. People have been wearing devices with antennae for almost a hundred years. MindWaves are more powerful than a smart phone, but the problem is still manageable. The antennae will be external, with ample shielding, so radiation won't be a problem."

Abril spoke up. "I trust you to figure out the safety issue, but, well, aren't these giant antennae going to look kind of goofy?"

"As for how they will look…" Laura spoke carefully. "Well…unfortunately that's not easy. We can't have subtly hidden antennae like people use for phone and internet networks, because for satellite reception we need something more directional. So, what we have in mind is something like this…" Two large antennae sprouted diagonally out of the back of Laura's head, each about twelve inches in length and connecting directly into the MindWave ports at the base of her skull.

Abril made a face, but Laura was not deterred. "I can't say they look great at first, yet if you add some fashion sense…" Laura's antennae morphed into golden horns, and then into a crown, and then into supports for a glowing golden halo. "...They can be a lot of fun!"

"How much is this going to cost?" asked Nick, barely believing the ambition behind Laura's plans. He closed his eyes while he accessed the data to answer the question. Behind him, numbers popped out into the air, for all four Aeons to see. Every mile of undersea cable would cost more than a new luxury car, and a typical intercontinental cable would take a full year to complete. He began looking into the expense of launching satellites.

"Never mind that stuff, *bra*, it's easy," interrupted Kobus, literally waving the numbers away. "I want to know how we shut down these *fokking miggies* who are interfering in our network. We can build network nodes and launch satellites, but we'll never know peace if there are a billion desperate *miggies* out to get us."

"I've got some ideas for that, too," Laura said assuredly. "The easiest way for us to start defending ourselves is to identify the most aggressive hackers and go after their money. People who have no money to pay rent or buy food won't have time or energy to hack into our communications. And going forward as we build our own networks, we must ensure that network security is absolutely first priority. And, we should of course take legal actions against hackers, file suit or press criminal—"

"*Ek se*, Laura!" interjected Kobus. "Would any *miggie* judge or jury ever take our side? *Nooit*. You don't really believe we can depend on the courts?"

He glanced at Nick and continued, "In fact, since that *bladdy* preacher Cruz inspired the riots over Christmas, governments all over the place are coming after us. What's the point of all that cash we slip politicians every month if they're intimidated the first time a church full of nats complains about us? The Federal Trade Commission and practically every other government agency coming after Sparkwise Energy and the Congress is reviewing a bill prohibiting MindWaves in securities trading. They call it 'leveling the playing field.' *Ek se*, I call it 'stifling competition.' What the hell happened to free enterprise?"

Nick wondered whether Kobus knew that Laura was diverting Sparkwise's own profits to fund the very initiatives he was complaining about. Even if he didn't know about Laura's activities, he must realize that Sparkwise's repeated increases in energy prices were driving people to desperation. Couldn't the other Aeons understand their own role in creating the hatred and fear they now faced?

Nick said "Can't we do anything to make those billions of people who hate us a little less desperate? My dad is wealthy but everyone loves him because he works hard to restore people's hope. Can't we do the same?"

"*Yo no sé*, Nick," replied Abril cautiously. "You saw the riots in New York. And did you hear about what happened to my friend Pierre in Paris last week? A bunch of nats broke into his house to steal food and fuel. In the chaos they started a fire and Pierre barely made it out alive, and lost his whole family estate and all of his cars.

When he went to the police, the Captain called him a Marie Antoinette and said thieves like him deserved the guillotine! It's *loco*; Pierre is the biggest employer in all of France."

Kobus joined in, "Nick, I think you're being a little naive. The *miggies* are at our throats and we need to fight back."

Laura held up her hands. "No, Nick has a point. There are eight billion humans and just dozens of Aeons. I've prototyped several tactical weapons systems that we can use to protect ourselves if it comes down to it. But even we Aeons can't take on hundreds of millions of humans each. We do need to bring some humans over to our side."

Nick noted that Laura was increasingly using the term "human" instead of "nat." He wondered whether she was trying to imply that Aeons were something greater than human.

Laura continued speaking. "We'll need to recruit *acolytes*. Devoted followers who will defend and serve us. We'll need to offer them a place to live and work. I suggest we build small communities designed to house acolytes and ourselves. These facilities will be called *havens*.

"A *haven* must be a place of comfort to deserve the name. And so, at each haven, we will build facilities specifically designed for the needs of Aeons. The facilities will include full medical and MindWave maintenance labs staffed by trained acolytes.

"Even more than comfort, a haven must offer safety. Offshore islands and peninsulas offer a strong defensive advantage. We'll have to fortify them properly, and develop our own sources of food and power." She gestured towards Nick. "And Nick's idea of having human allies will be critical in making these fortified havens safe. We'll train some of the acolytes as security guards."

For once, normally compliant Abril flashed Laura a skeptical look. "And how are we going to get nats to serve as acolytes? They seem to enjoy biting the hand that feeds them."

"We give them material goods they need. Food and energy," said Laura firmly, with a glance at Nick. "And beyond that, it's like Nick said. We need to give them some cause for hope. A belief in a higher power."

Kobus rolled his eyes. "A nice *oupa* in the sky is going to make everything *alles beter*? Reverend Cruz already owns that story."

Laura shook her head slowly and leaned forward, placing both palms on the table. "No, not some grandfather. Us. We are gods."

Nick stood in surprise. "No, Laura, you're twisting what I said. I didn't say we should create a fake religion. I said we can be a force for good! For one thing, Sparkwise needs to lower its prices so the people can afford to heat their homes and deliver food to the markets." He looked imploringly around the room at the other Aeons, who in turn looked to Laura.

Laura's eyes flashed with anger. "Nick, you fail to see the big picture because you're so focused on your own emotional needs. I'm sure you blame yourself for Sarah's death, and your childish emotional pain is clouding your vision. Nick, we are Aeons. We must not let simple human emotions distract us from our tasks."

Before Nick could protest, Laura continued. "Sure, if you'd like, there are enough carbon reserves to string things along for another decade or so. Artificially low energy prices supported by government subsidies. Dwindling stocks of oil, gas and coal being sold off as fast as they can be brought to market. Let the nats burn all the fuel, leaving nothing, and make no plan for what comes next."

"There must be some kind of technology, renewable energy…" Nick interjected. Even as he spoke, he realized that Laura had turned the momentum of the confrontation against him, deflecting his anger into a tangential argument he wasn't prepared to have, making him look foolish in front of Kobus and Abril.

Laura shook her head. "Nick, there's been a technology race for decades to develop renewable energy. Solar and wind never got there and uranium was too dangerous. Thorium reactors looked like they were going to save the day but then the Hurricane Reactor disaster derailed that idea. Now time's up. Humanity lost the energy race."

Before Nick could formulate a response, she continued, "And if you think the current chaos from high prices is bad, it's nothing compared to what will happen if we let the nats burn up the last drop of oil. You saw how mindless they are when they attacked you in the streets of New York."

Nick needed to get the conversation back on track. Kobus and Abril might not care about the plight of humanity, but they did care about their own self interests. "These are real people, billions who know they will suffer and die unless we lower our prices. Either we lower the prices ourselves, or they'll rise up and force us to."

Laura shrugged. "One way or another, the human population must be reduced by billions within twenty years. This is the great destiny for which we Aeons were created."

Laura's last statement caught Nick off guard. He was used to her making grandiose statements about Aeons, and showing callousness and contempt towards natural humans. But this was beyond anything she had ever said before. He stared at her in outraged disbelief. "What, are you mad? Are you now suggesting we commit genocide?"

Laura narrowed her eyes. She spread her arms and a powerful wind kicked up inside the closed ballroom, sending her bright red hair streaming almost vertically up. The floor shook and the walls fell away. Chandeliers crashed down onto the table and shattered.

The wind tore away all remnants of the banquet room, revealing Laura's mountain peak. Instead of the normally sunny weather, the sky was overcast and dark, with lightning flashing between the clouds. Laura stood at the very pinnacle of the mountain, with the other Aeons kneeling in a semicircle below her.

Laura pointed an outstretched arm at Nick. "Stand!" she roared.

Chapter 21

Against his will, Nick felt himself standing in front of the other Aeons. He saw Abril gasping with her hand over her mouth, and Kobus grinning and wincing. He realized, with sudden shame, that he was naked. He tried to cover himself but found his arms were pinned to his sides.

Laura's face took on a distant look. She spoke so softly Nick could barely hear her voice. "I remember, when I was a child, before I – before the MindWave... my father took me deer hunting. You enjoy hunting deer, don't you, Nick? I saw you hunting a buck in the ether on the day of the riots. Well, this was a real hunt, not just some simulation in the ether. I saw a beautiful stag with a great rack of antlers. I took aim and fired. My bullet went wide and hit him in the gut instead of the heart. My rifle jammed and I couldn't load a second round. How he struggled, that stag did, as he lay thrashing in the dirt. His marvelous antlers became tangled in the roots of a nearby tree, and he fought in vain to free them. I can still hear his panicked bleating now. It was pitiful to watch such a beautiful creature struggling like that. I tried to calm him but my touch only made him panic even more. Finally my father came and put a bullet between his eyes."

Laura's eyes lost their distant gaze and focused on Nick. "And then the stag looked so peaceful, so calm, so majestic. As if the horror of a few moments earlier never happened. I took his head and mounted it above my bed as a trophy."

Nick squinted back at her. "Laura… I don't – what does that have to do with anything?"

"Your feelings towards humanity echo my feelings towards that stag. We both feel pity when we see the death throes of a doomed animal. But when the moment of horror is past, you will learn to look at it with equanimity, just as I did."

"Mankind is not some wounded deer," protested Nick. "And even if it were, how could you suggest we shoot it again?"

"No, I'm suggesting nothing of the sort," said Laura dismissively.

"What the hell are you suggesting? Sterilization? Eugenics?" He needed to know what Laura's plan was, partly out of sick fascination with her psyche, and partly out of hope that she'd reveal some specific crime that he could take as evidence to the government.

Laura laughed as if amused by the simplicity of his train of thought. "No, Nick. We don't need to do anything at all. The population will collapse all by itself."

Nick's voice lowered to a whisper and he stepped backwards, experiencing an instinctive fear of Laura. "What do you mean?"

Laura gestured with her eyes towards the apple tree that stood at the top of to the peak. A leaf fell from one of its branches, was caught in the fierce wind and twirled into a detailed three dimensional map of the Earth's ecology. Nick watched as the map ran an animation.

The simulation displayed a counter of the Earth's population, which was initially a little under eight billion. The counter ticked precipitously down as the animation sped two decades into the future. The animation revealed that the key killer was dwindling supplies of unpolluted drinking water, although famines also became a major killer as the fuel used for transporting food became increasingly expensive.

At the end of the bleak animation, the population counter stood at 100 million.

"Good riddance," called out Kobus.

"My God, what can we do?" asked Nick. He felt his pulse racing, even though in the ether he didn't have a heart.

Laura responded impassively. "Even we Aeons can't *stop* it. It's inevitable."

He was reminded of his father's oft-repeated refrain that Langar Foods had just *delayed the inevitable.* He had never really considered what his father meant by that. Now the hard truth stared him in the face. Civilization would have collapsed a decade ago without the cheap foods created by Langar. Yet as his father had always hinted, that respite was only a temporary one.

Nevertheless, the Aeons had power, much more power than his parents had when they founded Langar. Laura was right that this was his destiny. It would become his life's mission. He would forge the brilliant future that his father had always dreamed of.

First he needed to get rid of Laura. And the way to get rid of her was not to provoke her but to pretend to be on her side, so that she would reveal her secrets to him. "Surely, Laura, beings as great as we are will do something to help. We can't just sit here and do nothing."

Laura gestured around her at the other Aeons with a cruel smile. "We could do nothing if we so desire." Then her face softened. "But we Aeons will *not* do *nothing*. I told you this is our destiny, our very reason for being. We will help the world weather the coming storm."

"*Weather* it?" Not *prevent*, but *weather*. Nick narrowed his eyes.

"Yes, by making sure we survive, and with us, civilization. And we will shelter some of the nats as well. With our intervention, perhaps hundreds of millions more can survive. Enough to preserve the knowledge and technology of the human race. But first, we ourselves must survive the impending chaos, no?"

Nick nodded hesitantly. He had been hoping to lure Laura into giving up some devious plan to speed up or profit from the disaster she predicted. Instead she'd promised to try to mitigate it. He still didn't have the information he needed to convict her of any crimes; he would still have to play along until he found what he needed.

She continued. "Instead of letting all the humans turn against us, we must recruit followers from among them. They will defend us today, so that we can save them tomorrow."

The group of Aeons suddenly reappeared in the banquet hall. They resumed their meeting. Nick noted uneasily that the other two Aeons sat in postures even more deferential to Laura than they had before.

Nick looked around the makeshift temple that had only taken three weeks for Abril's construction firm to complete.

Laura had selected the former Picnic Point on the grounds of Governor's Island in New York Harbor as the site. This location had a number of advantages. It was near a major population center, which was helpful for drawing visitors. But it was also on an island, making it easy to monitor access, and therefore ensure security.

Abril had put her artistic talents to work, ensuring the architecture made the most of the inspiring views not only of the New York skyline, but also of Ellis Island and the Statue of Liberty – icons of hope for past generations.

She had ordered her construction company to design and build a marble and granite structure with a three story façade complete with Greek columns flanking a high stone staircase that led to a flat dais. This façade was supported by a modular steel frame that her crews snapped together within a matter of days. Eventually, when the temple was finally completed, marble likenesses of Aeons would be installed to adorn the dais. Behind the majestic entrance, the temple had a more practical purpose.

Providing hope.

The temple included a large storehouse full of sacks of food and canisters of gas and kerosene. Visitors would be allowed to take generous measures of both free of charge.

There was also an acolyte recruiting center, offering jobs at the first of the havens to be constructed. Applicants would be asked to fill out a computerized questionnaire, and receive a quick medical and physical check. Those who passed these screenings would be subjected to intense interviews and psychological testing to make sure they would be sufficiently loyal to their new masters – especially once they were no longer driven by the desperation of starvation.

Finally, there was a fully staffed security center, and a total of two dozen elite mercenaries who had defended Sparkwise oil projects in dangerous locales. Their presence was necessary not only to protect the large amounts of food and fuel stored in the facility, but also because Laura and the other Aeons expected reprisals against their new religion.

Today would be the grand opening of the facility, and Nick had joined Kobus, Abril, and Laura at the temple.

Nick stood at the top of the staircase below the temple's façade, watching as the first ferry boat set out from a lock in the Hudson Sea Wall at Manhattan's Battery Park and approached the island. He tugged at the clothes Abril had instructed him to wear. "This outfit is lame," he muttered to Kobus.

Kobus smiled back, revealing normal human teeth instead of the polar bear dentures he sported in the ether. The two had not met in real life many times before. Nick noticed that Kobus, like himself, was well over six feet in height, and had sculptured features and an athletic build. In fact, Nick and Kobus were almost indistinguishable, except that where Nick had long black hair, pale skin and green eyes, Kobus had tightly curled hair, coffee colored skin, and blue eyes. Nick wondered if their parents had used the same medical team to conduct their genetic engineering, but decided he'd rather not know.

Kobus was attired in an outfit similar to Nick's. It was an updated version of what a Greek or Roman god would have been depicted wearing two thousand years earlier. A tunic, short enough to reveal the rippling muscles in his arms and legs, held closed with a thick black leather belt. Nick's tunic was green and Kobus' was scarlet. Both Aeons wore close fitting horned brass helmets. The helmets' horns held antennae, and their rims held discreet cameras that provided a 360 degree field of view. The backs of the helmets had holes that matched the wearer's MindWave cooling vents.

Kobus shrugged and grinned sardonically as he replied. "At least it's warm inside the temple, *bra*. What would we wear if the floor wasn't heated?"

"Aeons aren't supposed to worry about banalities like the weather," said Nick, careful not to let his voice sound too sarcastic.

"We're not used to dressing like *stukkies,* so we feel like a couple of *chans.* It's easier for Laura and Abril. They're real *choty goty.*"

Nick followed Kobus' gaze towards Laura and Abril. The female Aeons were dressed in more form fitting versions of the men's attire, Abril in black and Laura in pure white. In their real flesh and blood appearance, both women were tall and attractive, Laura statuesque while Abril was more curvaceous. In the morning breeze, Laura's long red hair blew outwards and mingled with Abril's dark brown locks.

"*Ja no,* they just look better," laughed Kobus. "Thank God for genetic engineering. It would be terrible, after all we've been through in the ether with them, to find out that they were ugly."

Nick agreed their two female companions were beautiful, but the thought just reminded him of Sarah. He felt a sick sense of relief that she was not witnessing today's events. If she had harangued him for trading oil, he couldn't imagine what she would have said about what he was doing now.

He reminded himself that it didn't matter what it looked like he was doing. He would play along with Laura's schemes just long enough to gain her trust and find evidence of her illegal activities. And then he would redeem himself by turning her in to the authorities and by convincing the remaining Aeons to use their vast wealth for good.

He realized he was glaring silently at Laura and Abril. To hide his ruminations from Kobus, he squinted and pointed at the colored tunics they wore. "There are, what, sixty Aeons now? Already, we've got red, green, white, and black outfits. Is Laura going to invent dozens of new colors as she gets all the other Aeons involved in this religion?"

Kobus chuckled. "Don't get your *broekies* in a knot, Nick. Abril already figured out we need to use sigils to distinguish us, instead of colors."

"How medieval," muttered Nick.

Laura saw them looking in her direction and called over. "All right, let's make sure we put on a show that impresses our visitors. Remember, we just have to stay during the consecration ceremony. I'll make a quick speech, and then we're out of here. No need to mix with the humans who come."

"You got it, *baas*," said Kobus, making a theatrical bow.

"The miracles we worked over the last few weeks will really draw the crowds today," gushed Abril. She was referring to the series of supposedly divine interventions the Aeons had made since deciding to found their religion, now formally called the Order of Knowledge. The emblem of the church was a golden circle with five interwoven lines coming out of its center.

In the weeks since Laura had proposed the new religion, Laura and Kobus had quickly released news across the multinet that the Aeons had intervened to cure terminally sick children, to provide new homes for dispossessed families, and to repair burned out factories. In some cases, the Aeons actually had done something positive. In others, the stories were entirely fabricated.

"My favorite was the story about the man who saw the device of the Order of Knowledge in a piece of toast and was cured of his tuberculosis," said Abril. "*Muy bien!*"

Nick noticed a shift in the stances of the security personnel that stood at the base of the steps. They didn't change position, but he perceived a new tenseness in their postures.

He used his MindWave antenna to connect to the audio channel they were using to communicate with each other.

"—wards the island. Repeat, four unidentified craft heading towards island" he heard a tense voice stating.

A calmer and more mature voice responded. "Eagle one, what is origin of four craft, and ETA?"

Eagle one responded. "Command, craft have departed from Clinton Wharf. ETA three minutes."

Clinton Wharf was in Brooklyn, directly across a narrow channel of water from the eastern shore of Governor's island. Nick arched his neck and squinted but could not see the approaching vessels because they were on the other side of the temple, and in any case were hidden behind the Sea Wall around Governor's Island. No matter. He linked his MindWave to the closed circuit security cameras around the perimeter of the building, and soon he could see four overcrowded vessels heading towards the temple.

Command spoke again. "Minnows 1 and 2, intercept unidentified craft and determine their intent. All points be aware we have unknowns inbound. Stallion 1, warm up for potential VIP evac."

Nick called out to the other Aeons, working to sound calm. "The security teams are picking up four boats approaching fast from Brooklyn."

"*Que*? Brooklyn?" asked Abril, nervousness in her voice. "Are you sure? I thought they were supposed to come from Manhattan." She pointed towards the slowly approaching orange ferry boat that had departed from Manhattan only a few minutes before.

"No, get on the security channel. These ones are from Brooklyn. Our guards are sending the speed boats to investigate."

The Aeons shifted uncomfortably. Behind them, they could hear the rotors of their helicopter begin to spin, as the pilots warmed it up for a possible emergency evacuation.

"This reminds me of my friend Pierre. Maybe we should head to the—" said Abril, taking a halting step towards the sound of the helicopter, yet looking to Laura for approval.

"Abril, stand your ground!" commanded Laura, holding out a long arm horizontally, as if to bar Abril's path. "We will not flee at the first challenge. Those boats may be bringing more believers. Or they may be bringing protestors. Nevertheless, today we unveil our first temple, and with it a new hope for our future. If we run away from a boatful of nats carrying placards, how can we form a new religion? No one worships cowards."

"Hal, are you still there?" Colonel Jaeger's voice was marred by static.

"I'm here. It's a sorry day when even United States Senators can't get a good phone signal," replied Senator O'Brien, trying hard to sound jovial.

"You must know the situation out in the Midwest and South is getting dire. It's not just heating anymore. People are starting to go hungry. And every day the Federal Government doesn't help, the Aeons look stronger."

"Laura Mayer seems content to turn the world against her. The National Unity Church has only gained followers since the Aeons launched that bizarre new cult of theirs," replied O'Brien.

"Laura believes she will profit from chaos. What the hell happened to all of those investigations and new laws?"

O'Brien grimaced. "It's hard to get anything constructive done. The Aeons are playing a game of chess where they use their money and influence to create different factions that they set against each other so no one's policies get enacted. As far as I can tell, they're tangling up every agency and every level of the Federal government. I can tell you they've brought the Senate to a complete halt. No one knows whom to trust. Governors who should be declaring martial law and cleaning up the mess seem to be looking to Reverend Cruz for leadership instead." He paused. "A lot of people in Washington have defected to Cruz' side."

"They're traitors. Forget about them."

"It's not so simple, Rad. Some of these are good, loyal people I've known for decades. They're defecting to Cruz because they fear the Federal government is too corrupt to protect the people against the Aeons. They think they can do more good from within Cruz' movement."

"Hal, we can halt all of this if we can make a real strike against the Aeons, and get the people the heating and food they need."

"What are you saying, Rad?"

"I have agents in place right now."

Chapter 22

Sarah and Michael were concealed in an old boarded up warehouse near Liberty State Park on the New Jersey side of the Upper Bay where the Hudson and East Rivers met the Atlantic Ocean. From here they had a perfect view of the temple. The augmented vision that had been implanted at the same time as their TacWaves allowed them to see the unfolding scene in detail. Sarah and Michael also had enhanced hearing, but the wind was unfavorable and made overhearing conversations difficult at their present distance. Instead, an array of carefully calibrated laser microphones detected and broadcast conversations within the temple.

Their position was hidden by a holographic projector that emitted a façade of normalcy over their location.

In addition to their surveillance equipment, they were also equipped with two tripod-mounted laser rifles with sights that interfaced directly with their TacWaves for precise targeting. They were to use these weapons only in an emergency.

The business of arranging the four boats that now approached the island had been carried out by Greg Silverstein's team of Demon commandos. Greg had rented the boats with cash, and then offered free passage to the Aeons' island temple. It was well known that the Aeons had offered free food and fuel to all comers. The boats had been filled to capacity with eager passengers within two hours, as news of the free ride spread by word of mouth through the dilapidated neighborhoods of Brooklyn. Some of the pilgrims crammed into each of the leaky craft were actually Greg's commandos, ready to take advantage of the Aeons' rare public appearance by arresting them while they were exposed in the temple.

This raid was possible because their spying on the Aeons had started to bear fruit. Michael was extremely adept at breaking into and navigating encrypted networks. His superiority to Sarah in this respect mirrored her advantage over him in using the TacWave for more physical tasks like hand-to-hand combat.

The Aeons, for all their care, could not protect every foot of the thousands of miles of cables they needed to communicate with each other. Michael had found a number of weak points to hack into.

Michael had not found any evidence of the terrorist attacks that they all suspected Laura had masterminded. But he had found strong evidence for insider trading on the public equity and commodity markets by Laura as an individual, and on behalf of Sparkwise.

Colonel Jaeger had decided to jump on the first concrete incriminating evidence his team had found. Moreover, he had insisted the strike proceed in secret, without even first obtaining a court warrant. Rather than risk the information leaking, he would have his commando team arrest the Aeons and then explain his actions later.

It had been almost a month since Sarah and Michael had started talking again, and by now the damage to their relationship that Sarah's affair with Nick had caused was mostly healed.

Michael turned to Sarah. "Are you ready?"

Sarah didn't pull her eyes away from the scene unfolding in the temple. "It's really up to Greg now." She was still heartbroken at losing her chance to convert Nick, yet also ashamed of her obviously unprofessional feelings for him. She wanted to crush her emotions and focus on proving she deserved to be a member of the team. "Let's see if the Aeons react the way we predicted from their psyche profiles."

As Michael had indicated from his first days tracking her, Laura Mayer was clearly the leader, holding influence over the other three Aeons through her strangely charismatic personality and an unwavering self-assuredness. Her preeminence was evident in the way the other Aeons unconsciously arranged themselves around her and, ever so slightly, dipped their heads when conversing with her. Sarah was sure Laura's dominance was just as strong with the more than fifty other Aeons who weren't present today. They might not be as intimately involved in her plans, yet they all looked to Laura for inspiration and direction.

Abril and Kobus were her key lieutenants. Abril tended to agree rather slavishly with Laura's ideas, but was nevertheless a good executive when given clear instructions. She also had a native artistic talent that made her a natural fit for her rapidly growing architecture and construction firm.

Kobus was more of a free thinker, who challenged Laura frequently. He was also a bit of a joker, even a hedonist, making full use of the worldly pleasures that a MindWave could simulate for its user. But when questioning Laura, he usually allowed himself to be convinced by her, and when his hedonistic desires were sated, he became a competent taskmaster.

And finally, there was Nick. Every time Sarah trained her eyes on him, she unconsciously grimaced and reached up to grasp the old necklace she had given him. She had replaced the old silver chain and icon with a new aluminum copy.

She was convinced he was trying to cooperate with the government's ongoing investigations into Sparkwise. And yet, here he was, standing beside Laura in a ridiculous outfit to help inaugurate her bizarre new religion. It seemed Nick had given up on fitting into the real world and was looking for a new place to belong.

Sarah remembered that feeling, from the time after her mother had died and she'd first been sent to an orphanage. She knew how desperate the need to belong could make a person. Unfortunately, whatever guidance Laura was providing Nick was leading him in the wrong direction.

She felt her heart opening up to Nick again. And she re-experienced her old desire to explain herself to him and bring him to her side. She squashed it. She was a professional, and Nick was an adult responsible for his own actions.

Nick was the first to pick up on his security team's focus on the four boats heading towards Governor's Island. After a moment, he notified the other Aeons.

Sarah noted with satisfaction that each of the four Aeons behaved as she expected. Kobus strode to the edge of the temple to see if he could get a view of the boats for himself but was careful to remain within earshot of Laura. Abril looked like she'd lost her nerve, and looked to Laura for orders. Nick almost seemed like he had his own plan, but then turned to listen to Laura, too.

Laura stepped to the front of the temple and commanded Abril to stand firm. She then exhorted the Aeons to face whoever was in the boats. She appeared fearless, and her leadership pulled the group back together.

In a few moments, the Aeons' two swift security boats had cut off the four slower moving ferries. Two men went aboard each boat. A sniper team was covering the entire scene from the roof the temple, ready to shoot anyone on the vessels who caused trouble. Sarah's TacWave allowed her to eavesdrop on the Aeon radio signals, and she overheard the security services talking on the radio to Laura. "Lady Laura, the passengers on the four boats appear to be pilgrims, but we can't confirm that without searching them."

Laura's response came back quickly. "How long will a search take?"

"As long as you want, my Lady. We can do a cursory search or a full one."

"Fine. Get it done in five minutes. I want these four boats landing at the same time as the ferry from Battery Park."

Several minutes later, Sarah estimated close to one thousand people had landed on the island and were filing onto the broad stairs leading into the temple. She scanned the faces and saw Greg was near the back of the crowd, dressed to look like just another desperate visitor to the island.

"Bravo squad in position," came Olivia Freeman's voice over the radio. She was in charge of Greg's second squad, whose members Sarah could see near the front ranks of the crowd.

There was less conversation among the throng than Sarah would have expected at such a spectacle, but then she remembered that these so-called pilgrims were hungry and tired. They had come for food and fuel, not entertainment or religious guidance. She saw the Statue of Liberty overlooking the scene, and was reminded of the words *huddled masses*. She ground her teeth in disgust at the borrowed symbolism.

"Surveillance team, give me a threat analysis," Greg ordered over the quantum-encrypted radio channel the Demon squad was using for this raid.

A row of a dozen guards armed with spears stood at the top of the stairway, impeding the crowd from stepping onto the dais where the Aeons stood. Sarah's enhanced vision allowed her to see that under their long white cloaks, the guards were also equipped with submachine guns. She transmitted the information to Greg in an encrypted signal.

Laura nodded to the captain of her guards, who stepped forward to the edge of the dais at the top of the temple stairway and rapped the bronzed butt of his long wooden spear on the stone floor. The sharp noise got the attention of the crowd.

"Pilgrims, we thank you for your visit today, a visit that will be rewarded in due course." At his words, a ripple of excitement went through the crowd, as spectators jostled to be first in line for food and fuel. "But first," he cried, his voice at a volume calculated to settle the crowd back down, "the Lady Laura will address you."

"Alpha squad, engage and detain Aeons on my mark," said Greg through the quantum-encoded radio. "Bravo squad, you handle the guards."

Sarah's radio crackled with a new signal. "Demon Team, this is Colonel Jaeger. Stand by."

Laura stepped forward to faint applause, holding her head high in a shining brass helmet and taking measured steps as if trying to appear majestic.

Sarah thought she looked like a fool playing dress up. Her façade of greatness would collapse the moment Jaeger gave the command for Greg's squad to act.

"Nice hat, Lady!" a huckster in the crowd called, drawing laughter. Sarah smiled. It appeared she was not the only one who thought the whole event deserved ridicule.

Laura gave no response. She simply stood at the edge of the dais, serenely looking down into the crowd with one foot slightly ahead of the other, her arms relaxed at her side.

Another person yelled out, "Where's the food? We're hungry!"

"Yeah, you robbed us so it's damn well time you gave something back!" came another voice.

A few members of the crowd picked up the reference and began chanting, "Give it back! Give it back!"

The crowd was significantly larger than originally planned by the Aeons, and people were jammed tightly into the half-built temple grounds. Some members of the throng were growing edgy, and Greg's squad members were struggling to hold their positions. Upon the dais behind them, three Aeons also shifted uncomfortably.

"Boo! Get off the stage and give us our food!" Some young men in the first rank of pilgrims were now trying to push their way past the guards, who held their spears horizontally in front of them to form a barrier. But pilgrims further back in the crowd were also pushing their way forward, perhaps afraid they would get to the food bank too late and return home with empty packs. The weight of the restless crowd was threatening to overwhelm the single line of guards.

Still Laura stood at the top of the raised platform unmoved, and unmoving.

"Colonel, give the command. We can't hold position," said Greg.

"Stand down, Demon squad." For once, Jaeger's tone sounded defeated.

Sarah saw that down on the dais, Laura was smiling.

"What's that Colonel?" Greg's voice registered a mix of outrage and disbelief.

"Stand down. I have orders for us to stand down."

"From whom?"

"From the very top. Now, stand down."

"To hell with this!"

Sarah's attention was drawn to a sudden movement from the crowd. It was Bob Eckers, winding up and throwing something at Laura. She saw knife turning end over end as it sailed straight for Laura's unarmored neck. Sarah saw Kobus leaning forward, intending to pull Laura back, but it was obvious he would not arrive in time save her from the weapon.

As the knife flew towards her, Laura calmly raised her hand. The blade stopped in mid-air and floated before her. There was a short gasp from the crowd. People who had been pushing forward took a step back to watch what was unfolding above them.

Laura inclined her head curtly and the knife dropped to the ground with a heavy metallic clank.

"Eckers, stand down. All Demons, exfiltrate immediately." In the crowd, Greg had lunged between several pilgrims to reach Bob and was physically forcing him towards the docks where the boats were waiting.

Sarah heard the Aeons' security team talking over the radio. "I see a dozen, no two dozen, individuals fleeing. Requesting weapons free."

"I got 'em." It was the voice of the sniper on the roof of the temple. "Permission to engage?"

"Demons, enemy sniper is engaging," Sarah barked into her radio as she reached for her tripod-mounted laser and zeroed in on the sniper.

Am I really going to kill this man? she wondered in disbelief.

Chapter 23

On the dais, Laura held out her arms, palms upward, to either side. Her voice came over the Aeon security radio network. "Hold fire. It would mar our religion's launch if we shot fleeing cowards in the back."

In a few more moments, Greg's team had overpowered the two guards that stood between them and the docks and hijacked the two speedboats to take them back to Brooklyn.

"Demon squad reports all friendlies aboard and unharmed," reported Greg. "Exfiltrating via lima zulu bravo. Request pickup in one-five mikes."

Sarah let out a sigh of relief turned her attention back to the island. The commotion was dying down and Laura signaled her guard to once again rap his spear butt on the dais to draw the crowd's attention.

Laura still stood with her arms extended to either side. Suddenly, from her left, a long, gleaming scepter flew across the length of the temple and landed in her hand. From the right came a heavy golden bracelet, which slipped over her outstretched fingers perfectly.

"How did she do that?" exclaimed Sarah. "And how did she stop Bob's knife?"

"I've seen her researching all kinds of electromagnetic technologies," answered Michael. "Diamagnetic levitation has been around for decades; that must be how she stopped the knife. And if you have magnets, making metal fly around is easy. The hardest part of what she just did was to align her wrist perfectly with the trajectory of the bracelet. But if her MindWave is coordinating, it seems possible."

"Well, whatever it is, it's gotten the attention of the crowd," said Sarah.

The crowd on the stairs had settled down and were now attentively looking up at Laura. She did not make them wait long.

"Downtrodden residents of New York," she began, in a deep and confident voice, "welcome to our temple. I come to you today to make a proposition.

"Your world is at a crossroads. A cataclysm is approaching, and it cannot be stopped.

"In the face of this disaster, your leaders, limited in their powers and faculties, have done nothing to protect you.

"So, we Aeons have descended to protect mankind, to carry the torch of life forward. When you are hungry, we will provide food. When you are cold, we will provide warmth. When you are desperate with loss and fear, we will provide love and comfort, until the danger has passed."

She gestured with her head and a number of guards came out from behind pillars pulled small cardboard boxes out of large sacks they carried. They threw armfuls of boxes out into the crowd. People pushed and shoved each other to seize the boxes that landed near them.

"Must be food," muttered Michael.

Sarah saw Kobus leering with amusement and licking his lips at the sight of the fighting within the audience. Nick was scowling.

This went on for a minute before the sacks were empty. As the pushing and shoving continued, Laura concluded her speech, now in a deep, powerful voice that carried even over the commotion of the spectators below.

"The cataclysm is inevitable. But I also spoke of a crossroads, and a proposition. You can listen to the counsel of the Aeons, serve us at the havens we are building, and support us in our great tasks. In this case, you will prosper and your children and grandchildren will remember your wisdom with gratitude.

"Or you can believe the lies told by the fellow men you appointed to protect you, yet who take every opportunity to steal your livelihoods and smear the names of those who would help you. These are the same men who have accused us of robbing you. The same men who just tried to kill me for daring to offer you gifts of food and fuel.

"Yes, you can join them. You can vilify us, jeer at us, even take up arms against us. But I warn you, the Aeons cannot protect those who forsake us. If you take this road, the souls of your unborn grandchildren will despair as you doom them to oblivion.

"People of New York, you can denounce the Aeons, and perish in darkness, or you can meekly seek our protection, and inherit the Earth."

With that, Laura stepped backwards out of sight of the throng on the stairs.

Nick started his presentation on haven construction. He had resigned himself to working towards Laura's plan for the moment, even though his long-term goal was to undermine it. "As you can see, acolyte recruitment is going ahead of schedule," he said. A 3-dimensional series of green bars sprang up from the table to illustrate the point.

"Boring, tell me something I don't already know," responded Laura. Kobus chuckled. Laura still insisted on holding these weekly meetings, but was always the first to complain about their uselessness.

The three Aeons' avatars were meeting in a secure conference room in the ether, though all three were physically resident in the half-completed haven at Calvert Cliffs State Park in Maryland. Calvert Cliffs was one of a series of parks on the sliver of land between Chesapeake Bay and the Patuxent River. The Maryland State government, in dire need of cash to support emergency economic programs, had sold the park to the Aeons in return for a ton of pure gold.

Nick continued his presentation, which was being beamed to other Aeons around the world. "Calvert Cliffs was a compromise – it offers an imperfect mix of the defensibility and self-sufficiency we want for our network of havens. The geography is broken up by tracts of land that carry low level radiation from the uranium plant that once operated here. The radiation levels aren't harmful to people, but can cause signal interference and, over time, might corrupt any data cable laid near it. This fact complicated our hookup to the intercontinental cables that Oceanic Cable, a company owned by Jakobus Van der Merwe and Abril Espinoza, already laid. The best solution to the problem was that we build a backhaul line to meet the main line at a terminal twenty miles north of the haven."

He brought up a three-dimensional map of the peninsula. "The peninsula itself is sparsely populated, in part because of fears about the radiation contamination. However, it has bridges connecting it to more heavily populated areas to the South, West, and East, eliminating much of the safety that comes with isolation. Its location inside Chesapeake Bay and the steep rocky cliffs that rise above the water make it quite safe from storm surges and flooding, though the soil is only passably fertile. The Patuxent River provides fresh water and a current that we can harness to generate electricity."

"I think you'll agree that despite its shortcomings, Calvert Cliffs is good enough to serve as a testing ground to build the first of our planned network of thirty to forty havens around the world. We have decided to name this location Sanctuary, to honor what it represents for Aeons and our followers."

Now he brought up a schematic of the Sanctuary facility. "Sanctuary deserves the name. Its walls are built high, and sophisticated sensors are installed throughout it. A food lab modeled on Langar Foods' facilities is being installed to mitigate the threat that the facility's inhabitants could be starved out. We have also buried the cable connection deeply, armored the cable with steel, and camouflaged the terminal building."

"How much time am I gonna waste every day running this *bladdy* Sanctuary of yours?" asked Kobus.

"Very little. As you know, our Order of Knowledge has seen its membership skyrocket. Newly recruited acolytes will be trained in every aspect of Sanctuary's upkeep, from running the cable connections to securing its perimeter."

"So what do I do while I'm there, *ek se*?"

"I'm glad you asked, Kobus. At the center of the facility will be our home, a building called the *divine residence*." He brought up a close up image of a squat forty foot tall structure, constructed of steel reinforced concrete modeled to look like granite. It had only one entrance, and was built like a military bunker with gun ports instead of windows.

"It may not look charming, but it's totally secure. The concrete used in its construction was mixed with iron and carbon fibers, to make it impervious to radio waves. This will prevent eavesdropping by satellites or attacks by radio frequencies designed to damage computer equipment.

"But the divine residence's most important features lie one hundred feet underground. In the unfinished subterranean chambers, our bodies will slumber in custom designed composite sarcophagi while our minds roam the ether." Nick secretly hoped that he could use his uninterrupted presence in the ether to locate and unlock some of Laura's dirty secrets.

"In addition to the undersea cable connection, a satellite receiver is being installed on the roof, giving the facility a backup way to connect to the ether."

"Do those satellites even work yet, *bra*?" asked Kobus.

"Not really yet," admitted Nick. "As you must know Kobus, since you're an investor in it, our first satellite is being launched today. It'll be another year or two until we have a full set in orbit."

Laura broke in. "Thank you for the update, Nick. Let's turn off the public feed and move to private Sparkwise matters. My source in the Attorney General's office told me the government's investigation into those energy riots—"

Her voice faded. She stared intently at a corner of the room. Nick followed her gaze, and saw nothing but a shadow.

"Who is that?" she demanded.

"Who?" asked Nick, straining his eyes to see. It was strange, he thought, that there was a shadow in the corner of the well-lit room.

"It was there," insisted Laura, standing up angrily. "I saw it!"

"*Bladdy* hell, Laura, are you seeing ghosts? I—" Kobus began.

He was interrupted by an explosion. Nick flinched and covered his face, waiting tensely for debris and shockwaves to tear him apart.

After a moment, Nick raised his fingers from over his eyes. He felt foolish. Of course he could not be hurt by an explosion in the ether. No form of physical harm was possible. At least the other two Aeons had clearly also been shocked by the blast, and were similarly recovering their composure.

Why had there be an explosion in their board room? As Nick regained his senses, he realized that their MindWaves had interrupted the business meeting with real time footage of an unfolding event somewhere in the real world.

Even has he figured that out, he was receiving additional information through his MindWave. The rocket upon which they had been preparing to launch their first communications satellite had just detonated on its launch pad in Florida.

"How the hell did that missile blow up?" cried Nick. He wondered if it was another scheme by Laura to convince the Aeons they were being persecuted. But he didn't dare to voice his suspicion. Not until he had some kind of concrete proof.

More information was already being fed to them by their MindWaves. Video footage from the launch pad showed a man wearing a workman's overalls pull a handgun out of a tool case and shoot two guards. The man then scrambled up an access ladder towards the rocket. He was out of the security camera's frame for a few moments before the image abruptly turned to static.

"A suicide bomber?" asked Kobus, clearly in disbelief. "Who was this *fokking* guy?"

Already, information to answer his question was becoming available as their MindWaves used face recognition software to cross-reference the video with personnel files, and checked security access records. The bomber was most likely a man named David Fisher, Nick's MindWave was now telling him. Fisher was a low-level technician working at the satellite launch facility. He had been employed by an engineering company owned by Abril for two years and had an unblemished record until now.

While the group sat in stunned silence, they heard Abril knocking on the conference room's doors. Her avatar needed permission to join the secure meeting, which was currently officially only open to members of Sparkwise Energy's board of directors.

"Come in," said Laura without looking to Nick or Kobus for their assent.

Abril slipped into the room without delay, letting the door close slowly behind her.

"You've seen the rocket explosion, right?" Abril asked in an unsteady voice.

"*Ja,* of course," replied Kobus through bared fangs. "A human technician named David Fisher blew it up."

"God damn it, Fisher's a member of Cruz' National Unity Church." Laura suddenly screamed, slamming her hand on the table.

"Those religious nuts have been talking about waging a holy war against us. I have a database of all their members; David Fisher was once an assistant Deacon at a church in Missouri that allied itself with Cruz three months ago. Damn it, Abril, we all have access to this information. Why didn't you check this human bastard's background properly? How could you be so careless!"

Abril looked down in muted acceptance of Laura's rebuke, her lower lip trembling.

Kobus interjected, leaning forward over the table so his bulk obscured Abril from Laura's view. He spoke to Laura. "It's all right. There's no use fighting amongst each other over a simple mistake, *ne*."

Laura took a deep breath, visibly working to calm herself. Nick suspected that she was also using her MindWave to release serotonin or endorphin into her blood, assuming the attack was truly a surprise to her. It all seemed a little convenient and staged. Since the riots in New York, Nick had watched Reverend Cruz' sermons and seen her advocating non-violence, not the radical messages Laura accused her of spouting. A suicide attack didn't seem to fit with the NUC's message.

Laura spoke. "I hope everyone has learned the lesson to take every precaution. We are under siege, and this is only the first of many attacks we should expect."

Nick could see that Laura was going to use this event to reinforce the Aeons' hatred of humans. He moved to speak before she could. If he could say something to dampen the passion in the room, Laura might again remember her commitment to work with natural humans. "Guys, let's all just keep calm. This was an isolated incident. We don't even know if the NUC was involved. We can't let it destroy our trust in all naturals. We need to—"

"Trust? It was hard enough to trust the nats before. But after this? This is like a declaration of war!" Abril's shrill words cut across Nick's voice.

Nick was stunned. Abril was the most timid of the Aeons. If even she was calling for war, what of the others? If he pressed too hard for a moderate response, he might lose what little influence he had over this group, and his chance of uncovering Laura's plots. Then again, maybe if he pushed hard enough he could provoke Laura into revealing her true intentions. He paused, unsure of how to pursue his cause.

Laura rose and leaned over the table, staring right at Abril. Abril shrank back under Laura's gaze, but Laura had apparently already forgotten her anger at her fellow Aeon. She smiled as if to reassure the other woman. "Yes, Abril. This is a war, yet it's one we've foreseen," she turned her gaze towards Nick and her smile faded. "And anyone who thinks this attack was planned by one or two isolated individuals is being naïve, or disloyal."

Nick felt a fiery anger burning in his gut at Laura's words. But instead of challenging her, he decided to play into her desire to explain her vision. Maybe she would finally reveal some violent, illegal plan. "What do you propose we do to fight this war, Laura?"

Laura turned back to Abril. "The cost of that satellite… My God, the impudence! We will strike back. But first we need to get our defenses in order. Abril, I need you to speed up the construction of the havens. And I have some improvements I want you to add. And all of you, there's training you need to start. Combat training."

"You mean…" Abril asked in a small voice. "You mean, we might have to be involved in the fighting *ourselves*?"

"We can't rule it out," said Laura sternly. Then she softened her tone into the reassuring voice of a mother. "But don't worry, Abril, our MindWaves, coupled with the right equipment, will make even the weakest of us into a powerful warrior."

"These guys have good protection," said Sarah, in a respectful voice. Despite Michael's exceptional skill at penetrating secured networks, even he had nearly been caught.

Michael piped in. "They've set up a sophisticated avatar-only virtual world. We can't eavesdrop without actually *being* there. I was able to sneak in when they were broadcasting to the other Aeons without being noticed. But once they moved to a private meeting, Laura switched on some kind of passive scanning ability that can see right through our cloaking procedures in a matter of minutes. If that satellite rocket hadn't exploded when it did, I would have been trapped. She might have traced me all the way back here to the ranch."

"How'd you get out of the secure room?" asked Colonel Jaeger, his brow scrunched up. As the campaign to spy on and disrupt the Aeons had stepped up in its intensity, he was attending the briefings and debriefings more and more frequently. Sarah wished he did not; his cold manner put her on edge.

"In all the confusion, they turned their attention to the explosion, Sir. When Laura opened the door for Abril, it gave me a chance to sneak out through the temporary opening in the security systems."

"If you can't track them in person, why don't you go back to the Sparkwise servers you almost broke into a few months ago?"

"Sir, we haven't been able to find a way back to those servers."

"How the hell—" Jaeger grimaced and recomposed his sentence. "You guys have spent months and months following Laura Mayer. You have the same equipment as her, and much better training. Why are you struggling just not to get caught?"

Michael looked down at his hands, his face a mask. Sarah didn't know what to say to defend him.

Willy stepped in, "Sir, I think—"

Jaeger brushed him away. "I am not blaming you or your agents, Johnson. Let's figure out where we're getting beaten so we can fix the problem and start winning."

Despite Jaeger's words, Sarah could tell that he did, in fact, blame Willy, Michael and her. She took the initiative to explain the challenges they faced to the Colonel. "Sir, they have a lot more time and resources to throw at this problem than we ever did. Laura's spent years building up layer after layer of overlapping security systems."

Jaeger rubbed his hands together pensively. "Is it possible they've broken into our networks and are spying on us?"

Michael responded. "I don't think so, sir."

"You don't *think* so?" Jaeger demanded. "Three months ago they somehow foresaw our raid on their damn temple and had it aborted at the last minute."

"We port all our sensitive communications through the NSA's photon entanglement encryption system, sir. I don't think even Laura Mayer has found a way to outsmart quantum physics. So the leak didn't come from our side." Michael didn't ask Jaeger who had aborted the raid. If Jaeger knew the answer to that question, he had not shared it with the rest of the team yet.

"Good. Keep investigating. I know Laura is up to something. For all we know, she blew up her own satellite to get her people pissed off at the National Unity Church." He rose and walked to the door, where he turned back and rubbed his hands energetically. "You don't have another year to bring her down. She's going to have a lot more blood on her hands soon."

Willy remained for a few moments. When the door had closed behind Jaeger, he turned to his two charges and winked. "Well, some good came out of this."

"How's that?" asked Sarah, shaking her head in confusion.

"We have a name for our little unit."

Sarah and Michael exchanged mystified glances and then turned back to Willy.

"The *Ghosts*," said Willy with a smile. "Didn't you hear what Kobus called you in the conference room? Now get out there and haunt the hell out of the Aeons."

Nick's father eyed him angrily from behind the wooden podium as he fielded questions at the evening press conference he had called in the seminar room at New York's Ritz Carleton Hotel.

"How can the nation trust the Lal Foundation to reduce energy costs?" asked a female reporter, amid a flurry of camera flashes.

Dr. Lal swallowed before speaking. "As I believe everyone knows at this point, our nation's energy prices have become too high for middle class families to afford—"

The reporter pressed deeper. "Yes, but it is Sparkwise Energy that has driven up prices. And isn't your own son one of the owners of Sparkwise?" Several holocameras swiveled to point at Nick.

"I'm afraid that's all the time Dr. Lal has to answer questions today," interjected one of Dr. Lal's assistants, easing himself between Dr. Lal and the podium. "Please contact the Lal Foundation media office for further comment."

Before he could respond to the reporter's sharp question or protest his aide's ending of the press conference, Dr. Lal was smoothly ushered from the stage, away from the pool of reporters and through the room's small back door. Nick quickly got up and hurriedly followed him out of the room, painfully aware that the metallic panels at the back of his head were glinting in the harsh light of the cameras.

"You can ignore my messages, Dad. But you can't ignore me here and now." he demanded of his father as they strode across the garage.

"There's nothing for us to speak about until you quit Sparkwise," responded his father tersely, over his shoulder. "But I'm glad you came so you could see firsthand the shame you are bringing to me, and the destruction you are bringing to the world,"

Nick heard the old chant in his head, taunting him. *Worthless*! *Worthless*! To drown it out, he raised his voice. "I'm working to make you proud of me, Dad."

"And yet we both know that you and your Aeon friends have caused the economic crisis by hoarding oil and throttling distribution," countered his father. "I haven't seen you lower energy prices."

"It's just more complex than you think. You'll see. You'll see soon."

His father waved a hand dismissively. "Yes. If the solution requires founding some cult religion that manipulates those you doomed to poverty into becoming your fanatical worshippers, and

378

retreating to your havens to hide from the chaos you've created, I agree that it's very complex." He turned away and strode towards the limousine that was to take him and his wife back home.

Nick angrily turned on his heel and walked towards the elevator to the rooftop helipad.

The explosion made a dull popping noise.

Chapter 24

It wasn't the kind of fiery blast Nick knew from *holomovies*, or from his own imagination, or even like the one that had felled his satellite rocket. Just a low crack.

The Mercedes his parents had just gotten into jolted backwards several inches, and then came to a halt. The only signs that anything had happened were the cracked windows and the smoke that was shooting through the chinks like the steam from a boiling coffee pot.

"Doctor! Call a doctor!" Nick screamed as he ran towards the car. He was simultaneously alerting emergency services through his MindWave.

Over Nick's satellite link, Laura's voice cut in. *Nick! Where are you, Nick? I've just found evidence the National Unity Church is going to attack your family.* Satellite coverage over New York was usually pretty good, but in this underground parking lot the signal was only strong enough to allow for low quality audio and video transmission.

Nick ignored her and kept running. He reached the car before any of the stunned security personnel and yanked at a door handle.

The handle was hot, and the door was either locked or jammed.

Nick needed to get the door open. He desperately bashed through the deeply cracked bullet proof window with his right hand. Broken shards of glass cut through his suit and into the flesh of his arm, and three of his knuckles felt like they were broken. After a moment of shock, he used his MindWave to dull the pain and help coordinate his panicked movements. He reached through the broken window with his uninjured hand, found the door lock, undid it, and pulled the door open.

His mother rolled out of the car and onto the ground. Her face was burned away, bone peeking through the blood and ash. Nick made a deep whimpering noise and nearly retched. Then he gathered himself, stepped over his mother's body and reached through the flames towards his father.

To do so, he had to reach across the length of the back seat, exposing his arms to the inferno within the cabin. Ignoring the pain, he pulled his father out and set him gently on the concrete ground of the parking garage.

His father's body was half burned, half untouched. He coughed and moaned weakly.

Nick's suit had burned away and his arms were covered with bloody blisters, strips of flesh sloughing off in some places, but he barely noticed.

"You can't remove a patient from this facility without the correct paperwork. And the patient currently is in no condition to sign the forms," a woman's voice cut through the blackness, followed by receding footsteps.

Nick stirred, and forced an eye open. He saw a familiar face framed by long red hair. "Laura…. What are you doing?" he mumbled through his stupor. Why was his vision so hazy? Had the doctors drugged him?

Laura gave him a reassuring smile. "Time to get you out of here."

"Out … of here? I need…hospital," protested Nick weakly. The image of his father dying in his arms came back into his mind and he blinked back tears.

Laura turned to the two suited men who flanked her, her movements and speech cursory and commanding. "Take the whole bed. Unplug the machinery. Just leave the IV in."

As the guards moved swiftly to obey her commands, Laura returned her attention to Nick. "This hospital is for humans. I have something better for you than the primitive care offered here. And also, the security here is terrible. If we can get into your room, anyone else can."

Nick groaned as he tried to sit up. Laura's presence made him wary.

Laura walked forward and put her hand on Nick's shoulder. "The painkillers you're on are making you drowsy. Use your MindWave to counteract them. Release serotonin."

Nick blinked as he accessed his MindWave and ordered it to release the hormone that would increase his alertness. In a moment, he felt the web of drowsiness fall away from his mind.

He saw that instead of one of her normal flowing white gowns, Laura was wearing what looked like a matte grey flight suit with padding around the shoulders and torso, and thick metallic bracelets around her lower arms.

"Do you remember what happened?" Laura asked.

Nick couldn't bring himself to say the words, so he just slowly inclined and declined his head. First Sarah, and now his parents. He had terrible fights with everyone he loved, and then they died. Now he recalled enough to make him not just wary around Laura, but furious at her. He suspected that she had been behind the bombing that killed his parents.

"It's good that you remember. And now, we have to get out of here."

A surge of fear helped him clear the remaining fog from his mind. He was acutely aware that he was helpless and Laura was accompanied by at least two men. "Where are you planning to take me?"

"A better hospital."

"You built a hospital?"

"No," she said with a wink. "Your father did."

Before Nick had a chance to respond, another suited man at the door spoke sharply. "My Lady!"

Outside the room, two police officers were arriving. "This room is under police guard. All of you out, right now!" one of them shouted, while the other dropped a cup of coffee as he spoke softly into a radio headset. Both had their hands on firearms.

The two suited men who had disconnected the monitors from Nick's body and were preparing to push his bed out of the room smoothly reached towards their jackets, as if preparing to pull out weapons.

With a flick of her eyes, Laura ordered her acolytes to stand down.

The two officers pushed their way into the room, hands still on their weapons. "All of you leave, now!" commanded the first one through the door.

A look of contempt and anger flashed across Laura's face, but she forced it into a smile and turned towards the police. She could not hide the haughty and condescending tone in her voice. "This patient wants to leave this hospital and is entitled to do so."

"I said get out of this room!" barked back the officer, drawing his pistol.

Laura calmly raised her right arm in the direction of the two guards. Her hand was open and empty, as if warding off the threat of being shot, and yet instead of flinching away, she leaned forward slightly.

There was a flash of light followed immediately by a sharp sound like a clap of thunder, which Nick felt in his bones as much as he heard with his ears. The two officers grunted and fell to the floor.

384

A nurse who had just run to the doorway also leaned heavily against the door frame and slid to prone position.

"What the hell was that?" demanded Nick.

Laura gestured towards one of the suited men. "Give Lord Vinicius the form to sign so we don't have any more drama."

The acolyte pulled a small folder out of a pocket in his suit and removed a neatly folded piece of paper and a pen. He smoothed out the paper, removed the cap of the pen, and, with a deferential bow of his head, carefully put both on Nick's chest as he lay in bed.

"What's this?" Nick asked, bewildered.

Laura walked over to his bedside and explained: "Just a petition to be released from the hospital's care. They can't keep you here against your will."

"I can't sign it." Nick gestured with his chin to his heavily bandaged hands.

"Easy," said Laura with a little grin. She briskly pulled a cord out of a side pocket in her flight suit, and used it to connect Nick's MindWave to her own. "You can use my hands."

Now that her MindWave was connected directly to Nick's, Laura spoke to him via the device, so her own guards could not overhear.

Don't worry about the police officers. It's just an electro laser.

Are they – Nick didn't dare finish the sentence.

Dead? No! Laura's tone suggested she was amused by the idea. *Just stunned, as if I used a Taser on them. Imagine the public relations disaster if we barged into a hospital and started killing nurses. It's all a misunderstanding over some silly paperwork. So please go ahead and sign the form.*

I'm not going to. I'm staying here. Despite her show of force, Laura couldn't actually kidnap him. As soon as she was gone, he would demand to speak to the police immediately.

She smiled at him, like a mother reasoning with a recalcitrant child. *Oh Nick, do you really think you have any choice?*

Chapter 25

The breakthrough happened suddenly.

Sarah and Michael had spent countless days trying to find any evidence of Laura's crimes. They had painstakingly investigated and reinvestigated the bombings of the Aeon satellite and Nick Lal's parents' car. As with the Hurricane Reactor disaster, they could find circumstantial evidence that an Aeon like Laura was probably involved. Yet they could never find any hard proof.

Sarah knew in her gut that Laura had committed all three crimes in cold blood. The Hurricane Reactor blowout had killed scores of civilians and started a severe economic depression. Conveniently, Laura had founded Sparkwise just months before the Hurricane disaster, putting her in a position to capitalize on the ensuing energy shortages. She had repeated the trick by buying up pipelines weeks before the Five Mile Creek blowouts that destroyed most competing transport capacity.

The bombing of the Aeon satellite had cost Laura a fortune and incinerated a team of engineers that were working for her. These losses would seem to put her beyond suspicion. Yet Laura had smoothly used the event to convince the other Aeons they were under attack. Maybe Laura valued their obedience above all else.

Most cold blooded of all was the murder of Nick's parents. Laura had clearly devised the bombing to remove Dr. Aakar Lal, who was working to weaken Sparkwise's grip on the nation's energy resources, and was the last remaining counterbalance against the weight of Laura's influence over Nick. Nick's injury in the bombing had no doubt seemed like icing on the cake to Laura, who had taken the opportunity to "rescue" him from an intensive care unit.

Sarah's hatred of Laura grew stronger every time she thought of the pain that Laura had intentionally brought to Nick. The prospect of uncovering Laura's misdeeds to discredit her in Nick's eyes had become a new motivation for her.

But no matter how hard they worked, she and Michael never found any evidence solid enough to prove Laura's guilt. Nor could they find any clues as to where she might strike next. Sarah and Michael both believed the answers lay in the secure servers of Sparkwise, which had recently been relocated to Sanctuary. Michael had even found hints that the memory address of the most secret files began with the letter "D". But the holes that Michael had found in the Aeons' systems had long since been plugged, and they had never been able to find a way back to those servers.

Until this morning.

"The construction firms working on the Sanctuary facility just installed a landline phone system around the worksite. They think this is more secure than using wireless signals to coordinate their work. But there's a good chance the landline installation was sloppy, and the temporary phone lines intersect with the data wires serving the internal servers," explained Michael. "There's no way to be sure, and we'll have to manually search the phone system line by line, but it's our best bet."

"Let's go, Ghost 2," said Sarah. Since Willy had given their small unit the name *Ghosts,* they used the call signs Ghost 1 and Ghost 2 whenever they were in the ether spying on the Aeons.

In a moment, they were within the main phone switch of the Sanctuary development site.

She looked around her surroundings. She was standing in a giant, perfectly spherical room whose shimmering white walls were evenly lit with bright white light. The curving walls were honeycombed with dozens of narrow, dark pipes leading in all directions.

Michael followed her gaze around the spherical room. "My theory depends on how they've wired their systems together. If they're smart, they won't have allowed any intersections."

"Let's hope they're not smart."

Michael flashed an imitation of one of Willy's winks. "Let's do it, Ghost 1."

Sarah didn't return the wink. It was too flirtatious. She didn't want to toy with his emotions. Michael tried to play down his attraction to her, but even if the depth of his affections hadn't been obvious from how hurt he'd been about her relationship with Nick Lal, it was apparent in the way he looked at her a little too long when they were talking, in his tendency to angle his body towards her, in his slowness to get up when they fell to the ground together during combat training.

She wished she returned his feelings the way she once had. That would be much easier than longing for Nick Lal.

Until she sorted out her feelings, she wasn't going to give Michael any misleading signs. Especially not in the middle of a critical mission.

Right now, she needed to focus on that mission. Laura was a murderer and she was set to kill again. And despite Sarah's efforts to stop loving Nick, she was still fixated on stopping Laura's damaging influence over him. Finally, after her many missteps, after doing little more than look over Michael's shoulder when infiltrating the Aeon networks, she needed to prove that she was good enough to serve in the Ghost squad with Michael. Prove it to Colonel Jaeger. To Willy. And to herself.

"Let's go!" She instantaneously flew across the spherical room to the extension opening that was labelled 01. But she stopped just outside of it, momentarily perplexed: It was much too narrow for her avatar to fit into.

While Sarah stared at the small hole, Michael took the initiative. He shrunk the size of his avatar by half, but this did not make him small enough to fit into the tunnel. No matter how he tried to contort his body, he could not fit into the tiny opening. He couldn't even fit his head through it, much less his shoulders.

"The phone system can't support enough data for a full avatar. We need to go forward in a diminished state," Sarah muttered. "Time to strip down completely."

Sarah arched her back and slowly pulled down the zipper at her throat that held together her single-piece body suit. She rolled her eyes as she saw Michael staring at her intently.

As the zipper opened, not just her clothes, but her body itself split apart and fell away, allowing a narrow, wormlike being to emerge from within. Her head, with its eyes, ears, and mouth, was discarded. So were her arms and legs. All that was left was the very innermost part of her being, a dim version of her consciousness.

For a moment, she had no vision, no hearing, and no touch. And she could not speak. She felt a terrifying sense of vertigo well up, followed by fear.

Most of the fear was primeval terror at the loss of control she was experiencing. There was also an element of fear of failing to complete the mission.

She steeled herself. The vertigo was a physical sensation, and could be mastered. Fear of failure could be recast as motivation to succeed. She inched forward into the mouth of the pipe.

After several moments, her ability to perceive her surrounding improved as her TacWave adapted to the stripped-down capabilities of the phone system. Some vision returned, but she could see no colors, just vague shadows in dim shades of grey. She could speak and hear, but only in a single tinny tone. Her movements were agonizingly slow and ungainly.

Nevertheless, now that she had some sense of sight and physical dimensions, she could at least be sure she was going in the right direction.

"Ghost 1!" exclaimed Michael from behind. "How can I do that? I don't have a zipper on my clothes!"

"Just get in here, will you, Ghost 2?" Sarah called back in her shrill voice.

In a minute, Michael crawled into the line behind her. "Ghost 1," he said, "Working through the phone system is forcing us to redline our TacWaves. We'll overheat if we're not careful."

Sarah tried to respond in a gruff tone, yet all that came out was the same high pitched voice. "Then we'd better hurry." She crawled through the new tunnel towards her goal as fast as she could. And yet the tunnel was narrow and winding, impeding her progress to a frustrating crawl. "Who knows how long it will take the Aeons to find this vulnerability and seal it. We might not get a second chance."

Finally, Sarah rounded the last bend of the pipe.

Nothing. She had wasted minutes pushing her way through the narrow pipe only to end up in a dead end. There were no connections to computers here.

In the cramped darkness, Sarah turned around and began the long crawl back out of the pipe.

Once back in the exchange, Sarah counted the number of extensions. There were 63 more. Considering how long it had taken her to search the research and development line, it would take her and Michael hours to search through all of them.

"Let's split up, it'll be faster," suggested Michael. "I'll do the even numbers, you do the odds."

Sarah headed into extension number 03. She squeezed forward in the dark, tight space as fast as she could, twisting through the tunnel until it, too ended in a dead end. *This is taking too long!* She thought in frustration. But there was nothing to do except keep searching. She turned around and headed back out of the pipe, intent on searching extension number 05 next.

Reverend Tracy Cruz sat in her old office at the National Unity Church's Kerrville headquarters. Today was the last time she would be using it, for soon she would be moving to new headquarters in San Antonio capable of housing her rapidly expanding staff.

A small helicopter would be arriving soon to take her to San Antonio. Then it would return and carry her husband Ricardo and an aide named John on a second trip. The use of the helicopter seemed like an extravagance, but her newly appointed head of security, Rosa Verde, had pointed out that the roads between Kerrville and San Antonio were plagued by desperate bands of economic refugees, and that Cruz would be a ripe target for kidnapping.

Cruz had been growing a team of highly capable advisors for months. Many of them had defected from positions within the United States government and military precisely because they hoped she would establish a new government free from the corrupting influence of the Aeons.

One of the most hawkish was a Brigadier General named James Widelane. Flattered that a flag officer had defected to her side, she had quickly appointed him to be her military chief. Now she regretted that move. Widelane constantly pushed her to prepare for and even instigate war with the Federal government.

Soon she would be able to heed his advice if she wanted: vast numbers of soldiers were defecting from the US military to serve her. And governors of a dozen states in the South and Southwest had indicated that they would follow her lead.

Cruz was deeply troubled by this enthusiasm for secession. Yet she often felt intimidated by the strongly felt beliefs of these devoted men and women, many of whom had experience and expertise far beyond hers.

Now she looked intently at Ricardo. "I can't believe you're siding with General Widelane. How can you be sure that secession is the right path?"

"Half the nation is on the brink of starvation. And you told me it's not just here in America. It's the same all around the world. It's all caused by Laura Mayer and her Aeons; they're bleeding the world dry. When they see the poor and the dispossessed, they don't feel sympathy. They use these peoples' desperation to mislead them into joining their cult."

"I know Laura Mayer is evil. I see that the Aeons have brought only misery to the world. I have denounced them. I have called the people back to the true faith."

"And the people have heard your call, and been inspired by your faith, and now you have tens of millions of faithful congregants, a government in waiting, and growing military might. All waiting for you to show them the path to salvation."

He pushed a sheet of paper into her hands. This was the document they all wanted her to sign. Across its top, in huge, boldfaced letters, was the title: *Declaration of Independence*. The body of the document was short.

We, representatives of the American nation, in order to protect the lives, liberty, and happiness of our people, hereby declare:

1. *Our formation of a new continental government, free of outside corruption, and devoted to the protection of all the American people.*
2. *Our establishment of a military to protect our people from all enemies, foreign and domestic.*
3. *Our intent and desire to peacefully coexist with all who would do no harm to our people.*

The declaration was already signed by many of her advisors. Yet they had left a large blank space at the top of the other signatures.

This was where Cruz was supposed to sign the document. So far, she had refused.

Cruz put the papers down, rose from the couch and looked out of the window at the children playing in the churchyard. "If you expect me to lead you to salvation by force of arms, I am a disappointing leader. I prefer to work with the Federal government, rather than depose it."

Ricardo shook his head. "The government is a creature of the Aeons. The government asks the people to suffer silently as the Aeons commit their evil."

"You've been spending too much time talking to Reverend Bacon," Cruz said in exasperation. "Congress is holding hearings into Aeon activities even as we speak."

Ricardo frowned. "I don't get along with Bacon. But on this point, he's right and I was wrong. Do congressional hearings provide food for the hungry? Do they provide jobs for the unemployed? No! The hearings have been going on since last year without one bit of progress. It's all a sham meant to lull us into silence, while the Aeons continue business as usual. The Federal government is just a puppet in the hands of Laura Mayer. We must replace our failed system with a new republic, founded on justice and faith."

Cruz watched two youths helping a younger child onto a tricycle in the playground outside her office. Evening was approaching, and the children were no doubt heading home. "I'm afraid to take such a drastic decision. What if it just ushers in more evil? What will the future hold?"

"The future will be dark if the Aeons still rule. We must make war and destroy these false idols."

Cruz felt as if she were the only bulwark protecting humanity from self-destruction. Now even her beloved Ricky had sided against her. She turned away from him and looked at the painting of Moses that Reverend Bacon had given her. It depicted the exhausted prophet seated on a rock, his loyal followers Aaron and Hur holding his arms up as a battle raged around them. Was Moses exhausted because, like her, he didn't know what God wanted of him?

She faced Ricardo. "I have no doubt that the destruction of the Aeons must be our end. But what are the proper means? The whole nation faces a common enemy. I am not convinced that the Federal government is merely a puppet. They are a potential ally, if we just give them enough time to sort things out. If we try to overthrow them, they'll definitely become our enemy. I don't want to doom us to a bloody civil war just when we need to unite. Regular humans cannot stand against Laura Mayer if we are divided against ourselves."

"Maybe signing the declaration will force the Federals to side with us once and for all," insisted Ricardo.

Before Cruz could respond, she was startled by a distant tremor that threatened to shake several items off the top of her desk.

"The chopper's here," said Ricardo softly, holding up his hands as if calling a truce. "It's time to go."

After exploring several extension lines, Sarah finally found a hole in the end of extension 15. She crawled through the hole and found herself in a large room. She intuitively knew she'd found a way into Sanctuary's servers and called for Michael to follow her.

Michael slithered into the larger space with her. "Why haven't you changed back to normal, Ghost 1?" he asked, even as he stuck one of his small grey appendages into an outlet in the wall, causing him to grow back into the regular Michael.

"We can do that here?"

"Now that we're inside the firewall, it's easy enough to find a safe connection via wideband data cables."

Sarah crawled to the same outlet and stuck a formless appendage into it. She found that Michael was right – now that she was inside the firewall, it was easy to disguise her full bandwidth connection as an innocuous signal. She sighed with relief as she reformed her body and her vision cleared.

She had her body back, yet she was starting to feel a headache. Her TacWave must be getting close to overheating from the exertion she was putting it through.

Michael was looking around the room carefully. "Of course, their guardian procedures will eventually find us, though I've developed a trick to confuse them if they attack."

"Let's just get out with the data before they find us," said Sarah, trying to ignore the pain in her head.

"Roger that, Ghost 1. The data servers are this way." Michael took a few steps towards a doorway across the room.

As Sarah was about to follow him, she saw a shadow and instinctively stepped back into the corner. "Ghost 2—" she whispered a warning.

It was too late. A giant cat-like creature burst into the room and pounced on Michael before he had a chance to react. The cat must have weighed five hundred pounds and it was moving at a full sprint. The impact alone was probably enough to snap Michael's neck.

If Michael wasn't already dead from the force of the cat's pounce, he was definitely dead once the cat dug its long fangs into his body.

Sarah looked away from the bloody scene in shock. Then she pushed away her fear.

It was impossible to be harmed in the ether. Michael was fine. He was back in the ranch, sitting in his cooling chair, cursing himself for messing up whatever plan he'd developed to confuse the guardian cats. Only his avatar here in Sanctuary had been destroyed.

Now was her best chance to complete her mission. The cat had dragged Michael's corpse to the other side of the room. She just needed to sneak behind it and run into the data server room.

Careful not to make any noise, she worked her way around the edge of the room towards the doorway. Thankfully, the cat was facing away from her, nudging and pulling at Michael's body, undoubtedly in an effort to trace his IP packets back to their source.

Finally, she reached the doorway and slipped through it.

Sarah saw the familiar four by four array of steel safes floating in the air.

Even as she walked into the room, Sarah nearly fell to her knees as a wave of pain and nausea hit her. Her TacWave was overheating and she would have to shut down soon or risk permanent injury.

But she was so *close*! She just needed to think clearly for a few moments to get the information she needed. She blinked to clear her head and summed up her situation.

She was in pain, alone, in an unfamiliar location full of enemies.

She finally understood the purpose behind the sadistic training sessions Colonel Jaeger had made her undergo. Jaeger had been teaching her how to think clearly and act precisely despite overwhelming pain and fear. He'd been teaching her how to cope with a situation precisely like the one she faced now.

It was time to prove she had learned the lesson. There were sixteen safes, and Michael believed the address began with the letter D. No doubt the address was in hexadecimal notation, in which the letter D corresponds to the number thirteen. She peered at the array of metal boxes.

Her heart sank as she saw that the one labelled D was at the top of the rightmost column. That put its lower edge about fifteen feet in the air. She'd have to climb the other safes to reach it. There was no use in waiting. Her headache was getting worse every moment.

She strode across the room to the lowest row of vaults. Just as she was about to pull herself onto it, she heard a growl coming from the far doorway.

Sarah looked up and saw the cat on the threshold. It had already seen her and was crouching as if about to pounce.

It must have finished with Michael and circled around. She'd have to outrun it and make her way back to this data room, she realized with grim determination.

The cat bounded towards her. Sarah pushed off the safe and sprinted towards the doorway she'd just come through. Behind her, she heard a tremendous clanging noise and a deep hiss. The cat must have rammed itself into the steel lockbox she'd been hiding behind. Hopefully that would buy her some time.

She was almost at the exit now. She'd get through it and hide and then find a way to double back into the safe room.

No! She saw the cat running directly at her, about to bound through the same doorway she was trying to exit. From this close, she could see the blood that still stained the cat's paws and mouth. *Michael's blood.*

Somehow the cat had circled around her again. She scrabbled to a halt, falling to all fours for a moment as she tried to stop from a sprint and begin running in the opposite direction all in a single stride. Her head was spinning from the exertion, but she pulled herself up and raced back into the room.

Now there was another cat coming around the lowest row of safes.

She realized with a jolt of fear that there were two cats, one by the vaults and one coming through the doorway!

She was trapped between them, and she was running out of time.

Chapter 26

Sarah knew she was doomed. But she wasn't going to give up yet. She kept running forward towards the safes. One cat was preparing to pounce on her from directly in front, and the other from behind.

As the cat to her front leapt at her, Sarah jumped as high as she could. The cat had aimed too low and its paws passed under Sarah's legs. She planted her hands on the bristly fur of the cat's forehead and pushed off hard, flipping herself over the cat.

She had expected to land on the left most of the bottom row of four vaults, but as she flipped through the air she realized the vault had been knocked out of the array by the cat's impact a few moments ago. Now the lockbox lay on the ground several feet from where it had once floated, its door busted open and its contents spilled out.

Sarah stretched her arms outwards and managed to grab onto the top edge of the safe in the column one over. She clawed at the slippery metal until she got enough purchase to pull herself onto it. Once on top of it, she had to stay crouched low, because the next row of vaults was only two feet above her.

Behind her, she heard the two cats hissing angrily. She spared a glance back and saw that they were entangled, as if they had collided into each other head on.

She used their momentary confusion to her advantage by rolling off the edge of the safe she was lying on. Just as she went over the side, she unbent her legs, launching herself up diagonally. She grabbed the edge of the box one column over and one row higher and scrabbled on top of it. Now she was kneeling rows and one column away from safe D.

The cats untangled themselves and returned to the hunt. One of them skittered towards the wall and began climbing towards the ledge that ran around the room at the height of the third row of safes. The other cat immediately pounced towards her.

Gritting her teeth against her growing headache, Sarah rolled to her side and pushed with her legs, allowing her to grab onto a vault on the next higher row just as the cat impacted with the cube of steel she had just been kneeling on.

The force of the cat's impact drove the safe out of the floating array and into the far wall of the room. It made a resounding clang before falling to the ground, its door broken open by the collision. The cat hissed and fell lithely back to the ground.

Sarah vaulted up to the top row. She was one safe over from where she needed to be. Without nothing directly above her, she was finally able to stand up and move more quickly.

She froze when she realized that she was staring right into the eyes of the other cat. It had climbed to the ledge and was now preparing to pounce the short distance towards her.

Sarah knew she was running out of time. Her headache was becoming unbearable and she was beginning to feel nausea and vertigo as her TacWave overheated. Soon she would not be able to jump between columns and rows anymore.

She stepped to safe D and stood still on it. "Here, kitty," she whispered.

The cat bunched its haunches and leapt.

As the cat flew through the air, Sarah jumped up as high as she could and drew her legs into her chest. The cat's momentum carried it just below her, into lockbox D, which was knocked out of the array by the impact.

As Sarah fell towards the ground, the vault flew across the room and smashed into the wall. Its door broke open and it fell to the ground in pieces. It landed so that its ruptured door was facing upwards.

As Sarah passed the third row in the array she pushed off of a steel wall just hard enough, and just in the right direction, so that she fell perfectly inside the broken doorway of safe D.

She pulled out the bag hanging from her belt even before she landed. Her head was spinning and her vision was fading, but she pushed the pain away and jammed everything she could find into the bag.

Everything she put in the pouch would immediately go to the ranch's computers, where Colonel Jaeger was standing ready to decrypt it. Sarah knew the hour was late, yet she still hoped there would be enough time for Greg's Demon Squad to prevent Laura's attack from succeeding.

As she jammed the last bit of data from the broken safe into her bag, she heard a woman's voice call out "Where are you?"

She pulled herself up inside the safe, so that her waist was even with its edge and her head and upper body were exposed.

She saw Laura Mayer striding into the room in her signature combat gear. The woman wore a white linen dress over which she'd strapped a silver breastplate. She carried a round shield embossed with a circle and five-armed cross emblem on her left arm. Her right hand was empty, but there was a long sword hanging from her belt. Her dress and her scarlet red hair streamed behind her as if she were in a strong wind.

The two cats turned towards Laura, growled, and charged her. Sarah could not understand why Laura's own guardians would turn against her, but she was grateful for the respite.

Laura ignored the approaching felines, fixing her narrowed eyes on Sarah. "Sarah," she uttered through a grimace of rage as she stepped into the room. "I know it's you, Sarah."

The first of the two cats pounced, sending its quarter-ton of sinew and muscle hurtling towards Laura's willowy form.

Without sparing it a glance, Laura backhanded the cat with her free hand. The cat shrieked as it was knocked backwards across the room. When it rolled into an upright position, Sarah saw that one of its long fangs was broken off at the midpoint.

"Do you think you can defeat me with these kittens, you nat bitch!" screamed Laura, taking a long stride forward.

Sarah gritted her teeth against the throbbing pain in her head and used her shaking limbs to start climbing out of the safe.

The second cat pounced at Laura. She ignored the beast as it rapidly closed the distance with her, until the last moment. She turned her face into the oncoming feline and head butted it right in the nose. The animal fell backwards and scampered into a corner.

"Sarah!"

By now the first cat had recovered and was again charging at Laura.

Laura let out a huff of impatience and the wind that was already swirling around her hair and dress magnified. Sarah felt the safe she was still half inside begin to move across the floor, emitting a high pitched scraping noise as it rubbed against the rough stone tiles. She rolled out of the safe and onto the ground just as it became airborne.

She looked around the room and saw that all of the safes – the ones that were still in the floating array and the ones that had been knocked to the ground by the cats – were trembling and moving. And then they were off, hurtling around the room as if caught in a tornado.

As the first cat leapt towards Laura, it was intercepted by one of the flying metal cubes. The force of the impact was enough to slam the lioness against the stone wall of the room, which trembled and cracked. The cat roared in pain or fury, but before could regain its feet, it was hit by another vault, and then another and another.

Sarah crawled along the floor towards a corner of the room, where at least she would be partially protected by the walls of the room. When she reached the wall, she turned back to see the second cat being battered by a barrage of safes. The metal vaults bounced off it without halting its charge toward Laura.

It reared up on its hind legs as if it were a bear or a horse and loomed over Laura, ready to strike.

A final safe smashed into its head with such force that bone and muscle disintegrated, leaving behind a cloud of red mist. Suddenly, the air in the room became deathly still. The blood-streaked safe bounced across the room until it finally settled against the wall near Sarah.

Laura was still walking toward Sarah. "Do you think I would allow a human such as you to interfere with my great destiny?" She drew her longsword and dragged its point across the stone floor, leaving a trail of sparks behind her.

Sarah was fighting her way to her feet, determined to fight the woman she hated. Her TacWave was too overheated to help her create any form of weapon. It didn't matter. She would fight Laura with her bare hands if she had to. As she used the wall to help pull herself up, her eyes fell on a broken fragment of one of the cats' fangs. She bent down and seized it in her hand. It was long enough that she could hold it in her fist and have the sharp point protrude three inches from between her index finger and thumb. It was no sword, but it was something.

"Don't you know I'm here to save you all?" shrieked Laura, accelerating as she closed the distance. The shower of sparks created by her sword cast flickering shadows against the walls of the room.

Sarah's field of vision was fading, but she could see that Laura's armor left her neck exposed. She took an unsteady step forward, holding the tooth out in front of her.

As Laura closed the last few feet, she let out a roar of rage and raised her sword for the attack. "Sarah!"

Sarah leapt towards Laura. "Come here, you bitch!"

As Reverend Cruz walked out of her office towards the landing chopper, she felt a hand pulling at her jacket.

"Reverend, there's a call you should take," yelled the young aide named John, his voice barely audible over the rotor downdraft.

"Can't you patch it through to the chopper?"

"Ms. Verde says you should take this one on the landline. More secure!"

Cruz grimaced. She didn't want to hold up the trip to San Antonio. "Can't it wait?"

"Not this one." John looked apologetic even as he shook his head.

Ricardo put his hand on Cruz's shoulder. "John and I will make sure we've loaded everything we need on the chopper. Take the call. Everything that happens is part of God's plan."

"Thanks Ricky. I guess Rosa wouldn't have asked me to delay the flight unless the call is truly urgent."

She blew a kiss to her husband through her window as he ran across the now deserted playground towards the helicopter.

Then she turned and stepped back behind her desk. The items on its beaten surface trembled with the muted beat of the chopper's rotors. Through her office window, past the playground, she could see the crew chief conversing with Ricky.

There was a light blinking on the secure landline holophone Rosa had ordered installed in the office. Cruz activated the call and a holographic image of Rosa sprang to life in front of her.

"Forgive the intrusion, Reverend, but a defector called."

"A defector? Rosa, I can't grant interviews to every defector who comes along, and certainly not on their schedules," protested Cruz.

"He's very highly placed in Federal intelligence. Knows something about the Aeons. And he said this talk happens now or never. Won't give his name, of course."

Outside, the chopper's rotors powered down so Ricky and John could load boxes its passenger bay without their contents being disturbed by the downdraft.

Cruz stretched her back and sighed. She wasn't sure the interruption was justified. Nevertheless, it looked like she had a few minutes to spare. "Fine, put him on."

"It's scrambled, voice only. He thought the call would be more secure this way," said Rosa's holograph before winking out of existence.

"This is Reverend Cruz. What are you offering me?"

"Reverend, let me ask you," the voice on the other end responded without missing a beat. It sounded strangely mechanical. Cruz assumed this was an artifact of the scrambling process. "Do you really believe the MindWave is the mark of Satan?"

"That's what I've said in my sermons."

"I've watched your sermons. But do you believe it?"

Cruz paused. Her eyes flitted to the painting of Moses. *Did he always know what the Lord wanted of him?*

The voice filled the silence. "I knew you were pragmatic, Reverend. You understand the MindWave is merely a tool. It can be used for good or evil."

"Keep talking."

"I can bring Aeons to your side, if you can assure me you will use the MindWaves for good."

"How can you bring Aeons to me? Tell me who you are," Cruz demanded. Her guard was up; the call could be fake. Maybe Laura Mayer or an NSA agent was on the other end of the voice scrambler.

"You can call me Kingfisher for now."

Cruz heard the chopper's rotors starting up again. She wanted to get this call over with. "Not your name. Tell me who you work for and how you can possibly do what you're offering."

"The only information that comes free is my offer, Reverend. The rest, you have to earn."

Before Cruz could respond, she found herself flinching away from a sudden bright flash. A fraction of a second later, a sharp, reverberating boom filled the room, shaking objects off of her desk.

Cruz turned to her office window in time to see an intense orange glow. The orange was split in half by a wildly spinning rotor blade that was coming directly at her at incredible speed. She stood rooted to the floor of her office as the long metal shaft slammed through the window, shattering it and taking most of the wall with it. The rotor continued forward and sliced through her desk half a foot away from her.

She stood there dumbly, trying to make sense of what had happened. And then she realized she was still alive but Ricky— Ricky had been in the chopper and the chopper had exploded.

She ran through the burning embers and scattering documents to the open wall where her window once had been, and felt a draft of hot air blowing into her face. The burning wreckage of the helicopter lay right below her window, where the playground had been.

"Ricky!" she screamed. She wanted to jump down and look for him, to find him, but a blast of hot flame forced her back into the room.

She felt her legs weakening and she sank to the ground of her office. She raised her tear-filled eyes from the orange flames below to the cold, dark sky above. She wanted to curse God, she wanted to deny His existence, and she wanted to be in His warm embrace.

She raised her hands towards Him, and she realized she would never again have an Aaron or a Hur to support her tired arms. She screamed a sound that was not any word.

Everything that happens is part of God's plan. Those had been Ricky's last words to her.

The Lord had taken him, yet spared her so that she could carry out His will.

But if so, what was His will? Why hadn't He told her?

As she leaned forward to cry, a singed piece of paper, one of many that had been blown into the air by the force of the explosion, drifted down and landed on her knees. Even through her tears, she could read its boldfaced title.

Declaration of Independence.

Sarah screamed in rage as she brought the tooth upwards towards Laura's throat.

Then Laura was gone. Someone was holding her shoulders and cradling her head.

"Sarah! Sarah are you all right? Dr. Lee get in here!"

Sarah opened her eyes and blinked several times to get them to focus. It was Michael, leaning over her, looking terrified. One of his hands grasped her network cable. He must have pulled it out to manually disconnect her from the ether.

She winced against her terrible headache and managed to croak out some words to calm him down. "Relax, you dork. We can't be hurt in the ether. And I was about to kick Laura's ass."

"You're hurt Sarah," he said, then turned to look over his shoulder at the doorway. "Dr. Lee, hurry!"

Sarah felt something warm dripping down her upper lip and curled her mouth in disgust. Had Michael really drooled on her in his panic?

She raised a weak hand to wipe her face and it came away slick with red blood. Shocked, she stared down and saw that there were more bloodspots on the front of her shirt.

Dr. Lee ran into the room with a medical pouch in her hands. "Michael get out of the way!"

"How can I be bleeding?" asked Sarah, fighting to keep her eyes open despite her migraine. "We can't be hurt in the ether. Michael was just eaten by a cat and he's fine."

"You overheated your TacWave," explained Dr. Lee as she pulled a small scanner out of her bag and waved it around Sarah's head. "Lean back and let me check where the bleeding's coming from."

Sarah felt a welt of fear rising in her gut. She knew she'd been pushing the limit but she didn't think she'd be bleeding profusely. Her eyes locked on Michael's. He was standing right behind Dr. Lee, wringing his hands and looking for a way to be helpful.

"Why did you stay in there after you got the information?" he asked.

"I told you. I was going to kick Laura's ass."

"What good would that do? You just said yourself that no one can be hurt in the ether."

"I would have shown her she's no goddess. And I would have felt good." Sarah didn't want to admit it to Michael, but she knew she'd been foolhardy to stay longer than necessary with her TacWave overheating. And now, she might pay a steep price for her bad decision.

Finally, the scanner beeped and Dr. Lee looked at the results. She let out a sigh of relief. "You ruptured a synaptic vein. You're going to be fine. Don't push yourself so hard again, or you might not be so lucky."

Michael crowded forward and leaned over her and asked tenderly "Are you all right?" Then he kissed her softly on her forehead.

Sarah was struggling to decide whether to protest when Dr. Lee jabbed something in her arm and everything faded away.

Nick tried to move but realized he was held by restraints in an uncomfortable sitting position. He must have fallen asleep. Maybe Laura had given him more drugs. He shook his head and blinked his eyes open against the strong lights.

As soon as his eyes were focused he screamed.

His arms were gone, cut off at the elbows. A series of straps and braces held the stubs of his arms motionless against a reflective wall that reflected his terrified features. "Laura! Laura, what did you do?" he screamed.

There was no response.

As he struggled for control of his frantic breathing he noticed that the reflective surface in front of him looked like the plastic walls of the vats at a Langar Foods factory. *What the hell was it doing here?*

He calmed himself down enough to realize that the plastic was transparent. He peered into the translucent fluid within the vat. He saw the vague shapes of half-formed bones, with muscles growing around them. *What was this place?*

"Nick," Laura said in an urgent whisper, running up from behind and placing a steady hand on his shaking shoulder. "Screaming within earshot of your acolytes is not beneficial to your reputation as a divine being."

"What the hell did you do to me?" he struggled to turn around far enough to see her, yet could not. "Where are my arms?"

"Your arms will be ready soon," she said, flashing a confident smile at him in the vat's reflective surface. "Your new arms. I already discarded the old ones."

"Discarded? You mean—"

"Yes, you'll have a new set of arms by late tomorrow night. In the meantime, I'll tell you about your new home. The divine residence is just about ready for you to move in."

"This is the Calvert Cliffs haven?" He finally remembered he could use his MindWave to release calming hormones into his blood. As his mind cleared, he looked around as best he could. The room he was in was a large square, lined with shining grey tiles and accented with stainless steel. He was in what looked like a small medical lab that was separated from the rest of the chamber by a long glass wall.

"Yes, you're in Sanctuary. It looks a lot better than it did last time you were here, doesn't it?" Laura put her hands on her hips and gave the room a self-satisfied look.

"This will make the perfect home for three lucky Aeons," she said with a wistful grin. "Of course, this is a first effort. We'll have to see what works and what needs improvement. We can apply what we learn here to future havens."

She looked excitedly at Nick. "For now, you, Kobus and Abril will inhabit this haven. I've got to head to Britain for a couple of days. We'll have another haven on one of the Scottish isles, you know.

"I know you've been indisposed, Nick, so I'm making sure everything is all settled for you before I leave. I even took the liberty of choosing your three acolytes. Don't worry, I selected them for their impressionability and willingness to serve. They'll be very good to you. I'll bring them by when your arms are ready."

Nick couldn't find words to respond. He kept seeing his father's face, half burned away, the white bone of his skull peeking out from under his scorched skin. And when he managed to get that image out of his mind, he saw the bones of his own half-grown forearms floating before him. He watched Laura continue to boast about the haven's facilities without really processing what she was saying.

"The sarcophagi tubes are finally installed downstairs. From the tube, you can connect directly into the ether, and remain there for days at a time. Your body will be kept at an ideal temperature, and fed and watered automatically. The tube will even bathe you periodically, and serve as an automated toilet. And it will slide up and down the wall in an arc, to prevent your body from getting bed sores or circulatory problems."

She smiled and clasped her hands together. "But even these wonderful sarcophagi cannot provide everything an Aeon's body needs. Once a week, your body will be guided back upstairs on autopilot, to undergo a full medical checkup right here. And over on the other side of this room, Nick, there's a full gymnasium. I suggest you make use of it to keep yourself in shape and practice your self-defense drills."

She gestured to the ceiling. "The facility is fully wired with motion sensors, video cameras, the works. They all link into your MindWave, so you can see anything and everything that's going on inside the walls without even opening your eyes.

Nick saw Laura looking at him for signs of approval and praise, but he shared none of her excitement. He wanted to flee, yet realized there was no escape from Sanctuary. He focused his gaze on the plastic wall of the vat, which held a translucent reflection of his face, and watched his green eyes moving up and down as he nodded silently at Laura's words.

She might have control over him for now. But he would turn the tables on her as soon as he was healed.

Hank Green's voice blared over the intercom. "Ghost Squad, report to the briefing theater immediately."

Sarah sat up in her cot. She'd been resting in the infirmary for a full day, and already she felt much better. Michael had just come to visit her when Hank's announcement came. It was Michael who had confused the Lionesses into attacking Laura and destroying the safes. When he'd been tackled by the cat, he'd injected it with a virus that had disabled the friend-foe identification function of the server's guardian protocols.

Now, Michael helped her get out of bed and walk the hundred feet through underground passages to the briefing theater. She probably didn't need to lean on him as much as she did, but she liked the sensation of his broad chest and strong arms helping to support her. She wasn't sure what she was feeling, and she wasn't sure what it meant. For now, it was good enough to feel safe.

Inside the theater, Hank was standing by the doorway. Instead of the faded combat fatigues Sarah normally saw him in, he was wearing a sergeant's dress uniform.

"What's going on, Hank?" Sarah asked him.

"Wait here for the General, Ma'am," he responded.

Sarah felt regret rising from her gut. She and Michael had finally gathered incriminating intelligence from the Sparkwise servers. But their success hadn't come in time to stop Laura's assassination of Reverend Cruz' husband, which was sure to destabilize the nation even further. Now Jaeger was going to reprimand them. Punish them. Maybe even kick them out of the program. He'd even called in a general to add to her humiliation. She was going to be alone again. She took a deep breath and steeled herself for what was coming. She promised herself she wouldn't let Jaeger see her cry.

"Attention!" barked Hank as Jaeger strode into the room, also in a dress uniform. It was the first time Sarah had seen him in formal military attire. Her eyes played over his row upon row of medals. Her defiance melted into intimidation as she stood at attention in front of him.

Willy was behind Jaeger, but he was looking at his superior and Sarah couldn't catch his eye.

Jaeger made a sharp turn and walked right up to Sarah, so close she could have stuck out her tongue and licked his nose. He gave her a once-over, his severe expression only softening slightly as his gaze met her bloodshot eyes.

"I'm sorry, sir, people died because we were too slow," said Sarah stoically, though she knew it was a useless statement. Jaeger would still mete out whatever punishment he had planned.

"A lot more would have died if you hadn't been so fast," offered Willy from behind Jaeger.

Jaeger gave Willy a glance and the trace of a smile on Willy's face was replaced by a set jaw. Willy handed two small black boxes to Jaeger with a strange, robotic motion.

Jaeger's heels clicked as he brought himself to attention in front of Sarah, and opened the first box. "Second Lieutenants Fenton and Kang, I have been instructed to convey the President's personal gratitude to you for your meritorious duty. You are each promoted to First Lieutenant with immediate effect. Furthermore, you are each to be awarded the Silver Star for gallantry in action against an enemy of the United States."

He pinned a medal on Sarah's shirt, then shifted over and pinned another just like it on Michael's chest. Then he stepped backwards alongside Willy, and the two officers saluted Sarah and Michael in unison. Sarah belatedly realized that Jaeger was wearing a Brigadier General's single star and Willy was wearing the silver oak leaf of a Lieutenant Colonel. Evidently they had been promoted, too.

After returning the salutes, Sarah smiled at Willy. He winked back at her.

She felt tears trickling down her face and cursed herself for breaking her promise not to cry. She struggled to stay standing at attention as a wave of elation overcame her. Finally, she had made up for her mistakes. Finally, she had proven herself. Finally, she had found somewhere she belonged.

"However," said Jaeger, his voice losing its stilted formality and taking on a sense of urgency, "the President has also personally ordered you back into action immediately, on a mission of the highest importance."

"What's the mission, sir?" asked Michael.

But Sarah didn't need to ask. She already knew. They were going after Laura Mayer, and this time they wouldn't just be spying on her in the ether. This time the raid wouldn't be cancelled at the last minute. This time they would bring her in, dead or alive.

To be continued...

Dear Reader,

I hope you've enjoyed reading *False Idols* as much as I enjoyed writing it. Please check out the included sneak peek of the next book in the trilogy, *Do No Evil.* I'm working to finish the full novel as soon as possible. In the meantime, why not take a moment to recommend *False Idols* to a friend or even review it on Amazon.com? I would really appreciate your support!

-Alexis

www.facebook.com/falseidolsbook

@Alex_M_Grove

The Aeon Trilogy

Sneak Peek at Aeon Book II: Do No Evil

It was 3AM precisely and the computer in Sarah Fenton's brain told her she had a five percent chance of dying before 4.

She shut down her brain implant so it wouldn't overheat. Five percent was a small number. One in twenty. But now that small number loomed across Sarah's consciousness, overwhelming her with a desire to flee.

Sarah had fought some virtual battles and observed an aborted commando raid, but tonight would be her first time going into real combat herself. And she'd be going in alone. Despite her ability to adjust her mood and stress level by consciously secreting hormones into her bloodstream, her stomach was curdling and she hadn't been able to eat all day.

Willy might understand if she ran, Sarah guessed, but General Jaeger wouldn't.

"Are you ready, Ghost leader?" Brigadier General Rad Jaeger was addressing her over her radio headset. His voice, even now, retained its normal tone of condescension.

"Yes, I'm ready to go, sir," Sarah responded, driving back the urge to say "no."

Sarah was surprised that Jaeger had assigned her to spearhead tonight's raid on the Aeon facility, given he had been disappointed by her relationship with one of the Aeons. Nine months ago, she had been assigned to gather intelligence on the Aeons by going undercover and beguiling Vinicius, or *Nick* as everyone called him. But instead of coopting Nick, she had fallen in love with him.

She'd loved Nick because despite his vast wealth and power, he was compassionate and unassuming, even meek. And because he was so good-natured he wasn't capable of understanding the evil his compatriots were committing in his name. Her intimacy with Nick, while not part of her assignment, would eventually have helped her bring him over as a double agent.

But General Jaeger hadn't seen it like that. He'd been furious about the affair, and forced her to end the surveillance by faking her death during one of the energy riots shaking New York.

"Good," replied Jaeger. "Just get in and take down their sensors, Ghost Leader. The rest is up to Silverstein's Demons."

"Yes, sir!" she answered.

"Go get 'em, Sarah. Or should I say, Ghost Leader!" Michael Kang had walked up behind where she stood on the pitching deck of the boat. He looked at her intently with his black almond-shaped eyes and forced a smile. Sarah knew Michael was unhappy about her dangerous role in the upcoming raid. Hopefully he would not let his emotions affect his judgment. Sarah would be counting on him to help her make sound decisions to keep the whole team safe.

"I'll get the assault squad in safely. Hopefully we'll drag Laura Mayer out in handcuffs," Sarah said. Laura Mayer was the target of tonight's raid. At 20, Laura was just two years older than

Sarah. But as leader of the Aeons, Laura was arguably the most powerful – and most dangerous – person on the planet.

"Sounds like you're going to have all the fun," continued Michael.

"Don't worry, I'll leave some Aeons for you, Ghost Control," replied Sarah, finally managing to smile slightly.

Despite her show of bravado, Sarah's hands were shaking. To occupy herself and calm her nerves, she began to check her equipment, one last time.

She started with her weapons. She had a laser rifle, a silenced 9MM automatic handgun, two fragmentation grenades, and a flash-bang stun grenade. She also had a self-heating serrated knife, primarily meant to cut through metal barriers yet usable in combat.

In her backpack and pouches on her hips she carried a first-aid kit, a silenced cement drill, three small charges of plastic explosives, a wand-like device custom designed for cutting into data cables and hijacking their signals, and a matching set of gloves and overshoes with multiple functions.

All of these items were held to her body by black straps and webbing that matched her body armor. The protective suit, custom made to match the curves of her body, was made of a prototype alloy of titanium and ceramic called DualProtect. It was dense enough to stop a high powered bullet or to absorb the shock of an explosion. When heated by a laser beam, its matte black surface melted and became mirrored, diffusing the beam harmlessly.

Sarah's once long blonde hair had been given a utilitarian cut, the bangs short and the longest strands barely reaching her shoulders even when not wound into a tight bun inside her helmet. The back of her helmet held a bulky cooling system that would allow her to use her TacWave brain implants for about fifteen minutes straight without fatally overheating her skull.

Her equipment was all in good order, of course. In her earpiece, she heard Greg Silverstein running through the final roll call of the Demons. The Demons were comprised of two squads of ten commandos, and would be making the arrests tonight.

For the raid to go smoothly, she'd have to coordinate closely with Greg, without the benefit of being able to see or communicate with him. She respected Greg as a comrade who would protect her no matter what. But she had hardly talked to him in the fifteen months since she and Michael had been made Ghosts and Greg had been assigned to the Demons.

She'd confronted Colonel William Johnson, General Jaeger's deputy and the senior officer she was closest to, with the need for more time to jointly rehearse the raid with the Demons. She'd seen his characteristic look of guilt flash across his face, and then he had shaken his head and said, "The orders to attack now come straight from the Commander in Chief."

"The President?"

"Yes. Since Laura Mayer bombed Reverend Tracy Cruz' chopper, Cruz has hardened her view of the Federal government. She thinks we're in bed with the Aeons. The President wants a visible strike against the Aeons to assure Cruz we can all cooperate.

"Fine, we'll give the President a win. But we still need more time to prepare."

"The President doesn't have more time. Cruz is on the verge of declaring independence from the United States. Her husband died in that bombing. It's personal for her. The President sees a need to strike hard and strike fast."

"I understand it's a crisis. But can't we just have two or three more days? Our chances of winning will go up a lot if we can prepare properly," Sarah had pressed.

"Sorry, Sarah. Michael's intelligence suggests Laura is at the haven now. But there's no telling how long she'll stay. The President can't risk letting her get away," Willy had explained.

Soon after that discussion, General Jaeger had removed Willy from the mission planning process and Sarah hadn't been able to get straight answers about anything.

Jaeger made no secret of his contempt for Sarah, which was hard to square with the fact that he'd given her the most critical role in this urgent raid. Then again, she knew Jaeger didn't have much choice. After all, only a Ghost equipped with a TacWave would have a chance of knocking down the defenses of an Aeon haven, and she and Michael were the only two Ghosts. Sarah had always had stronger command of the TacWave's tactical functions than Michael. And her feelings for Nick Lal would not be a liability: intelligence gathered by Michael indicated that Nick, who had been badly injured in a recent fire-bombing targeting his parents, was not at the facility.

Jaeger would be supervising the mission from the small, blacked-out fishing boat in Chesapeake Bay that the entire strike force was currently squeezed into. He would monitor the raid via radio and via an interface that gave him a limited ability to use Michael's TacWave to communicate directly with Sarah. But much of the mission would be conducted in radio silence, leaving Jaeger unable to communicate with his troops. Once their boots were on the ground, Sarah and Greg would be in tactical control of the operation.

The timing of the raid would require precise coordination between her and Greg. They were attacking at low tide, so that the water level would be below the narrow beach that was completely submerged most of the time. Sarah would land first on Western banks of the bay, a quarter mile from the walls of the Aeon compound, and advance along narrow trails through the rocky, forested terrain. Ten minutes later, Greg would lead his team to assault Sanctuary's walls and arrest its inhabitants.

The intelligence they had, mostly gathered by Michael, told them that the Aeons called the facility Sanctuary. It was the first of several fortified redoubts, or *havens*, they planned to build around the world. They had built sophisticated security systems throughout Sanctuary, which could be used to coordinate a spirited defense. Sarah's objective was to make sure she destroyed those systems right before Greg's team struck. If Greg moved his men in while

Sanctuary's defenses were operational, he would face a deadly tactical disadvantage against the Aeons.

Conversely, if Sarah shut down the security systems too long *before* Greg struck, the Aeons would be alerted to the attack and have time to organize their defenses. Even without functioning security systems, the dozen armed guards who resided at the haven would be a strong defensive force. If Sarah's timing was off, whether too early or too late, the intended surprise raid would turn into a shooting match.

"Roll call complete. Initiate mission Golden Calf, and begin radio silence," ordered Jaeger.

That was Sarah's signal. She nodded to Greg and Michael, and flexed her shoulders as she pulled tactical goggles over her blue eyes to protect them from sand blown off the beach by the night's stiff breeze. Then she stepped into a small black rubber raft and pushed it into the dark waters of Chesapeake Bay. In the inflated boat, it was a fifteen minute sprint to the shore, across confusing currents, in pitch black on a moonless night. She ought to be worried about missing the beach entirely. But she wasn't worried about that at all. Her TacWave would guide her.

Nevertheless, she felt a deep sense of foreboding as the small motor pushed her towards the shore. She was used to being alone, and tonight was not the first time she'd been in danger. But it was the first time she'd sought danger out. And now she was risking not only her own life, but also twenty-one others. She reached up to rub the silver cross necklace her dying mother had given her when she was seven. Of course, the necklace was gone; she had secretly given it to Nick as a sign of her love.

She would have felt better if Willy on the mission. She trusted Willy. Even more than Michael, Willy had become her closest confidant in the last few years.

Sarah remained anxious until she landed her raft on a narrow beach covered in coarse sand. As she stepped into the shallow surf, she felt a transformation like those she'd felt as a teenager competing at track meets. Before a race, she'd be horribly nervous. Then, as soon as she stepped up to the starting line, her apprehension would melt away and be replaced by alertness and determination. She straightened her shoulders and set her jaw. She didn't need Willy to hold her hand. This was what she'd been trained to do.

She pulled the vessel onto the beach as quietly as she could, settled her backpack, and deftly climbed up the rocky cliffs to the flat ground above. It was easy enough to make her way across the forested terrain that led inland, even in the pitch dark. Thanks to artificial retinas and the image enhancement powers of her TacWave, her night vision was almost as good as her day vision.

From two hundred feet out, she saw the two sentries, pacing around the outer wall, smoking, chatting. *Amateurs.* Getting past them wouldn't be a challenge. Every fifty feet along the top of the wall, she also saw tiny cameras silently swiveling on their bearings. They were the outermost of several layers of security systems that protected Sanctuary. But the haven had been constructed in haste, and there were vulnerabilities in its design. Sarah would be taking advantage of many of those weaknesses tonight.

She quickly slipped from tree to tree, timing her movements to coincide with momentary holes in the view of the pivoting security cameras. She reached the base of the wall a minute later.

Now the hard part would begin. While the cameras' view of the terrain outside the walls had holes, they maintained an excellent view of the top of the wall and the inside of the haven. Sarah would need to disable them before she climbed the wall.

The escarpment was made of two foot thick concrete, reinforced with metal rods. The power and data cables that controlled the cameras ran up and down the inside face of the wall. At the top was the parapet that the sentries traversed. It was five feet wide and supported on its inner edge by steel columns every thirty feet.

Sarah slipped on her gloves and activated their electromagnetic sensors. Now she worked her way along the wall, feeling its surface with her hands. Two feet along from where she started, she felt a strong magnetic surge. She halted for a moment, probing carefully with both hands, hope beating in her heart. Was it the wire she needed?

No, it was too big to be a wire. It was one of the metal reinforcements inside the concrete.

She kept working her way down. A step further, she felt a fainter magnetic field. She paused and concentrated on its size and shape. Not a wire. It was one of the thin steel supports that held up the parapet above her.

The clock in her head was ticking down. Greg was now eight minutes behind her.

Sarah kept sliding her palms across the concrete surface. Finally, she was sure she'd found a set of camera wires.

She removed one of her magnetic gloves and pulled her drill out of a large pouch on her waist. It looked almost like a small megaphone: a pistol grip with a plastic trigger. Instead of a gun barrel or drill bit, the front of the device was a large cone, with soft rubber around the edge. The drill bit was concealed within. She positioned the device, being careful to ensure the shell of the megaphone was flush against the wall.

As she pulled the plastic trigger, the sound of the drilling was completely muffled by the combination of the cone-shaped shell and the white noise emitters built into the device. Sarah leaned into the drill, willing it to quickly bite its way through the two feet of concrete.

When the drill had cut a narrow shaft that exited the wall's opposite face exactly half an inch to the right of the camera wires, Sarah shut it off and pulled the bit back out.

In its place she slipped her metallic wand. As the probe's head cleared the other side of the wall, she squeezed a button on its handle. The head of the wand opened into six narrow strips of metal that slowly bent backwards against the wall. Two of the six heads hit the video data wire and cut through the rubber insulation. They stopped as soon as they pressed up against the copper core of the wire.

A light set into the base of the wand in Sarah's hand blinked red twice to indicate it had connected. This signal was redundant, because Sarah already knew. Her TacWave was connected to the probe by a narrow black wire, and her mind was now inside the camera control system.

Each camera had a six second transverse period – the time it took for them to rotate left, rotate right, and then come back to the center again. She waited for five full periods, grimacing as thirty valuable seconds ticked away. By now the microchip in the wand had collected enough data. She could climb the walls and walk around inside the haven, but the microchip would make her invisible to the cameras.

The cameras along the wall were now useless. Even worse for the defenders, they appeared to be working properly. The security team inside the base still had no warning that they were under attack.

Sarah quickly disconnected from the device, which she left hanging from the wall, and put away her drill. Now she activated the grip functions on her gloves and overshoes. Forests of nano-sized hooks sprouted out of her glove fingers and her boot soles. These allowed her to scale the smooth concrete of the wall as if she were an insect.

Unlike Greg's Demons, Sarah was not equipped with a powered exoskeleton, so she had to rely entirely on her own physical strength to climb the twelve foot wall while bearing the weight of her equipment and DualProtect armor. Soon, her arms and back were burning with lactic acid. But she was strong enough to clear the obstacle, a testament to the value of the intense physical training Jaeger had insisted Willy put her through during the past several months.

It was easy enough to slip past the sentries when they were on the far side of the wall. She dropped down, deactivated the grip functionality and oriented herself inside the compound. She stood at the edge of a large central courtyard with a roughly circular pattern of buildings around it. As she'd expected, most of the haven's buildings looked incomplete, like they were still being insulated and fitted with pipes and wires.

The large concrete building with large antennae obscuring half of its roof was clearly her target. She recalled that the Aeons called it the *Divine Residence*. She needed to get onto the residence's roof and break into the antenna, which would allow her to infiltrate and disable the haven's central security systems.

The only person she saw in the courtyard with her was a tall figure in a scarlet tunic standing near the thick steel front door of the Divine Residence. Its back was to Sarah so she couldn't identify it, but given its abnormal height, the horns that curved above its head, and the glints of metal she saw through its hair, she knew it was one of the Aeons. Probably Jakobus Van de Merwe, though the man's fingertips were obscured by his body so she couldn't zoom in with her enhanced vision for a positive ID.

Regardless of who it was, she knew most Aeons had night vision nearly as good as hers, so she'd have to be careful as she moved towards the Divine Residence.

But she now had only five minutes' lead on Greg's team, so she'd also have to be fast.

Sarah slipped across the compound, staying in the darkest patches, making sure the lone figure did not turn and see her.

Finally, she made it to the most shadowy face of the Divine Residence. She reactivated her nano grip devices and pulled herself up the side of the three story building quickly and silently, sliding across the slightly sloped roof to the side of the antenna opposite to the metal roof access panel. From her elevated perch, the night's stiff breeze seemed even stronger, and loose strands of her hair whipped around inside her helmet.

Her gloves were supple, yet they were still stiff enough to impair her manual dexterity, so she stripped them off. The clock in her head told her Michael and Greg's first squad would be arriving on the beach now.

She took a deep breath and calmed herself. The next bit would require precision.

The antenna she was pressing herself against sent its signals through wires protected by an aluminum tube running down its side. The Aeons should have shielded these wires better. This was another design flaw, attributable to the hurried construction of the haven. All Sarah had to do was penetrate this tube, connect to the control wires with her TacWave, and use the opening to infiltrate the building's security systems.

If there were any security systems she was unable to disable via the antenna, she'd have to slither inside the roof access panel and find her way to them. But surely that would not be necessary. Michael's careful intelligence had shown that all of the systems would be accessible from here.

She pulled her knife from a pouch on her belt and activated its heating function. The blade was designed to cut through just this kind of metal tubing.

Greg must be getting close; she needed to have the security systems down for him. Impatient, she glanced down at the knife. It was almost fully heated; the serrated blade giving off a faint red glow.

Just as she was about to cut into the tube, she heard a clicking noise and then a hollow metallic bang on the other side of the antenna.

Someone had opened the roof access panel.

This close to the Aeon antenna, she couldn't risk using her TacWave or radio to access a spy satellite video feed or even to ask Michael what was happening. Her communication signals would definitely be picked up by the antenna and alert the Aeons of the attack. She would just have to proceed with the plan.

She pushed the knife's edge into the metal antenna pipe and sliced at it. But the knife did not catch in the aluminum. Instead, it scraped down the side of the metal, making a noise that sounded to Sarah like a gunshot in the silent night.

"Quién es?" *Who's there?* It was a startled woman's voice, coming from the other side of the antenna. She heard the rustle of a person turning around quickly.

Damn! thought Sarah. Someone was on the roof with her, on the other side of the antenna. She needed to avoid discovery or the whole raid would be compromised. It was probably already too late, but maybe, *just maybe*, whoever was there had not tripped the alarm yet.

She heard footsteps coming around the antenna from her left.

Sarah gripped the knife carefully in her right hand to avoid letting it clink into the roof and spun around the right side of the antenna. The receiver was about three feet wide; just big enough for her to hide behind.

She crouched there trembling for a few moments. Then she took a deep breath and risked a peak around the antenna, to the far side. It was empty, and the access panel was open. *Oh no,* she thought. *Whoever it was has already reentered the building to trigger the alarm.* She stepped forward to look inside the access panel. *Maybe I can stop them.*

Just as she stepped forward, a figure stepped around the other side of the antenna. Sarah saw a curvaceous woman about her age, dressed in a long black robe, the sigil of a golden eagle emblazoned on her breast, her long dark hair blowing wildly in the night's stiff wind.

The two women confronted each other for a moment from a distance of only several inches. Then the woman screamed in alarm and shoved Sarah's left shoulder.

Instinctively, Sarah thrust out her right hand to ward off the woman. The knife she held in her right hand, with its blade hot enough to cut through metal, slid behind the woman's ribs and into her heart. There was a sharp gasp of pain, and there was a violent spray of steam and red blood.

It all happened so fast Sarah didn't realize what she'd done until the woman was already dead.

As Sarah let the body slump backwards into her arms, she noticed with a jolt that the back of the woman's head was metallic, and there was a cable coming out of one of the jacks between the cooling fans, winding its way down through the open roof access panel. *One of the Aeons!* She peered closer at the face that now pressed against her chest, its mouth lolling open and its dead eyes locked wide in fear.

She remembered the face. It was Abril Espinoza. *Dammit!* She almost said the curse aloud. Abril was little more than a timid errand runner for Laura Mayer. And Sarah had just killed her.

At the sound of the screams from inside the wall, Greg Silverstein didn't hesitate. He snapped his fingers softly, just loudly enough to be heard by his sniper team.

Dispatching the two sentries who stood atop the wall 200 feet distant was quick work. One moment the sentries were there, silhouetted against the bright lights that illuminated the interior of the wall, raising their weapons to aim inwards. The next moment they had both jerked and collapsed, so simultaneously the scene appeared choreographed.

Greg gestured with his hand and the ten black clad Demon commandoes with him silently raised themselves from the knee high grass. As they moved forward in a crouch, dull glints of matte black metal pierced the moonless night.

Behind them, faint splashing could be heard over the night's stiff breeze as the second Demon squad moved through the water. But Greg couldn't sit and wait, not even for the three minutes it would take for the second squad to catch up. Sarah was in danger. She had screamed, and then her screams had *stopped.*

His team moved quickly through the low vegetation towards the walls where the sentries had stood. Greg knew there was a clearing between the edge of the forest and the wall. In the life-sized model he and his Demons had used to practice this raid, the clearing had been 100 feet across, well lit, and monitored by sentries and cameras. *A kill zone*, too dangerous to cross in the open.

But his team had just eliminated the sentries and Sarah's first act would have been to disable the cameras. And since the screams he'd just heard indicated that Sarah had been discovered, speed was now more important than stealth.

He signaled the team to advance. Relying on the powered exo-suits that enhanced their strength and speed, his team sprinted to the wall and easily jumped the twelve feet to its top.

Greg's orders had been to avoid violence. *But it's too late for that now*, he thought with relish. Maybe he would get to kill one of the Aeons himself.

As he landed on the wall, there was a moment of eerie silence. The only noise the faint sounds of the water behind him and the whirling torrent of the warm wind. As he raised his laser sights to his eye, he knew the silence would be short lived.

www.ingramcontent.com/pod-product-compliance
Lightning Source LLC
Chambersburg PA
CBHW060339260626
47160CB00006B/2135